D1000705

HONORING Anna

BOOK II: THE WINDS OF TIME

DOUGLAS H HOFF

Illustrations by Molly Hoff

William F. Laman Public Library System
Argenta Branch Library
420 Main Street
North Little Rock, AR 72114

Honoring Anna: Book II The Winds of Time
Copyright © 2021 by Douglas H Hoff

All rights reserved. No part of this publication may be reproduced, distributed, or transmitted in any form or by any means, including photocopying, recording, or other electronic or mechanical methods, without the prior written permission of the author, except in the case of brief quotations embodied in critical reviews and certain other non-commercial uses permitted by copyright law.

ISBN
978-1-954168-57-2 (Hardcover)
978-1-954168-56-5 (Paperback)
978-1-954168-55-8 (eBook)

Table of Contents

PART I
AGAINST THE WIND

Preface

Honoring Anna started as a history project for my wife Marlene (Molly) some forty years after her Grandmother Anna's death. I had met Anna before she passed and liked her a lot, but at the time I had absolutely no idea of the complexity and depth of her life. As I uncovered the layers of Anna's life through interviews with her daughter Marjorie, who was my principle source of information, and her sons Obert and arthur, along with other relatives and friends from South Dakota to Norway, the family history that I had thought would be brief became so captivating that I decided that it needed to be memorialized in book form. Anna's story is fascinating, but the level of faith, honor, and love that she and her fellow immigrants exhibited drew me so deeply and unexpectedly into their lives that it made me want to hold them up as examples for all people to emulate.

As I was writing *Honoring Anna*, I found that there was too much material for one book, thus this second book, *Honoring Anna: The Winds of Time*, which will help bring Anna's story to a conclusion. We found some of arthur's old journals and some letters in an attic in Anna's house, along with Anna's trunk stamped "Ellis Island," contributing further to the story. My prayer and goal in writing both books were that I would do justice to Anna and her fellow immigrants. Anna's story desperately needed to be told and remembered. It just couldn't die with our generation.

As the first book ended, Anna's amazing life was, in many ways, just beginning. In it she had immigrated to america, traveled through it, and was married to Iver with their first child, Obert.

The second book is centered around her life with Iver on their South Dakota homestead and is packed with adventure along with many trials that tested their faith and endurance to the limit. Nice, orderly, and scheduled days are rarely found on a ranch where nature and live animals often dictate what you do on any given day, which can often be spent "putting out unforeseen fires" rather than what had been intended to be accomplished for the day. Having been a rancher for virtually all of my life, I know firsthand how chaotic and episodic that lifestyle can be. This book may be unique in that aspect as it endeavors to capture Anna's daily life on the prairie and the true heart and soul of her homesteading and ranching lifestyle.

Molly remembers that her grandmother Anna liked to sit in her rocking chair, pull the shades down, and turn off the radio, thinking back on her life without any interruptions. I have introduced this book in that fashion as a way of capturing Anna in one of those very rare moments in ranching when she actually had some free time to relax, and as a way of briefly reviewing the events that led to this book.

Anna and Iver experienced the Great Depression, the Dirty thirties, World War I and World War II firsthand, along with Mother Nature at her very finest and very worst. This book will give you a glimpse of what homesteading in western South Dakota and living from day to day at the whims of the weather and the dictates of the land was like. We owe so much to these pioneers that paved the path on which we now walk. They were true american heroes, and I will forever be in awe of what they accomplished under those unforgiving conditions.

PART I

Against the Wind

A Time to Remember

Anna couldn't keep from smiling. She was experiencing a rare sense of freedom and independence, something not often found on her prairie homestead. Life there had its brief encounters with beauty, but Anna's thoughts were usually concentrated on just surviving or trying to finish whatever task was at hand. Her husband and son, along with their livestock and small ranch acreage, were always her first concern they weighed heavily into her every decision, and seldom did she consider doing something just for herself today, however, was one of those extremely rare days when Anna had some time that she could call her own. She briefly thought about using the precious time to tend to her huge garden behind the house in which unwanted weeds were regularly and tenaciously springing up in the rich and fertile prairie soil.

The weeds will wait, she thought, as she headed to her bright and cheery enclosed porch, her favorite spot in the house the creaky oak rocking chair was lazily waiting for her there as the sun shone on it like a beacon, inviting her to her sanctuary, that little piece of heaven on earth from which she could see much of their ranch. Anna was extremely proud of their ranch and everything that lived on it, but along with her feeling of pride came the burden of having living creatures and the land depend on her for survival. Even in a moment of happiness like this Anna was aware that smiles could quickly turn to tears if time or nature turned the tables on her.

On her way to the porch Anna looked around at her home, which was almost a year old. Its creation and existence still seemed like a fairy tale to her, something from her imagination, and she feared that she would wake up and find it all just a beautiful dream the hardwood floors, the oak hutch integrated into the wall between the dining room and kitchen, the elegant crown molding, and the well- planned kitchen with built-in flour and sugar bins and hand-crafted cabinetry all seemed surreal two years before, she and her family had been living like badgers in an earthen dugout with rock walls, dirt floors, and two tiny rooms. She had truly loved those meager accommodations because she had shared them with her husband Iver and her son Obert. But now she was living in what she considered a castle, a miracle, a gift from God—and from rasmus, her long-ago love who had fulfilled his promise to build her a house even after they had parted.

Reaching the porch, Anna slowly took in the panorama, which seemed magical to her since everything on the prairie is so much prettier after a rain. The air was still fresh from the water's purifying affect, and because autumn had already arrived, the prairie was in the process of changing from green to gold. The grasses had turned into various shades of tan, brown, and red, but the trees were still trying to decide if it was time to change wardrobes. Anna smiled with satisfaction as she looked southward toward their horse pasture on Gap Creek, then her gaze turned to the west in the direction of a long column of pine-covered buttes that abruptly rose up out of the flat prairie surrounding them. The buttes were interspersed with huge and magnificent battleship-shaped formations, which to Anna seemed like silent sentinels placed there to protect the prairie from unknown invaders through the centuries. The region was called the Slim Buttes because it was fairly narrow but several miles long.

Since the prairie had been blessed with the gentle fall rain, Anna's husband Iver had been able to put off some other chores and find sufficient time to ride his favorite bay gelding to their horse pasture out on Gap Creek, checking on their colorful colt crop. After Iver left, reidun Larson, Anna's closest friend and neighbor, had stopped by with her two young children and asked if she could take Anna's nearly two-year-old son, Obert, on the short buggy ride with her family to the general store in reva. Anna had happily complied, and now she was all alone in her beautiful new house although the roaring '20s were a rather carefree time for most americans, Anna and other homesteaders in western South Dakota were still without electricity and the luxuries that their city cousins enjoyed.

Their lives were tremendously difficult, affording little, if any, time for repose, so this truly was a precious moment for Anna Smiling to herself, she contentedly sank into her welcoming old rocking chair. She closed her beautiful blue eyes and slowly rocked back and forth, mesmerized by the warm sun, and made the most of her stolen time. As she listened to the colorful meadowlark singing by her window, Anna relaxed and allowed her thoughts to slide back in time and meander through her past life. She was napping by the time her memories drifted to Norway and the small North Sea Island on which she had been born. It was there that her beloved mother, Karin, had died when Anna was nine, to be replaced by a stepmother who abused Anna and her siblings. In her dream Anna saw her mother furtively reaching out for her but being pushed away by her father and stepmother.

By the time she was sixteen, the already beautiful Anna had hidden sufficient money to pay for her secret passage to paradise, to america. On the ship she met her first love, the handsome and engaging rasmus Johnson. Being with each other felt wonderful and natural, but it was especially exciting for Anna who had never before had a boyfriend. They eagerly shared their dreams and aspirations, mapping out their future together, soon becoming engaged with rings rasmus carved out of a block of oak wood that he found onboard. His family in Norway made everything from ships to houses, and rasmus was a master craftsman. He promised Anna that after their marriage he would build her a house as beautiful and as strong as she was, a home in which they would live together for the rest of their lives as they raised the family they both dreamt of having.

When they were almost to their final destination, the shores of america, a good friend that they had made onboard the ship became ill. Fearing that the american authorities would send him back home due to his illness, he committed suicide rather than face the firing squad that would have been waiting for him in russia. This might have been a bad omen, because rasmus received a telegram from Norway right after they made their way through Ellis Island, on the very day that he and Anna were to be married. The news from Norway tore their world apart and forced them on their own paths rather than to their planned marriage. Neither thought they could survive without the other, but they did. They had no choice.

Unbeknownst to Anna, rasmus had been engaged to a childhood friend in Norway, but when his fiancée changed her mind and refused to follow him to america, he decided to leave without her. Her family had other ideas, however, because when they found out what she had done, they sent rasmus a telegram telling him that they had placed their daughter on a ship bound for america so that they could be married as planned. It was a matter of pride and honor to the girl's parents, but that telegram crushed Anna and rasmus. Heartbroken, Anna decided that the honorable thing to do would be for rasmus to marry the girl whom rasmus knew was too weak to survive in New York by herself.

Rasmus remained in New York to become involved with the thriving construction industry there, but Anna decided to follow her original dream of traveling to the american west, to South Dakota. Every day that she spent in New York would be filled with dreams of what her life with rasmus would have been. Anna knew that if she was ever going to move on with her life, she would have to leave the city where everything reminded her of rasmus. She desperately wanted to see him again, even just a glimpse, but at the same time she knew that her heart might explode if she did. In order to leave him behind, she would have to flee from New York. Anna found herself running away for the second time in her young life—this time from love rather than from cruelty.

Working her way from New York to Minnesota, she found a loving family that took her in as if she were one of their own relatives. There she met Obert, a lonely old man that she came to know and love. She would even name her first son after him. She was still using the Winchester rifle that he had given to her as a parting gift, and she was still occasionally riding Blue, the horse that he had secretly put on board the train that took her to Dakota. In her sleepy dream, Anna was smiling and crying simultaneously as she dreamt of that old man and how much she loved, honored, and respected him.

Anna's train trek across america ended at Hettinger, North Dakota, where she was met by reidun Larson who would become her best friend, as close as a sister reidun and her husband, Odd, eventually introduced Anna to Odd's best friend, Iver tenold, Iver was another immigrant from Norway and was a few years older than Anna. Although they hadn't known each other in Norway, he had followed a nearly identical path to america a few years prior to Anna's journey. Like Anna, he had traveled in steerage on a steamship, gone through Ellis Island and New York, and ridden the rails to North Dakota. With similar backgrounds, hopes, and dreams, Anna and Iver felt like they had known each other forever. Within a few months they were married and living in a crude rock-and-earth home. Both he and Anna agreed that building a ranch and cow herd were their highest priorities and that a real house would have to wait.

Some years afterward, an unexpected and astonishing event forever changed their lives. Anna's former fiancée, rasmus, unexpectedly showed up at the doorstep of their little prairie home with wagon loads of lumber and helpers. When they had been engaged and planning their life together, rasmus had promised to build Anna a house, and he was in South Dakota to honor that promise if Anna and Iver would give him permission. The astounded Anna hardly even remembered the promise and never would have expected rasmus to honor it, let alone travel across america with lumber and men to somehow find her and fulfill his pledge. Anna and Iver were now living in that house. It was a house of honor, lovingly built by rasmus and Iver as a tribute to Anna.

Iver had been jealous and mistrustful of Anna's former fiancée when he first arrived, but by the time rasmus and his crew went back to New York, Iver and he had become very good friends. Whenever Iver thought of rasmus now, he was in awe of the honor and selflessness the man had shown in keeping his promise to build Anna a house. It was a promise that no one except rasmus and Anna knew about, a promise that most men would have forgotten the day after he and his fiancée parted. Honoring that pledge had required an enormous sacrifice, keeping rasmus away from his family and construction business for nearly a year.

As Anna awoke from her nap and dream, the beautiful and serene images of her home were gradually replaced by the realities of the hardships that came with her life on the prairie. It seemed like almost every day new challenges presented themselves, some of which were life or death debacles. Every time Iver rode out, she knew there was a chance that he wouldn't come back or would return injured. The country was riddled with perils, any one of which could be lethal. Every crop they planted was subject to the weather and the whims of Mother Nature. Every animal they owned depended on them to provide health care, food, and protection—from predators, severe weather conditions, and sudden storms. Her young son Obert needed to be guarded from the plethora of lurking dangers and illnesses that kept homestead mothers marching to graveyards with the caskets that held their children, graves that were usually placed on a hill overlooking their homes. Even Father time seemed to work against them, because there were never enough hours in the day to get the necessary tasks finished and never sufficient days in the season to accomplish their work.

Anna knew her life would never be easy, but she was strong and resilient and possessed a faith that seemed unshakable. She had already faced down many seemingly insurmountable challenges in her young life, and she was as strong and beautiful as the prairie she was living on.

A Time to Forget

Anna was prioritizing her long list of tasks to finish and thinking of ways to make life easier for her family when she heard the sounds of reidun and three little children at the door. She sprang out of the rocking chair and, trying to look busy, wiped the sleep and worry out of her eyes while hurrying to the door. Napping wasn't allowed in Anna's diligent and hardworking life, and she didn't want to be caught loafing. "Is there anything new at the store, reidun?" she asked. "Was Obert any trouble?"

"Not at all, Anna. I love having him along—and I really do love pinching and kissing his fat little Norwegian cheeks!"

"Can you and the kids stay for a while? I know Iver would like to see you and hold little Esther. He's been dreaming of having a daughter of his own ever since I told him that we were expecting another baby late next spring."

"Wish I could, but Odd is depending on us to be back mid- afternoon to help him move the yearlings and work on the corrals. It's getting close to weaning time, and he wants to get things in shape before he and Iver start the process. I think they plan to get the calves to the Belle Fourche livestock market the week after next if the weather holds."

"Ok," Anna said, "but promise me that we'll have some time to ourselves one of these days. I really do miss you, especially when I don't get to see you for days at a time. Some of my best and most cherished times were the days that I lived with you and Odd. Say Hi to him and give the big lug a hug for me."

Iver got home late. He was a handsome man by most standards, not very tall but sturdily built and muscular to Anna his most enduring qualities were his quick wit and sense of humor, even when the situation was dour. Norwegians just seemed to be able to shrug off the bad and cling to the good, poking fun at themselves in either situation. Iver's Uncle Chris, who lived close by, had helped Anna finish the milking and other chores, and Anna was trying to keep Iver's supper warm. When he arrived, he was mud from head to toe and smelled terrible. Knowing that Anna wouldn't let him in their new house in his condition, he undressed by the horse water trough, scraped the bulk of the mud and slime off, and skinny-dipped in the water tank sufficiently to remove whatever remained.

"What in the world happened, Iver?" asked Anna. "I was getting ready to saddle up and come looking for you. Chris has been wondering too."

"Found one of the colts bogged down in a water hole that had nearly dried up. The mire had enough hardened mud on top to support him for a ways, but he fell through the crust in the middle and couldn't get out. Lucky I found him. Poor critter, he would've been dead before morning. I managed to rope him, and when I got him to within reach of the edge, I bailed into the mud hole with him and was able to lift him out. He was so exhausted from thrashing in the mud that he didn't even try to fight me. I scraped most of the muck off to help his mother recognize him and allow the poor creature to dry off and warm up. He regained enough strength to stand, and, thankfully, the mare let him nurse. I was a bit worried that she wouldn't claim him, looking and smelling the way he did" "You should have come and got one of us to help before jumping into that muck hole by yourself," replied Anna. "What if you hadn't been able to get out? We never would have found you"

"You're right, Anna, but I wasn't thinking straight. I just saw that poor little guy in need of help and did what first came to me. Another hour or two and he might have sunk out of sight, never to be found in his slimy grave."

"You never were one to ask for help, Iver. Anyway, I have the chores done, and supper is getting cold. As soon as you get the rest of that pungent mud washed off, you need to get some food in your belly and go to bed, so you can rest those weary bones of yours. By the way, reidun said Hi. She was here with Esther and James, and she mentioned that Odd was getting ready for weaning."

"Yeah, we're planning for the week after next if the weather and the market prices hold. Wish I could have seen reidun and the children. You promised me a little girl next spring, and I could have had some practice holding Esther Anna."

The following day, after the milking and chicken chores were finished, Anna strapped Obert to her back, then saddled and bridled Blue. Blue was showing his age, but he was still the most trustworthy horse on the homestead. Anna couldn't keep from thinking about Grandpa Obert whenever she rode Blue. She wiped the tears from her eyes and replaced them with a smile and a prayer:

> *Lord, if you have time, please let Obert peek down from heaven and see his trustworthy old horse and this young child that is named after him. He'd be so proud to know that I have named my first son after him. If he were still alive, and if he wanted to, I'd have him living with us in that new house that Rasmus came back to build for me. Grandpa Obert might be better off with you in heaven, Lord, but I sure would have loved to have him here with us a little longer. Thank you for taking care of him, Father.*

With Obert strapped to her back and his chubby cheeks bouncing with every stride that Blue took, Anna rode out to check on the foal that Iver had pulled out of the mud bog. Iver wanted to go along, but he had some geldings in the round corral that he was working with, and, like Odd, he needed to repair the corrals and get them ready for the big roundup that preceded weaning time.

Weaning was always chaotic and noisy. Frantic cows searched and bellowed for their missing calves, and bewildered calves cried hysterically, looking and longing for their mothers' love and warm milk. The corrals had to be in perfect repair to hold the already four- to five-hundred-pound calves. They searched assiduously for a hole in the corral large enough to squeeze through, walking and crying for hours until they were too tired to stand, finally collapsing into a deep sleep. If they were startled out of their slumber by a loud noise or a wild animal—such as a fox—the terrified calves sometimes leaped up as a group and stampeded. The frightened critters would go through the corral like it was made of match sticks causing the hapless rancher to have to gather the calves—which were scattered over hundreds, sometimes thousands of acres—and start over.

It wasn't difficult for Anna and Obert to find the colt. The last time Anna had seen him he was a brilliant blood-bay with four black knee socks. Now he was a muddy gunmetal gray from head to hoof and smelled like rotten eggs. The dried sludge rattled when he walked, frightening the other colts, so Anna decided to name him rattles. She and Obert laughed as the other foals shied away from him. With their ears perked forward and their eyes bulging, they cautiously studied rattles from a safe distance, ready to flee from the bizarre looking and noisy stranger in their midst.

Baby Obert was getting hungry, and when he was hungry, he let the world know, so Anna stopped and dismounted by a Juneberry thicket to let him nurse. As he hungrily sucked her breast, she warned him, "Weaning time is coming, and you will soon be old enough to get weaned right along with the calves and the colts. Drink up, my little milk monster; this won't last forever. Besides, you have a brother or sister coming in a few months that will need this milk more than you do." She smiled at him as he smacked his lips, but he didn't even look up. When Obert was having lunch, nothing else seemed to matter.

Weaning came and went, as did the flocks of sandhill cranes that both Iver and Anna loved to watch and listen to as they flew south for another winter. The sight of them was a thing of wonder and beauty, especially to Anna, but it was also a harbinger. Winter was trailing in right behind the cranes, and if the fall work wasn't finished in time, Mother Nature and Father time would take from them what they hadn't gathered. Iver still had grain in the field and hay in the meadows. The grain crops needed to be cut and bundled, and the grain in their heads would be thrashed out to be either hauled to the elevator and sold or stored in the wooden grain bin that Iver had recently finished building. The hay had to be moved to the locations where it would be needed for winter feeding.

By the first of November, Iver, Chris, and Odd had sold their calves in Belle Fourche in a steady but weak calf market. The wheat price per bushel was down, but Iver decided to market then anyway rather than store it over the winter and sell the following spring. To Iver trying to outguess the market was like going to the casino in Deadwood. Sometimes you were right and congratulated yourself, but if you did, you were almost certain to be proven wrong the next time.

Moving the hay out of the fields and into the hay corrals and barn for winter feeding was extremely time consuming and strenuous. The hay, which had previously been stacked in the field, was pitch-forked by hand onto a horse-drawn wagon and taken home. Once there, it was pitched off the wagon in the location where the cows would be wintered, or by the barn to later be placed in the barn's upstairs haymow. Getting the hay up and into the upstairs, second-level haymow was an arduous, dirty, and backbreaking task. It was accomplished by filling a large basket with hay and then using ropes and winches to hoist it up and through a door to the hayloft. Once there, it had to be restacked by hand to allow the loft to be filled to capacity. It was hot in the loft, and dust from the hay filled the sultry air rapidly, sticking to Iver's sweat-soaked skin and clothes. The sweat and dirt, along with the hay needles, made his skin crawl and itch, while the dust filled his lungs causing him to cough it up for hours after the job was completed.

Iver also pitched a few loads of hay into a small hay corral that he had made out of pine-pitch posts and small trees by Gap Creek where the horses wintered. The horses were very self-sufficient—if they had good grass and the winter wasn't too severe—but Iver liked to take good care of them and be prepared for any bad storms that might arise. When the water in the creek was frozen over, the horses were actually better off to graze through the snow rather than to be fed hay. With their hard and sharp hooves they could paw through the crusty snow and find the dried grass beneath, taking in sufficient snow with the grass they ate to provide the water their bodies required.

There were only a few stacks left in the field, and Anna knew Iver was feeling pretty good about being prepared for winter, when it started raining. This was unusual for November when any precipitation usually came in the form of snow the event started like a warm summer thunderstorm with thunder and lightning. As the temperature dropped, the rain became cold and icy and poured from the clouds. The cold rain continued relentlessly for four days, soaking the prairie to the bursting point and sopping the drenched animals living on it to the bone. On November 10, the mid-day temperature dropped from just above freezing down to ten degrees, and the rain turned to snow. Lightning and thunder continued throughout the snowstorm, which was quite uncommon. It snowed for another three days, accumulating three to four feet of snow on top of the already wet, muddy, and super saturated soil, before the storm gradually cleared up and allowed the sun to shine.

Anna was hoping that it would warm up again and melt the snow, but it just kept getting colder with nighttime temperatures dropping below zero. With that much snow on the ground they had to start haying the cows since even the hardy horses were laboring to get through the deep snow to the grass underneath. To make an already impossible situation even worse, and add to the workload and pressure, many of their colts and heifer calves—even some of their older animals—started coming down with pneumonia and other stress-induced respiratory illnesses.

Ranch animals are resilient but being soaked to the bone with cold rain and snow for several days, along with the extreme cold and wind, is more shock and stress than they can endure. Anna and Iver worked around the clock trying to save them—moving the sickest and weakest animals to the barn, trying to dry them off and warm them up, and administering every home remedy they knew of. Penicillin and other antibiotics hadn't been invented, so all they had to rely on was their blood, sweat, tears, and what warmth they could generate in their barn to try to save the sick animals. Many of them died despite Anna and Iver's heroic efforts. Others survived but remained chronically ill for the rest of their lives, never fully overcoming the respiratory problems that had developed during this period of extreme stress. But, as nature intends, the strongest and most durable animals survived and lived to pass their genetics for stamina and hardiness on to future generations.

With each death Anna mourned, and with each survival she rejoiced. The animals were her extended family and the lifeblood of the ranch. Death was a common occurrence on the prairie, but Anna was always deeply saddened by it, whether it was the smallest or largest of creatures. Many people who lived on the land became accustomed to death and were able to steel their hearts against it, but Anna was never able to. She took each death to heart, praying for her animals as if they were human, and asking her Lord to care for them when she couldn't.

Chris was getting too old and worn-out to be working day and night. With this in mind Anna helped Iver as much as she possibly could—to the extent that she was probably endangering herself and her unborn baby that was due in the spring. She knew this, but when her family or her animals needed care, they always came first. Putting her own needs at the head of the line, even this late in pregnancy, was never an option with Anna the worry and stress were etching lines on her face, but when she caught Iver looking, she always found a soft smile to bless him with.

With so much snow on the ground, even doing the simplest of chores became extremely difficult Every step the cattle, horses, or humans took meant sinking through the three- to four-foot deep snow to the mud beneath it. With that much snow insulating it, the muddy prairie soil didn't get cold enough, even in subzero temperatures, to freeze. When Anna and Iver took the team and wagon out to feed the stock, they often got stuck—not in the snow, but in the mud hidden beneath it. Getting a stuck wagon out of the mud with thirty to forty inches of snow on top took hours of exhausting and frustrating work. On many of those long, cold, miserable, and overwhelming days, Anna and Iver came in from feeding and caring for the animals too depressed and too tired to feed their own bodies, with sleep offering their only escape from the wrath of the prairie snow and mud.

Anna weaned Obert, as she had promised, and made mashed vegetables, eggs, and ground meat for him to chow on, along with milk and cream from their milk cows. Her happy child didn't notice the long, exasperating winter while sleeping in his warm and cozy crib by the sunny window in his bedroom—with Chris often watching over him. He was too young to perceive the worry in his mother's eyes or know how guilty and neglectful she felt while she was out helping Iver in their battle for the survival of their little prairie ranch rather than caring for him.

On one very cold, frosty, and foggy morning, Anna went to check their heifer calves after feeding Obert and doing her chores. As was her habit, she stopped and listened to the sounds of the cattle when she was close to them. Listening to the cattle gave her volumes of essential information. If it was nighttime and all she heard was grunting, snoring, and heavy breathing, she knew that all was well with the herd, bringing a smile to her face. If it was during calving season and she heard some soft cooing and mooing, it usually meant that one of the cows had just calved and was telling her newborn baby, *I just had you, but I already love you more than anything on earth.* On a nice night when Anna could leave momma and her baby by themselves, it was a beautiful sound. All she needed to do was to make sure the calf got up and had its first, all important, life- sustaining meal. On the other hand, if was freezing, snowing, or conditions were otherwise too harsh for a newborn calf to survive, she faced the arduous and often almost impossible task of getting the cow and her baby to shelter. The new mother frequently—usually— mistook Anna's motives and instinctively tried to protect her baby at all costs. When that happened, it was a battle of life or death between a twelve-hundred-pound cow and Anna, with both of them desperately trying to save the baby calf.

If Anna was out riding through the pasture and there was a lone cow bellowing, she knew that it usually meant that mom was missing her calf, and it was her job to help the often-frantic mother find it. Sometimes her baby was just playing hooky, but usually it was sick or lame and needed help. If the cow's voice was a little shriller, it sometimes meant that she was impatiently looking for a boyfriend. When the bull answered in his distinct and heroic manner, it meant, *I'm coming babe, be patient. I have a whole herd of cows here to keep happy.* When Anna went out in the morning and started filling the wagon with hay, she was generally greeted by a group chorus of moos which meant, *Hurry up! It's breakfast time and we're starving.* This was a happy chorus to Anna, knowing that it would be replaced by the sound of cattle contentedly chewing on their hay as soon as they had been fed. Anna had no smile, only a concerned frown, if she discerned an angry or chaotic chorus. This always meant that something was horribly wrong, and she needed to take care of the problem immediately.

On that particular morning Anna's pace and heartbeat quickened when she heard some low moaning and groaning—sounds of trouble and distress. One of the sick heifers they thought they had cured of pneumonia and turned out of the barn two days earlier had gotten herself bogged down in the snow and mud during the night. As her warm body melted the snow, a muddy, icy hole was quickly formed, rendering her trapped. Anna ran over to help, only to discover that wolves had already found the helpless heifer during the night. The merciless wolves had literally eaten her alive, gnawing the meat out of her hindquarters and her rectum, leaving her to die an agonizing death. Anna was sick to her stomach at the bloody sight and horrified at the thought of the pain and agony that the heifer had undergone and was still suffering. She hurried back to the house to get her rifle so that she could put the poor dying creature out of her misery. Anna sobbed deeply as she put the rifle to her shoulder, wiping her frozen tears away so that she could see clearly enough to do the painful deed with one shot. Anna loved all creatures, but she vowed to never feel sorry for another wolf again. After checking the rest of the herd, she slowly walked back to the warmth and security of her house and told Iver the heartbreaking story through her tears of sorrow.

It was nearly Christmas before it warmed back up to normal temperatures. Slowly, the livestock, along with Anna's family, regained their strength and stamina. Odd rode in one day to check on them. He and reidun had also lost several head of cattle, and Odd had shed so much weight that he looked like a skeleton, a shadow of his former self, as did Iver. Anna prepared a delicious and hearty stew for dinner that day, and the three ranchers visited about their losses while they ate, managing weary smiles at the thought of the coming Christmas season. They knew that it could have been worse—the two families and most of their livestock had survived. Other neighbors that hadn't been as diligent had reported losing up to half or more of their livestock.

The winter hadn't actually been so much different than other winters. It had just been the early and freaky storm that drenched them with icy rain, and then quickly covered them with several feet of snow, that had turned it into a disaster. When the temperature finally turned back to normal, their ranch work became easier, and the health of their animals improved greatly, meaning that Anna and Iver no longer had the added daily chore of doctoring sick cattle. But even after it warmed up, the ranchers and their animals fought the mud under the snow for most of that long and arduous winter. Anna would never forget the harrowing year that they had to pull their wagons through feet of snow only to get mired in the mud hidden beneath it.

3

Another Year, Another Rancher

With the added work of a harsh winter, Iver hadn't had time to go to the buttes and chop their usual family Christmas tree, so Anna found a large tumbleweed in the fence corner and took it to the house to decorate. On Christmas day they completed their chores early and then came in to celebrate with Obert and Chris, who was babysitting. After reading Obert the Christmas story, which he seemed to be delighted with, they put him to bed early and said goodnight to Chris.

Anna said a long prayer to her heavenly Father, and Iver joined her. They didn't grumble about their losses or the wicked weather, but thanked God for the moisture and the fact that they and most of their herd were still alive. They thanked Him for each other and for Obert, for Chris and the ranch, and for their baby that would be born in the spring. Anna and Iver fell asleep in each other's arms as a team that didn't know defeat. They had become an integral part of the prairie, taking its punishment and pain along with its recompense and rewards. They knew that eventually the beast that was winter would morph into the beauty that was spring—a time of the year that they both loved—and that with it the prairie and pastures would be replete with new life.

New Year's Day came quickly, and Anna and Iver celebrated it by working until dark and then taking time after supper to list everything in the past year they had to be thankful for. Each of their lists of thankfulness started with each other. Both Anna and Iver admitted that by themselves—without their partnership—the prairie and its capacity to so randomly produce unyielding hardships might have broken them. They went to bed together, drained but determined.

As if to show them the sweet side of Mother Nature, the sun came out brightly the next morning, and the temperature soared to above freezing. A Chinook wind followed, melting some of the snow that had plagued them since early November. The warm wind energized Anna and Iver, breathing life back into their souls and encouraging them to keep going. Spring was coming!

When spring finally arrived, the prairie displayed its sweet and stunning side, bursting forth with new life. The grass, the hay, and the flowers had a head start from all the rain and snow that had made the prairie dwellers' lives so miserable all winter. Little white-faced Hereford calves were peeking out from under the sagebrush, their mothers licking their brilliant red hair, proud of and in love with their newly born babies. The mares, along with Anna, were bulging, showing their pregnancies and preparing for birth. Anna knew that Iver was proud of everything on that ranch, but most of all, he was proud of her. A winter like that would have broken many women, but not Anna. If anything, it made her more determined to make the prairie their home.

With the calving season behind them, they began preparing for foaling, planting, and haying. Anna was getting closer to her due date, and Iver wanted her to take a couple of days off and make the trip to see Dr. Townsend in Belle Fourche.

Anna agreed but asked Iver if they might be able to ride over to the Slim Buttes for a picnic first. "I can hardly remember the last time we were there, Iver. It would be so peaceful and beautiful this time of the year to ride up to the top plateau and enjoy the splendor that God has placed all around us."

Iver looked at Anna, smiled, and replied, "I'm looking at all the beauty a man could ever want or need in a lifetime right now, dear, but if a trip to the buttes is what you'd like, I'm all for it. Anyway, I feel like I've been neglecting you and Obert in favor of the demands of the ranch and livestock. Maybe some time off and a trip to the buttes will help make up for my lack of attention to what matters to me the most, my family."

After chores the following morning, with Obert in his backpack, Iver led the little prairie family of three on horseback to the top of the Slim Buttes. Life was abundant there, and they saw baby turkeys and sage hens, new fawns and antelope kids, and even a rare litter of red foxes. The mischievous and playful pups were frolicking near their den, completely disregarding their mother's futile pleadings to get inside and out of possible danger. Anna laughed—the pups reminded her of Obert.

The vista from the top still took Anna's breath away. To the east, fertile farm ground and grassland stretched to the Missouri river and beyond—to Minnesota, Iowa, and the Mississippi. To the west, the horizon was filled with a never-ending sea of grass and prairie, dotted with trees, sagebrush, ravines, and draws, along with an occasional antelope. The Cave Hills, another ridge of pine- covered hills, cropped up in the distant west. Hidden amongst them was a large cave covered with petroglyphs which had formerly been occupied by ancient people who had lived there long before the settlers or even the Sioux, arikara, Mandan, Cheyenne, or Crow. To the south, the Black Hills of South Dakota arose with all of its beauty and majesty evoking a profound sense of awe. The Black Hills had once been occupied by the proud Kiowa Indians, but the Lakota Sioux had savagely and fiercely forced them out and claimed it for themselves, soon coming to believe that they had received it from "The Great Holy" Himself. Just two valleys to their southeast was where Iver had first taken Anna to view his secret, the wild mustang herd that they had miraculously captured. Anna still called it their miracle valley and smiled when she thought of her first glimpse of that beautiful wild herd of horses.

Obert had lunch first—he never ate last—and then Iver and Anna got their beef sandwiches out. After a short prayer of thanks, they enjoyed this little piece of heaven that they had found, nearly a world away from the North Sea Island where Anna had been born. "Do you feel like an american yet?" Anna thoughtfully asked Iver.

"I think so, Anna, but I often dream of my family, friends, and the farm in Norway. I still miss them desperately, and my dream would be to see them and the family farm one more time. Especially my mom, who cried for days when she knew I was leaving. For all I know, she might still be there at the docks in the harbor town of Vik, crying for me. But at the same time, I do know that she and dad were happy for me, and without their assistance and sacrifice in paying for my voyage, I never would have been able to make the trip. I couldn't possibly have received more love from my parents. I guess they knew it would have to be enough to last me a lifetime. Now all I have is you, Obert, Chris, this ranch, and our american dream—but that is so very much more than I had ever imagined or hoped to have. I came here to be an american, and, except for the occasional oofda and missing lutefisk, I think I feel pretty american. How 'bout you, dear?"

"I'm not sure either, Iver. Sometimes my life in Norway seems like yesterday; sometimes it feels like it was just a dream in another lifetime. Except for my mom and my two sisters and brother, I really didn't have anyone in Norway who loved me. I surely would like to see my brother and sisters again, though. I would give anything to know how they're doing and to tell them how much I love and miss them. I think that the worst part of being separated from them is the not knowing."

"If I could send you back for a visit, Anna, I would, but the ranch and I wouldn't survive without you. Besides, you have someone living in that tummy of yours to look out for."

The three of them just sat for a while, looking out over the vast prairie and listening to the wind whispering its stories of days, lives, and customs long gone. Tales of the times when the arikara, Mandan, Crow, Cheyenne, and Kiowa Indians lived there and claimed the great Dakota country as their own. Legends of the days when the warring Lakota Sioux rode in and conquered those tribes, taking their land and leaving only their memories and their ghosts behind to tell their stories. Almost silent sounds of the 1700s when a French explorer named Verendrye planted a lead plate 180 miles to the east of where Anna and Iver had lunch, claiming the vast Dakota land for France. Memories of a Lakota warrior named Crazy Horse and his prophetic dream, depicting his rise and fall and foretelling the fate of his people. Stories of explorers like Lewis and Clark and of the Custer expedition which came through the Dakota country in 1874 and found gold in the Black Hills. Desperate echoes of the mighty Sioux crying out that the land of Dakota was still theirs, only to be drowned out by the clamoring flood of gold-hungry miners and settlers.

The battle-seasoned Sioux won the Battle of the Little Big Horn but lost the 1876 Battle of the Slim Buttes waged right between the little family's current picnic spot and their house. Anna and Iver could

William F. Laman Public Library System
Argenta Branch Library
420 Main Street
North Little Rock, AR 72114

have watched the entire melee from their vantage point. Eventually, in what history called the Great Sioux War and the Black Hills War, the tide turned against the overwhelmed and divided Sioux Nation, and the Dakota wilderness once again changed ownership. Railroads inched their way through what was then the Dakota territory, followed by more settlers and more fortune seekers.

The same prairie wind that now teased little Obert's hair once ushered in the great blizzard of 1880 in which countless school children and homesteaders had frozen to death. But even its mighty force and fury couldn't halt the enterprising american souls and their lust for land and hunger for fortune. In 1889, South Dakota became a state, along with North Dakota. It was still a wild frontier in the late nineteenth and early twentieth century when Chris, then Iver, then Anna came from Norway to call this wild Dakota country home. Like their predecessors, they were determined to tame it and make it their own.

"All good things have to come to an end, Anna. We'd better be heading home and get the cows milked before dark. I should have checked the mares this afternoon, but," he thoughtfully looked at Anna and Obert, "I had more important matters to tend to."

"You're right, Iver. I asked Chris over for supper tonight, so I'll need to whip something up when we get home."

"How about some pancakes, eggs, and sausage? I'm starving and so is this handsome son of mine!"

The trio arrived home late but refreshed. Anna had been able to enjoy her Creator's magnificent work, and she thanked Iver by giving him a nice rubdown before bedtime and some extra snuggle time. Tomorrow was Anna's favorite day, Sunday, and if possible, they would be going to church. Anna could regularly feel the movement and stirring of the life inside her, and she knew that delivery was imminent. The child in her womb was getting ready to make an appearance.

After church service the following morning, their neighbor ruth asked Anna if she was going to Belle Fourche to deliver her obviously due baby. Anna said she would be leaving soon as she suspected the baby's arrival any day. Ruth told Anna that she had a sister in Belle that she hadn't seen for a long time and asked Anna if she could possibly ride along. Anna happily accepted because she had been wondering how to convince her occasionally

William F. Laman Public Library System
Argenta Branch Library
420 Main Street
North Little Rock, AR 72114

stubborn husband to stay home and let her make the trip by herself. The mares had started foaling and needed daily attention, another field needed planting, and Iver needed to get ready for haying. Without Anna there he would also have the daily chores of milking the cows, gathering eggs, feeding chickens, checking the cows and their calves, doctoring sick animals, repairing fences, and handling whatever the latest emergency was that happened to present itself. Iver obviously needed to stay home and tend to the ranch, and having ruth go with her to Belle, Anna figured, would allow him to do that gracefully.

"Ruth is riding with me to Belle, Iver, so you won't need to go along," Anna said. "I could do this on my own anyway, but now ruth will be there to help if I need it. I sometimes think I should just stay home and deliver our baby here. It would sure make things a lot less complicated, and you could stand by with the calf puller and be my assistant. One thing is certain, you absolutely need to stay home and take care of the ranch. If you don't, we'll both worry and fuss about what is going wrong at home the whole time we're gone."

Iver agreed. "I'll feel terrible if I don't go with you Anna, but you're right. I wouldn't be a lot of help to you in Belle Fourche anyway, and the ranch needs me here to watch over it. Chris can't even keep up with the milking, let alone all of the other chores and emergencies that come up without warning and need to be taken care of. It seems like every time I turn my back on the cattle something dies or gets sick or some crisis crops up. And as for letting you stay here and standing by with the calf puller, I think I'll nix that idea."

He chuckled at Anna's practical Norwegian humor.

Two days later, Anna, Obert, and ruth packed up the wagon and took the reva trail west to Buffalo where they stayed overnight with ruth's brother and his family. Her brother commented that it was nice that he and ruth got to see each other so often, and the remark made Anna realize that ruth probably saw her sister in Belle quite often too. Anna felt thankful and was humbled that out of the goodness of her heart ruth had sensed her predicament and probably fabricated the story about needing to see her sister so that she could gracefully help a neighbor in need.

"You are a Godsend, ruth," Anna told her friend. "Iver never would have let me make this trip alone. It is imperative that he stay at home right now with all that could have gone wrong on the ranch while both of us were away. I suspect that you are neglecting things at home to help us out and that you didn't really have to see your sister." "Don't even think about it, Anna," ruth replied. "My family is old enough to get along without me for a week or so, and I really do enjoy seeing my sister, so please don't feel obligated to help us out in return. I'll be the very first of the neighborhood women to see and hold your new baby and that will be reward enough for me!"

Dr. Townsend was happy to see Anna and gave her a brief checkup in between other patients. He pronounced that she was as healthy as a horse and that her baby was very close to making its grand entrance into the world. Anna told Dr. Townsend that she would be staying with ruth's family and that she would check in with him when the time for delivery came. He said that would work fine, then asked if she and Obert could stop by his house for supper later so that he and Minnie, his wife, could catch up with the reva community gossip. He was anxious to hear how Iver was doing, along with Odd, reidun, and their two children, James and Esther Anna. Anna told him that she would love to and asked what time to be there.

"Why don't you two just go over this afternoon?" he suggested. "Minnie would love the company and that would give you time to bake me a pie. Just kidding! that isn't at all necessary—it just sort of slipped out."

"The hint was well taken, Doc—you just might have a hot, fresh pie waiting for you after work. Any preferences? I know you like apple."

Anna and ruth did some shopping the next day, and then Anna took her friend to the local diner for their noon meal. The waitress recognized Anna right away and asked how everything at the ranch was. While she had been in Belle waiting for Obert to come into the world, Anna had helped the café by serving as a waitress and even baking them bread and pies. The chubby old cook came out of the kitchen, greeted Anna, and asked her if she had time to make a few more of her deliciously famous pies. He grumbled that his customers were still asking for her pies months after she had left the last time. Anna told him that it depended on how soon the latest addition to her family arrived, but that she would do her best to fit in some special baking for his customers.

Anna and ruth had arrived in Belle on thursday, and on Monday of the following week Anna's water broke. It conveniently happened in the middle of the day rather than the middle of the night as it had been with Obert, so she walked over to the doctor's office and informed Dr. Townsend. By five o'clock, the weary but ecstatic Anna brought another rancher into the world, a second son whose name would be arthur. She studied her new baby carefully, holding him and loving him while thanking God for her healthy and hungry baby boy. This time Anna didn't ask the mailman to deliver the news to Iver as she had done with her first son. Early the next morning she and ruth wrapped arthur up securely, put their bags and Obert in the wagon, and pointed the team north toward reva. They pushed hard enough to make the entire trip in one day, and Anna was able to drop ruth off and arrive home before bedtime.

Iver couldn't hide his happiness and pride. His smile was as broad and bright as the prairie sunrise. "I thought this would take at least another week," he smiled. "You are so beautiful! I've missed you every minute that you've been gone. Obert almost seems more grown up. You must be tired to the bone. Did you have any trouble on the way home? What's hiding under that blanket? Did I get my little girl, or do I have another son? Either way, I'll be thanking God all night that you're back here with me. There are four of us in this family now, Anna. Did you ever dream of such a miracle? You are so amazing! I had to travel halfway around the world to find you, but I'd do it a hundred times over again if I had to"

Anna interrupted her husband to proudly show off baby arthur, but arthur was more interested in having some milk than in meeting his dad. After he was through nursing, both he and Anna dozed off while Iver told them everything that had transpired on the ranch when they were away. Iver was still talking when Anna woke up and reminded him that it was past bedtime.

It had been a very long but rewarding week. Father time had treated them well, and their prayers to the Lord for a healthy baby had been answered. The prairie had another creature to care for, and Anna and Iver now had two beautiful baby boys to share their love and their ranch with.

4

Summer Surprises

Anna thought that it had been an unusually wet winter and spring, but now the summer season was proving to be hot and dry. The wheat that they had planted germinated well and popped out of the warm soil evenly, but the plants were beginning to show the stress of too much heat without sufficient rain. Iver had finally gotten another quarter of land broken and had planted flax in it. It was also showing heat stress, so Anna was diligently praying for rain. She often wondered how their crops could go so long without water but knew that most of the prairie soil on their ranch was structured in such a way that it required minimal moisture. The prairie usually had about a foot of rich topsoil on top of heavy clay. This was the perfect soil combination for semi-arid lands that didn't receive an abundance of rainfall. The rich topsoil soaked up every precious drop of rain that it received and provided plants and crops with all the nutrients they needed for growth. Any excess rainfall went through the topsoil to the clay where it was held like water in a jug—waiting for the crops to use every last drop.

Anna disliked wind, the one commodity of which the prairie had an abundant supply. Invariably, it seemed like the wind was their mortal enemy because it made the hot days hotter and the cold days colder. A hot summer wind seemed to suck the moisture out of the prairie soil as fast as a cold winter wind sapped the heat out of it. Anna and Iver had just about given up on their crops when a bank of clouds started forming on the western horizon. When the storm got to reva, it turned out to be what Iver referred to as a "politicians' storm," providing an abundance of wind, thunder, and lightning, but nothing in the way of the rain that they desperately needed. They were extremely disappointed, but early the next morning, an overnight formation of cumulonimbus clouds produced what Anna had been praying for—a nice, refreshing summer rain.

The crops, the land, and the people on it immediately perked up, and Iver and Anna took Obert and arthur out to check on the fields after chores the following day. It was their first flax crop, and it was just now blooming. Anna had never seen a flax crop before and was astonished at the beauty of the field which had blossomed and transformed from a dark green color to deep blue. The plants were waving in the morning breeze, and the field looked stunningly like the North Sea to Anna with the waving plants simulating the blue-green ocean waves that she had so loved to watch as a child. The only things missing from Anna's seascape were some fishing boats and a few flaxen fish. "Oh, Iver," she exclaimed, "I've never seen such a beautiful field of grain. It makes me feel like I'm in Norway. Why did you plant flax instead of wheat?"

"It seems to do the best in freshly broken soil, Anna. Or at least that's what Chris told me. The seed is expensive, but a bushel of flax sells for double to triple what a bushel of wheat does. If you mix some flaxseed with your flour, it will make that homemade bread I love so much even tastier and give it a nice crunch."

"We need to say another prayer of thanks, Iver. That last rain saved our crops and our bank account."

They enjoyed one more late-summer rain which gave their crops and the land another life-giving drink and boosted Anna's spirits. She enjoyed watching the summer surrender and the days shorten as the season stretched toward fall, her favorite time of year. One sure sign of autumn was that there was only one mare left to foal, and another was that their cows and calves had been out on the summer pasture for over a month, and the calves were getting noticeably larger and heavier. Like Anna, they loved the cooler weather and seemed to grow much faster after the summer heat had dissipated.

Iver, Anna, and Chris had done their branding by themselves this year, though it was usually a community affair with neighbors going from one ranch to the next and taking turns helping each other out. Branding was a complex and difficult task, but the ranchers made it more enjoyable and easier by turning it into somewhat of a social event. Sometimes they organized it to the extent that there was a crew of men to get the corrals, chutes, and branding fires ready, another crew to do the rounding up, another crew to do the sorting and push the calves through the sorting alley and chute, and a final crew to brand, dehorn, and castrate the bull calves Well, it wasn't really the *final* crew—that was the women who prepared the feast for the workers at the end of the day these banquets almost always included an assortment of baked beans, a dish of vegetables from the garden, fresh bread and butter, roast beef, and heaps of mashed potatoes that the cowboys floated in rich and greasy gravy. After all of that came the goodies: cakes, cookies, pies, and sometimes homemade ice cream. If there wasn't any ice left in the root cellar to make ice cream, there was always fresh cream—thick, heavy, and sometimes whipped up with sugar in it. And, of course, gallons and gallons of coffee and lemonade to wash it all down.

This year was so busy that Anna and Iver just didn't have the time to go around helping all of the neighbors, so they made their branding a one family affair. Anna, Iver, and Chris saddled up before daylight for the roundup. Art—as his family had taken to calling baby arthur—was pretty little, so he rode in Anna's backpack. Obert, who loved to eat and was getting heavy, rode in Iver's backpack. Chris was getting pretty old, so he rode Blue, their most faithful and trustworthy horse, by himself. After rounding up the herd, successfully trailing them home, and securing the cattle in the corral, Anna started the branding fire and put the branding irons in it. Their brand was 2-T, called the two Bar T, which required three separate branding irons: a 2, A –, and a T.

Iver and Chris were the sorters. Instead of sorting the whole herd, they just sorted ten to twelve calves off of the herd at a time, which were then branded, castrated, and placed in a separate pen before sorting another batch of calves from their mothers to be worked. Between groups, Anna would quickly check on the two boys and nurse art if he was complaining. They had placed high sideboards on the wagon to make sure the boys couldn't fall out of it and penned them there, securely away from the rattlesnakes and anything else that might harm them. As she left, Anna gave them a stern warning to stay put until she returned.

Iver and Chris caught the calves and carefully threw them down on the ground and held them securely while Anna applied the brands to their left ribs, the calves bellowing and kicking and the air filling with smoke and the pungent odor of burning hair. Anna often alternated jobs with Chris to give his aching body a break. The smaller calves were fairly easy to hold down, but the older and stronger calves were much harder to wrestle to the ground and hold them there. If a leg that wasn't held tightly got loose, the calf either got away or kicked the dickens out of the person holding it. The wranglers that wrestled the calves and held them while they were being branded usually—always—went home black and blue from head to toe and weary to the bone at the end of a day of branding.

The proper placement of the brand was important since other ranchers were allowed to have the same brand if it was on a different location on the animal.

For the bull calves, Iver whipped out his carefully sharpened and disinfected jackknife, slit each side of the scrotum and, one at a time, squeezed the testicles out and surgically removed them. A little more disinfectant was splashed on to complete the surgery which turned the bull calves into steer calves.

One calf at a time, from daylight to dark, they toiled relentlessly until they finally finished. The kids were howling, the men were famished and nearly too tired to stand, and Anna—worn out and weary as she was—was expected to feed all of them. It was too late and too dark to trail the cattle back to their summer pasture, so they decided to finish in the morning and let the herd stay in the corral overnight. The cows, calves, and ranchers all needed some time to rest.

The next morning before daylight, Anna, Iver, and Chris saddled up and repeated what they had done the day before in reverse. Anna stowed Obert and art in the wagon and tied her horse to it so that it could follow behind. The family moved the cattle slowly since the former bull, now steer, calves were extremely stiff and sore. The wounds from surgery usually clotted up quickly, but there was always the danger of a calf bleeding to death, so Iver and Chris frequently checked each of them very closely for signs of bleeding. The cows were in no hurry, trying to devour as much grass as they could fill their hungry mouths with along the way back to the pasture.

When they reached their destination, and the cattle were securely in their pasture, Iver and Chris circled the herd and held them there until each of the cows had found her calf and let it have lunch. Art was also nursing, and Anna warned him that if he headbutted her like those calves were doing to their mothers, he'd get weaned pretty fast. He giggled as if he knew what she was talking about and nuzzled over and found the other fountain.

Anna was relieved after the herd had been worked and was back in the summer pasture because it meant that most of the cattle chores had been finished for the spring and summer. All that was left was to check them—daily if possible—for any illness, rattlesnake bites, injuries, or any of the other maladies that occasionally arose, and make sure they were all in the pasture where they belonged. Of course, they had to wean and market the calves before winter set in, but that would wait until late October or November.

It was now august, and an early fall rain had caused a brief respite from the haying that was underway. Anna had a project that she wanted Iver to help her with, but he was nowhere to be found. He finally showed up with a mischievous grin on his face, telling her that he had a surprise for her and the boys hidden in the porch. Anna was a little leery since the last surprise Iver had presented to her had been a pretty little box that she eagerly opened, only to find a baby skunk peeking out at her. Iver had laughed all day about his great prank but was pretty cautious all week because he knew payback would probably be coming in one form or another. It did. A few days after the skunk incident, Anna told Iver at breakfast that he would be having hot pie with cream for afternoon lunch. Iver's mouth had watered all day at the thought, and he came running when Anna called out for him to come to the house for some fresh pie. With his belly grumbling in anticipation, he quickly sat down at the table, eagerly awaiting his fresh pie. Smiling at her husband, Anna had appeared with a fresh, steaming "cow pie" from the barnyard. "Want some cream on your pie, dear?"

"Guess I deserved that," Iver had conceded.

"Yup," Anna agreed. "Momma always gets the last laugh."

As if he was reading her mind about the past skunk surprise, Iver spoke up, "I promise you that this isn't another prank, so you don't have to worry, dear. On my honor, there aren't any rattlesnakes or badgers or skunks in the porch. You'll love this surprise and so will the boys."

Anna cautiously opened the door to the porch and peered around the corner. She saw some black and white fur protruding from a box in the center of the floor and, at first, thought Iver had found another skunk. Then the animal cautiously and shyly peeked over the edge revealing a six-weeks-old border collie puppy. Anna quickly went and found the boys and brought them to see the cute little black and white puppy. It was love at first sight for everyone—the puppy, the kids, and Anna.

"Oh, Iver," Anna smiled as she gave her husband a hug. "You can't imagine how much I've wanted the boys to have a puppy, and you know how much I love dogs. You've told me about your childhood dog named Buster, and I know that story didn't have such a happy ending, so thank you so much for trying again. Where did he come from?"

"Where did she come from," Iver corrected her. "Those ranchers from north of Buffalo by the Cave Hills raise them. They told me that this was a purebred litter and that I could have the pick of the pack if they could get a discount on their next horse purchase. This little sweetie was the first to come over and smell my hand, and she just seemed to be smarter than her mates. I have to admit that I fell in love with her too. She cuddled with me all the way home, but my feelings for her were dampened a little when she puddled on me! What should we name her?"

"I think she looks like a daisy. The daisies were so beautiful this year, especially in May, and they just seemed to be everywhere. Let's call her Daisy May."

"Daisy May it is, Anna. I like it, and it really seems to fit the little girl."

Obert already had Daisy May out of the box and was lifting her tail to inspect her bottom.

"Obert tenold!" Anna laughed. "Don't be pulling her tail."

As if to make it all right, Daisy quickly turned and licked Obert's face, and then she did the same to art. Both of the boys giggled, and Anna and Iver laughed out loud. They were one happy ranching family that night, and Anna was so excited that she got up every other hour—just as if it was calving season—to check on Daisy. Early the next morning, Obert was missing from the boys' bedroom, but Anna quickly found him in the porch snuggled up to Daisy May, both of them sleeping peacefully.

"Looks like you got your baby girl, Iver, and I think her brothers highly approve," Anna smiled.

"She favors your side of the family, Anna." "Go milk the cows, Iver."

After the milking and other chores were finished, Iver went to the west pasture to check the cow herd. He could see some smoke coming from the east side of the Slim Buttes, so he thought he'd ride over and investigate. It was fire season, and if a fire broke out in the buttes, it could quickly spread to the nearby ranches. Iver rode into the pine trees and followed the trail of smoke to a small, freshly made log cabin and an outdoor moonshine operation. It was prohibition time in america—the Eighteenth amendment to our Constitution prohibited the making of, or distribution of, liquor—and many American entrepreneurs had sprung up around the country making homemade moonshine liquor.

Iver surprised the two scruffy-looking lawbreakers, and they bolted for a rifle that was sitting against a tree. "No need for the gun, fellas!" Iver exclaimed. "I ain't the law. I just spotted the smoke and was worried that a fire had started. If you let me have a trial sip of your liquor, I promise not to give your operation away. You need to be more careful with that smoke because I spotted it a few miles off to the east while checking my cows. It is fire season, and anybody that sees your smoke will come to investigate."

The two guilty looking moonshiners gladly gave Iver a sip. He hadn't had liquor for a long spell—Anna prohibited it too—and it hit him like a smack in the face. "Great stuff, guys! If my wife hadn't put me on the wagon, I'd try to bargain with you for a gallon or two. This tastes a lot like the brew we used to sneak from our dad back in Norway. By the way, I'm Iver tenold and hale from a few miles east, close to reva. I got nothin' against 'shine, but I do like having a warm bed partner at night, if you get my drift."

"Nice meeting you, Iver," One of the moonshiners laughed. "We're the, err, uh, the Miller brothers from the Deadwood area. If you got any neighbors that need a bottle or two, send them by—just make sure they don't tell the law"

Iver doubted that they had given him their real names and location but couldn't blame them for fibbing. "I will. Just be careful with your fire and that smoke; it could lead the law here."

It was already late afternoon, but Iver couldn't resist the pleasure of riding through their horse herd on his way home. Just the thought of those horses brought a smile to his face. The broodmares had increased to around fifty-five head, and they had only lost two colts that spring and summer. There was nothing more therapeutic for Iver than to ride through that amazing wild horse herd, which he had found grazing in a deep canyon in the buttes. During one of the harshest winters in years, he and Anna had rescued the horses from the wolves and starvation by coaxing the emaciated and wolf-ridden herd out of the buttes and to their ranch with trails of hay.

Iver reached home just as his diligent and dependable wife was finishing the daily chores. "What's for supper, gorgeous?" he cautiously asked Anna, knowing that he should have been there to help with the chores.

"If you don't get home in time to help with the chores, I don't have time to make supper," Anna forced a frown.

"I'm sorry," Iver apologized. "How 'bout I help you whip up some pancakes? I just saw Chris, and he wanted to come over tonight to play with Obert and art. Maybe he could join us?"

Anna pretended to be irritated. "The more the merrier; just make sure that Chris knows that because my husband is such a loafer and gets home *after* the chores are finished, it will be a pretty modest spread at our table tonight."

After their meager but delicious supper, Chris, Daisy, and the boys ended up on the floor playing. Daisy was growing rapidly and was almost six months old. She was already showing off her collie herding instincts and was trying to keep Chris and the boys rounded up in the middle of the room. Iver bent over laughing while he watched her futile efforts. Anna finished the dishes and joined in the fun, rolling on the floor with the rest of them. Daisy had given up on herding and was now behind Obert, pulling his pants down. Obert, who was just starting to walk, got up and tried to move but quickly fell over, shackled by the pants around his ankles. Iver and Chris howled, tears in their eyes from all the laughter. "This is the most fun I've had in years!" Chris commented. "Sure is nice of you to share the family with me, Anna. Makes an old man mighty proud and content."

Anna smiled at the old man. "They're your family as much as ours, Chris, and they love you as much as Iver and I do." Daisy proved it by giving him a lick on his face. Chris tried to hide the tears of happiness in his eyes and turned for the door.

Later in the evening, after art was finished nursing, Iver helped Anna put the boys to bed. Daisy was already familiar with the bedtime drill and went to the porch and curled up on her blanket.

Iver and Anna then sank into their own bed, smiles still on their faces from the evening's activities.

"You tired, honey?" asked Iver.

"Maybe. Maybe not. What you got in mind? More than a back scratch, I hope."

"Whoopee!" exclaimed Iver.

That fall was one that Anna would remember for the rest of her days. It turned into what she called an Indian summer—which meant an extended fall with nice weather through to Christmas. Her hardworking family finished nearly all of their fall work before winter came, which was almost a first for them. The markets were good, and their fatter-than-usual calves brought top dollar. Wheat prices were above average, and their flax seed brought over twice as much per bushel as the wheat did, just as Iver had predicted. Iver sold several yearling geldings, and, as usual, the buyers asked him to "Please top them off and work with them a little. You are so good with colts, and they'll be a lot easier for us to handle if you work your magic on them for a few months."

With their better-than-average income Anna's family was able to pay off some of their loans at the bank, and the banker congratulated them on how their hard work was paying off. When their banker was happy, Anna knew that the year had been productive. Life was good, if only for a moment. Anna was content and silently rejoiced in the victory. Their diligent efforts were producing fruit, and her prayers were being answered since both Mother Nature and Father time were being kind to them.

One afternoon Iver was on a two-year-old gelding that he was just starting to ride. Daisy was on the other side of the corral watching, so he called her over to get the horse habituated to dogs. Nearly all of his horse customers had ranch dogs, so getting them familiar with having a dog run behind and around them was part of their training to become ranch horses. Daisy came running over, and instead of stopping like she usually did, she made a wild leap for the horse and scrambled into Iver's lap. Iver was as surprised as the horse was, which was so shocked that it didn't even start bucking. Daisy looked at Iver as if to say, "I'm tired of running behind; time for me to get to ride too."

Iver rode over to the house and yelled for Anna to come out. She brought Obert and art along to see what the commotion was. Obert spotted Daisy on the saddle and immediately wanted to be on the horse too. Anna said he couldn't, thinking that it might be too dangerous. Iver agreed and Anna asked him how he had gotten Daisy onto the horse with him. "I called her over to get the horse used to dogs, and the crazy little pup just leaped up and landed on board! I was as shocked as the horse was. I had no idea a dog could jump that high. Guess she's tired of following behind and thinks that she should get to ride too!"

With the unseasonably nice weather, Christmas and New Year's Day were special that year. Anna invited the Larson family over for a celebratory Christmas dinner. Iver had bagged two turkeys in the buttes, and they were as fat as butter. Of course, he checked in on the moonshine boys while he was at it, taking a sip of their 'shine to make sure that it was still tasty. reidun brought some suet pudding and her specialty, baked beans. Together, the prairie families shared their past year and its high—and low—points while Obert, art, and James, along with Esther and Daisy, played outside on the grass. To have weather warm enough on Christmas day for their kids to play outside was a first for both families. Odd helped Iver saddle and bridle Blue, and they were able to get all four children and Daisy on his back, leading him around the yard with his passel of passengers. Blue perked up, enjoying the attention and looking forward to his own Christmas dinner—the gallon of oats that was waiting for him back in the barn.

It turned cold by New Year's Day, but there still wasn't any snow, so Anna and reidun decided that they should do Christmas day in reverse. Anna's family, including Daisy and Chris, rode over to the Larson place where they had a dinner of beef and venison stew and Anna's pie for dessert.

Reidun was pregnant again, and Odd couldn't help but boast a little to Iver, "I'll soon be in the lead again, old-timer. Guess you just can't keep up, huh?"

Iver had a come-back, "I don't have to have my wife pregnant to keep her home. I'm so handsome she'd never look at anyone else."

"Or so ugly she locks her bedroom," kidded Odd.

"Boys, boys, would you two try to behave yourselves and set a decent example for the children!" Anna laughed at the two Norwegian juveniles.

"Yes, Anna," they chimed together. "We'll try to behave." Iver and Odd winked at each other.

Anna's family arrived home early enough to get their chores finished before dark. Daisy had already gotten the hang of bringing in the milk cows from their little pasture by the barn. Anna could clearly see how proud Iver was of her. He hadn't done any training because working with cattle was bred into her and came as natural as sleeping or eating. Daisy silently and effortlessly flitted around the cows, moving them to where they needed to be so gently that the cows hardly knew they were being chased. Daisy would edge into the cattle's flight zone—a distance just close enough to urge them in a given direction without being too close to frighten them. Unlike most other dogs, Daisy needed no reward to reinforce her good work. She did, however, love praise and hearing the words "good girl." She was just happy to help whenever or wherever she was needed and to please her masters. When the work was finished, she was ready to play with Obert and art or whomever she received attention from. Her energy seemed endless—she could help Anna and Iver and Chris all day and play with the kids all night.

By mid-January there still hadn't been any snow, and Anna remarked that if all of their winters were like this life would be like a walk in heaven. It did turn cold enough to freeze over the creeks and ponds, which meant that they had to chop holes in the ice for the cattle to drink. They even chopped ice for the horses since there wasn't any snow on the ground for them to take in while eating the dry grass. Chopping ice was a chore that Iver usually did and actually enjoyed since he could often take the wagon around to the water holes, bundling the boys up so they could ride along. If she had the time, Anna loved riding along and helping. She could wield the axe almost as good as Iver, saying that it was "good for the figure."

Daisy could clear the side of the wagon without touching the sideboards, so getting in was no problem for her. One of her favorite commands was "Load up, Daisy," whereupon she would jump into the wagon or onto the horse, whichever was the current mode of transportation. Her next favorite command was "round-up," which meant to bring the milk cows in for milking, or perhaps it was "Sic 'em," which meant to chase whatever it was out of wherever it was that Anna or Iver didn't want it to be. With Anna it was usually chickens or pesky rabbits scratching and eating in the garden. With Iver it was usually cows in the haystack or out of their pasture fence.

Anna knew that a mild winter meant that she would have extra time for her family and friends and helping Iver with the numerous jobs that had been put on the back burner. These jobs included things like cleaning the grain bins, cleaning the barn, mending corrals and fences, cutting trees in the buttes for lumber and firewood, cleaning the chicken coop, sharpening saws and axes, mending and softening leather items such as saddles, bridles, and harnesses, reloading old ammo cartridges with new gunpowder and projectiles, trimming the horses' hooves or re-shoeing them, working on the ranch records, and a whole sundry of other tasks that running a ranch required.

Iver hated bookwork, so he usually tried to persuade Anna to do it. "Are we rich yet, dear?" he asked, hinting that she should do the books.

"How would I know?" She didn't take the bait. "If you get the books caught up, you'll know."

"Good try, Iver. Maybe I'll work on the books while *you* nurse arthur."

"I figger I got the wrong equipment for that, Anna," Iver laughed.

"Since you're already 'figgering,' you may as well do the books yourself, Iver," Anna grinned.

Seasons

February followed the same weather pattern with above normal temperatures and below normal precipitation, but March came in, as Anna noted in her journal, like a lion. A winter storm dumped over a foot of snow which turned their world into a giant icebox and made everything in it colder. Daytime temperatures were barely reaching the high teens, with nighttime temperatures falling well below zero. The snow meant that Iver and Chris had to start haying the cattle, but it also meant that they could quit cutting ice for the horses, an almost even swap. Having adequate hay for the winter was always a battle, but this year—for the first time in his ranching career—Iver knew that he would have several haystacks left over. The thought of having leftover hay brought a huge smile to his face. Extra hay was almost as good as having more money in the bank.

Iver and Anna had decided to move the calving season later, back into april. Moving the calving season was accomplished by turning the bulls into the cow herd earlier or later in the breeding season. The timing of the calving season was an important decision. They wanted to be sure they were finished with calving before the mares started foaling because it was just too much work—and there weren't sufficient hours in the day—to do both the calving and the foaling at the same time. On the other hand, they didn't want to start calving too early in the year and take the risk of having newly born calves when there was still a good chance of snowstorms and freezing temperatures. Fighting Mother Nature by trying to calve too early was, as Anna stated, as difficult as finding good lutefisk in South Dakota.

Anna was glad to see the end of March bring mild temperatures and sufficient sunshine to entice the spring into staying until summer arrived. The first two weeks of april, like the rest of the winter, were uncharacteristically mild and made their calving season copiously more tolerable. If possible, Anna and Iver liked to have their heifers calve a little earlier in the season than the cows, giving them more time to deal with the frequent calving problems associated with them. Since heifers had never calved before and were smaller and less mature than cows, delivering their first calf was difficult and often complicated, requiring Anna and Iver to check them throughout the day and night. They locked them in the milk cows' pasture by the barn so that it was easier to get one of them into the barn if she wasn't able to birth the calf by herself. When this happened, they brought the heifer in and put her in the doctoring alley, a task that could be hard in the daylight and was especially difficult on dark nights. All they had to light their path was a kerosene lantern which wasn't a lot of help in the pitch-black darkness and created shadows that scared the already bewildered heifers.

After getting her into the alley, they felt around inside until they found the calf's legs and hooked straps or chains to them so they could assist her in calving. Ideally, the front feet and head were properly positioned to come out first, since breech—backward— calves were a lot harder to pull. With breech presentations the calves came butt-first rather than head-first, and had to be pulled out faster because they often started breathing before they were born. If they did this they sucked the placental fluids and slime into their lungs, causing them to drown. When the heifer pushed, Anna and Iver pulled, usually by hand unless the calf was really large. In those cases, they attached the calf puller. It was a pole with a winch and rope, the rope having a hook on the end to attach to the straps already secured to the calf's legs. Once attached to the calf, the rope and winch were used to "crank" it out.

Calving season, especially heifer calving season, was a time when sleep was a very precious commodity. One night, after three days of little or no sleep, Anna woke up and noticed Iver just standing by the bed as if he were contemplating what to do. "What are you doing, Iver?" she asked her puzzled looking husband. "Do you need some help?"

"Yeah," Iver replied. "I'm so tired that I can't remember if I'm undressing to go to bed or if I'm dressing for the next check. My brain just doesn't seem to be working."

"Go to bed, Iver. I'm pretty sure that you were getting dressed to go out and check the calvers. I'll take this one for you."

Iver was too exhausted to reply, and he was asleep before he hit the bed—still dressed. Anna quickly got out of bed and put her winter clothes on, hating the thought of leaving her warm house to go out in the cold. Daisy, however, didn't mind; she was wagging her tail and eager to go. When they were out of the house, Anna could hear some loud mooing, a sign that there was probably a new calf in the corral. Sometimes heifers were comical—seeing their first calf get up and wobble around actually scared them! *What is that thing!? How did it get here!?*

Since the temperature was below freezing, Anna and Daisy took the heifer and her calf to the barn so that the calf could warm up out of the wind and get its first meal. That meal was extremely important because it contained colostrum, a type of milk rich in antibodies that helped the newborn calf fight off infections and disease. Anna carried the slippery and slimy calf, and Daisy worked the heifer into the barn. When both of them were inside and in a small pen, Anna nudged the wobbly calf toward the heifer's bag and helped it get a teat in its mouth. Soon the happy mom was proudly licking the nearly frozen slime off her beautiful baby while it nursed its first meal. When a newborn calf or colt got up and haphazardly wobbled around in search of a teat, finally finding it by chance and nursing, it seemed like a miracle to Anna. If animals out on the range failed this difficult test, there was no forgiveness—they simply starved and perished.

When they got back to the house, Anna gave Daisy a treat— another of Daisy's favorite words—of venison and thanked her for the help. Daisy was proving to be one of the best ranch hands the family ever had. Then Anna happily went back to bed and put her frozen feet on Iver to warm them up. Her husband didn't even flinch. Anna was delighted when calving season was finally over and she and Iver could get a little more sleep. With the calving season finished, the mares, almost on cue, began to foal. This was undoubtedly one of Anna and Iver's favorite times of the year. Every trip to the foaling pasture was like going on an Easter egg or treasure hunt, and they eagerly searched for the new wonders they would discover. Sometimes there would be a paint foal, sometimes a palomino. Sometimes they'd find a bay, sometimes a gray, sometimes a filly colt, sometimes a stud colt. The weather was usually nice by the time foaling season started, and mares rarely had trouble foaling, so it was almost an entirely enjoyable event. If Iver was busy with planting or something else, Anna loaded the boys and Daisy in the wagon and checked the horse herd for him. If she couldn't do it, Chris got the job, but it was a chore that nobody minded having handed down to them.

Late summer had arrived, but reidun's baby hadn't, so Anna, Daisy, and the boys ventured to the Larson ranch to see how she was faring. She and Anna had gone to Belle together when Esther and Obert were born, and Anna had been living with reidun and Odd to help out when James was born. Although she didn't know how she would manage it, Anna offered to take James and Esther for a week or two while Odd took reidun to Belle to see Dr. Townsend. Since reidun was so close and possibly even overdue, they knew the next Larson should arrive very soon.

After discussing Anna's proposal with Odd, reidun asked Anna if she really wanted to do it. "I know that you once managed to take care of two ranches for a few days all by yourself, Anna, but having four young kids to manage along with all of your other work might just drive you to the nut house. Are you sure that you want to tackle this?"

Anna didn't even hesitate. "You know that I'd do absolutely anything for you, and I'm hoping that the children, with Daisy's help, will pretty much entertain themselves. It's time to wean art, and this will give me an excuse. Besides, I might be pregnant again myself. I haven't told Iver yet, so don't spill the beans, okay?"

Anna loaded the wagon for home, this time with two more children than she came with. She had to stop twice to break up their boisterous games and get them to sit still—giggling while trying to hold a sour face and reprimand them. Daisy backed her up by barking at the kids and then giving Anna a doggy kiss in the face.

Iver and Chris were in the yard when the troops arrived. Iver took a headcount and declared that there were too many children in the wagon. "I think you'd better turn around, Anna. There are more kids in the wagon than you left with. Can't you and reidun count?" "I just thought that you didn't have enough work, dear, so I brought a couple extra kids home to keep you busy and out of trouble." Anna turned to Chris and smiled, "Don't you agree that he's been loafing and needs some more work to keep him out of mischief?"

Chris smiled back, "You know I'd agree if you said the earth was flat, Anna, especially if a piece of pie was part of the bargain."

"Ok guys, here's the situation," Anna explained. "reidun and Odd are going to Belle tomorrow, and hopefully they will soon be coming home with another Larson. In the meantime, I get two extra kids to care for, and you two have the pleasure of riding over to their place daily to check on their stock. Too bad they don't have a few cows for you to milk, Iver!" Anna laughed.

"Sure, you get to play with the kids while I get extra work to do," grumbled Iver.

"I'll happily trade with you," Anna challenged him. There wasn't a reply.

For a little over a week about all Anna's family accomplished was keeping the kids under control, doing chores, and checking livestock—the Larsons' and their own. Anna actually enjoyed most of the time, but it did make her wonder how women with large families managed to get all of their work finished. It helped that she had established a regular routine, playing with the four children part of the time and acting like a drill sergeant the rest of the time.

Anna had about figured out how to best manage the "herd" when the Larson wagon pulled into the yard. Odd was whooping and generally making as much noise as he could, and he threw his hat in the air when he saw Anna and the children come out of the house. They ran out to the wagon to greet Odd and reidun, and Odd jumped off to give everyone a hug while Anna helped reidun get off—very slowly. reidun was still pretty stiff and sore, as much from the wagon ride as from the delivery, but, nevertheless, she still wore that wide hallmark reidun smile. She uncovered their newest family member, a little bundle of boy that they named John. Anna took him out of reidun's arms and held him for a while, instantly loving the little baby as much as she loved reidun and the rest of her family.

"Can you stay for supper?" Anna asked. "Here comes Iver."

"I wish we could, but we'd better get home and settled in before dark," reidun replied. "We'll let Iver meet his new neighbor, and then we need to head down the road. Thanks so much for taking care of the kids and the ranch all this time. What would we do without you?"

"And what would we do without you? We did nothing that you wouldn't have done for us, and we enjoyed every minute we had with Esther and James. Now I think that we need to catch up in the baby department," Anna winked at reidun.

As Odd turned their team around to leave, Daisy, even though uninvited, jumped onto their wagon. She wasn't one to turn down a ride, even if it was with someone else. Iver called her back, and the Larson family of five headed north to their ranch.

Iver turned to Anna and smiled, "I caught that remark about catching up, Anna. Anything you want to tell me?"

"I've been meaning to, Iver. I'm nearly certain that we're pregnant again."

"Whoopee! I can't wait to tell Odd that we're catching up!"

"Is keeping up with the Larsons all that you're concerned about?"
"Sorry, Odd and I just have this guy competition going. You surely know that you and my family are my first concern, and that I love you more than everything else in this world put together, don't you? I already have all that I could possibly want, and more than I ever deserved."

A flock of sandhill cranes were flying above them in the dusky evening sky, so Iver quickly took the opportunity to change the subject. "Is that what I think I hear? Do you see them? It's the cranes heading south for the winter, telling me to get my work done while I still can."

Anna had asked Chris over for supper, and Iver told him that Anna was pregnant. Chris had Obert on one knee and art on the other, bouncing them in accordance with the words of an old ranching game:

> The rich man's horse goes trit-trot, trit-trot.
> The poor man's horse goes hobbledy-gee, hobbledy-gee.
> The hunter's horse goes pacety-pace, pacety-pace.

Chris smiled broadly at the good news and added that he would just have to get another knee.

Fall passed quickly and gracefully turned into winter, allowing Anna and her family sufficient time to market the calves and bring the hay out of the meadows. Anna was already swelling up noticeably but was past her morning sickness episodes. On a fairly nice morning in December Iver asked her and the boys if they would like to bundle up in their warm clothes and ride along with him to open the ice holes for the cattle. If so, he would hitch the team to the wagon and come back and pick them up in an hour or so. Anna thought it sounded fun, and Daisy wagged her tail in agreement, so Anna told Iver that he had a date.

They had recently purchased a foot warmer for the wagon, so Anna heated it in the oven while she and the boys got out their winter gear. She only had one winter coat for her sons, so she put it on Obert and wrapped a big quilt around art. They had a heavy and warm buffalo robe in the wagon that they all could snuggle under if they were cold. Obert was almost three, so he was getting around pretty good and nearly potty trained. Art was barely walking, but he could already say a few words. Iver complained that his first word sounded a lot more like Daisy than Daddy. It was cold and humid outside with frost in the air, but once they were all in the wagon, snuggled together under the buffalo robe and taking turns putting their feet on the foot warmer, they felt toasty and warm.

On the way to the pond where they needed to chop ice, Anna and Iver talked about their cow herd and how some of those cows were almost like family members. Two summers earlier, Anna had raised an orphaned calf which she called a "bucket-calf" because it had to be fed milk from a bucket until it was old enough for hay and grain. The calf had become a family pet, and although it was now a grown cow, Anna still looked forward to scratching her back and seeing how she was doing whenever they checked the cows. Anna named the cow rain in the Face—"rain"—because she had an eye that always watered, especially if the wind was blowing or if it was cold outside. Anna was eager to visit her friend on their trip, knowing that when they got to the herd, all she had to do was call out her name, and if rain was close enough to hear, she would come trotting out of the herd to meet her.

When they popped over the hill above the pond, Anna and Iver noticed something very unusual. A lone cow was lying by one of the holes that they had been opening for the cows to drink. When they arrived, they could see that the cow wasn't sleeping but had somehow slipped on the ice and fallen headfirst into the watering hole. Unable to get sufficient traction on the slippery ice to get out, she had drowned. The cow had been dead for quite a while as the ice had frozen solid around her head. Anna didn't recognize her at first, but when they pulled the cow out of the hole, she realized it was her friend, rain. Tears ran down her face as she felt the pain of losing one of her most dearly loved cows. She would have hated seeing any of them die, but she wondered why, in a herd of so many cows, it had been the one that she loved the most.

Anna looked away, trying not to display her sadness and emotion in front of Iver and the children, but Iver noticed, finally deducing that the cow must have been rain. He gave Anna a hug, and she sobbed into his shoulder for a few minutes. Knowing that they had work to do, she gave him a slight smile of thanks, dried her tears, and silently helped him open the rest of the watering holes. The balance of the cows had already arrived, eagerly waiting for a drink, and shoving and pushing to be the first in line. Anna figured that was probably what had happened to rain. She was taking a drink, and another cow pushed her from behind causing her to slip into the water hole headfirst.

Losing a cow in a hole cut in the ice had never happened at their ranch before. It was just one of those freak accidents that all too often occurred when you lived on the prairie. Normally, Iver would have butchered the cow rather than waste the meat, but under the circumstances, he didn't. He asked Anna if she would mind if Odd came over and got the cow.

She gave him permission. "That's what cows were given to us for, Iver, but I just wish it hadn't been one of my best friends. I'll dearly miss rain. But speaking of meat, our supply is getting a bit low. Could you spare the time it would take to go on a hunt and bring home some fresh venison?"

Since conditions had been so bountiful for the past two years, deer were plentiful along with turkeys, grouse, rabbits, and antelope. This provided a plethora of food for the wolves, so they hadn't been a problem for a long time. It was only in those lean years when game was scarce and winters challenging that the wolves preyed on livestock. Sheep were the easiest to target and kill, followed by cattle, and, finally, horses. If the wolves were desperate, there was nothing they wouldn't try to kill. No creature was too small or too large to escape the ever-menacing wolf pack.

Iver decided to start his venison hunt in their north pasture. It had deep tree and brush-lined canyons and was where the whitetail and mule-eared deer were the most abundant. Iver preferred to hunt "mulies" the best since they were usually easier to shoot and had bigger, meatier bodies. He was in the deepest canyon on the ranch watching about twenty deer when his peripheral vision caught a flash of movement behind him. He turned quickly to look and saw that a mountain lion was stalking him! He pulled his rifle up to take a shot at it, but, like a ghost, the big cat had already disappeared into the shadows and brush.

Iver just stood there for a few minutes cautiously looking in every direction to make sure the large lion wasn't still hunting him. He was shaking, and it took him several minutes to regain his composure and get back to the work at hand. He scrutinized the valley, and the deer were still there, so he resumed stalking them while fearfully looking around for the lion. When he was close enough for a shot, he chose a big, fat dry doe. Nursing does were generally pretty thin this time of the year, and bucks were often gamey tasting, so a dry doe was the animal of choice. Iver took careful aim trying for a neck shot since he was close enough not to miss and didn't want to ruin any of the precious meat.

After a short prayer of thanks for a successful hunt, Iver bled and gutted the deer, leaving the entrails in hopes that they would appease the lion if it was still nearby. He then began the arduous task of dragging the carcass up the steep and wooded hillside. By the time he finally reached the top and found a place accessible to the team and wagon, his legs and arms ached, and he was winded. He left the deer there and alternately walked and ran about a mile to where he had left the wagon. Fortunately, the horses hadn't seen the cat or been aware of its presence and were still where Iver left them, tied to some buffalo berry bushes. Iver was anxious to get back to the carcass, fretful that the lion might have returned and found it. Thankfully, the deer was still there, and he hoisted it onto the wagon and headed the team for home, grateful that he was taking dinner home with him—rather than having something taking him home for dinner.

Winter very gradually warmed into spring, which was slow in arriving. Anna wondered if it would come at all that year. Every time it seemed to get there, another cold snap slipped in from the north and froze the country over again, but it finally turned nice permanently—or at least as nice as northwestern South Dakota gets. The sun was peeking over the eastern horizon just enough to wake Anna. Since she was the first one out of bed, she turned Daisy out for a romp in the yard. Daisy immediately began barking, which was unusual for her. She was usually very quiet around the livestock and the barnyard, hardly ever sharing her opinion with anyone. Anna woke Iver who found his shotgun and ran out the door suspecting that Daisy was trying to alert them to some unknown danger. Sure enough, right there on the front steps was a big, angry rattlesnake warming itself in the morning sun. Daisy had it on the defense, and it was coiled up, shaking its rattles, ready to strike out at any intruder. Iver told Daisy thanks for the warning and put her back in the house where he grabbed their longest broom so that he could safely sweep the snake off of the steps and shoot it in the yard—away from the house.

"Good girl! thank you for the warning! One of us could have easily gone out and stepped right on that snake," Anna told Daisy while giving her a hug. That was music to Daisy's ears since she loved praise of any kind but hated it when she thought that she had done something wrong. Daisy smiled her biggest doggy smile and wagged her tail in appreciation.

As Obert grew, Daisy became especially watchful of him since he had begun to wander when Anna wasn't there to watch him closely. One morning Anna thought her son was in the porch, but when she went to check on him, she found that the porch door was partly open. Obert had escaped, and Anna was distraught with fear of where he might be. After frantically searching the nearby areas, she thought to call Daisy who was also missing. Daisy came bounding from the creek that led to the windmill. Anna ran to her, and Daisy led her back to where Obert was happily playing in a mud hole. Life on the prairie was strewn with danger, especially for the young, but Daisy had been diligently watching over her charge.

"What would I do without you, Daisy May?" Anna asked her faithful dog.

Daisy looked up at her with those huge, soft brown eyes as if to say, "No worries, Mom. It's all in a day's work. I'm just doing my normal dog duty, and I love every minute of it."

Blessings and Burdens

On the way back to the house from Obert's escape to the mud-hole, Anna felt a little queasy. "Maybe it is just from all of the worry and excitement," she thought to herself, but when she arrived at the house, she discerned that it was more than just the excitement. Her lower back had been aching horribly for the previous few days, but she had dismissed it as strain from carrying too many buckets—or any one of a number of her other backbreaking farm chores. Now she was starting to cramp and spasm, and Anna knew that her baby was coming.

Fortunately, Iver and Chris were in the corral working with three geldings that Iver was training, so Anna called out to them, "Iver, could you please come to the house as quickly as possible? Please hurry!"

"What's the matter, Anna? Got a mouse in the closet or something?" grinned Iver.

"Just get to the house," she insisted. "The baby is coming!" Iver ran in almost out of breath. "What should I do, Anna?"

"Would you ride over to the Larsons and see if reidun can come over and help? I'd like to have her here to assist me just in case I need it."

"Should we head for Belle and take you to Dr. Townsend?" Iver asked.

"You're not listening to me, Iver. We don't have time. Please go get reidun right away!"

Iver didn't need to be told three times. He ran back to the corral and mounted the horse he had saddled there. Quickly explaining the situation to Chris, Iver asked him if he would stay with Anna until he and reidun got back. Chris ran to the house and hurried through the door where he was met by Anna. She explained to him that her water had already broken, and the baby was going to make its appearance a little sooner than she had predicted, so she didn't have time to go to Belle—or anywhere else, for that matter. She asked Chris to help her boil some water while she gathered clean sheets and towels and sterilized the washbasin. After Chris helped her get the items to the bedroom, Anna asked him to leave, but to watch for reidun and send her in when she arrived. She was praying that reidun would get there in time to lend a hand but wanted to be prepared in case she had to deliver the baby by herself. She knew that this child was in a real rush to get out and see the world.

Anna tried to remain calm, breathing in and out slowly, pushing gently instead of bearing down, and doing her best to hold the birth off until reidun arrived. Finally, when she felt like she couldn't hold back any longer, reidun and Iver came running into the bedroom. As soon as the aid arrived, Anna relaxed and after a few easy pushes, a beautiful baby girl entered the world and their lives. The relieved Iver, who had been shuffling aimlessly around the room and was usually getting in the way, didn't argue when reidun patiently told him that he could leave, and she would finish. He just thanked her and retreated as quickly as he had entered.

"Men," reidun exclaimed as she started cleaning the newborn baby. The content and happy little girl was breathing normally, so reidun didn't see the need of spanking her. After she had bathed the child with warm water and dried her off, she carefully wrapped her in a dry towel and handed her back to Anna. It was love at first sight. Anna's dream had always been to have her very own daughter, and here she was in her arms, a precious little gift from heaven. It seemed surreal, and Anna breathed a silent prayer of gratitude.

"Thanks so much for coming over, reidun. This one was coming out whether I was ready or not, and I felt so much better knowing that you would be here. I knew there was no way that I could get to a doctor in time and immediately thought of you. Who is with James, Esther, and John?"

Just then a wagon pulled into their yard. It was Odd and the whole family. He ran in with John in his arms and Esther and James trailing behind, almost beating Chris and Iver through the bedroom door which reidun had just opened.

"It's a girl!" Anna and reidun harmonized.

"Okay, everyone," reidun said after each of them had admired the infant. "The show's over so let's allow Mom and her baby to have some alone time, so they can catch some rest. That precious child of yours looks hungry, Anna."

"I'm famished," Iver and Odd said in unison at the thought of being hungry. "This having a baby is mighty hard work for us guys." Over her objections, Anna let Iver name their new daughter Marjorie. She had wanted to name her Karin, after her mom, or reidun. Marjorie was petite at birth, but she grew nearly as fast as the new foals that were being born about the same time. By the time fall rolled around, she had gained at least ten pounds and had inherited Obert's chubby Norwegian cheeks. She was the daughter that Anna had always wanted, but she was also the "Apple of Iver's pie"—his version of "Apple of my eye." He was as smitten as Anna, and Marjorie had both parents wrapped around her pudgy little fingertips from day one.

Even Marjorie's brothers seemed pleased, and they, along with Daisy, admired their sister and kept watch over her all year. Obert couldn't wait until she was old enough to play with, and art thought they should all have horses to ride. When Marjorie started crawling, Daisy instinctively transitioned into her guard and herding modes, never letting the little girl out of her sight. Anna appreciated having Daisy there to assist with Marjorie and keep the boys occupied.

She knew how much Iver liked having Daisy with him to help with chores, but he was letting Anna keep her full time.

Anna hadn't told Iver yet, since only a few months had passed and she didn't know how it could be possible this soon, but she was pretty sure that she was pregnant again. It seemed like only yesterday that Marjorie had been born, and Anna wasn't prepared to endure another pregnancy quite so soon. The thought of going through labor, and the responsibility of bringing another child into the world so hastily, felt overwhelming— almost depressing. Where would she find the time and energy? How could she get all of her work done and care for her three children while being pregnant again? Knowing that she should have been overjoyed rather than having these gloomy feelings filled her with guilt and added to the pressure, making her almost wish it hadn't happened—at least not so soon.

The autumn season brought shorter days, allowing the family fewer daylight hours to get their work done before winter set in. Anna's emotions about being pregnant again were still ebbing and flowing. One day she would be depressed, the next she would summon her faith and strength and feel better. On one of those feeling-better days, she decided that she needed to confess and tell Iver that she was pregnant again. It should have been such an easy and happy task, but something about this pregnancy just didn't feel right to her.

After another battle with her conscience, Anna put a smile on her face and finally told Iver and Chris about her pregnancy. They were excited, and their jubilance lifted her spirits enough to think about a shopping trip to reva. It was a sunny and cloudless day, and Iver didn't currently need any help, so Chris volunteered to watch the children while she was gone. Marjorie was sleeping and had just nursed, so Anna figured that she had two or three hours free before she awoke. This would give her sufficient time to gather what she needed at the store and catch up on some of the neighborhood gossip with whoever else might be shopping.

When Anna got to reva, Mrs. Fischer was in the store, and they struck up a conversation. After inquiring about Anna's family, Mrs.

Fisher asked Anna if she or Iver could possibly come over and check their sick sheep. Anna and Iver often went to help neighbors with their ill animals since they were the closest thing to a veterinarian that the reva community had. Anna knew how busy Iver was and didn't want to bother him, so she decided to forego her shopping and followed Mrs. Fisher—Mary—to her ranch.

Mary told Anna that the sickest sheep were in the barn, so Anna checked on them first. The sheep appeared to be extremely agitated and nervous, and Anna asked Mary if they were normally that skittish. Mary replied that they were usually pretty calm since they were used to her and her husband walking through them and working with them. Anna put one of the sickest animals in the chute, and upon closer examination she found that it had a high fever, so she showed Mary how to bathe the animal in cool water to bring its temperature down. Anna remarked to Mary that the ewes had huge udders and that they must be milking extremely well. Mary looked and said that she hadn't noticed it, but, yes, their udders were much larger than normal, so Anna decided that something must have been causing their udders to swell and fevers to set in.

They went back into the corral to examine the ewes there, and Anna noticed a small, pinkish-red blob of something foreign looking lying on the ground. She asked Mary what it was, and Mary replied that she hadn't noticed it there and had no idea what it was. Anna picked it up and examined it closely, and when she did, she told Mary that she thought it might be an aborted fetus since it resembled a miniature lamb. On their way to the gate, searching the grounds more closely, they noticed several more of the tiny pink forms scattered about. Knowing that they were probably baby lamb fetuses saddened Anna deeply. She kept thinking that in another month, maybe less, they would have been beautiful baby lambs. How horrible for them to die when the tiny living creatures had been so close to birth.

Wiping away the tears that were forming in her eyes and trying to clear her mind, Anna said, "I think that something is giving your ewes a high fever, and that either it or the fever is causing them to abort their lambs. With the swollen udders I first thought of milk fever, but that only happens after they lamb, and even then, it is rare. Maybe the extremely high fevers are creating enough stress to cause the abortions, Mary. Let's look at what you're feeding them to see if that could be the cause."

They examined the oats and hay used to feed the sheep, and both looked fine to Anna. She was hoping to find some moldy hay or grain, or some poisonous seeds or weeds—anything to point to what the problem might be. All Anna could do was shrug her shoulders at the mystery illness. She instructed Mary and her husband to keep ample cold water in the corral so that the sheep could drink their fill and to bring their fevers down by bathing them with cold water. Anna asked Mary if all of their sheep were in the corral, and when she said no, Anna advised her to keep the rest of the herd away from the ones in the corral. "It might keep it from spreading to the whole herd, Mary, if it is being caused by something in this corral or something contagious. Other than doing that, and taking diligent care of the sick ones, I don't know what to tell you. I feel terrible since it looks like you've already lost a portion of this year's lamb crop."

Mary was grateful for the help. "Thanks, Anna. We didn't know who else to turn to. I guess we'll just have to wait this out and see what happens."

"That's what neighbors are for, Mary. I just wish that I could have been more helpful. Please let me know how this turns out, okay? If it gets worse, either Iver or I will come over again. I'll say a prayer for you and your flock tonight."

Anna rode straight home at a full gallop, desperately trying to erase the sight of those pink fetuses from her mind. They haunted her all the way and made her feel uneasy about her own pregnancy again. She arrived home just barely in time since the children were hungry and Marjorie was already crying.

Chris looked like a fish out of the fish bowl, trying to figure out how to placate them.

"I have no idea how you keep up with this crew of yours, Anna. It's way more than I could ever handle. How you manage them and all the other work you do is beyond my comprehension."

Anna heard Iver coming, so she answered Chris's question loud enough for him to overhear. "I had lots of practice taking care of Iver."

"I heard that, Anna."

A couple of weeks after her trip to reva and the Fischer ranch, Anna started feeling ill again. At first she thought that it was just a reoccurrence of her morning sickness, but this seemed much more severe. It started with a headache that just kept getting worse, followed by a fever with chills and sweats. Her joints ached so severely that she wondered if she could still take care of her three children and do the cooking and barnyard chores. She didn't want to bother reidun, so she asked Iver if he could spare Chris for a few days until she recovered. She told him that this was probably just a relapse of morning sickness coupled with, and probably compounded by, a cold or the flu.

"Are you sure, honey?" asked a concerned Iver. "You look pretty sick and tired to me. Maybe we should take you to the doctor?"

"I'll get by if you can spare Chris to help me get over the hump until I feel a little better, but thanks for asking," she replied. "I'll be fine, and we certainly don't need to run to the doctor every time I'm not feeling well. Besides, it's a two- or three-day trip, and we don't have that kind of time to spare."

Later that week, Mary Fischer rode in to tell Anna that their sheep had recovered and that the group they had left in the pasture had never even gotten sick. They had lost a portion of this year's lamb crop, but Anna's advice not to mix the healthy ewes in the pasture with the sick ones in the corral had probably saved the remainder of their lambs. Mary was so thankful that she told Anna that her children could come over and pick two or three lambs to keep as their very own. The two boys were thrilled. Marjorie even seemed to smile at the thought, although she was too young to know what anyone was talking about.

"Great," Anna thought to herself. "Now I'll have bum lambs to take care of along with all the other chores." She was finally feeling a little better but didn't relish the thought of more work. "Thank you so much, Mary," she said forcing a smile. "That isn't necessary, but I'm sure the children will love playing with them. Let us know when you want us to pick them up."

All through the remainder of autumn, Anna kept losing weight and wasn't her usual vigorous self. The fevers and chills kept returning and then disappearing along with occasional headaches and pain in her legs and back. Iver again suggested going to see Dr. Townsend, but Anna still scoffed at the suggestion. Taking time off to see a doctor and letting the work slide just wasn't something that she could do. She informed him that she would be fine and that whatever was bothering her was gradually getting better. She kept telling herself that she didn't have a choice in the matter. She *had* to get over whatever it was that kept nipping at her heels and gain some weight and strength.

Mary stopped by and told Anna they could choose their lambs anytime, so Anna took the boys and Marjorie to the Fischer place to pick them out. They were given their choice of about twenty lambs, choosing the ones that looked the cutest or that were the tamest. Anna laughed that they had probably picked the poorest five lambs in the pen, two for each of the boys and one for Marjorie, but behind her laugh the horrific sight of the pink fetuses kept creeping into her mind. She somehow couldn't get over the deep feeling of sadness that thinking about those dead, premature lambs gave her.

When they reached home and turned the lambs loose, Daisy went to work making sure that they stayed together and in the yard. She cautiously herded them, keeping them rounded up while the boys helped. This daily routine gave Anna a little time to relax until the day that she left them alone for a couple of hours while she was in her garden picking weeds and harvesting some peas and onions. When she returned to the house, she found the boys and the sheep bouncing on the bed with Daisy innocently and intently watching. Anna didn't know whether to scream or laugh. Seeing how much those baby lambs enjoyed bouncing on the bed with their stiff little legs appearing to have springs attached made her smile. She went back around the corner, replaced her smiley face with a stern face, and re-entered the room. She then told the boys that the lambs were not house pets and to keep them in the barnyard from now on. Daisy seemed to understand, and as soon as Anna got the lambs off the bed, she herded them out the door.

With the illness that came and went and the baby girl and two robust boys to care for—along with all her cooking, cleaning, and chore duties—Anna felt like her family needed to get off of the ranch for a while. They hadn't been to church for three weeks, and she made Iver promise to take his family to church when Sunday arrived.

"We have so much to be thankful for, Iver, and it's getting close to thanksgiving time. remember when I reminded you that we shouldn't just pray for what we want and need, but that we should also take the time to tell God how thankful we are for what we already have? We need to do that this Sunday, and I need to get out of the house and yard for a spell." Anna recited her favorite bible verse, "This is the day the Lord has made, let us rejoice and be glad in it."

"You are right, Anna," Iver thoughtfully replied. "We should go to church every Sunday and remember to be thankful, even when things aren't going our way—which seems like the case more often than not. No matter what is going wrong tomorrow, I promise you that we will go to church."

"The last time you promised me that, two heifers started calving just as we were getting ready to leave for church, and one had back legs sticking out," Anna reminded him. "It took us two hours to get the breech calf delivered. And do you remember last Easter? We did chores the night before so we could get to sunrise Easter service on time, and a late spring storm came up during the night forcing us to tend to baby calves all day and miss the service. It seems like Satan is always bringing some catastrophe upon us on Sunday mornings to prevent us from going, but tomorrow we will close our eyes to the ranch and take our family to church."

They skipped chores in the morning, and Iver helped his wife get the children dressed for church. He didn't even check the pasture for fear he would find something amiss. As promised, the whole family was in church that day, and thanks to Obert and art, not a person in the congregation missed that they were there. Anna apologized after the service, promising to get her two boys a little more church- broken before they came again. The two boys had entertained the parishioners as much or more than the pastor who wasn't used to so much competition. Iver offered to take his belt off and have a little of his own preaching and teaching moment with the boys, but Anna declined, telling him to leave his belt on for fear that his pants would fall off of his skinny butt.

On their way home the boys got a lecture about proper church behavior, and then Anna said a family prayer. She thanked God for their family and her pregnancy, still trying to eradicate the feeling of guilt over not accepting it sooner. She thanked Him for Jesus, for their family, the ranch, their house, their horses and cattle, and good neighbors. Iver joined in, and they recited the Lord's Prayer together. Their faith was cemented, their roots went deep into the prairie, and they were ready for any storm that might come their way. They would need every ounce of this faith, every tiny bit of this courage and perseverance, to get them through the next few years. The beauty and bliss that was today could become beastly at any moment and with very little warning. Ill winds were stirring, and Anna somehow subconsciously sensed that something seemed amiss.

The days grew shorter and the nights grew longer as thanksgiving passed and Christmas approached. It was colder and wetter than usual, and the ground froze up as hard as the granite stones that kept popping up in their fields every spring. (Iver swore that someone must be sneaking out and planting a new crop of stones for them to have to carry off the fields every year.)

Late in December, between Christmas and New Year's Day, Anna started having labor pains. It was too soon, but she couldn't stop the contractions. Praying to herself, she opened the front door and called out to Iver, but he was haying the cows and couldn't hear her. Chris was probably in his house, but she didn't think that she could make it there and back. So, she went back inside and boiled water and gathered clean towels between her labor pains. She continued to pray while she went to the bedroom where the beautiful baby Marjorie had been born and, by herself, delivered two stillborn baby boys. At first, she was in shock, horrified at the sight of the two dead babies, but then the tears started flowing as the realization of what had happened set in. She lay there crying and sobbing for two dreadfully long hours until she gathered enough strength to get up and take care of the bodies.

By the time Iver came in for lunch and found her, she had lovingly cleaned the boys, wrapped them in clean white dishtowels, and placed them in her wicker basket. Finished, she lay back down with them, prayed for them, and cried more. Even in their cleaned-up condition, it was a shocking scene for Iver to walk into. Seeing his lovely Anna lying there sobbing uncontrollably alongside of their silent sons nearly broke his heart. Anna and Iver cried together for a long time with Iver holding Anna closely and massaging her, trying his best to console her.

After a long while, Anna asked Iver if he would finish cleaning up the bedroom while she went and fed Marjorie who had been sniveling in her crib for some time. Anna tried to will her sons to life one last time, said another prayer, and then reluctantly left, trying her best not to show the two boys waiting outside her tear-stained face and swollen eyes. Unaware that there was anything amiss in her happy little world, now that her mother had shown up, Marjorie nursed and then wanted to play with her mom. Mom tried, but there would be no cheering her today—or for a long, long time to come. *What happened today would haunt her for years, dominating her prayers and thoughts, bringing her an ocean of tears. What had she done to bring this horror to her family? Was it because she had secretly wished she hadn't been pregnant so soon? Was it because she hadn't been as thankful as she should have been? Should she have heeded Iver's advice and gone to see a doctor? Had she somehow offended her Father in heaven?*

At evening chore time Iver told Chris what happened, and together they tried to dig a small burial plot on the hill overlooking the house and barn. They chipped and axed and pounded and chiseled at the frozen ground for a long time before giving up. When Iver went in after chores, he sadly told Anna that they weren't able to dig the graves and that burial would have to wait until the following spring.

After a short conference with Chris, they decided to have a small family service for the boys even though they couldn't bury them. Their sons were already wrapped in linen, and Iver said he would build them proper wooden caskets before spring to bury them in.

Since it was below zero outside with a twenty-five mile an hour wind from what felt like the North Pole, they held the service inside. Anna's little prairie family asked Jesus to take care of their boys for them until they could meet again, and they thanked Him for their three healthy children. Chris kept Obert, arthur, and Marjorie in the house while Anna and Iver took the twins to the grain bin, the only place they could think of to store them until spring. Leaving them wrapped in the linens and in the wicker basket, they wrapped the basket with a sheet and—through tears—buried their sons in the wheat. They planned to uncover them as soon as the ground thawed in the spring, when they could put them in their new caskets and properly bury them. returning to the house, they sternly warned Obert and art to keep out of the granary which was to be strictly off limits to them.

A week later Obert and art, who had never before gone into the granary or even wanted to, tested Anna and Iver's patience. They just *had* to see why they were forbidden to go into the granary, so, making sure their parents weren't watching, they snuck across the yard. Slowly and cautiously they entered the grain storage room, the hair standing out on their scrawny necks for fear that any minute a ghost or goblin might strike out at them. Finding nothing out of the ordinary, and certainly nothing that looked like it should be forbidden, they sighed a breath of relief and jumped into the grain, playing in it like it was a giant sand box. Working in the barn, Iver heard them laughing and caught them just as they uncovered the basket that contained his other two sons.

This time he didn't wait to counsel with Anna, and his belt quickly came off. Obert was first. The frightened art had to endure watching his older brother get thrashed while waiting for his turn. Afterward, both boys ran to the house bawling and shrieking with Iver following behind them. He explained to Anna what had happened. She hadn't thought that she could generate any more tears, but they came anyway. *More tears, more remorse, more heartache.* Obert and arthur didn't know what they had done that was so horrible, but they fully understood and felt their mother's sorrow. They silently and solemnly went to their room and behaved themselves for the rest of the day. Anna retreated to her porch rocking chair and silently rocked, cried, and prayed.

The following spring, as soon as the ground had thawed sufficiently to dig two small graves, Anna and Iver retrieved the frozen bodies from storage and tenderly placed them in the wooden boxes that Iver had made, ready for burial. This time they arranged for a more formal funeral with the minister from the reva Lutheran Church. Odd, reidun, and their family gathered with other friends and neighbors to solemnly help Anna and Iver carry the bodies up the hill and listen to the minister say a few words of prayer over them. Through more tears, Anna and Iver silently and lovingly covered their sons with the dark prairie soil.

Anna felt like it was the second time that she had buried them and silently said her own prayer over the grave. She didn't blame God or anyone else for their misfortune; *she blamed herself.* She didn't ask Him why this had happened since she had already decided that it was because of her actions. She just thanked Him for them and her other children and asked Him to take care of them for her so that she could meet them in heaven. Her heart was heavy, her soul was sad, her eyes were swollen, and her body was weary, but just the same, she invited everyone to the house for pie and coffee and thanked them for coming and sharing in their sorrow and grief.

Anna still had occasional bouts of flu-like symptoms that summer and fall, and although she was no longer losing as much weight, she hadn't gained any back either. She was very thin and didn't feel as strong and resilient as she once was, often being depressed and tired. She hadn't been resting, almost fearful to sleep since she continued to have reoccurring nightmares. Her dreams were plagued with those dreadful pink sheep fetuses, often combined with dead babies, the scenes so horrifying that she woke up screaming and was too terrified to lie back down. All of this weighed on her, but she vowed to regain her strength so that she could hold her own on the ranch and take care of her family. Marjorie was old enough to be weaned, and she was still in diapers. Anna was hoping to end both of those chores— nursing and diapers—before fall. She did, and it really seemed to help her get going again. She finally re-gained some weight along with some strength and stamina. She was resilient; the old Anna was returning.

7

Iver and the Wolves

Spring had warmed into summer, and Anna was slowly but surely recovering. She made regular trips to their little graveyard on the hill overlooking the house and barn, and the wildflowers she had planted there were blooming brightly. The flowers, along with the beauty of the prairie, lifted her spirits and made her feel better. She could actually make the trip without crying now. Anna was even milking and doing other barnyard chores again, along with her household duties.

They were getting in short supply of meat, so Anna asked Iver if he would mind a day or two of hunting. She knew that he enjoyed hunting and that it would be a brief time of reprieve from the usual drudgery of the ranch work. He ventured out to get an antelope or some fresh venison that week, but there was none to be found. He knew that the late and extremely vicious spring storm that had gone through had killed nearly all of the newborn deer fawns and antelope kids, but he didn't know that it had been as serious as it was proving to be. All he brought home from almost a full day of hunting were a grouse and two cottontail rabbits. He told Anna that they would have to butcher a beef or one of the children's lambs if the hunting didn't improve. She suggested trying the Slim Buttes, but Iver and Chris had ridden through that area the week before without spotting any game there either—not even any turkeys or coyotes. One thing they had seen was a lot more wolves than normal.

"Not a good combination," Iver told Anna. "It looks like the wolf population is up, and the prey population is down. We'll have to watch the stock closely this winter. The wolves will be starving, and our livestock will be their targets if this situation doesn't improve."

It didn't. The summer continued to be hot and dry, and even rabbits were scarce. The shortage of game brought Anna's thoughts back to the vicious wolf attack in their heifer pen. She knew that Iver was right and that the ever-menacing wolves would be back. She silently vowed to protect her children and the ranch animals from them. The dry spell continued into fall with Anna vigilantly watching for wolves and doing the chores while Iver and Chris scraped every meadow and ditch and low spot on the ranch to gather some hay for the winter. Chris, always in tune with the seasons and the weather, predicted an early and hard winter, and Iver agreed.

One autumn day Iver hitched the team to the wagon to bring home a load of hay from the field, and three wolves followed him back to the ranch. He couldn't get a shot at them, but witnessing those wolves, brazen enough to follow him home, felt like a harbinger. He asked Chris about the incident, and Chris said that in all the years he had been in South Dakota he had never seen the wolves as fearless and hungry as they were this year. To his knowledge, they had never before been so bold as to come into someone's yard in daylight. It was indeed a bad omen.

Iver advised Anna to keep Daisy and the children in the house or the yard and to have her rifle close at hand. Anna didn't need to be told because she already had the rifle loaded and ready. She loved God's creatures, but wolves were the lone exception, especially since the morning that she had to kill the heifer that the wolves had partially eaten alive. They were only doing what nature intended them to, but they were vicious and indiscriminating killers. Anna certainly knew this and told Iver that she would guard the farmstead and the children while he patrolled the livestock. The calves were big enough to wean, and the horse herd knew how to deal with wolves, so Iver wasn't really worried yet. Wolves always preyed on the old and the weak first and almost always on easy targets like sheep before cattle.

The next few days went by uneventfully until the Fischer family reported losing several of their sheep. At first they thought they were just missing, but a day later they found one hamstrung and a few more absent with the telltale signs of a massacre. No doubt it was wolves as there hadn't been any mountain lions reported since the time when Iver saw the one stalking him. Wolves and lions were the only two species in western South Dakota that could do that kind of damage, and this had to be wolves. The ranching community was alerted, and everyone prepared as best they could, knowing that the bloodthirsty wolves would graduate from sheep to cattle and horses. The sheep ranchers began bringing their flocks closer to their homesteads and keeping as many as they could in their corrals.

Iver and Chris decided to wean and market their calves right away. Other than barnyard critters like the pet sheep and chickens, the calves were their most vulnerable animals to wolf attack, so it was best to eliminate that likelihood before it happened. They usually kept around forty head of heifer calves to replace the older and less productive cows that needed to be culled from the herd, but this year they would cut the number of calves retained to fifteen or twenty so that they could keep them closely guarded in the corral by the house. Iver told Odd that they intended to wean right away, and Odd thought it was a great idea, so they worked together with weaning as they had done in the past. Anna, Chris, and reidun were put in charge of home guard duty while Iver, Odd, Daisy, and two neighbor boys trailed the calves to the Belle Fourche market which had become the nation's leading shipper of cattle.

About halfway to Belle, six large gray wolves followed them for a few miles. They were close enough to be seen every now and then, but out of gunshot range. Iver circled back on them in an attempt to try for a shot, but they must have caught his scent in the breeze and disappeared. Even with the threat of wolves they stopped to rest the calves several times since they didn't want them to lose any weight.

The more pounds that went across the scale, the more money that lined their pockets since calves were usually sold by the pound.

The trail drive paused at the Belle Fourche river before entering town, letting the calves get a good drink and add a few precious pounds before they took them to the stockyards for weighing. Although they were marketing earlier than normal and the calves didn't weigh as much as usual, the price per pound was better. Iver and Odd were both extremely happy with the outcome.

After selling the calves and collecting their paychecks from the stockyards, the men stopped at the bank to cash them. It was what they had always done. They weren't worried about thieves, and they preferred to keep the money under their own supervision rather than trust the bank. Iver and Odd paid their helpers and then made their way to the hardware store where the only thing they purchased was more ammunition to use on the wolves during the winter. Iver wanted to get Anna something special, so they went to the dress shop where he settled on a brightly colored silk scarf. Not to be outdone, Odd purchased one for reidun.

By the time Iver and Odd were done shopping, the two boys that helped them drive the cattle to town had already filled their saddlebags with candy and other goodies. When they were all saddled up, they aimed their horses northeast. The ride home would be a lot easier and faster than their ride to town had been, and they were all in a hurry. The boys were missing school, and the men were missing their families. The four rode as hard as they could without pushing the horses. Daisy rode with Iver part of the time and ran behind the rest of the time. She sensed the wolves and was never more than a few feet from Iver and his rifle. Iver and Odd safely returned the boys to their homes and then continued to their own ranches and families.

"About time you got home!" Anna and Chris said in unison at the sight of Iver. "What's in that saddlebag you're bringing in?"

Iver proudly opened the saddlebag, smiled, and spread the fresh hundred-dollar bills on the table. The steers and heifers had averaged over twenty-five dollars each and had been the highest selling set of calves that week. To top the market was the best bragging rights a rancher could have, and Chris beamed at the news. Iver gave Anna her new silk scarf and presented Chris and the boys with hard candy and licorice from the general store. All was well in their prairie home that night. Selling calves and bringing home the cash was a highlight of their meager ranch lives.

After supper Iver visited with Anna about purchasing some more land. There was a small ranch for sale a few miles east of them, and he figured if they bought it, they could run another fifty to seventy- five cows and their calves. The seller wanted cash, so if they made the purchase, they would have to go to the bank in Buffalo for a loan. Iver explained that he had already asked their banker for a land loan, and the banker had said he'd loan them the money.

Anna pretty much threw cold water on his idea, explaining that they already had more work than they could handle and that she was against borrowing more money. "We finally have Chris paid off for the Herefords, and as soon as I go pay our bill at the reva store, we will be debt-free. Just think of it, Iver! this is the first time in our married life for that to happen. Let's enjoy what we have for a while and not jump into purchasing another ranch that we don't have the money for, okay?"

Anna had always been conservative and detested being in debt. She was very liberal with her love and generously helped others but hated owing someone something. She didn't believe in interest either, saying that it just wasn't biblical. Taking on another loan, after finally being out of debt, just didn't feel right to her. Maybe it was just a premonition, but she also had the feeling that their time of prosperity could soon come to an end. She felt like she was disappointing Iver and battled with her conscience over the decision. She was still struggling with the loss of the twins and still having nightmares. That, plus worrying about her family and the ranch, all weighed heavily on her mind and conscience. Anna wondered if that was why she felt so uneasy about the future.

In the morning—after gathering the eggs, milking the cows, feeding the replacement heifers in the corral, and separating the cream from the milk—Anna went to the general store with her three children and Daisy. She could hardly wait to have the pure pleasure of paying off their bill which had been accumulating over the past several months. Marjorie was old enough to crawl and walk a bit, and the boys were—well, they were boys. Going to the store was a great adventure to them, but Anna made them promise to stay on their best behavior. They were *not* to touch anything in the store, and they were *not* to whine and beg for candy and toys. They were to be polite and say "yes ma'am" or "yes sir" if anyone talked to them.

They actually did pretty well until Obert spotted the BB gun. It was a Little Daisy Model 20, and he excitedly proclaimed that he *really needed* it to help hunt the wolves. He explained that he had outgrown his stick gun and was a "big boy" now and that he could guard his brother and sister if he had that BB gun. Anna told him that he would have to ask his dad about having a gun, and Obert—surprisingly—settled for a stick of peppermint candy without complaining.

The store owner reported that there had been a few more wolf attacks, but only on sheep herds. Anna loaded the supplies and her children in the wagon, and Daisy effortlessly jumped over the side and almost landed on Obert who gleefully giggled and gave her a lick of his peppermint candy. Anna smiled all the way home, inside and out. She had been feeling much better, and this was a glorious day. They were debt free! *Thank you for all of your blessings, Lord*, she said silently as she smiled toward heaven. Her smile turned into a concerned scowl when she noticed the four wolves watching them from the hill overlooking their barn. The wolves left when she pulled into the yard.

Anna could feel it in her bones; winter was right around the corner. So far they had only received one snow, which had mostly melted, but the temperature had turned permanently colder. There was a small coal mine six miles north of their ranch, and the cold weather prompted Anna to ask Iver to go and get their winter supply of coal before more snow came and blocked the roads. She thought the trip might be a good father-son bonding experience, so in the morning she bundled the boys up so that they could accompany Iver on the ride to the coal mine. The trio of "men" loaded up, leaving Daisy home to guard the sheep and keep Anna and Marjorie company. Daisy looked disappointed as they drove off, hoping to hear Iver tell her to load up. She watched intently as they left, saddened not to be riding on the wagon with them.

Anna also watched while Iver and the two boys turned out of the yard and headed the recently broken team of horses north toward the coal mine. Iver had been working with the horses for two months, and he told Anna that he thought it would be a good learning experience for them to have a long and tiring haul. Anna went back to her chores until about an hour later when little art came walking home, crying and screaming that his daddy needed help. "Daddy needs help, Momma! Daddy needs help, Mommy!" he cried and sobbed to her repeatedly.

Anna instantly knew there must have been an accident, so she took Marjorie and ran out to look for Chris with art doing his best to keep up. Finding Chris in the barn, she hurriedly told him that something terrible must have happened, and she thought that Iver and Obert probably had a wagon accident. "Art came walking home by himself, crying to me that 'Daddy needs help.' Please ride out and find them, Chris. Please hurry! I'll come with the buggy and Marjorie and art."

Chris quickly saddled up and galloped off to the north. Anna ran to the corral to get Babe, their buggy horse, and then hitched the bay mare to the buggy, willing her hands to work faster. She helped art into the buggy and held Marjorie on her lap, whipping the mare into action. Daisy didn't load up in time, so she came running behind wondering what the excitement was about and why Anna hadn't waited for her to load. Anna drove the buggy over the hill with Babe at a gallop, frantically searching the horizon for the rest of her family. She first saw the wagon and team about a mile and a half to the northwest in the corner of the fence that kept their cows out of the field. As she started to turn that direction, she noticed Chris's horse to the northeast. Chris was off the horse and appeared to be looking at something on the ground, so Anna turned her buggy back to the north toward him. When she got closer, her heart sank as she perceived that the something on the ground was someone. Anna slid the mare to a stop, set the hand brake, and leaped off, running to where Chris was standing over Iver.

"Iver! Iver!" she screamed at her husband as she ran. There was no response. She fell on her knees beside him and called again. Still, there was no response. The fear of losing her husband turned to shock as she continued to will him to speak or get up. Was this another nightmare? Was it really happening? How could she lose Iver so soon after the deaths of her twins? She felt the blood draining out of her head, her spirit with it.

"I'm afraid that he's gone, Anna," Chris whispered through dry lips, obviously in shock.

Anna, her tears falling on Iver, leaned over to kiss her husband. As she was kissing his lips, she felt his soft and warm breath on her cheek. It filled her with joy and shocked her back to reality. "He's alive, Chris! He's just unconscious! It looks like he hit his head on this big rock. Do you have anything to help me clean up the blood? Where's Obert?"

Chris seemed not to even hear the question, clearly in shock over what he had perceived to be Iver's death. Anna tried to get through to him once again. She desperately needed help. "Chris, can you hear me? Iver is alive!

We must find Obert! Hurry over to the wagon and see if he is there. Hurry, Chris, please hurry!"

Chris finally regained his composure, climbed on his horse, and galloped toward the wagon. When he got closer, he could see that Obert was still in the wagon, sitting there with the reins in his hands but not knowing what to do with them. His boyish, tear-stained face looked up at Chris with an expression of fear and helplessness. The horses were still stamping their feet nervously and snorting their fear but had calmed down enough that Chris could softly talk to them and keep them from stampeding off again. The fence corner was probably the only thing that had saved Obert, and it was a wonder that the horses hadn't plowed right through it. Maybe the soft earth in the field had helped too, slowing them down and tiring them faster. Chris tied his horse behind the wagon and drove the still panicky team, along with Obert, back to where Iver lay at the other edge of the field.

Obert leapt off the wagon at the sight of his parents. "Daddy, Daddy! Is Daddy dead? the wolves were chasing us, Mommy, and Daddy shot them!"

That was when it all started to make some sense. Anna knew that something out of the ordinary must have happened to stampede the horses. "We have to get Iver on the wagon, Chris. We have to get him home."

It was not an easy task. Iver was in his prime, probably weighing around 180 pounds. Chris was old and weak and not nearly as strong as he once was. He and Anna carefully dragged Iver to the back of the wagon and folded the railing down. Thankfully, it was on hinges so that when the back railing was down, it created a ramp that made it easier for them to load Iver. With Anna at one side and Chris on the other, they pulled and hoisted Iver to the ramp. Little Obert helped hold him in that position until Anna could get on the wagon and grasp Iver's shoulders. With her pulling and Chris and Obert pushing, they somehow managed to get Iver up the ramp and into the wagon. Then Anna loaded the boys and Marjorie. Daisy was already in the wagon, not wanting to get left again, faithfully sitting beside Iver. Anna headed the wagon toward home with Chris following in the buggy.

When they arrived, they discovered the problem of how to get Iver into the house. Chris volunteered to go to reva and get some help, so Anna and the children waited until he returned with a neighbor, Nels, and Charlie, the owner of the reva store. Iver was still out cold, so the three men and Anna carried him into the house and laid him on the bed. Anna was at a total loss of what to do. She sat with Iver, dressing his head wound and washing his face and body with warm, clean water, talking to him and holding his hand.

The boys and Chris solemnly stood by, patiently waiting for Iver to get up and talk to them. Eventually, Anna remembered that Nels and Charlie were still there, so she thanked them and told them that they might as well go home. There was nothing more they could do anyway except have their families say a prayer and petition God for Iver's swift and complete recovery.

When the men left, Anna realized that none of the chores had been done and that she had three hungry children to take care of. She reluctantly left Iver alone on the bed and asked Chris if he would help her milk tonight so she wouldn't be gone from Iver's side for so long. They hurried through chores, skipping many of the details. Anna hastened her pace as she ran back to the house, then she sat with the still unconscious Iver and rested for a few minutes, giving him a few more kisses before leaving to make supper for the family and Chris. It had been a horrific day, but in Anna's resilient mind it was still salvageable. After what could very possibly have killed all three of them, Obert and art were fine, and Iver was still alive. Anna had a lot to be thankful for.

She stayed up most of the night fending off sleep while singing and talking to Iver, holding his hand, and rubbing his shoulders. The head wound had clotted and didn't appear to need stitching, although the wound looked pretty deep. Anna cleaned and disinfected it once more, then carefully wrapped his head with a piece of linen to keep it clean and hopefully help it heal. She finally lay down beside him and tried to close her eyes. The horrific scene kept going through her mind, and as she fitfully went to sleep, she put the pieces of the puzzle together, discerning what had probably happened and later remembering it like this:

> Iver and the boys were about a mile north of the ranch when Iver spotted a few large gray and black wolves skirting around the wagon as if they were getting ready to attack. Iver had never heard of wolves assaulting a

wagon and horses, but without thinking, he dropped the reins and loaded his rifle, taking a few quick shots at the lean and vicious-looking wolves. Before he knew what was happening, the partially broken team of horses—not familiar with gunfire and sensing and fearing the wolves—spooked and bolted through the ditch, stamping off to the northwest.

Just as Iver dropped his rifle and jumped up to take the reins, the wagon hit one of the many rocks that he had removed from the field and placed along its edge. The wagon bounced wildly, and off balance, Iver flew out, his head smashing into another of the jagged rocks as he landed. Little art, now about three-and-a-half years old, was also ejected and sailed right alongside his dad, luckily staying in flight for a few feet farther and missing the rocks. Only Obert managed to stay with the wagon, fearfully riding behind the stampeding horses for almost another mile until they ran into a fence corner at the far end of the field where they were boxed in and finally stopped.

Art was bewildered but not seriously injured. Seeing his father lying on the ground motionless, he cried out, "Get up, Daddy! Get up, Daddy!" all the little boy could do was cry in fear, but that wasn't getting any results, so off he plodded, his almost white hair flying in the wind, his short little legs working assiduously to take him home. Miraculously, the gunshots must have frightened the wolves away, or both my son and my husband would most likely have been killed and eaten by the ravenous pack. Just as miraculous was the fact that tiny art was able to find his way home without getting lost.

As she restlessly slept beside Iver, Anna dreamt. In her dream Iver had regained consciousness and was laughing at her for being so concerned. She was scolding him for not being more careful. It was a wonderful dream, but she woke from it only to see him still lying beside her, breathing but not showing any other signs of life. She now realized that he had to go to a hospital. There was no medical help in South Dakota until you reached Belle Fourche, and Dr. Townsend was just a country doctor without a hospital. Iver needed full-time attention. There was nothing available—unless—her good friends in Minnesota and Doctor George Christman came to mind.

The sun was just beginning to peek over the horizon, but Anna immediately got off of the bed and went to Chris's house. She pounded at the door until he got out of bed and, in his long johns, came to the door. Anna's tone was urgent, "I need you to ride to reva and get Nels and Charlie again, if they can come. Iver is still unconscious, and we have to get him to a good doctor and medical facility. We need them or anyone else that's available to help load him back into the wagon. I should have done this right away, but I was so certain that he would get better on his own overnight. Please hurry. I'll take him to Hettinger, and if there isn't any help there, I'll put him on the train to see Dr. George Christman in Minneapolis."

Chris wanted to know who Dr. Christman was, so Anna hurriedly explained. "He's a friend that I met on my way to South Dakota. He's a wonderful doctor with a clinic, and he will know what to do. Just hurry over to reva. If Nels and Charlie aren't up yet, pound on their door! I'll have the team hitched to the wagon and ready to go."

Anna rushed to the barn, got the harnesses and halters, and then ran to the corral to retrieve the horses. Getting them hitched to the wagon was not an easy task, especially this early in the morning. The horses were cold and hungry and didn't want to cooperate. Anna promised them that if they were patient, she would give them some oats after they were hitched up, while they waited for the men to arrive. True to her word, she gave each of them a gallon of oats after she was finished, then hurried back to the house, worried that the kids might already be out of bed.

Obert was awake, but the others were still sleeping. After checking in on Iver, she made breakfast for all of them, plus some extra pancakes and sausage for Chris and the men coming to help load Iver. While impatiently waiting for help to arrive, Anna sat with Iver, talking to him, telling him how much she loved him, wetting his lips, washing his face with warm water, kissing him, and praying for him. Her prayers were also questions. *"What did I do to bring all this grief to my family? First the twins, now Iver. Please forgive me, Father. Please help me, Father."*

The men finally rode in, tied up their sweat-lathered horses, and ran into the house. Anna looked at them thankfully, deeply relieved that they had been able to come and help, and said, "I'm so sorry to bother you guys again, but Iver needs to be loaded back onto the wagon. He's alive but still unconscious, and I need to get him to a good doctor who can take care of him. I have a stack of pancakes on the table and coffee in the pot. Grab a quick bite, please. I'll sit with Iver until you're ready to load him."

They chowed down on the buttered, syrupy hotcakes as rapidly as they could, gulping the hot coffee as they ate. Anna already had blankets, sandwiches, and water in the wagon. All that was left was to load Iver and her children and head for Hettinger.

After quickly eating, Nels offered to go along with Anna to Hettinger. Charlie thought a bit, and then he volunteered to go too, saying that the store could get along without him for a day. Then Nels carefully added, "You know, Anna, it will be an extremely difficult trip for you and three children. It looks like Iver is in God's hands right now anyway, and there isn't anything that any of us can do except get him to help. You might be better off staying here with the children. You never know, we could have snow any day, and being caught out in the cold and snow with little children wouldn't be wise. What about your livestock and your milk cows? and have you thought about what might happen if the wolves attack the wagon again? I know you want to be with your husband, but Charlie and I can make this trip on our own, and I think you should stay here, Anna. That is what Iver would want."

Anna hadn't thought of anything but getting Iver to Hettinger as quickly as possible, knowing that she would have to take the children with her. After evaluating what Nels had just said, she knew that he was right. She would be endangering the children to take them out on a long trip this time of the year, and she hadn't even considered the wolves. Two men would be much better equipped to handle an emergency, and Iver would be safer and in better hands with the two men than with her and three children.

She went to Nels and hugged him first, then Charlie. "I will always love you both for doing this for us. You couldn't be more right, Nels. Iver will be much better off with you two taking him, and I must put his safety and the welfare of my children first. I am nearly positive that there isn't anyone in Hettinger equipped to take care of Iver, so you will probably have to put him on the train for Minneapolis."

While the men carried Iver to the wagon and placed him on the buffalo robe and then covered him with all the spare blankets that Anna had, she wrote a note to send with Iver.

To the train conductor and to whoever reads this letter:

My name is Anna Tenold, and this unconscious man is my husband, Iver Tenold. He was injured in a wagon accident where he hit his head on a rock yesterday. He has never regained consciousness.

If there is no help in Hettinger, please take him to Minneapolis and deliver him to Dr. George Christman or to Dr. Christman's clinic on the west side of town. Dr. Christman is a family friend and will know what to do. Please leave this note pinned to Iver for Dr. Christman to read. I pray that in your kindness and mercy you will please help us.

Most sincerely and thankfully,
Anna Tenold

P.S. George, this is my husband Iver. Please do whatever it takes to get him back home to me, alive and well. Greet the family for me.

All my love,
Anna

Anna ran the note out and pinned it on Iver's shirt under his coat. After giving her husband another kiss and whispering to him, "I love you my darling Iver; please hurry back to me," she gave the two neighbors another hug and told them that there were sandwiches and water packed in the wagon.

Daisy was faithfully sitting by Iver's side, but Anna asked her to get off. "I need you here to help me, Daisy, but thanks for offering to go along with Iver."

8

The Winter of Wolves

The wagon pulled out of the yard, and Anna went into the house and cried. She knew that there was hope, and she believed that her prayers would be answered, but it somehow felt like Iver was leaving her and would never be coming back. She was distraught with the feeling of losing him and terrified at the thought of trying to survive alone on the ranch with three children. The notion that she might never see Iver alive again kept running through her mind. Somehow, she remembered first meeting him and how she had thought he was trying to trick her with the wild horse story.

There were so many things that she loved about Iver. Had she told him how much she appreciated his tenderness and sense of humor? Had he heard her tell him how much she loved him and how desperately she wanted him to return to her? She wondered if he had been able to hear any of her parting words as he lay there unconscious. "Please, Lord! Let him have heard me! Please let him live! Please bring him back to me and his family!"

The sound of Marjorie's intermittent whining and whimpering brought Anna out of her remorse, so she wiped away the tears and went to the kitchen to make breakfast for the children. Then, sitting at the breakfast table, she slowly explained to them that their father had been seriously injured and that he might be gone for a long, long time. She told Obert that he was now the man of the house, and he would be responsible for helping her take care of his younger brother and sister. Obert proudly told his mommy that he would help her, and art importantly added that he would be a big boy too. Marjorie was just starting to talk, and she almost acted as if she comprehended the conversation and was trying to be helpful too.

Then Anna turned to Chris and said, "Chris, I feel so terrible that you have been burdened by all of this. At your age all you should have to do is sit on your rocking chair and read a book or watch the birds in the bird feeder. Worrying about the ranch should no longer play a part in your life, but now it seems that I need you more than ever before. We know that the wolves are starving and that, sooner or later, they will come knocking at our door. I aim to shoot every one of them before I let them kill another animal on this ranch. We need to use every ounce of our strength as efficiently as possible. I think we should bring the cows closer to the homestead, to their winter pasture, and patrol them and the horses daily. The best arrangement, if you agree, would probably be to keep you on your horse checking the livestock with me doing the barnyard chores and the milking. I can keep the kids in the barn while doing the chores, and Daisy will be in charge of watching over them and keeping them rounded up." She paused for a moment. "What do you think, Chris? Can we make this work? We *have* to make this work."

Chris replied thoughtfully, "Most of the burden will be on you, Anna. I can't see well enough to shoot straight, and my heavy-lifting days are over. But like you suggested, I still can ride a horse and check the livestock. I think your plan will work Anna, and please don't worry about this old sack of bones. They've seen better days, but they ain't giving up yet. You have a lot more important things to think about than fretting on me, like those three beautiful children sitting here and your husband. We must never give up hope that he will come home. That hope is what will keep me—and you, of course—going."

"Well said, Chris, we must never give up hope, and we must never stop praying." Anna felt some of her courage and strength returning and continued, "I'll do the dishes and put some soup on for dinner. As soon as I'm done in the house, I'll take the children with me to the barn and start milking and doing the chores. You saddle up and check the cows and the horses. We need to pray ceaselessly that Iver lives through the day, and that Nels and Charlie get him safely to Hettinger and find help. Nels promised to give us a report first thing in the morning if they make it back tonight."

Anna paused, deep in thought, and then added, "We'll never be able to get it done today, but let's plan to bring the cattle home to the winter pasture tomorrow after chores which will make it a lot easier for you to check them. Thank God that Iver already has the hay moved in."

Early the next morning, Nels rode in to report to Anna and her worried family what had happened in Hettinger. "You were right, Anna; there wasn't any help for Iver in Hettinger, so we took him to the train station. The train folks were real nice to us. They remembered you and wondered how you and the big blue roan horse that rode the rails with you were doing. They put Iver in a special bunk on the train, and we watched the train leave, taking him to Minneapolis. God must have heard your prayers, because there just happened to be a nurse on the train. She said it was important to keep his lips moist and try to get him to take some water to prevent dehydration. She promised to watch over Iver and do whatever she could to help him survive until they reached Minneapolis. The train conductor even said that he would personally deliver Iver to the doctor that you wrote about on the note."

"Thank you so much, Nels," Anna replied. "At least I had one brief moment of sound judgment when I thought of pinning a note to Iver. If it hadn't been for you, I probably would have rushed off in the wagon with the children and Iver, and heaven only knows what all could have happened. You are a truly good person, Nels, a saint. When Iver returns, he may owe you his life."

Anna had just finished the morning chores when Nels came riding in with his report, and Chris rode in right behind him from checking the horse herd, so it was time for them to move the cows home to their winter pasture. Nels asked if he might be able to go in and see the boys and Marjorie for a while before he left, and Anna one-upped him by saying that if he wanted to, he could stay with them for about three or four hours—while she and Chris moved the cows home. He happily stayed, and Anna said one of her numerous silent prayers, thanking God that things somehow just seem to work out when He is involved.

Anna, Chris, and Daisy moved the cattle home with no difficulty. Anna knew it would be easy since cows know that there will be free food waiting for them and are always eager to come home to winter pasture. Daisy was a great help, as usual, circling cautiously around the cattle, nudging them along when they needed it, and keeping them going in the right direction. Chris remarked that, "Next year we might just have Daisy do this all by herself."

When they got home and had the cows securely in the pasture by the barn, Anna went in to see how Nels was doing. He was having so much fun with the children that he didn't seem to want to leave, so Anna invited him and Chris to stay for supper if they didn't mind waiting until she finished the chores. She hadn't seen any wolves that day, and the livestock were content. Life was *almost* normal at their homestead on the prairie.

That night, the weary Anna couldn't go to bed before writing a letter to Dr. George Christman, the doctor in Minneapolis whose hands she was putting her husband's life into. Anna was almost too tired to write, but she wanted to get her letter off with the morning mail. She also remembered that in all of the confusion she hadn't let Odd and reidun know what had happened. Maybe she could get Chris to ride over there tomorrow and catch them up. She sat down and by the light of her lantern wearily began composing her letter to the beloved family in Minneapolis that she had lived with on her trip to Dakota.

Dear George and Sarah,

I have wanted to introduce you to my husband Iver, but certainly not in this manner. He and our two little boys were going to the coal mine to get our winter supply of coal when wolves started following them. I'm not exactly sure how it happened, but the team stampeded, and Iver and Art went flying off the wagon when it bounced over a rock. Iver apparently hit his head on another rock, but little Art was uninjured and managed to make it all the way home on his own.

We took Iver to Hettinger and placed him on the train and sent him to you, the only people in the world that I know who would care for him and make him well, if that is possible. I pray that he is already there in your care, and that you will know what to do to help him. I hope this isn't a burden, and

I pray that the Christman family is all well and happy. I miss all of you so much and am still hoping that I can come out to see you sometime when Gert is also visiting.

It is late and I must get some sleep as I have a ranch to run and three children of my own to care for. Please let me know that Iver has arrived safely. Also, please give those six beautiful children of yours a hug from me.

All my love,
I miss you so much,
Anna

She started her bedtime prayer but fell asleep in the middle of it. Morning came swiftly. Anna could have used a few more hours of sleep, but she was up with the sun and prepared breakfast for her family. She had already fed them and started on the milking when Odd pulled into the yard with a load of coal.

He entered the barn and gave Anna a big hug. "One of the neighbors stopped in yesterday and told me what happened. I don't know what to say Anna. Have you heard anything about how Iver is doing?"

"We haven't heard anything yet, but it's too soon. Iver is probably in the hospital in Minneapolis by now, and it will take a few days before I get a report. I've heard about that new invention they have in cities called the telephone, and I sure wish we had something like that here to communicate with in times like this. The waiting is harder than anything I've ever had to do, but the children, chores, and livestock keep me so busy that I sometimes don't have time to think and worry. Or sleep. right now, that is probably a good thing, except for the sleep part. How is your family doing?"

Odd began, "reidun is pregnant again, and the children are growing so fast it makes my head dizzy. James is getting to be a pretty good assistant. We talked about sending him over to lend a hand, but I'm afraid that he and Obert would probably just get into mischief, and it would do more harm than good. I plan to come over and help whenever I can, and reidun wants to but realizes that she and the kids would create more work for you than they would get accomplished. I decided to get you a load of coal after finding out about Iver's accident and the events that happened on the way to the coal mine. Thank God the boys are okay. It could have been a lot worse, I guess. Can I put the load in your coal bin? How are you holding up, Anna?"

"I'm doing okay, but I desperately miss Iver. I could sure use some of his strength and courage right now. Odd, how did you find the time and energy to get coal for us? You are so generous and thoughtful. I pray that Iver will be home soon to repay your kindness."

"I'm not keeping track, but if I were, I know that you and Iver would be way ahead of me in the kindness and good deeds department, Anna. Being able to help you out is a blessing, not a burden. Are you sure that you're ok?" Odd added with a brotherly hug.

Like a dam bursting it all came suddenly pouring out. The worry about whether Iver would live or die. The weariness of trying to care for her children and the animals with virtually no sleep. The pressure of all of the decisions that had been forced on her. Wondering how she could possibly run the ranch by herself while protecting her children and the livestock from the ruthless, bloodthirsty wolves. The guilt of the deaths of her twins. Anna's shield had cracked, and when she let her guard down, the tears flowed like a cloudburst.

Finally regaining her composure, Anna helped Odd unload the coal. Doing their best to mitigate Anna's numerous problems, the two friends visited about all the good times they had together. Odd mentioned how much reidun missed having Anna there, and Anna said that she missed it too. Odd and reidun had become Anna's extended family, and she considered them her american brother and sister.

After Odd left, Anna gathered her children and went back to the barn to finish milking and do the rest of the chores. The replacement heifers were already accustomed to getting fed, so they gave Anna a chorus of moos when they saw her coming with the pitchfork. In spite of everything, it somehow made her smile.

It was nearly the end of November, several days after the accident, when Anna received a letter from George. She trembled as she opened it in fear of bad news, but to her great relief Iver had arrived in Minneapolis. He was still unconscious but alive and was safely in George's care. George promised to write again as soon as he knew more. Anna said a prayer of thanks. Iver was still alive! It was her first glimpse of happiness since the accident and a great relief to know that her husband was still alive and being cared for. Through tears of gladness she reported the good news to Chris and her children.

November gave way to December and soon it was Christmas, with average winter temperatures and snowfall. Anna had received another letter from George that Iver was still unconscious but alive, giving her continued hope to go with her non-stop prayers. The wolves had come calling a few times, but Anna and her rifle kept them at a distance. The sheep ranchers were taking the biggest losses. Anna and Chris didn't have time to go to the buttes for a pine tree for Christmas, but no one seemed to miss it. Marjorie was too young for gifts, and the boys mostly received promises. Obert was still hoping for that Daisy BB gun, but Anna told him that it would have to wait until his father returned home. Guns were gifts from fathers, not mothers. Obert had to settle for some new gloves.

Art got gloves too, but he also got some "stick horses" from Chris. They were wooden slats about four feet long with leather reins for the rider tacked to the horse's imaginary head and some horsehair attached to the other end, simulating the horse's tail. These play horses proved to be the start of another almost famous horse herd. Within a year or two little art would have as many stick horses in his collection as the ranch had real horses.

Their best Christmas present by far came right after Christmas in the form of another letter from George and Sarah. Anna tore it open, a little fearful that it had bad news, but more hopeful that it contained good news. The news was mixed but included a little hope, which was something that Anna desperately needed. At this point in her life she might not have had the fortitude to withstand more bad news.

Dearest Anna and family,

Iver has been here for over a month now. I should have written again sooner, but I wanted to wait until I had more to report. Iver is still alive. That is the best and most important news. He hasn't regained consciousness, though, and remains in a coma. His head injury has healed nicely, and all of his vital signs are good. We take turns sitting and talking to him and waiting for him to respond. He is getting fluids and nutrition through a tube and needle inserted into his vein and seems to have responded well to this. As I told you in my first letter, he was very dehydrated when he arrived. It is a wonder that he got here in time, Anna, and probably a miracle that he is still alive. You have a strong-willed husband, and your prayers are apparently getting through.

I have heard of a doctor at Mayo Clinic in Rochester that has had excellent results with patients like this that are in a trauma-induced coma. If Iver doesn't respond in another day or two, I think we will send him there. By the time that you get this letter, he may already be at the Mayo Clinic. If Iver responds, I will try to get word to you, even if it means dispatching a pony express rider. Almost anything would be faster than the mail. We have telephones here now, but that doesn't help you.

Please don't give up hope, Anna. I think that if Iver was going to die, he already would have. Our bodies have a way of healing themselves, and the state of unconsciousness that Iver is in may be his body's manner of protecting itself while it heals.

Our family is well and doing fine. Everyone sends their love and their prayers. We miss you so much.

Lovingly,
George and Sarah

Between chores, checking for wolves, and baking bread, Anna wrote back that same day.

Dear George and Sarah and family,

Thank you so much for your last letter. It was the best Christmas present that our family could have hoped for. The only better news would have been that Iver had recovered and was on his way home. Please send him to Mayo—maybe you already have—if you think that would be the best.

It is cold here, and we are still battling wolves. There isn't any wild game for them this winter, so they are preying on livestock. The children are doing great, and I wish I had some of their never-ending energy. I don't know how I will possibly keep up with all the work this ranch requires. I sometimes feel like giving up, but something always comes along to encourage me, like your letters.

Not much else for news.

All my love,
All my thanks,
Anna

Anna received another letter from George in January. Iver was still alive and all his vital signs strong, but he was still sleeping. They had sent him to Mayo Clinic and hadn't heard back yet. George promised to keep in touch with Mayo and let Anna know if there were any changes in Iver's condition.

February rolled in with more snow and news that Iver was still sleeping but seemed a little stronger. Anna was managing to keep the wolves away, but other neighbors were reporting mounting losses. Anna was holding to her vow not to let the wolves kill one more animal from their herd. Iver's decision to sell most of their young stock along with all of their older cows last fall in Belle Fourche had proven to be amazingly wise. They still had a few older mares, but horses banded together, and unless one of them was injured or too old to stay with the herd, they were pretty safe. The wolves would usually attack as a pack, depending largely on fear and chaos to scatter their prey and make it easier to kill the weak and slow individuals that got separated from the herd. The wild mustangs were accustomed to their tactics and had a solid line of defense.

The snow hadn't been deep this year, and the wind had blown it off of the open areas, gathering most of it behind windbreaks and into draws and other places that the wind couldn't reach. This made foraging much easier for the horses—and life better for Anna and Chris because they could let the cattle graze on the days when there just weren't enough hours to get them fed. The dried winter grass didn't have as much nutritional value as the lush, green spring and summer grass or the hay, but it helped fill their bellies and provided adequate energy to keep them content.

As Anna liked to say, March came in like a lion, but it turned out to be a cub as the storm only dusted them with another two inches of snow. She had received two more letters from George and Sarah, with no change in Iver's condition. Anna felt despondent, like she was slowly losing Iver, and her life was seeping away with his. It didn't help that calving season, the most complex time of the year in terms of labor required and of difficulty in protecting the stock from predators, was right around the corner. Fortunately for the cattlemen, lambing time often coincided with calving time, and lambs were much easier prey than calves. A cow would protect her calf with every last ounce of energy she possessed, while ewes were helpless and unable to do anything to protect their lambs.

Chris suggested that they let most of the milk cows keep their calves after they calved rather than taking them away from them like they usually did, which would eliminate most of the milking chores. It would mean less cream and butter, but it would give them more time to guard the cows as they calved and to protect the newborns. Anna agreed wholeheartedly and felt fortunate to have Chris's advice in helping her make those difficult decisions. He may have been too old to do any hard work, but he had accumulated an abundance of wisdom during those strenuous, unyielding ranching years. Anna was nearly always exhausted and forever facing new challenges, so every little energy saver was immensely helpful. She had been close to giving up several times, wondering if she could muster the stamina to continue. Thinking of not having so many cows to milk, and all of the time and energy it would save, brought a thankful smile to her weary and worried face.

March was a memory, Iver was still in a coma, and april arrived too soon for the fatherless prairie family. With it came cold, wet rain and the dreaded calving season. The first two weeks were uneventful, and Anna let her guard down. They had pushed the cow herd closer to the barn, and she had been doing wolf patrol every hour, almost around the clock. Not having seen any sign of the wolves and being worn out, weary, and sleep deprived, she finally gave in to total exhaustion and slept through part of a night. Like that of an addict falling off the wagon, her fatigued body demanded more sleep, and she missed her checks entirely the following night.

Anna awoke, alarmed at missing all of her checks, and drowsily hurried out before sunrise. She stopped to listen, and all she heard were the sounds of chaos. The cows were fearfully bellowing and highly agitated, and she immediately knew something terrible had happened during the night. She found two cows that had recently calved, the afterbirth still hanging from one of them. There was no sign of their calves, and from all of the tracks and scattered blood it was apparent that wolves had stolen in during the night. The two newborn calves had apparently been killed and devoured, along with several more recently born calves. Anna was beside herself with disgust for having slept through the carnage and felt rage and sorrow at the thought of letting the hated wolves kill what she should have been protecting.

She was nearly drained of energy, and her body was numb from the morning's revelation. But since the wolves had disappeared, she reluctantly decided to leave the cattle and go back to the house to take care of her children. She sat down in the kitchen and cried with grief, very near the breaking point again. She loathed herself for giving in to sleep and questioned her abilities and character. How could she have put her own needs ahead of those whose lives depended on her? How would they survive if she wasn't strong enough to go a few nights without sleep? Daisy seemed to share her anger and sorrow, the dog's mood a reflection of her master's. She licked Anna's numb fingers and searched her master's eyes sorrowfully. Obert came trailing in with his blanket and that, plus Marjorie's fussing, helped bring Anna out of her fury, rage, and remorse—and her feelings of confusion and helplessness.

Chris came over for breakfast, and Anna sorrowfully shared the night's events with him. He wisely consoled her, seeing that she had been crying and was desperately close to giving up entirely. "Water under the bridge, Anna. Don't waste your energy beating on yourself and pondering over it. If a few calves are all we lose this spring, we won't even notice it by fall. We'll just have some more dry cows to butcher or sell with the calves when we market them. Without you protecting that herd, half of it would be gone by now. You've single- handedly saved most of them."

Obert told his mom that if he had that Daisy rifle, the wolves wouldn't dare come around. Anna smiled weakly at him thinking how much he reminded her of Iver. Art had gotten out of bed, and proudly added that he still had all of his horses—meaning his stick horses—and was "'tectin' them from the bad wolfies." Chris and Anna both smiled at the small boy who wanted so much to act like a man. It was a release that Anna desperately needed, but art seemed a bit perturbed at her lack of seriousness about his work. Marjorie just ate another pancake.

The wolves came back looking for another easy kill a few nights later on a cold and moonlit night, but this time Anna was ready for them and waiting in ambush. She screamed her abhorrence while she emptied and reloaded her rifle. Like a demon she ran at them without fear, stopping only to shoot and reload again. She attacked them with a vengeance and fury that was enhanced and fueled by all of her pent-up frustration and hatred for them. As her battle cry echoed over the prairie, the wolves that weren't dead or injured scattered and ran off into the shadows. Finally satisfied that she had won and that all of the wolves had fled, the exhausted and battle-weary Anna went through the cattle to make sure they were all okay, and then walked home to check on her children.

The Long Wait

Easter came and went with no change in Iver's condition, and anna was too immersed in work to take her children to church services. May Day arrived soon after and was beautiful, sunny, and warm. Spring flowers had begun blooming, and green grass was starting to peek through the fertile prairie earth. Anna was weary to the bone but pleased that calving was nearly finished. She was still checking the cows around the clock even though only about twenty- five stragglers were left to calve, and the wolves hadn't made any more attacks. Anna spotted about three of them lurking on the east ridge one morning, but they quickly disappeared when she started in their direction. As often as time allowed, she posted ranch reports to Iver at the Mayo Clinic with requests that the doctors and nurses read them to her unconscious husband in hopes that he might respond to them. Since she couldn't be there to talk to him in person, she prayed that he might hear her letters.

Tthe wolves had almost vanished, probably not wanting to confront the screaming demon that lurked there again. Apparently, the prairie ranch, protected by the ever-vigilant anna and her blazing rifle, was proving to be impenetrable even for the wolves and their tenacious tactics. Anna looked forward to finishing the calving and knew she could handle the foaling but was dreading the branding, farming, and haying seasons. She had never helped prepare the soil for seeding nor even planted any of the crops. She worried about it but hoped that she could rely on Chris to guide her through the process—if she could gather sufficient energy and find the time that it would require. Time and energy were two commodities that were in desperately low supply. How anna longed for Iver to return. How sweet it would be to have him home to share the incessant pressure and workload.

Late one afternoon Chris came galloping into the yard waving an envelope. It was another letter from George and Sarah, addressed to anna. Together they tore it open, their hearts and minds leaping, yearning for some good news about Iver. It wasn't exactly what they had hoped and prayed for, but it was very encouraging. George had just heard from Mayo, and while Iver was still unconscious, he seemed to be having more reflex actions, blinking his eyes and even wiggling his fingers. It was June, seven months after the disaster, and the prognosis, the hope, seemed to be that he was finally recovering. Of course, there was still the concern that his brain had been damaged and that he wouldn't fully recover when and if he did wake up, but the situation was looking the most optimistic it had since the accident.

Anna asked Chris to join her in a prayer of thanks and hope— thankfulness that Iver was still alive and hopefulness that he would soon come home completely mended. She didn't say it out loud, but she also prayed for the strength to get through the rest of the year. The letter was the impetus anna so desperately needed to tackle branding and the farming and haying seasons without Iver. It brought renewed optimism and faith, the two mainstays of her prairie existence. Anna dared to dream that she and her family would survive.

Anna was still convalescing from occasional flu-like symptoms and fevers herself, but with the good news about Iver she seemed and felt a little more like her old self again. The fact that she and Chris had finished the entire calving season with less than twenty percent of their calves lost also helped. There had been times during those long nighttime calving hours that she was so weary, so worn out and drained, that she just felt like going to bed and giving up. Now she felt herself fighting harder again. She felt like she could actually accomplish the seemingly insurmountable events she faced and survive, along with the ranch and her children.

With calving season virtually over, anna thought that she could take a little more time for her energetic family. At milking and chore time she had been corralling them in the barn with Daisy standing guard, but now she felt like she could let them trail along and help. She still kept the rifle with her just in case the wolves showed up again. Art loved feeding the chickens, and Obert learned to gather the eggs by himself. The occasional hen would peck his fingers when he searched under them for eggs, and he was jumpy at first but soon got the hang of it, saying that no old hen was going to scare him off.

In the meanwhile, Chris was teaching anna the ins and outs of driving the team and pulling the farming equipment. They decided to use their own seed left over from the previous year's crop. Anna also decided that she would only plant wheat and oats since she was a novice and didn't know if she could even accomplish that many acres. Nels and Odd were aware of her dilemma and came over to help. With their assistance and encouragement anna finished the planting just in time for a nice June rain. When Chris told her that Iver himself couldn't have planted straighter rows and done any better, anna beamed with joy and pride. She couldn't wait to have the seeds germinate and watch the plants push through the rich prairie soil into the spring sunshine, so she went back to her first field a few days after planting it. There were already long rows of green plants, their color contrasting beautifully with the dark black prairie soil. Anna was overcome with happiness and thankfulness. It felt like a miracle, and she looked up to heaven and smiled her thanks.

Another job that anna dreaded was working the calves and branding. It was backbreaking, daylight-to-dark work, and although she participated, she had never actually done it by herself or organized it. The job ahead hung over her head like a storm cloud until the day that Chris informed her that she was going to have help—*lots* of help! Knowing her predicament, their neighbors, their ranching community family, came to the rescue once more. Every single friend from miles around came to their ranch at branding time. They rounded the cattle up, sorted and worked the calves, and took the herd back to their pasture. All that anna had to do was to watch in awe and admiration and make meals for the famished crew.

Anna was used to helping others rather than being helped and felt extremely humbled by the labor of love her neighbors brought to her and her family that day, dropping their work to do hers. She shed tears of happiness and gratitude as she thanked each of them. After they had all left, she said a prayer of thanksgiving to her Father God for providing for her in her hour of need. Then she gathered the children and the milk buckets. It was already dark, but the chores were still there waiting for her. The children slept in the barn on hay while anna worked. She felt bad because they hadn't even had supper. After chores she carried her sleeping children to the house and lovingly put them in their beds. She could barely hold her pen for weariness, but wrote a short note to Iver sharing how their friends had been there to do the branding today. It had been one of the happiest days of her summer and such an immense relief to be able to cross that chore off of her list!

The children were healthy and growing, as were the calves and the crops. Foaling was well underway with still no sign of the wolves returning. Meanwhile, Chris and anna were preparing for haying, which was another first for anna. She asked Chris for advice, and he told her that they wouldn't get nearly as many acres hayed this year, but they'd just do what they could. He had hardly spoken the words when Odd and another neighbor came over and mowed for three days, promising to return after anna had raked the fields, and they thought the hay was ready to stack. Anna got up several hours before daylight to do the chores before sunrise, devoting most of the daylight hours to raking. When it was too dark to rake, she headed home to do the evening chores and feed the family. For three long and grueling days she rode the rake behind their team and gathered the freshly mowed hay into windrows. right on cue, the neighbors returned to help gather and stack the long ribbons of raked hay that were lying in the field. Such was the rhythm of the prairie. It ebbed and flowed like the great ocean tides, with times of beauty and times of beasts. Neighbors helped neighbors get through their trials. Their common goal was survival. Their enemy was time. There was never a sufficient quantity of it, and it preyed upon them, stealing minutes, hours, days, and sometimes entire seasons.

By the end of July, a successful haying season was behind them thanks to Odd and their neighbors. The men made anna blush, complimenting her on those straight and uniform windrows and her first-rate raking job. She returned their compliments by serving fresh pie piled with whipped cream along with her wide-as-the-prairie smiles of thanks and appreciation.

Every single day on the ranch brought new challenges and more problems which anna tackled with gritty determination. A good hay crop had to be transported home and stored before Father time brought winter weather and snow. A healthy grain crop had to be harvested before Mother

Nature brought hail or strong winds to harvest it herself, and marketing it at the right time was often merely guess work. Calves had to be weaned and taken to market. Colts needed to be halter-and-saddle broken and shown to buyers. Anna still didn't think they could get it all accomplished, but somehow, day by day, job by job, they managed to do at least most of it. She learned to prioritize. There were tasks that absolutely had to be taken care of, but there were also jobs that she came to realize could be left for another day, maybe for another lifetime. Her earlier experiences in operating a ranch alone for a few days had helped, but that had been child's play compared to this.

Anna doggedly labored through the rest of the year without Iver, finally getting the wonderful news late in October that he had sat up in bed and was trying to talk. The hospital was doing therapy on his body, which had been motionless and speechless for nearly a year and needed to re-learn how to function again. The best news of all was that the doctors at Mayo were hopeful of a slow but full recovery. That day anna, Chris, Obert, arthur, and Marjorie celebrated life, exuberant that Iver would soon be returning home. It took another month for him to will his body to board the train and ride back home to South Dakota. He had been gone for what seemed to be an eternity to anna.

She had written to him at every opportunity her weary body allowed. In late October she wrote this:

My dearest Iver,

I have said a thousand, maybe a million, prayers of thanks that you are recovering. Don't worry about the ranch; everything is just fine and dandy here. You will not recognize the children since they have grown so much and have seemingly changed from babies to almost young adults. Obert is waiting for you to approve of a BB gun for him so that he can guard the livestock with it, and Art already has a herd of stick horses large enough to compete with yours. Marjorie is a beauty. You will fall in love with her all over again.

Chris is worn out but optimistic about everything. All of our neighbors were here to do the branding and castrating, and next week we will wean with the help of Odd and two of the same neighbors. I have hired some neighbor boys to help me bring home the hay that our neighbors so graciously cut and stacked for us and move the calves to market. I noticed some of the older cows bulling this fall, so I'll send them to Belle along with the calves. Chris helped me choose our replacement heifers which we already have sorted off. Reidun is nearly ready to have another baby, so be prepared to listen to Odd bragging that they are winning the baby contest.

George and Sarah write often, and George is in contact with your doctors at Mayo weekly. He was the only person I knew of who could help us out, and I think we owe your life to him. I won't bore you with all of the details. We can go through everything piece by piece and day by day when you get home. My dreams have turned from nightmares to delights knowing that you will soon be back here with us where you belong.

We love and miss you so much,
Anna, Obert, Art, Marjorie, and Chris

When they finally got word that Iver was ready to return home, anna was almost as giddy as she had been in anticipation of her first date with him. She had waited and prayed for this day for what seemed like forever. At times she had thought that it would never arrive, and that the only way that Iver would return was in a casket. Only her never-ending faith, optimism, and determination had gotten her to this day which was late in November, just before Thanksgiving.

To anna there was absolutely no doubt that it was a miracle when Iver walked off of the train that day in Hettinger, ND. There to greet him were anna, Obert, art, Marjorie, Chris, Daisy, the Larsons, and Nels. Some of the same train personnel that had helped anna and her horse, Blue, off the train a few years earlier were also there eagerly waiting. A year ago, these same men had placed the comatose Iver on the train, wondering if he would ever come back home to his wife and family. They clapped and cheered when they saw him and watched as anna and her children surrounded him, and now that their family was united, they all dissolved into hugs, tears, kisses, and pure love. They shared in the jubilation and helped anna and her once-again complete family board their wagon. Anna and Iver thanked them and waved as they and their entourage of neighbors headed south and disappeared into the prairie grasslands. It was a deliriously happy trip back to their ranch on the range, and anna's family was at last whole again.

Iver was still walking with a limp, and his body didn't always respond in the way that he wanted it to. He was also having difficulty speaking and finding the right words and couldn't account for some of the events leading up to his injury. Anna tried to catch him up. The ranch news was easy since she had experienced all of it firsthand. She relayed to him every detail of the winter of the wolves, the weather, calving, farming for the first time, the colt crop, haying for the first time, what the neighbors had done to help, how the kids had fared, how Daisy had been there for her through all of it, how Chris had managed to do the work of a younger man, and everything in between.

What anna didn't know was that amelia Earhart had flown over the atlantic, that al Capone was on the rampage in Chicago and had killed dozens of people, or that the post-war prosperity had ended with the stock market crash and that americans were going into the worst depression in their nation's history. She didn't even know—or care—that women could vote now, that prohibition was still the law of the land, that folks in the cities were reading *Time Magazine* and *Reader's Digest*, or that people were driving motor driven buggies called automobiles. ranches and ranchers in western South Dakota were very isolated, and news like that reached them slowly. When it did arrive, it was of no consequence. All that mattered to them was living through another year, desperately holding on to what they had, and finding a sufficient amount of that elusive thing called time to get their work finished. To anna, everything in the world that mattered had happened. Her husband was alive and well, and her entire family was safe. They were all together again on their prairie home.

Into Hard Times

In January, Anna reminded Iver that he usually visited with the banker about money needs and plans for the coming year. They had done this in previous years, lining up credit for seed grain and other supplies before the seasons came. Since Iver was having some difficulty with remembering and still getting caught up with all that had transpired while he was gone, Anna decided to accompany him.

They were surprised to see the bank nearly deserted. They greeted the bank president and asked if he could help them with their yearly planner again. "What's going on, Mark?" asked a puzzled Iver. "The bank is nearly empty. Usually I have to wait in line to see you."

"Where you been the past few months, Iver?" asked Mark.

"That's a long story, Mark. I had an accident and have been in the hospital an extended time. Actually, I was gone for about a year."

"Then you haven't heard about the bank closings?" Mark replied. "I'd guess that over half of the nation's banks went bust and closed their doors. The unfortunate folks that kept all their money in those banks went under with them. It isn't much better here. Many of my best customers are either already out of business or in the process of going broke. I was barely able to keep the doors to the bank open and had to let all of my employees go except one. It all happened after the stock market crashed."

"What do you mean *crashed*? Where are the ranchers selling their livestock now if the stock market in Belle Fourche is gone?" asked a puzzled Iver.

The banker had to explain to Anna and Iver that the *stock market* that he was referring to wasn't the livestock market in Belle Fourche where they sold their cattle, but that it was a place where investors put their money. It was difficult to explain since all Anna and Iver knew was that ranchers invested their money in cattle and land and had a difficult time paying off their bill at the local general store. They didn't have time for foolishness like putting good money in some unseen stock market across the country in New York. This Wall Street and stock market that Mark was telling them about was virtually unknown to the ranching community. They couldn't understand how something so unimportant to them that was so far away could affect them so deeply.

Mark went on to tell Iver how wise he had been not to take the big land loan he had offered him the last time they met, and how, because he had sold his calves early in the fall and a few weeks before the crash, they had gotten good prices. Other ranchers that sold after the crash had received pennies on the dollar for their cattle in comparison. Several ranchers that received those poor prices weren't able to pay back their bank loans, and many of them weren't even able to pay their property taxes.

Iver interrupted Mark to explain again that he had been in Minnesota in a coma, and Anna had been the one that sold the calves early. He even admitted that he wanted to get the loan, but Anna had wisely thought that they shouldn't take on that much debt. Mark warned them that the situation would probably get a lot worse, and it did. The era that would become known as the Great Depression had landed on america's doorstep. The prairie couple went home remorseful but thankful that they hadn't borrowed the money to buy more land. They owed no one, and desperately needed to keep it that way.

On their way to the bank Iver had stopped at the reva store and ordered the little Daisy Model 20 BB gun that Anna told him Obert wanted so badly, having to pay for it up front. It didn't cost very much, but after visiting with Mark, Iver already regretted the decision. Every penny counted.

Even in isolated western South Dakota, which was usually the last frontier to benefit from national prosperity—and one of the last to suffer from the lack of it—everyone started feeling the effect of the Depression. The severely stressed national economic climate, coupled with extreme drought and acute weather patterns, was taking its toll on Dakotans. The year 1931 was a miserably sparse time on the ranch, and the prairie people hunkered down, hoping that the worst was over. Anna and Iver hardly had any hay, grain, or grass that year. Iver traded some colts to a neighbor for some hogs hoping they would garner more money than his cattle had been bringing. Colt sales and even the market for broken horses were drying up as more and more ranchers either abandoned their ranches in search of work or didn't have money to buy them.

By 1932, there were twelve million unemployed americans. Transients and other drifters began walking and hitchhiking across the country in search of a job or food and shelter. Since their house was less than half a mile from the road, many of those unfortunate souls landed on Anna's doorstep. The first few drifters were somewhat of a novelty, but they soon became a burden. Most of them meant well and offered a day's work for something to eat and a place to sleep. Anna accommodated them as best she could, but Iver worried there might be thieves and criminals amongst them, so he informed all of the hapless hikers—truthfully—that there was no money to be found on the ranch. Already tired from her ranch work and taking care of their children, Anna tried her best to feed them at least a bowl of soup and some freshly baked bread. She welcomed the first several to stay in their house, but after a dozen or so, Anna made living quarters for them in the barn. The travelers at least had a roof over their heads and shelter from the storms, and they greatly appreciated even this meager accommodation. It was far superior to sleeping in the road ditch with no protection at all, either from the weather or from the occasional lawbreaker that preyed on the weakest of them.

One night there was a commotion in the barn, and Anna and Iver ran out to see what was happening. A fire had started, and the two strangers that were staying there were frantically trying to put it out. Anna and Iver found some buckets and started hauling water from the well. They soon had the fire extinguished, but Iver was furious with the man who had started it by throwing a cigarette butt on some hay. Iver told him that he had best leave, and he did. From that time forward, Iver made a rule that there could never be any matches or lit cigarettes in the barn. The barn was an integral part of the ranch that they couldn't afford to lose. A loss like that could wipe them out in stringent economic times like this.

One of the roadies that came through was an Irishman named Patrick reilly. He was a talker with a penchant for storytelling. His tales fascinated the family, especially Obert and art who eagerly listened to them until their parents put them to bed. Pat liked to pull the boys' legs a little, and one night told them about a fellow traveler he had been walking with. The two of them were mighty thirsty and stopped at a water hole for a drink. Pat's partner was gulping the water so fast that he accidentally swallowed some rattlesnake eggs that had been flushed into the pond by the last rain. A couple days later the eggs started hatching, and every time the poor fellow tried to swallow some food, the hungry snakes slithered up his throat and ate it right out of his mouth. The snake-ridden guy couldn't get any food past the hungry reptiles and ended up starving to death. Horrified, Obert and art went to bed with visions of rattlesnakes and woke up several times with nightmares, so Anna had to ask old Pat to tone down his tall tales!

Pat also proved to be good help with mending fences and other odd jobs around the ranch. He never asked for money, which he knew they didn't have anyway, and was always appreciative of anything Anna had for him to eat. Art followed him everywhere, and he helped the boy refine his horse herd by painting some of the stick horses. Art was thrilled! He now had paints, bays, blacks, and even a few greens and yellows. His horse herd was even more colorful than his dad's.

Art loved riding those stick horses, and one morning he brought three of his best steeds out, giving a black to Obert and a bay to Marjorie. He rode a white horse and wanted his siblings to ride with him to see their neighbor and friend tom. Tom's house was beside the path that Obert and art took—Marjorie was still too young—when going to their small country school when it was in session. He often gave the brothers a piece of candy or a cold drink as they trailed by on their way home. They hadn't seen tom since school let out in the spring, and art just knew he still had some of that sweet and delicious candy hidden away for them.

Off to the east this fearsome gang of candy monsters charged, shooting robbers and rogue Indians and wolves along the way, generally terrorizing the neighborhood with their dastardly deeds. They rode their horses wildly, sometimes galloping and sometimes trotting or walking. They were in a hurry to see if tom was home, and their only fear was that he might be out of candy—or that they would get home late for dinner. If that happened, they would have to face the wrath of their parents, especially Anna. They tied their horses at tom's door and knocked loudly.

Tom wasn't in, but he heard their pounding and knocking from the corrals. "What are you three mean and ornery desperados up to today?"

"Been out shootin' wolves and bank robbers and rattlesnakes," art slowly and seriously replied. "Our horses was tired and we're mighty hungry, so we thought we'd stop in for a bite and give our horses a rest, Mr. Tom, sir."

Tom knew what they were looking for, so he thought he'd pull their little legs a bit, maybe even stretch them some. "Golly, I'm all out of candy right now kids, but I do have some delicious skunk meat in the house. Since you're so hungry, that might taste really good to you. Skunks taste a little better than they smell, you know? Come on in."

Obert spoke up first, "Well, uh … Well, we'd better get home and tend to the chores. We don't want to be a bother, and I'm not nearly so hungry as I was a while back."

"That's too bad," tom replied. "I just remembered that I might still have a sack of candy in the pantry that I had put away for a rainy day. Sorry you lost your appetite and need to leave."

All three of the wicked outlaws spoke up this time. "We got time to stay for candy, Mr. Tom!"

Fully refreshed and full of tom's candy, the three desperados headed their horses back to the west, raiding ranches and blowing up banks along their way. They knew they'd get a licking if they were late for dinner, and they made it home just in time.

Tom was a good neighbor and family friend, a fellow Norwegian from the home country. He was a bachelor and never did marry, but he loved the Lutheran church and hand made the pews, lectern, and baptismal fount for it. When he sold his land, he donated the money to the church. He kept his John Deere GP tractor which he continued to drive to reva for his mail, supplies, and candy for any neighborhood kids that stopped in. Tom walked with a severe limp which was the result of being thrown into a fence by his horse. He had quit riding horses after that incident, but he still trusted his John Deere which was his only means of transportation. The neighborhood children—especially Obert and art—never missed an opportunity to visit their good neighbor and friend, tom.

Anna's family had two other bachelor neighbors, Jake and John, who lived north of them and west of reidun and Odd. The brothers lived with their parents until their dad died, then with their mom until she passed away. One brother was a bit feeble minded, and after the deaths of their parents they had a difficult time in managing their small half-section place and keeping up their sod house. Anna often took the two old bachelors a pie or cake and usually some fresh baked bread. Their sod home had two rooms, a tiny kitchen with a place to eat and a bedroom with one bed. The shabby bed looked as though someone had hit the hay a few too many times as the middle sunk almost to the floor, making one wonder how the two slept together without falling on top of each other. The house wasn't very warm or windproof, but the two old homesteaders piled enough blankets on top of themselves to keep from freezing in the winter. The interior looked like it had never been cleaned, but when Anna offered to clean it for them on a visit, they just replied, "Naw, that's fine, Anna. We'll clean the place when it needs it."

Anna stated that 1933 was hot as a branding iron and dry as a bone bleached in the scorching sun. She planted a garden, but there wasn't even an adequate amount of rain to germinate the seeds. She kept herself busy caring for travelers and her family, doing her chores, and helping Iver when time allowed. The wind-driven dirt and dust grated at her nerves as she tried to keep things clean. Anna worried about how they would survive another dry year and felt sad when she thought about the livestock which didn't have sufficient grass and were forever hungry and thirsty. Every creature on the prairie was restless, relentlessly searching for food and water.

History called 1933 the year the Dust Bowl began. Hot, dry winds were whipping through the Dakotas, and they unsympathetically sucked up the fertile farm soil that was meant to be in the fields. The wild, wicked winds ate the topsoil like a hungry beast, devouring it and spitting it high into the atmosphere where it formed menacing black clouds. Farmers and ranchers would longingly look at what they thought was a rainstorm brewing in the western sky only to find themselves and their farmsteads rapidly deluded in dirt and dust when the clouds arrived. The dirt filled their lungs and their barns and their homes. Some women literally went crazy listening to the relentless wind howl at their doors while trying to keep their houses clean and the dirt out, and men lost their minds trying to keep food on the table and pay the bills.

Eastern South Dakota, with its miles and miles of horizon-to- horizon farm ground, was hit harder by the dust storms than the western part of the state. The grass in most of western South Dakota had thick and deep roots that helped preserve and protect the soil that gave it life. But the hot, wicked wind dried the grass and everything else to a crisp, sucking it up along with the dirt and dust. Anna and Iver had to sell large numbers of both their cattle and horses since there wasn't enough forage to keep them from starving. They tried to console each other with the very small compensation that they received. Anna said that it was closer to giving away their animals than it was to selling them, but every penny counted in those dire Dust Bowl and Depression days.

The boys and Marjorie continued to grow, filling the otherwise cheerless days with excitement and adventure. Obert had become an excellent marksman with his BB gun and often brought gophers and mice to the house, wanting Anna to fry them for him for supper.

"I'll fry them for you if you skin and gut them, Obert." Anna tried to hold a serious face.

"What else we having?" he wondered. "Maybe that will be enough. I'm too busy hunting to have time for skinning and gutting." One day Marjorie came running in tears to Anna, claiming that her brother had shot her with the BB gun. Anna doubted the tale, but upon inspection she found a big, red swelling on Marjorie's neck. She went and found Obert and picked him up by his ear, setting him down on a chair in the corner of the kitchen to await punishment from his father. Obert was yelling before Iver even got his belt out, and art was furtively peeking around the corner in fear for his brother. Marjorie, however, was happy to see the justified punishment being doled out.

Iver traded one of his old mares for a pony for the kids that year. It was an ugly little Shetland pony and knew every dirty trick in the bad pony book of dirty tricks. When the kids tried to catch it to play with it, the horse turned its butt and kicked at them. When they went to put the bridle on, it tried to bite them and struck out at them with its front hooves. Getting the pony saddled was almost impossible, and when the children finally managed to accomplish it, they left it saddled all day knowing how long it took and that they might not be able to do it again. When they tried to ride, the pony jumped away just as they attempted to put their foot in the stirrup, seeming to laugh at them as they fell on the hard barn floor. If one of the children managed to get their foot in the stirrup, the horse lunged ahead before they could get fully mounted, leaving them half hanging on and half hanging off as it tried to run away. Iver named the horse Nuisance, but Anna called it Nasty.

It was mid-morning by the time the boys got Marjorie in the saddle for her turn to ride Nuisance, and as soon as they did, Nuisance promptly ran out of the barn with Marjorie barely hanging on. He galloped over to the only pond that wasn't dried up. The only reason it had water in it was because the windmill well water flowed into it when the tank that the windmill filled ran over. Nuisance immediately lay down in the water in an effort to make Marjorie jump off his back. When Nuisance lay down, Marjorie fell beneath the horse, her head held under the water. Seeing what was happening, Obert and art ran to the pond, yelling at Nuisance to get up. Nuisance did, and then trotted down the road with his tail arching over his back as if to say, "Ha! You'll never catch me!" Marjorie's head popped out of the muddy water just in time. She had come very close to drowning. Obert pulled her to the water's edge where she lay for a long time trying to catch her breath and coughing the water and mud out of her lungs. The three walked back to the house and told the story to their mother.

That night Anna repeated the saga to Iver in a not-so-nice, you'd-better-take-care-of-this-immediately tone. Nasty old Nuisance was never again seen on their ranch. Iver took him back to his prior owner early the next morning. When Iver returned, he told the children that since they had been taking on some of the ranch responsibilities, they were being rewarded with a *real* horse now, and that he would give them one of the gentle ranch geldings that he had been riding. Obert, art, and Marjorie were pleased to get rid of Nuisance and proud to know that they were big enough to have a *real* horse to ride. Anna was even happier than the children to be rid of Nuisance. It was one less thing to worry about on her never-ending list of worries. She even found herself doing something that she had never in her life done before—wishing that the year would hurry up and end so they could just start over. Every day of that year had been a trial. The heat, drought, and dust just seemed to go on and on with no end in sight. *Was she still being punished?* For what? Anna prayed for forgiveness, and for better times.

Lightning, Snow, Drought, and Death

Franklin D roosevelt was the american President in 1933, but Anna, Iver, and other South Dakota ranchers barely noticed or cared. To them the fact that Prohibition had ended, and they could finally have a legal sip of corn liquor was more important than who was their president. None of those overworked and weary ranchers knew or cared about the World's Fair in Chicago, or that roosevelt was confiscating american's gold and prohibiting them from owning it. ranchers didn't have gold anyway. Their gold was their land and their livestock, and they desperately needed some rain for both of those commodities.

The year 1934 just brought more of the same devastating weather patterns. Anna thought it felt like hell had descended on their ranch and wouldn't leave. It was virtually a repeat of 1933, and the Dirty '30s just kept getting dirtier and drier. The year started with a dry and cold winter, and dirt flurries filled the air, replacing the usual snow flurries. What little snowfall they did receive immediately turned brown from all of the dirt in the air. Anna and Iver called the combination of dirt and snow "snirt."

More of their neighbors were forced to abandon their homes and land when they couldn't pay their taxes, and when their credit ran out at the general store, they generally departed, leaving behind their bill at the store and whatever they couldn't get on their wagons. Anna mourned for those families and prayed that they would be provided for on their journey and that they would find happiness somewhere. Anna and Iver were in constant fear that they, too, might lose their ranch and clung to it like mothers to their babies. They worked together as a team and tried their best to find feed for their stock and food for the table. It was easy to get depressed, so they used Norwegian humor to ward it off. The Norwegian's favorite ethnic group to poke fun at was fellow Norwegians, so the Ole and Lena jokes were their favorites. With no crops to harvest and no hay to speak of, they did what they could to keep their hands and minds busy. That elusive thing called time, the item that they were always short on, had turned the tables on them. They suddenly had too much of it on their hands and didn't know what to do with all of it. If only they could store it for one of those years when there weren't nearly a sufficient number of hours and days to finish their long list of jobs to do!

Anna kept planting gardens that didn't grow, while Iver kept training horses that he didn't have buyers for. He used some of his idle time in the shop making gadgets out of whatever raw materials he could find. He invented a gate opener and closure latch and made a few of the devices to sell, but he didn't have any paying customers for them. He did manage to trade some of them for a few items that he needed, though, so it wasn't a totally wasted effort.

July was as hot as a branding iron in the branding fire, and more dust and rainless clouds filled the skies reinforcing Anna's earlier thoughts about hell moving to South Dakota. Storms would build, and lightning would light up the prairie skies like a 4th of July fireworks display with both sheet lightning and ground strikes, but no sign of rain. Anna and Iver were back to ten milk cows, and one of those lightning storms came up when Anna had her children in the milking parlor with her. Obert was now big enough to milk a cow by himself, and he and Anna were milking their cows when a flash of lightning came crashing through the barn. The barn instantly filled with smoke. The cow Anna was milking jumped and tipped Anna's bucket of milk over, and Obert's cow kicked wildly at him, her foot landing in the middle of his nearly full bucket. Art was frightened, Marjorie started crying, and Anna immediately jumped off of her milking stool to gather the children and get them and the livestock out of the barn, thinking that with that much smoke it was surely on fire. They never did know what saved the barn, since there was a hole in the roof where the lightning hit, and the studs were charred black. For some reason the wood smoked a lot but somehow didn't burst into flame.

Anna viewed the incident as just one more miracle to add to the mounting list. If they had lost the barn, they wouldn't have been able to replace it, and without a barn it would have been nearly impossible to run a ranch. Without a barn, where would they milk the cows, keep the sick animals, and deliver the calves? Where would they saddle, bridle, and brush down their horses when it was raining or snowing out? Where would they keep their saddles, bridles, harnesses, and other supplies? Where would they store hay for the saddle horses and milk cows? Where would the homeless strangers that wandered into their yard stay? a barn was almost as essential as a house, maybe even more. If need be, they could sleep in the barn, but they couldn't milk the cows in the house.

Anna came to hate lightning almost as much as wolves, and the children were deathly afraid of it after the day they witnessed the strike on the barn. These fear-provoking lightning storms that contained mostly dry, static lightning with no precipitation started building almost every night. The lightning that struck the ground usually started a fire since everything was dried up and ignited easily, and there wasn't rain to extinguish it. Anna, Iver, Odd, and reidun sat up night after sleepless night watching for lightning strikes, hoping and praying that it wouldn't hit their houses, barns, or one of their precious few haystacks. Iver filled some barrels and every bucket he possessed with well water and strategically placed them by the house, barn, and stockyard so that he had water ready just in case a fire broke out in one of those places. When lightning started a fire, they doused it as quickly as possible with wet gunnysacks and then hoed, raked, and shoveled dirt onto the fire to extinguish the flames. Getting to the fire immediately before it got ahead of them was their best defense. With many harrowing and sleepless nights watching for lightning strikes and fires or actually fighting prairie fires, the exhausted ranchers usually made it home in time to start the morning chores. If there weren't any major crises after chores were finished, they tried to get a few winks of sleep in, usually before or after dinner and before the next storm formed.

Late in the fall, on a similarly cloudy afternoon, Obert went with Daisy to gather the milk cows. A few minutes later he came running home, leaping over the four-wire fence by the barn and screaming, "I'm struck by lightning, I'm struck by lightning!"

Iver laughed at his terrified son and exclaimed, "Boy, if you were hit by lightning, you'd be dead!"

The following morning, while Anna was working at setting the breakfast table, she noticed Obert's baseball cap sitting on it. His cap had several little round metal buttons that he had collected at the store pinned on the top and around the brim. The metal buttons were all charred black. It probably hadn't been a direct strike, or he would have been dead, but Obert surely had been struck by lightning—and he had a blackened baseball cap to prove it.

Anna thought that she was possibly pregnant again, which made her more fearful than cheerful. *She couldn't keep from thinking about her twin sons and distressing that she had done something wrong that had caused their premature deaths. It weighed heavily on her conscience and sometimes consumed her thoughts.* She wasn't positive about being pregnant yet, as it was early, but she decided to tell Iver anyway rather than hold out like she had with the previous pregnancy.

Iver didn't share her trepidation and was ecstatic. "I'd sure like another girl for Marjorie to play with, but whatever you have will be just fine with me, dear. This almost feels like our first baby to me. I think that my memories are mostly all back now, but sometimes I still feel like I'm starting over. A year was a long time to be gone—that missing year somehow seems surreal, like it never happened, but I know it did. Have I told you lately how beautiful you are, Anna? I think that is the reason that I recovered from the coma. I just couldn't die without seeing my beautiful wife again."

Anna gave her husband a sweet smile. "I thank God every day that you're back, Iver. I know it was a miracle, or should I say a series of miracles. It was a miracle that art made it home on his own without being detected by the wolves, another that we got you to Hettinger and to the train, and it was a miracle that I knew George, and he got to you in time to hydrate your body. And it sure wasn't just a coincidence that he found a doctor in Mayo Clinic that knew what to do to help your body and mind start working again."

Anna paused in reflection, then continued, "There is so much that I haven't told you like how tiny little art made it home after the wagon wreck to find me. I shudder to think about what would have happened if the wolves had returned and found you before we did, or if they had seen that little boy walking home by himself. 'Daddy's hurt, Daddy's hurt,' our little boy kept crying to me when he arrived at the house. When you hadn't regained consciousness the next morning, I was determined to take you to Hettinger by myself. What a disaster that could have been. Nels and Charlie kept me from making what possibly could have been a grave mistake. I nearly rushed off in the wagon with you and the children, not even considering all of the dreadful things that could have gone wrong." Anna held her husband's hand and looked into his eyes. "The wolves were nipping at our heels all winter. It was a wonder that Chris and I were able to fend them off and save most of the stock. One night when I let my guard down, they killed several calves. The cows were terrified, and there was chaos in the calving yard that morning, but there was nothing I could do. I felt so helpless and hopeless. When spring and summer finally arrived, I had to learn to harness and handle the team, plant fields, rake hay, and do all the things I had totally taken for granted when you were here, Iver. Not to mention trying to keep food on the table for those always ravishing children of ours. Every day was a new challenge, and it was only with God's help that we survived that year without you. There is no way that I could describe how desperately I missed you and longed to have you back home."

Iver was touched. "Chris has told me some of the stories, Anna. You are the only reason that we still have this ranch. What you did the year that I was gone was almost beyond human endurance and ability, so I know the Lord must have been helping you. I even think He gave you some sort of premonition about what was going to happen to this country since it was your decision not to take out the loan that saved us from bankruptcy. As it is, we can barely keep our taxes paid now. I sometimes wonder if I did something to bring the wrath of God down on us like this, but you remind me that God has nothing to do with our troubles. I guess I like to look for someone else to blame for my problems when I should be looking in the mirror. You always point at our children, the cow herd, the horses, and at me and say, 'What more could I ever want?' You make me feel special, Anna, and you are the one consistent thing in my otherwise inconsistent life that keeps me getting out of bed in the morning. Just looking at you reminds me of how blessed I am."

The two of them sat and talked for a long time. Anna finally opened up about all they had been through, and just talking about it made her feel better. She confessed to Iver that she didn't know if she wanted to be pregnant again after the death of the twins. She also admitted that she felt like all of their misfortunes had been her fault, and that she had somehow brought all of this evil into their lives. She shouldered the blame for the death of the twins, Iver's wagon wreck, and even the weather. They both bared their souls to each other, and they both were better for it. Iver finally confessed that he was a bit apprehensive about another pregnancy too, but he wisely said that they'd just have to see what happened and let the Lord have control over those things. Anna was so proud of her husband when he made such profound statements of faith.

Milking the cows had become a family affair. Even art now had his own cow to milk—a little Jersey they had acquired in one of Iver's horse trading schemes. With her sons and husband to help with the milking, Anna decided that it was almost fun. On one typically dry and windy October afternoon Anna and Iver were in the round corral working with two yearling colts, trying to prepare them for the saddle. It was milking time and Obert and art volunteered to start without their parents. When Anna and Iver arrived at the barn, they caught the boys having a milk-squirting fight with Marjorie giggling and cheering them on. Iver normally would have scolded them, but there was nothing normal about the thirties. He made some loud noises to warn the boys that he and Anna were coming, and they immediately stopped and aimed the milk at their buckets again. Iver even let it go unnoticed when the boys squirted milk at the occasional cat that got within range. Daisy really enjoyed those moments too and seemed to be laughing at the cats that got squirted while she patiently waited for her bowl of milk. In the summer and fall cow flies filled the air, and they landed on the rim of the milk buckets wanting some of the sweet liquid. The boys had great fun trying to spray those flies—washing them into the milk and drowning them with a few more accurately aimed squirts. Of course, *most* of the flies and the hairs from the milk cow, along with the occasional bits of manure and debris, were strained out of the milk before drinking it! Since it was October, Iver thought the lightning episodes were over, but there was one more incident to come. Another ominous black cloud came up in the west, and, as always, Anna and Iver were hoping and praying that it had some rain in it. A few drops fell but not enough to even begin to moisturize the parched prairie. The lightning flashed and the thunder crashed with sheet lightning lighting up the skies like it was the grandest 4th of July fireworks in the history of america. If it hadn't been so frightening and threatening, it would have been beautiful. Anna and Iver hiked up the hill to watch for fires. Iver had been able to make a few small haystacks and was terrified that lightning might hit one of those precious stacks of hay, or the house or barn. When the storm—which seemed to last forever—was finally over, they came home so relieved that they still had their haystacks and buildings that they cried with happiness while saying a prayer of thanks.

Their celebration was short-lived. When Iver checked their cows a few days later, he found seventeen head of beautiful Hereford cows and calves dead in a little ravine, crowded around a tree. The tree was charred black and had apparently suffered a direct hit from a powerful flash of lightning. The animals had either bedded down by the tree or had crowded around it for shelter from the storm. Either way, they were close enough to it to get a sufficient amount electricity through the ground to kill all of them. Scavengers had picked their bloated bodies, and there wasn't any salvageable meat. Iver was heartbroken, and he didn't tell Anna about what had happened until November when they were rounding up the cows to wean their calves. He knew Anna would discover the dead cattle during the roundup anyway, so he relayed what had happened to her.

"You should share those dreadful moments with me, Iver," Anna told him. "It's best to share our sorrows and console each other."

"I cried enough tears for both of us, Anna. I didn't think you needed to see that dreadful scene, especially being pregnant, even though I knew that sooner or later you would run across the dead cows or their bones. I try to avoid that section of the pasture if I can. I still have to turn away rather than watch the vultures and predators gorge on our once beautiful cattle. It was a heartbreaking and sickening sight. Those cows were like our family."

"You're right, Iver; they were our family. Thanks for protecting me from the horror of seeing them sooner. You saved me a month of tears and sadness. I sometimes wonder how we can still create tears, as dry as it is."

Anna's prairie family suffered through the rest of 1934, hoping and praying that the worst of times were in the past and that better weather and economic conditions were ahead. Their optimism and faith were great treasures. They made the unbearable bearable and were the lifeline that they and their ranching community clung to in those desperate times.

When Anna asked Iver if he thought it would ever rain again, he replied seriously, "You know, Anna, it rains after every drought is over."

"Brilliant, Iver. How did you figure that out?"

"Didn't know you married such a clever Norwegian, did you?" they laughed together, their best way of coping with their dire circumstances.

When New Year's Day of 1935 arrived, Anna asked everyone in the family to write out some of the good things that had happened in 1934, forbidding any of the bad events they had suffered through. It wasn't easy. Iver thought a long time and finally offered this: "Well, I guess that since we didn't have any grain to harvest or any hay to speak of, I had more time on my hands to spend with what I love the most—my family. We even went fishing a few times, and although the river was mostly dried up, we did catch a couple of catfish. The kids and Daisy had a great time playing in the mud holes that used to be the river. Do you remember the puddle that still had a couple of live fish in it and how Daisy bailed in trying to catch them? I laughed so hard I cried. Of course, the kids jumped in too, trying to help her catch them, and created more chaos—and more mess for you to clean up, Anna."

Anna smiled and said, "Yes, that was a highlight of the summer for sure, Iver. And while we are speaking about what we *didn't* have ... since there wasn't any fruit or berries or garden this past year, I didn't have to do any canning. The one thing that I *do* have and am, by far, the most thankful for is having my husband back! and although I am a bit apprehensive about it, we can't forget to be thankful that I am pregnant and due next spring."

Obert was next, and you could tell that his little mind was thinking really hard. "I'm just so *really* happy that Mommy discovered that I *really* had been struck by lightning. I got to have the last word with Daddy after he laughed at me so much and said I'd be dead if I had been struck by lightning."

Art was thankful for Pat reilly, the drifter that had come through and stayed with them for almost a month, helping art improve his herd of stick horses. "I'm happy that I have more horses than Mommy and Daddy!"

Marjorie was still thinking about what she was the most grateful for but agreed with her mother that having her dad home was the most important. "I'm just happy to help Mommy and Daddy when I can." It was Chris's turn.

"At my age," Chris grinned, "I'm just fortunate to still be above ground and not fertilizing daisies, to be able to enjoy watching these kids grow up, and to have enough teeth left in my mouth to chew my food. Without the five of you I would have had to grow into an old man without anyone to talk to or love and nobody to love me. Times may be tough, but I wouldn't give up a single day of what we've gone through. It somehow makes better folks of us, I think, and makes us realize how much we need and love each other. That is what really counts."

No one could top that, so they ate their meager New Year's Eve meal while singing a few old songs. They were optimistic that 1935 would bring better times and better days—and if that didn't happen, they were getting to be experts at turning the worst of times into the best, or at least better, times.

No sooner had 1935 arrived than it snowed a little. Not a lot, but enough that Iver announced that the drought must be over, and their family actually celebrated the cold weather and snow. One day, a drifter came in and surprised them. Anna wondered how he could be out walking in this kind of weather. He told them that he just had to keep walking to keep from freezing. Anna felt sorry for him and asked Iver if he would let the forlorn hiker stay in the bedroom above the kitchen rather than in the cold barn. Iver relented, and after Anna gave the man some hot soup and coffee, she showed him the upstairs bedroom which had a real bed in it. The traveler was ecstatic and said that he hadn't slept in an actual bed since he had left his home in Ohio to look for work out west.

Anna was making breakfast when she noticed water dripping down the kitchen window. "It's raining, Iver!" she exclaimed. Iver discovered that the rain was yellow and ran upstairs in time to catch their new boarder peeing out of his upstairs bedroom window. The guy apologized, saying he just couldn't hold it any longer. Iver moved him to the barn anyway.

He stayed another day and walked out with a short break in the weather, heading west toward Buffalo. Anna brought a bucket of well water to wash her kitchen window and outside wall. It was so cold that her water froze almost immediately, but she somehow managed to clean the window with her icy water. Iver couldn't keep from kidding Anna about the incident. "Seen any more yellow rain lately, dear?"

"I'll let you know, Iver."

"Don't eat any yellow snow, honey."

"Would you please find something constructive to do?"

There were still a couple of watering holes for the cows, but rather than open ice for all of the animals, Anna suggested they move some of the herd close to the well. Even with the drought their deep well was still producing a good supply of fresh, clean water. Nevertheless, Iver was concerned about drying up the well, so they continued to open ice for most of the herd. The horses didn't need to be watered since they were eating the snow that came with the paltry supply of grass they found while grazing. Anna and Iver had cut the horse herd numbers down to about forty percent of what they had been in good times along with a similar reduction in the cattle herd which was partly due to the lightning strike.

The cattle they had sold in the sale barn the past fall had only brought pennies on the dollar, so Iver was eyeing his recently accumulated hog herd. Someone told him that hogs had recently sold for good money in Chicago, so he decided that he'd disperse his swine enterprise. They needed some cash for supplies, and he had already decided that he didn't like hogs anyway. As a matter of fact, he pretty much couldn't stand them unless they were in the form of bacon, ham, pork chops, or sausage. He kept a few of them for butchering along with a pregnant sow and asked Odd to help him take the rest of his hog herd to the train in Hettinger for delivery to the Chicago livestock market.

Neither of them had ever conducted a trail drive with hogs, so getting them to Hettinger was quite an adventure. It was February, and they were fortunate that the weather was fairly nice and there wasn't very much snow on the ground. The weather wasn't their biggest concern though. They were fearful that one of their neighbors would see their "hog drive," knowing that if they were caught, neither of them would ever live it down. Cowboys herding hogs with horses was quite a rare sight in South Dakota!

They took Daisy—Odd called her Daisy the Wonder Dog— along to help. They probably wouldn't have gotten the pigs to Hettinger without her. The hogs just ignored the horses, but if they didn't go where Daisy wanted them to, she could get their attention with a nip on their hind leg or curly little tail. They squealed in their high-pitched hog voices when she did and soon learned that they needed to go where Daisy wanted them to. Iver had to laugh at one old sow that squealed every time Daisy even got close to her. By the time they reached Hettinger, Daisy was a real hog-dog, and the two cowboys weren't even trying to help her.

After the train stopped, Iver negotiated the terms of freight charges, and then he put Daisy the Wonder Dog to work. She rounded up the hogs and herded them into the rail cars with virtually no help. The railroad personnel were so impressed that they asked Iver what he'd take for her. They had never had such an easy time getting hogs into the train cars and wanted to keep her to help them load and unload livestock. Daisy could have had a professional railroad career, but Iver wouldn't part with her. After all, Daisy was a member of the family, not just a dog.

Iver, Odd, and Daisy rode back toward the Slim Buttes with Iver dreaming about how much money he'd be getting for the hogs all the way home, while congratulating himself for finally getting most of the smelly swine off of his cattle and horse ranch.

Reaching the Larson ranch first, Iver went in with Odd to greet the children and see how the new baby was doing. "She's so beautiful," he complimented reidun. "I'm in awe of how you can create such handsome children with Odd as the father!" He ducked out before Odd could get back at him.

When Iver got home that evening he sang praises for Daisy all night, telling Anna and the children about how good she was at herding hogs and how the railroad men wanted to buy her. He went to bed that night with a big smile at the thought of getting rid of his hogs and dreamt about all the money he'd be getting from the sale. Three weeks later, Iver finally got a letter from the railroad. He tore it open to see how fat the paycheck for the hogs was. There wasn't a check. There was, instead, an invoice for freight charges. The railroad company wrote to Iver: *"We regretfully inform you that the sale of your hogs didn't bring in enough money to cover our freight invoice. We deducted your paycheck from our bill, and this is what you still owe us."*

Anna wrote back to the freight company for Iver since he was still learning to write.

> *Dear Sirs,*
>
> *We are so sorry that the hogs didn't bring enough money to cover the cost of their freight. We were hoping to make enough from their sale to pay the freight, cover the cost of supplies for the winter, and pay some of our other creditors as well.*
>
> *We regret to inform you that we don't have any money to pay you the difference, but we do have some more hogs. Would you like to have them as payment? We could bring them to the train in Hettinger whenever you want them.*
>
> *Sincerely yours,*
> *Iver and Anna Tenold*

Anna and Iver waited for a reply from the railroad, but they never did get one. The episode did give Anna a chance to get even with Iver for his yellow snow jokes though. "Any more brilliant ideas on how to make us rich, Iver? Maybe you could start raising chickens? I hear they're bringing good money in Chicago. Maybe even enough to pay the freight bill!"

"I'll check into it," Iver grinned. "You think Daisy would herd chickens?"

It was the spring of 1935, and Anna started getting the chills and sweats again with her bones aching to the core. It worried her desperately knowing that the same symptoms had occurred before the twins had been stillborn. She prayed frantically that the same thing wasn't happening again. The old questions of doubt and the fear of losing another child kept racing through her mind. She even had a reoccurrence of her old nightmares, waking up in a sweat from one of them that dreadfully displayed a garden with rows of sheep and baby fetuses where fruits and vegetables should have been. "Please, God, not again," she pleaded.

Anna had these episodes off and on for over a month, but the current one was more severe and lasted much longer than usual. After a few hours of wrenching pain, she went into labor. She knew that it was still too soon, but there was no holding it back. At least this time she had Iver with her to help. He mainly occupied the children and kept them out of the bedroom while Anna did what came naturally. She pushed with the pains and rested in between. It was over quickly, and the two tiny twin girls that she delivered were indeed too early and stillborn.

Anna was beside herself with heartache and grief. Iver heard her crying and came into the room knowing what probably had happened. He cried with his wife wondering what they had possibly done to deserve another blow like this. Together they grieved for the little girls that should have been. They had lost two sets of twins in three years. They now had three live children and four dead children. Anna was inconsolable for days. It felt like God had turned his full wrath on her and her family again, and she had no idea why. *She prayed daily, and she believed in Him with all of her heart. Wasn't that sufficient? What could she have possibly done to deserve this unbearable punishment? What more could she possibly do? Why would God take these beautiful baby girls from her? Hadn't the dead twin boys and the drought and the depression been sufficient punishment?*

Since the weather was already warm and little bodies would decompose quickly, they had to bury the girls right away. Iver quickly made two more wooden boxes for them, and then Anna, Iver, Obert, arthur, Marjorie, and Chris somberly carried the boxes containing their infant daughters to the little knoll where the twin boys, their brothers, had been laid to rest. Chris said a few words, as did Iver. Anna felt like the spirit and life had been drained from her body and buried with her daughters. She remained silent, still trying to absorb her shock, anger, and grief. Once again Anna's unyielding faith had been shaken to its foundation and put to the supreme test. Other than a few words to the children and Iver and crying out at night when she experienced more nightmares, she remained silent for days.

Along with the warm weather, the wandering travelers returned, lost souls looking for some solace. They walked in like clandestine and silent zombies. The life had been sucked out of their bodies, and their eyes were empty, devoid of any expression. Anna empathized; she felt lifeless and empty too. Still, she fed and cared for them as if they were her own family which suffered when some of their meager rations went to feed others. One day, in exasperation, Iver made a sign and put it on the road to reva: "We don't have enough food for ourselves. Please keep on walking."

Anna saw the sign a week or two later and asked him to take it down. Somewhere from deep within her soul she was able to find and recover some tiny remnant of her old self. "These are God's children, Iver, and we will help feed them as long as we are able to. Let's butcher those two old cows that are about to die of starvation anyway. We can share what meat is left on their bones with whoever comes walking in. When the meat is gone, we'll make soup out of the bones."

That day, old Pat reilly, whom Iver had befriended the year before, came drifting in. He hadn't found any work in Montana and didn't think he could make the long trip to California, so he just turned around and started walking east, retracing his footsteps. Iver was actually happy to see him and so was art. He had long outgrown stick horses, so Pat taught him how to whittle. It was great fun for art and gave him the opportunity to use Pat's knife which was something that he had always wanted. Iver promised to buy him one when they could afford it.

The dust storms weren't over and kept coming in like mirages, fooling Anna and those watching them build into thinking that they might actually bring rain. Iver said it could drive a man crazy, hoping and praying for rain but getting drenched with dirt instead of water. One hot summer day an even more menacing form of cloud developed. It came like a thief in the daytime. This time it was a cloud of locusts that rained down, devouring everything in their path. They ate the paint off of houses and the clothes off of the clotheslines. They ate the gardens, the grass, and the weeds. They devoured everything and anything that they could get their greedy and tireless mouths on, even happily munching on their own deceased relatives. When all was devoured and the land lay bare, they flew away leaving only their destruction and the carcasses of their kin behind.

Anna thought that it was almost like God was sending plague after plague upon the prairie, destroying everything that He had created. The plague of the flying insects came and went, like the prairie wind. After several sieges of their random destruction, even they disappeared, their carcasses littered across the prairie, nourishing it for the future. Along with that plague Iver and Anna had experienced the year of the wolves, livestock diseases, drought, and the death of four babies. There was no water left to turn to blood, no water holes for frogs to live in, and it was just plain too dry to generate any hail, so those plagues would have to wait for another day. Anna told Iver that she'd even be happy to have a plague of hailstorms because there was moisture in the hailstones.

Anna gradually began doing what she had always done in the past. She prayed for their survival and for their souls. Then, as if to try her mighty courage yet another time and beat her down once more, she discovered that Blue had died in the corral. He had been her gift from old man Obert, one of the grandest surprises and gifts of her life. Blue had accompanied her to the Dakotas. He had been her friend and faithful companion, the horse she could always trust to do anything she asked of him. He trained her children and Odd's children to ride. He was the friend that always did his best for her and her family. Even Chris had loved to ride him, both of them being too old for foolishness. Anna knew it would happen, but why now? Why now, along with everything else?

Iver and Chris helped Anna dig a grave large enough for her horse, which was more work than they needed, but Anna couldn't just leave her faithful horse in the sun for the coyotes, wolves, and crows to devour. Blue deserved a grave and a headstone. Daisy saw the sadness in Anna and tried to console her. She lay at Anna's feet with her head on her paws turning her big brown eyes up and focusing them on Anna's. Anna sat down beside the faithful border collie, and they shared the loss together. Blue was Daisy's friend too, and he seemed to enjoy having her ride on his back.

"True Blue" would truly be missed by everyone on the ranch, especially Anna. She looked toward heaven and prayed that the old horse and his former owner, Obert, would ride together again. She also prayed for better days and for rain and for the survival of her family and their ranch. In closing, she asked God to forgive her sins and thanked Him for her husband and family.

The Cold of '35, the Heat of '36, the Hope of '37

Anna heard them before she spotted them and called to Iver to hurry out of the barn. It was the fall of 1935, and after a dreadfully long, hot, and dry summer the sandhill cranes were making their annual flight. It was the event the prairie couple loved to watch, even though it meant that winter was coming. But it also meant that the days were getting shorter, and the air would get cooler, a much desired relief after the extreme summer heat.

As the cranes warned them it would, fall faded into winter, and the Dakota family braced itself for whatever else Father time and Mother Nature might have in store for them. Optimism, the lifeblood of the prairie, was becoming extremely short in supply again. Brutally cold weather swept in from the north to rapidly replace the excruciating summer and fall heat. It started snowing in late November, and Iver again declared that the drought was over. After the first several snows Anna and Iver stopped celebrating the moisture and the end of the drought. The ranch had turned into a gigantic icebox with knee-deep snow everywhere and the temperature dropping daily.

By the middle of December, it was taking them over an hour to ride to the horse herd. Checking took another hour or two, and then it was another hour's ride back home. Taking a wagon anywhere was impossible since mountainous banks of snow had drifted over the roads and trails and had almost covered some of the buildings. Anna thought that the entire world had turned into a frozen, white ice sculpture. Iver rode to reva one day in another snowstorm only to find that there hadn't been any mail for a few weeks and that the bare-shelved store was virtually out of supplies. He took the last pound of sugar and the last can of coffee and was happy to have found anything at all.

He asked Charlie when he expected more supplies, and Charlie just shrugged, "I've heard that the roads from here to the Missouri are blocked with snowbanks up to twenty feet deep. There might not be any travel or supplies until it melts in the spring. Even the trains have stopped running from what I've found out." Iver believed him, since there were fifteen- to twenty-foot snow drifts in his yard. The two-mile ride to reva had become a four-mile ride, circumventing the mountainous snow drifts.

Anna gave her husband a hot mug of coffee and put him by the furnace to thaw out when he arrived from reva. They had shoveled a tunnel through a giant snowdrift to get to their house, but the wind kept drifting it shut. Sometimes they had to shovel it open every time they left and every time they came back. The snow went with the wind, blowing past them from the northwest one day and then returning unwelcome to where it came from with a southeast wind the following day. They moved Chris into their house since they didn't have the time or the energy to shovel to his home and get him for meals. He was too old for this kind of work—for any kind of work, really—and they worried that he might have a heart attack shoveling snow in the icy cold wind. Anna did her best to keep her family healthy knowing that if any health problems arose this winter, there would be absolutely no way of getting help. They were totally isolated and on their own, as were all of the ranchers that were living in western South Dakota. They were used to isolation, but this winter was taking it to a record extreme.

Iver came in grinning one morning when it was minus thirty degrees after helping Anna with the milking and chicken chores and separating the milk from the cream. "You always tell me to look at the bright side, Anna. I didn't see a single fly or mosquito or bum today." He thought that Anna would be laughing at his humor, but she actually looked sort of irritated.

"I don't like that term *bum*, Iver. They're just folks like us, down on their luck. We could easily be homeless too, just like they are, and the

Lord knows that could still happen. They don't have any money, and they don't have any work. They're just wandering down the road of life looking for something better—a job, a home, and something to eat. They aren't *bums*, Iver. They're just unfortunate and unlucky and trying to live with the hand that was dealt them. Some of them had homes and families and lost everything. We need to treat them with compassion and kindness."

"You're right, Anna. I should take more time to help them with their problems and be more patient with them. I do ask them their names and call them by it, and I honestly do figger' they're no different than us, maybe just not as fortunate. I know that I'm certainly no better than they are. I guess that I'm used to jokes about us Norwegians and don't mind the Ole and Lena stories and being called a lutefisk lover or paleface. I really rather enjoy it. If I can't find any humor in life and laugh at myself, I guess it's time to quit, but that doesn't mean I can poke fun at others. I didn't intend any harm, Anna; I just wanted to bring a little laughter into this hapless day. I promise that I'll never use the word *bum* again, even when they're calling each other bums."

Anna gave Iver a long hug, sorry that she had scolded him. He was a good and decent man and had just been trying to spread a little cheer and humor in their often-cheerless world, and she had done the same as thrown cold water on him. Anna vowed to be less grumpy. Maybe it was just because of all the snow, cold, and gloom and being ranch-bound? Maybe it was the loss of her babies? She had never quite gotten back to her old self after carrying her children up the hill to the graveyard.

The year 1935 gave way to 1936, and with the New Year Anna desperately held the hope that everything would get better. But it didn't. On New Year's Day the temperature dropped like a sledgehammer coming down on a finish nail. It was so cold that it couldn't snow, and a shower of frost filled the air instead. Iver came in after chores, his fingertips white, and Anna knew he had frozen them. She wondered how the livestock could possibly survive in temperatures this cold. They both remarked that it had never been this bitter cold before for this long, and it just seemed to keep getting colder. Anna couldn't keep from thinking that since the dreadful summer heat and drought had failed to finish them off, the winter cold and snow were doing their best to complete the job.

Iver needed to get to the horses and see how they were doing, but he knew it would take most of the day to navigate around the towering snow drifts and the snow laden draws which were nearly impossible to cross. Anna and Chris volunteered to do the chores and take care of the cows so he could make the ride on the first day that the sun came out and the wind let up. Finally, after waiting almost a week, they had a sunny day without wind. It was bitter cold, around minus 35, too cold to be out riding—or anything else for that matter. But they were desperately concerned about the horse herd, so Iver saddled up to leave, and Anna met him with the buggy robe. He already had his horsehair coat and his horsehair mittens, but she wrapped the blanket around him and let it drape over his legs. She told him it would help keep both him and his horse warm.

The ride was so difficult that Iver almost gave up. He had to lead his horse almost as much as he rode it. When he finally got to the herd, both he and his horse were totally exhausted. The wild horses were out on the hilltops where the wind had blown some of the snow off, making it easier to paw their way through it to find the meager grass underneath. They were pretty emaciated but didn't show it with their long winter hair all fluffed up. It added a thick layer of insulation, and they didn't seem to mind the cold.

One of the mares was on the next ridge all by herself away from the others, so Iver rode over to investigate. She was standing so still that she appeared to be a statue. She was. The old mare, one from the original band of wild mustangs who had been one of their best producers and had two roping horses to her credit, was standing there frozen solid as if even in death she was still keeping watch over her herd. Iver was shocked by the ghastly sight. He started back for the ranch almost wishing that he hadn't come, with the vision of that stoic and statuesque old mare haunting him all the way home. Anna had tears in her eyes when he relayed the story to her. She should have been hardened to death, but the loss of an animal, especially one of their mustangs, still deeply saddened her.

Even in their land of extremes, February was the worst winter month they had ever experienced. It snowed more, and, impossibly, it got even colder. The daytime temperature didn't get up to zero for the entire frostbitten month. According to Anna's log, they had over forty continuous days with their high temperature not reaching zero, and ninety continuous days that the temperature never went above the freezing point. That winter would be written about in the history books, when the average temperature for February in South Dakota was minus twenty degrees and the winds blew incessantly. Back then, they hadn't invented chill factors yet. If they would have, the temperatures would have been off of the charts. The ice age was bearing down on them. The cold and the wind relentlessly swept in from the north like an arctic invader conquering the land and seeping into every corner and crevice of the homesteading family's life. The cattle and the people were still alive but barely hanging on with day after endless day of the same frozen misery.

Then, finally, when Anna and Iver were down to their last ounce of strength and ready to give up, the first day of March in 1936 changed everything. It got up to 32 degrees! the sun was shining! the winds had died down! Anna proclaimed that heaven had descended upon the earth and driven the wicked invader out. Mother Nature was finally smiling on them. Their dwindling optimism had paid off. The temperature hung at around 32 for a few glorious days, and then toward the middle of March it just kept getting wondrously warmer. It seemed splendid. Anna smiled and found the few remaining garden seeds they had, thinking that she could start planting any day. She took the children and Daisy up the hill to visit the graves, then loaded all of them on the makeshift bobsled that Iver had made and slid back down. For half of the glorious afternoon they tried to make up for the months of gloomy and housebound days, frolicking and playing in the sunshine, trying to soak every last ray of the glorious heat into their bodies. The mountains of snow and the valleys of ice were melting, and the surviving cattle and horses had drinking water everywhere.

Anna's world had turned into a paradise, but it was a very short- lived paradise. It kept getting hotter, and the ice and snow kept melting faster, and suddenly, almost overnight, there was too much water. Ponds were becoming lakes, and draws, that normally sported a trickle of water, were now becoming rivers. Anna wished they had one of her dad's fishing boats from back in Norway to navigate with. Chunks of ice the size of their chicken coop were careening down the Grand river, tearing out trees that had been there for over a hundred years. Iver waved at Odd far off on the other side but didn't dare try to cross the raging river. The same river that he and Anna had laughed at when they first saw it because it had been just a tiny stream was now making some of the rivers in Norway look pretty tame. This was indeed a land of extremes. Anna told Iver that they needed to look on the bright side. At least the drought had finally ended, and the ice-age was in rapid retreat.

It had swiftly warmed up, and the temperatures soared from severely below normal averages to severely above normal averages in a matter of days. Flooding was everywhere, and the animals that had survived the excruciating winter were forced to high ground. The cattle and horses that didn't get caught in the floodwaters and drown were found on islands, starving from lack of forage. The ranchers and the livestock that had been trying to adapt to and live through the coldest winter in history were now faced with the hottest spring they had ever experienced. The continually dreary and snowy weather that Anna and Iver had endured day after day all winter had turned, almost instantaneously, into a sunny, hot, and dry spring. Anna felt like they were trapped in a nightmare. She and her family had escaped from the freezer but now found themselves in the frying pan. The grass started growing quickly from all of the moisture that came with the snow melt, but it dried up almost as rapidly when the hot, dry, rainless, and cloudless days that immediately followed sapped the remaining moisture out of the soil and sent it off into the atmosphere. South Dakota hastily transitioned from the coldest winter in history to the hottest, driest summer ever recorded. Summer temperatures in 1936 soared to 120 degrees and Anna thought that the red stuff in her thermometer would boil out the top. Along with the sustained heat wave, that year also witnessed the strongest hurricane ever recorded in american history and rare nighttime tornados that killed 446 people in four states. The Dust Bowl continued in the Dakotas with near hurricane force winds that drove the dirt through Anna's house and into their lungs and every aspect of their lives, enhancing the heat and drought. She longed for any moisture, even a hailstorm, but it was too dry to even generate hail. Cracks formed in the desiccated prairie floor sufficiently deep and wide to lose a cat or small dog in. Animals hid in them, trying to find some shade and relief from the scorching sun.

Anna and Iver were almost at a complete loss of what to do. Some of their cows had aborted their calves during the harsh winter, their bodies not being able to support their fetuses with all the stress. But the few that carried their pregnancies through the winter and survived the floods experienced the warmest calving weather in history. There weren't any storms, just day after day of nice, sunny, and very hot weather. Foaling for the horse herd was about the same with the exception that, by then, it was too hot for the baby colts to do well. Many of the mares had lost their foals during the winter with premature births due to stress, but some of them—the youngest and the strongest—had been fine. If more of their stock had survived the winter and spring, Iver and Anna would have tried to sell some of what was left, but there wasn't anyone to buy them anyway. Even their stock market had gone out of business. They were stuck between a rock and a hard place with almost nothing to feed their remaining stock and with no market to take the starving animals to. Even Anna was out of ideas, but she wasn't out of prayers. Prayer was her way of never giving up, her way of solving her problems and making decisions.

The winter of 1935-36 and the summer of 1936 had taken survival of the fittest to the extreme. By then the only ranchers left were either the extremely hardy or the foolhardy. Those were indeed the times that stole women's and men's minds and souls. Women went crazy listening to the wind howl at their doors day after day, week after week, and month after month—with virtually nothing to feed their families. As for Anna and Iver, they thought that it just *had* to get better. They possessed eternal optimism and a fountain of faith, and they still had each other, their faith, their family, and what little was left of their livestock.

President roosevelt and his administration had organized the Works Progress administration (WPa) in 1935 to help put unemployed americans to work building schools, hospitals, roads, sewers, airfields, bridges, and dams, and planting trees for shelterbelts. Farmers were learning how to control erosion, both from water and the wind, and plants and trees were a major component of the solution. They desperately needed windbreaks and vegetation cover to protect the precious prairie soil and keep the wind and water from scooping it up and carrying it off.

WPa dams were being built to control rivers and supply electricity. Anna learned from a neighbor that one was being built in western South Dakota near Sorum, which was fairly close to their ranch. In the summer of 1936, she asked Iver if he wanted to go and see if he could get employment there and earn some WPa money. When the construction manager found out that Iver had a team of horses, he immediately hired him. They needed wagons to haul dirt when and where it was needed and later to haul rocks to cover the face of the dam and keep it from eroding away. Anna's family was ecstatically happy to have a little money coming in. The new work gave them new hope. Work and a paycheck were what americans desperately needed.

While Iver was working for the WPa, Anna was pretty much in charge of the ranch again. There was no haying or harvesting that year because there was no rain to grow the hay and grain crops. Still, there were cows to milk, chickens to care for and eggs to gather, and what was left of the cattle and horse herds to check daily. There was also the occasional fence to fix, animal to pull out of a bog, wire-cut horse to stitch and mend, colt to halter break, cow to doctor, hens to butcher, garden plants and house to haul well water to, and barn to clean. Obert and art were old enough to help, and Marjorie was growing quickly and doing her best to be of assistance. The year 1936 may have been one of the worst in the history books, but with Iver bringing home a paycheck and Anna and her children being able to take care of the ranch, it was tolerable.

When unfortunate souls drifted in, Anna did everything she could to feed them and make them feel better about themselves and their situation. She figured that through the 1930s they had probably helped about twenty to thirty wandering souls per year, amounting to hundreds of drifters through the Depression. In all of that time and with all of those strangers coming and going, they never once had anything stolen that they knew of or had one of them give them any more trouble than almost setting the barn on fire or peeing out the bedroom window.

Iver made a good friend who was also working for the WPa on the Sorum Dam. His name was Murel Watson from a little town east of reva called Prairie City. Murel had been a sort of jack-of-all- trades, at one time owning the Sorum store and eventually starting a cattle ranch of his own. The two quickly became good friends and usually shared their lunchtime and dinnertime together. Both had wives that were good cooks, and the other workers looked hungrily at the lunches prepared by Anna and Doris. Iver and Murel often generously shared their meals with the drooling onlookers.

A welcome fall arrived, and other than taking time off to help wean the calves, Iver worked for the WPa until things froze up, and his job ended for the winter. Anna had proven before that she could run the ranch on her own, and on a year like this with hardly any stock and no hay or crops to harvest, she said it was easy as eating *lefsa*. Iver came home before Christmas with his final paycheck for the year in his pocket, hoping that it would be sufficient to get them through another winter. The store had supplies again, and Anna spent every penny as if it was their last. If there were to be any Christmas presents this year, they wouldn't be store bought.

Iver found and shot a lone antelope that December, butchered one of his last hogs, and mixed the two meats together, making sausage out of everything except the steaks and loins. They loved sausage, and every ounce of the hog fat went into it along with some spices and as much garlic as they could gather. They enjoyed many meals out of fresh eggs, sausage, and Anna's still-famous pancakes. When friends or neighbors stopped by and knew that Anna was having pancakes and Iver's sausage for supper, they almost always found an excuse to hang around until after they had eaten.

Another scant Christmas went by with Anna's family hunkering down and making the best of the situation. ranch kids didn't complain when they weren't given a new train or a new dress for Christmas; they were happy to just get to come in from work earlier than usual. On New Year's Day Anna proclaimed that it was 1937, and, as always, her eternal optimism took over and she forecasted that it would be a great year—and it truly was! Well, not even close to great, but at least a huge improvement over the first six years of the 1930s. Obert was almost a teenager, art acted like a teenager, and Marjorie seemed to have her mom's way of making things happen. She certainly had her way with her brothers, knowing just what button to push when it needed pushing, and she was equally as adept at manipulating her father into seeing her side of any quarrels with her brothers.

After the winter of 1935-1936 and the summer and fall of 1936, anything would have been an improvement, but 1937 was actually a semi-decent year in western South Dakota. The temperatures were about normal, and the precipitation was sufficient to at least get them by. Nothing in South Dakota seemed to ever be normal or average, but this was beginning to look like one of the years prior to the '30s and the Depression. Hay and grain yields were still well below pre-1930 averages, but they were much better than the new normal average of virtually nothing that the family had become accustomed to. Having some hay to stack and a little wheat and oats to harvest for the first time in years was wonderful. Anna welcomed the extra work and thanked God for it. There was even a small, albeit still very meager, market for their cattle. They actually sold—really almost gave away—three horses that year, but getting anything for them and just selling something was a gratifying experience.

A few game animals began appearing on the prairie again, another welcome and long overdue sight. As she had the previous fall, Anna heard the beautiful birds before actually seeing them. She called to Iver, but he already had his eyes on the heavens. The sandhill cranes were making their annual debut, flying lower than usual this year. It almost looked like you could reach up and touch them. They had never seen them this close up, and Iver optimistically stated that it was a good sign. The large, graceful birds chattered happily as they flew by signaling the end of fall and the beginning of yet another winter. Anna couldn't decide whether to pray for snow, so she just prayed for a nice winter.

Anna had regained a little weight, enough that Iver teased her about getting fat although she was still pretty gaunt. She returned the compliment by asking why his hair had quit growing on his head and instead was coming out of his nose and ears. "Must be that hard Norwegian head of yours, Iver; the hair can't get through it anymore so it has to come out in other places."

"It's just getting older and wiser like me and doing things the easy way, Anna," he laughed. "You have to fight gravity to go uphill, so it's easier for it to grow down and sideways rather than up. Even my hair is smart."

Obert and art were pranksters, and one spring day Daisy discovered a group of skunk babies and alerted the boys to their presence. They thought that it would be fun to put a couple of them in Anna's hat box and place the box in Marjorie's room. Marjorie came into the room and eyed the hatbox on her bed. The boys glued themselves to the door waiting for their sister to scream so they could come running in and make fun of her and then rescue her. They waited ... and waited. Finally, they peered around the corner thinking that Marjorie must not have taken the bait. There she sat petting the little skunks just like they were kittens. The joke was on them!

the skunks actually made fairly good pets, and the kids named them Puey and Louie. Marjorie fed them with a baby bottle until their eyes opened, at which time they followed her around everywhere she went. Anna made the kids take the skunks out to the north trees when they got a little older, thinking that sooner or later either Puey or Louie or both of them would get excited and spread some of their powerful perfume around her house.

That seemed to be the year of skunks. Iver was moving his replacement heifers to another pasture and ran across a lone skunk on his way home. Since he was on the horse and up and away from danger, getting sprayed didn't concern him, so he amused himself by chasing the skunk with his horse. The skunk got tired of being chased and suddenly stopped and looked back over its shoulder at Iver. Planting its hind feet, it let loose with a burst of perfume that hit Iver squarely in the chest and face. Astonished, he galloped his horse all the way home gasping for breath and wondering how in the world that skunk managed to spray him sitting way up on top of his horse. Upon getting home, he dove into the water tank and scrubbed and scrubbed, but with little effect. Anna tried a few home remedies on him that didn't work either, so Iver had to sleep in the barn with the wanderers for a few smelly nights. One of their guests moved out of the barn and slept under the tree in the yard, complaining that his room at the inn needed airing out.

A week or so later, Anna and the boys were going to milk the cows, and a skunk came out from under the shed and brazenly paraded in front of them. Daisy was on guard duty and immediately jumped between her family and the skunk. She managed to run the skunk off, but of course she got perfumed in the process. There was a pile of poop—manure—by the barn, and she rolled in it for a while, trying her best to get the burning smell off of her face and out of her eyes. The manure seemed to work a little better than the soap and flour that Anna had scrubbed Iver with, but Daisy was still demoted to the barn just as he had been. Anna laughed about it and told Iver that the next time he got sprayed she'd have to scrub him with manure instead of soap since it seemed to work a little better.

"Now that's a really dirty joke, Anna—shame on you," Iver chuckled at his wife's dry Norwegian sense of humor.

Later that week Anna and Daisy watched an entire family of skunks strolling leisurely across the yard like they owned the place. Anna thought they were so cute, especially the little ones, but Iver said, "Enough is enough." He and art went out to the shop to make a skunk trap. They used chicken wire and wooden slats to create a box with an entrance door that only opened in one direction. Then they put some scraps from dinner in the box and placed it by the hole under the shed that the skunk families were regularly frequenting. Iver attached a long rope to the box in case they actually trapped one of the critters so he could pull it out of the yard without getting within spraying range of the trapped skunk. The very next morning there was a big, fat skunk in the trap. It worked really well, and almost every morning art would find some unsuspecting skunk in the trap box which he would release in the draw where they had turned Puey and Louie loose.

The Sorum Dam was nearly completed by the summer of 1937, so Iver knew that his work would soon be ending. It was easy work compared to what he did at the ranch, and he and Anna would miss the paychecks. They thought of his job there as getting paid to train new teams of horses. In true government fashion, twice as many workers were hired than were needed, and the loafers among the workers mainly watched the others toil. Iver joked to Anna that they had two watchers for every worker.

Iver told a story about one old geezer who had been watching him and his team all morning and came over to visit with him when he stopped for lunch. "Howdy, mister," he addressed Iver. "That's a mighty fine team that you have. Where did you buy them?"

"I raised them and trained them myself," Iver proudly answered. "I noticed you watchin' me haul rocks to the face of the dam."

"Ya," the old man smiled. "I really enjoy work. I could sit and watch *others* do it all day!"

Iver laughed, and after rubbing the horses down, he invited the old freeloader to share his lunch. They exchanged stories, and Murel came by to visit. Murel loved a good tale, and Iver shared this one with him.

"Yeah," Murel said. "I could get used to working for the government. Good pay, don't have to work, and I've never seen anybody get fired. Too bad that this job is almost over. We've already stretched it a few months longer than it should have taken; maybe we could make it last until fall."

"If I worked this slow at home, it'd take me all day to milk two cows," chuckled Iver. They both laughed. Iver really enjoyed Murel and told him to bring his wife by the ranch some day for a piece of Anna's pie.

The WPa workers did manage to stretch the work into the fall months, giving all the men a few extra, desperately needed paychecks. Anna loved taking those paychecks to the reva store and cashing them. It was a great feeling of independence to have cash to pay for their supplies rather than having to charge them. For that feeling alone, Anna would gladly have done all the ranch work by herself for the rest of her life!

In the spring of 1938, a brief but very strong storm went through the area and dumped over two inches of rain in about ten minutes. It flooded rabbit Creek which fed the Sorum reservoir, filling it in a matter of hours. There was even water going over the spillway, and neighbors came for miles to see the sight. Anna and Iver packed their family and Daisy in the wagon and took them to the dam so Iver could show off his work. He and all of the men that worked on the dam were proud of their accomplishment, especially now that it had water in it, and they could see the spillway in action. The dam had been designed such that it also served as a bridge across rabbit Creek, making the face of the dam part of the Sorum road which allowed the workers to drive across it to better show their families their handiwork.

A few days later, the son of one of Iver and Anna's friends came home to visit his family after being away for several years. He had earned enough money working in Iowa for a down payment on a car and was driving his DeSoto home to show it off. When he didn't show up on time, the family went looking for him and found part of the DeSoto sticking out of the water in Sorum Dam. Their son had been driving late at night and hadn't known the dam was there. Apparently, he had driven right off the face of the dam and into the water, probably hitting his head on the steering wheel and drowning in his new car. It almost made Anna and Iver wish they hadn't help build the dam.

That same spring, Iver was out fixing a fence with Obert and art. Iver had purchased a new fencing tool called a golden rod. It was a piece of flat iron with notches and attachments at each end for clamping on to and holding barbed wire. Once the wire was clamped at each end, a handle was used to ratchet the arms to the middle, stretching the wire from both ends. The rancher could then splice the wire and detach the tool, leaving a tightly stretched fence. Iver thought it was the best invention ever and liked showing off how tight he could stretch the wire. He was in the process of splicing the overly stretched barbed wire when the grabber on the golden rod gave way allowing the tightened barbed wire to slide through his hand. The barbed wire sliced through part of his palm and nearly completely cut off the end of his middle finger. Iver dropped the fencing equipment, wrapped his hand and finger in his t-shirt, and headed home with the boys.

Iver was whining and thought that Anna should take him to Buffalo where it was rumored that a new doctor had moved in. However, Anna inspected the injury and promptly told Iver that there was a doctor on the ranch. She washed and disinfected his wound, got out her needle and thread, and told Iver to buck-up while she stitched it shut. First, she reattached the end of his finger, and then she sewed up the cut through his hand. By then Iver had an audience—all the kids and Daisy were watching—so he had to act like it was nothing and he was tough enough to take a little stitching on his hand and finger. Finished, Anna admired her sewing, re-wrapped the sewn-up finger and hand, and told Iver to go back to work. Grumbling that he should at least get the day off Iver reluctantly headed for the barn. A few days later Anna removed the wrap, wondering if the finger had rotted and would come off with the wrapping. It didn't. It was a healthy pink and almost as good as new.

There had been adequate rainfall that year to put some water in the ponds but not enough to fill them. One morning in late October, after another fairly hard freeze, Iver and Anna decided to check the cows and make sure they were still getting water. The first pond they came across was a total disaster. The water had frozen hard enough that the cows couldn't get a drink, so they tried tromping on the ice which had finally broken with several of them on it. The cows that were on the ice went into the water and couldn't escape. There had been sufficient freezing and thawing to build up a rim of ice around the outside edge of the pond, and the cows couldn't get over that rim of ice. They were trapped in the freezing water, and some of them were so frigid and fatigued that they were no longer even trying to escape. To make matters worse, the cows that weren't in the water were thirsty and crowding the narrow opening to get a drink, pushing even more cows into the icy water.

All that Iver and Anna had with them were a couple of ropes and their saddle horses. Fortunately, both of them were riding well- broken roping horses that day. Iver tied one end of the rope to Anna's saddle horn and jumped into the icy water, disregarding his own safety. One at a time, he put the loop end of the rope around a cow's neck, and Anna nudged her horse ahead until the slack was out of the rope. Iver pushed and lifted, and Anna and the horse pulled, dragging the cows over the rim of ice and out of the water one at a time. Sometimes another cow would get shoved and pushed into the water by the thirsty cows behind her, and for a while, Iver and Anna were hardly gaining. They first tried to pull out the cows that appeared to have been in the water the longest before they perished from hypothermia and shock in the muddy, frigid water.

Finally, after a few hours of excruciating work, the ranch team had the water clear of cows. Iver was nearly in shock from being in the frigid water so long. Anna had some matches in her saddlebag and made a fire from some sagebrush and thistles to warm him up for the ride home. He looked blue, and his teeth chattered all the way. When they arrived, he quickly stripped off his clothes while Anna gathered some well water and put it on the stove to heat for a hot bath. Anna was worried that he would come down with pneumonia, but he didn't.

Iver stayed in the hot water while Anna and the boys went back to the water hole to see if any more cows had been pushed in, but thankfully none had. Two cows that they had pulled out were still lying on shore even though the rest of the herd had left, so Anna rubbed the cows while her sons went home for blankets to cover them. They died later that day, apparently from stress and hypothermia. Anna was sad for them but trembled at the thought of how many cows might have died if they hadn't by chance happened upon the scene when they did. They had precious few cattle left as it was and losing more would have been devastating.

Father time had actually treated them with favor that day—a few more hours and it would have been too late to save their cows. Before going to bed, Anna said a prayer of thanks to Jesus for being able to save what was left of their cattle, but, subconsciously, she wondered what else could possibly go wrong on their prairie ranch. It felt like the worst of the weather was behind them and that the economy was rebounding, but nothing could be taken for granted when you lived off of the land. As she was drifting to sleep, Anna let her mind wander back in time to the almost ethereal past, back to Norway and how Chris and Iver had immigrated a few years before her voyage to america. Her thoughts drifted back to her mother and family and the many friends whom she had left behind. Would she ever see any of them again?

PART II

Faith and Forgiveness

We Stand Here Today

Anna was wondering whether to make stew for supper or to fry some venison steaks. She already had an apple pie in the oven. It was Chris's favorite, and Anna wanted this day to be as special for him as it was for her. The winter of 1938 was fast approaching, and Chris was too old to be shoveling snow, so they were moving him to their upstairs guest bedroom. Anna had his room ready and decided to go over and get a few of his things while she was waiting for the pie to finish baking. She knocked with no answer and then went in. She called to Chris to let him know she was in his house, still without getting an answer, and then she spotted the old man sitting in his chair by the stove. She called again with no response and went over to him, thinking that he was probably taking a nap. But Chris wasn't napping. He had died in his chair, probably of a heart attack. It was the last thing Anna had expected, and after the shock of it wore off, the sadness started setting in. Anna truly loved the old man. He had been so much nicer to her than her real father had, and she had grown to think of him as her actual dad. They had gone through so much together, and their bond had grown tighter and stronger each year. Anna was convinced that without Chris she never would have survived the year that Iver had been recovering from the wolf attack. Without him she and Iver might never have even met nor had a ranch. Now he was gone, and the ranch and their lives would never be the same. It would seem empty without Chris there. She sat with him a while longer, her sadness gradually turning to thankfulness. Anna dried her tears and said a prayer for Chris before leaving. He had lived a long and good life and had been loved. He had a content look on his face, and Anna knew that although his body was there, his soul was in heaven.

Since Iver was out checking cattle, there was nothing Anna could do except go home and take her pie out of the oven. While waiting for Iver, she sat down in her rocker and thought about the old man that they loved so greatly and were going to move in with them that day. She was sad, but Chris had lived a long and good life, and she even managed a smile as her mind went back to the past and his story went dancing through her mind.

Chris had voyaged to america a few years before Iver, in the 1880's, but for similar reasons. The economy in Norway was meager, and there just weren't any jobs. In addition, Chris had been ambitious, intelligent, and had an adventurous spirit. Unlike Iver, he hadn't come to be a farmer or rancher, but simply to find a better life and do and see something new and exciting. Upon arriving in america and going through Ellis Island, Chris found some work at a factory in New York but decided that he didn't like the crowded conditions there. He worked his way to Chicago where he toiled in two of the slaughterhouses and another factory. After a few months in Chicago, he determined that he really hated that city, especially the filthy and foul-smelling slaughterhouses with their harsh working conditions that seemed to trap his fellow immigrants.

In Chicago he learned that scores of fellow Scandinavians were settling in Minnesota, especially Minneapolis, so Chris thought that might be the place for him to call home. He rode the rails in an empty livestock car from Chicago to Minneapolis, just as Iver would do a few years later. He worked in construction in downtown Minneapolis and then for a farmer on the outskirts of town for about a year before his wandering spirit took over again. He checked out some maps and decided that Pierre, South Dakota, looked like a good destination. When he reached Pierre, he worked for a blacksmith for a few months, and then he delivered goods for a general store.

On one sunny and pleasant spring day, Chris delivered some supplies to a local carpenter whom he had gotten to know. Chris visited with him for some time, and the friendly German immigrant, Henry, told him that he needed to hire some help since two of his sons had left town to acquire some of that free government land. Chris didn't understand what he meant by free land, so Henry, who had studied the subject extensively before his boys left, tried to explain it to him. "The homestead business all started with the Homestead act of 1862 which gave settlers a free quarter—160 acres—of land if they would live on that land and farm it for five years. Since my sons are immigrants, they also needed to apply for american citizenship. I think the law originally excluded black folks and Norwegians since the Democratic landowners didn't want the market competition."

"You telling me they excluded us Norwegians?" Chris asked, bristling up.

Henry laughed, "Just joking with you, Chris. I heard you Norwegians were always up for a good joke. On the other hand, we Germans take life too seriously most of the time."

"You got me good with that one, Henry! Please continue," smiled Chris.

"By the time my sons went searching for land, the best and most productive spots, those along the rivers and valleys, were already taken. However, they found some good farmland east of here about thirty miles and set up their homesteads there. I visited them a few months back, and it is very fertile soil, but even that area has been nearly all taken. Now you'd have to go looking in the western region of the state where there is still a large amount of land available."

After thanking his friend Henry, Chris gave what he had just learned some serious thought. Although he hadn't intended to be a farmer, the Homestead act sounded like a great opportunity. What could possibly be better than free land? after more consideration, he decided to look for land in western South Dakota. Making his way to Harding County in the late 1800s, Chris laid claim to 160 acres of prairie grassland in a beautiful spot just east of what the natives called the Slim Buttes. All that was required of him was to be over 21 and the head of the household, pay the government an $18 filing fee—which was the only thing they really seemed to care about—and sign and file a declaration to become a United States citizen. If he stayed there for five years, the land would be his, free and clear. The Enlarged Homestead act of 1909 doubled the amount of acreage to 320 acres, which both Chris and Iver eventually took advantage of. Before he left Pierre, Chris posted a letter—with the help of the owner of the general store where he was working—to his family in Norway telling them that he was doing fine and that he was going farther west to acquire some of america's free land. Iver's father read the letter and told his family about his brother Chris, his travels across the ocean to america, and the free land that was available there. That was Iver's first introduction to america, and the notion of the government giving an immigrant free land had implanted in his mind and grown throughout his youth. There was no land available in Norway, and even if there was, it would cost a fortune. The prospect of free land in a paradise like america was almost too good to be true.

When Chris laid claim to his first 160 acres, he needed shelter for the winter, so he made a crude little dugout in the side of a knoll. It was little more than a hole made of rocks and soil with a few wooden beams placed across it to help support the roof which was made out of strips of sod cut with a plow. That little dugout, which resembled a large badger hole, would later become Anna's first home.

A family from west of Chris's claim came by one day on their way to Dickinson, North Dakota, to see family members that lived there. There was a post office in Dickinson, and the family graciously waited while Chris wrote another short letter to his family in Norway. In it, he described his free land, probably making the property and the environment sound a lot better than they actually were while at the same time omitting anything negative. This second letter was the one that totally set the hook in Iver's mind, and the reason that he came to america when he was merely a boy.

Since his homesteader neighbors offered to pick up and deliver mail for him, Chris told his family in Norway to send letters to him to Mr. Christian Olson, Dickinson, North Dakota, USa. The rural post office was accustomed to holding mail for settlers until someone came in and claimed it. Chris and Iver both had been Olsons in Norway, but Iver had his last name changed to tenold by the officials when he went through Ellis Island.

Chris had become seriously lonely and several times had almost left his homestead to look for a wife or move to a town where at least he had someone to talk to. A couple of years later, when he was on the verge of leaving his homestead, the same neighbors that had taken his letter to the post office in Dickinson came by with a letter for him. Chris was crazy with happiness just to receive a letter.

Dearest Chris,

We hope that this letter finds you healthy and happy. We have so enjoyed your letters from America, and we can only imagine how beautiful it must be there. Conditions in Norway have not improved, and life here continues to be a struggle. My son John wants to be a farmer, and as the oldest son, he will inherit my land and the farm. My other son Iver also wants to be a farmer and have some land of his own. As you know, that is virtually impossible here in Norway. Iver has read your letter until the pages are almost worn out and dreams of going to America to live with you. To have his own farm and land is his only desire.

Although he is only fourteen, we have purchased passage for him on a steamship that will take him from Vik Harbor to New York City in America. Once in America, he will make his way across that immense country to find you in South Dakota. Will you please help him get started with some land of his own? Can you teach him how to find the free land? We would be forever indebted to you for your help. Since it takes so long to send letters back and forth, and since we have no idea whether you will even get our letter, Iver will be leaving without having heard back from you. We pray with all of our hearts that your friends will go to Dickinson again and find this letter addressed to you and deliver it. Iver is a good son and is smart and a hard worker. I think that you could make a good team and build a large, wonderful farm together. We don't know how we will possibly be able to part with him, but we must think of his dreams, not our own.

Have you found a wife? Have you built yourself a home? We hear stories of wild Indians that take settlers' scalps. Do you still have your hair? What do you do for a living besides farm? Do you have livestock? Are there wild animals? We are sorry for all of the questions but living there and having *the American government give you, an immigrant, free land sounds almost too good to be true.*

As for us, we are doing fine with the exception of the dreadful Norwegian economy that shackles us. Nevertheless, we still have food on our table, and we are healthy. It could be so much worse. Hundreds of others like you have left Norway for America in search of work and prosperity. I pray that it is as nice there as you have told us and that our fellow Norwegians are finding their dreams and all of that milk and honey they talk about. Lutefisk and lefsa would be better, but we can't be too fussy.

We have no idea how long it will take Iver to get there, but he is a very resourceful young man and will do his best to get to South Dakota with haste once he reaches America. He is worried that the free land will run out, so he will hurry.

We love you and pray you are still doing well,
Please write back to us,
Your brother Olav and family

Upon reading the letter, Chris threw his hat in the air and started dancing a jig. The family that dropped the letter off looked at him as if he was deranged, so he explained to them, "I was about to leave this desolate place 'cause I'm so lonely that it hurts to my heart. I was depressed and feeling blue just this week and had made up my mind to give up my claim and move back to Pierre where I'd at least have some company and someone to visit with. I had decided to work for the nice German farmer I met or a feed company again. Now, this letter that you so kindly brought to me has changed my mind and given me hope and something to look forward to. I'm going to stick this old homestead out and wait for my nephew to arrive. With his help and company we'll make this claim into a real ranch. Your kindness has changed my life! Would you like to stay for something to eat? I don't have much, but I'm pleased to share it with you. If you can stay, I'll shoot a couple of those pesky rabbits behind the house and fry them up real tasty for you. If it weren't for you and your goodness and helpfulness in delivering that letter to me, I'd 'a been packing my bags this week."

Surprisingly, they did stay for the meal. Perhaps they felt sorry for the lonely man living by himself near the Slim Buttes.

It wasn't until years later, after he met Anna, that Chris told Iver and Anna this story. He told them that if he hadn't gotten that letter, he more than likely would have abandoned the claim and moved to Pierre. He even told them about dancing the jig and making the visitors think he had lost his mind. They all laughed and told him how blessed they were that he stayed. When Anna heard the story, she said one of her thousands of silent prayers, thanking God for getting that letter to Chris before he left. She said another prayer now for Chris, who she dearly hoped was in heaven, as she continued to think back on his life.

After getting the letter from his brother and learning that his nephew was coming to live with him, Chris put his newly found energy into the homestead. He went to the Slim Buttes and chopped several trees to use for lumber for a real cabin and barn and went around meeting his sparse supply of neighbors. One of them was giving up his homestead and going back east to his family. He had some beautiful Hereford cows, and Chris purchased the small herd from him since the man had no way of taking the cattle with him. For little more than he had paid for the filing fee for his first 160 acres, Chris also purchased the man's land which adjoined his homestead. Chris didn't have nearly enough money to pay for the land and cattle, but he promised to send the balance of what he owed to the seller as soon he could. They finished their business with a handshake, the contract of the west. Chris proved to either be lucky or have a good eye for cattle as that turned out to be one of the highest quality Hereford herds in South Dakota. The grass on Chris's ranch was nearly as good as he had described it to his family in Norway, and it fattened up cattle almost like grain would.

It was another two years before Iver finally arrived, and by then Chris had the makings of a real western ranch. He was so happy to see some kin that he probably would have given it all to Iver just to have someone there to visit with. As soon as Iver was old enough, Chris took him to the courthouse to file another claim which bordered Chris to the southwest.

They probably would have ended up as two old bachelors living on the prairie if Anna hadn't arrived there a few years later. Iver and Chris worked well together, making future plans and acquiring more land as it became available. right after he made it to South Dakota, Iver wrote a short letter to his parents and family in Norway to let them know that he had arrived safely. It was in Norwegian since he didn't learn to write English until much later in his life. He told them a little about his trip across the ocean and arriving at Ellis Island in New York where they changed his name from Olson to tenold, as well as his train trip across america to Dickinson, North Dakota. From there he had traveled about 130 miles southwest to his uncle's homestead near reva, South Dakota, and the Slim Buttes. In his letter Iver informed his family that when he was old enough, he was going to apply for his own homestead—160 acres—which would adjoin Chris's land. He wrote that he was happy that he had made the choice to come to america although he missed his family so much that he often broke down and cried at night thinking of them. Iver rode all the way to Dickinson, North Dakota, to get the letter mailed to his family in Norway.

There was another settlement with a post office in Deadwood, South Dakota, and, at first, he thought that he might take his letter there since it was closer. He had asked Chris about it. "What do you think, Chris? I'd like to get this letter in the mail right away to let my family know that I have arrived safely, and I've heard that Deadwood is closer than Dickinson."

Chris thought for a while and then said, "I'd definitely go to Dickinson for more than one reason. First off, you have traveled that route and know how to get there and back. I might add that it is a much easier route since it takes you over flat prairie plains, whereas to get to Deadwood you'd have to go through mountains. But the main reason to avoid that area is safety."

"What do you mean?" asked Iver.

"Deadwood is known for its lawlessness," explained Chris. "There are gamblers, thieves, prostitutes, opium, and maybe even some rogue Indians left in the Black Hills. The Indians thought that the 1868 Ft. Laramie treaty gave them that land, and they still aren't happy about Custer's expedition and the way the war turned out. On top of all of that, the region has forest fires and smallpox."

"really?" asked Iver. "They still have smallpox, prostitutes, brothels, robbers, and such?"

"It's getting better, but that's where Bill Hickok was killed, and they have brothels and gamblers galore. It is said that you'd better have eyes in the back of your head if you want to safely travel through Deadwood. I think the pox has run its course, but I wouldn't tempt fate."

Deadwood, indeed, had had a long and colorful history and wouldn't have been safe for someone like Iver. It was founded in 1876 after gold was discovered in the southern Black Hills by the Custer expedition. Named for a gulch that was full of dead trees and a creek that was full of gold, Deadwood quickly rose to over 50,000 inhabitants. It even had a Chinese population which had to traverse Deadwood through underground tunnels since it was legal for the cowboys to shoot them. The famous Deadwood brothels thrived, and the state of South Dakota didn't close them down until 1980—not for being brothels, but for not paying their taxes!

About six months after Iver sent that letter to his family in Norway, he received a letter from them, delivered by the same neighbors that had relatives in Dickinson and had helped Chris with mail delivery in the past. Iver's family hadn't received his letter informing them that he had made it to South Dakota, and they were beside themselves with worry about how he was doing. Iver quickly wrote another letter to them:

Dear Mom and Dad and family,

I have safely arrived in America and am living with Uncle Chris. I wrote you one other letter which it appears you didn't receive although you may have gotten it by now. Maybe our letters crossed paths somewhere. I hope so. We have to rely on friends to deliver and pick up our mail from our closest post office which is 130 miles from where we live. I have heard that there is a town starting called Hettinger, North Dakota, since the railroad is going there. That will be a lot closer for us to send letters and pick up our mail.

When I am old enough, I will file for 160 acres of free land for the ranch that Chris and I are building. He already has a nice herd of Hereford cattle, and we have been cutting trees for lumber for ranch buildings and corrals.

I think about all of you every day and night, Mom. I hope that you have stopped crying for me and can smile now. Dad, every time I have a problem, I ask myself what you would do in the same situation. I am truly doing fine thanks to everything that you and Mom taught me. Thank you both again for the money and the help to get me to America to realize my dream. This never would have happened without your love and support.

Brother John, I worry that the economy there is too poor for you to make a living on the farm. I know that you felt bad that you got the family farm and that I couldn't have a farm in Norway too, so now you can quit worrying about me. With the help of Chris, I will soon have more land here in America than you ever would have imagined possible in Norway. If it gets to the point that you can't make a living there, you are welcome to come and join us here. The government has more free land, and it is easy to apply for. All you have to do is pay a small filing fee and become a citizen.

I pray that you get this letter. When I have time, I will write you a long letter and describe my entire journey to and through America and tell you all about the land and the customs here. It is a wild and wide-open prairie country, and the weather isn't dependable, but the ample supply of opportunity and farmland make up for it.

Please write to us soon. The family that has a homestead north of ours goes to Dickinson regularly to visit their relatives and always checks to see if we have mail, delivering it to us if we do. If you write to me, address it to Chris since the post office is familiar with his name and used to holding mail for him. When I went through Ellis Island, the officials there changed my last name to Tenold, so that might be confusing for the post office. Uncle Chris sends his love and best wishes and asks that you get word to the rest of our family on how he is doing.

> *I love and miss you all so very much,*
> *I see all of you in my dreams every night,*
> *Your son Iver*

Thinking about Iver's letter reminded Anna that he should be home from the pasture soon, and they would have to decide what to do with Chris's body. She thought about telling the children about Chris now but decided to wait until Iver was home. They were working on a project in the basement, and supper was on the stove, so she continued her journey back through time, remembering how she had met Iver.

Anna's friends, reidun and Odd, had arranged for a social gathering to introduce her to the neighborhood, especially the bachelors, and Anna and Iver had hit it off almost immediately. They found that they had almost everything in common, especially their love of livestock and land. They might have even come to america on the same shipping line, and they had followed the same route across america to reach South Dakota. Anna, who thought that she would never be able to love anyone except rasmus, found herself admiring and appreciating—possibly falling in love with— this handsome and independent rancher. Later, when Iver proposed to Anna and she accepted, Chris was just as excited with the prospect of having Anna on the ranch as he had been with having Iver. He later admitted that he was probably even more excited. The thought of having some female company and little children around—and especially homemade bread and pie—was more than he had ever hoped or prayed for.

As she thought back, Anna was stunned at how fast those years had passed and how quickly Father time had turned Chris into an old man. Yesterday, he had been a young man searching for a life in america. In a few blinks he had become old, his life spent, and now he was dead in his rocking chair next door. Life was a fleeting moment, a conundrum, here today and gone with the prairie wind tomorrow.

Anna was still deep in thought when Iver came in and smelled the fresh pie and stew. "How did I ever manage to find a beautiful woman that could cook too!" he asked, smiling at Anna. She smiled back, but quickly invited him to sit with her for a moment. After telling Iver what had happened to Chris, Anna gave him a hug and kiss and said how sorry she felt. Iver couldn't believe it at first, but in his heart he had known that Chris had been failing and that his health wasn't very good. They sat together for a while longer, shedding tears and consoling each other in the loss of their beloved Chris. Their children interrupted their remorse, coming up from the basement and asking when supper would be ready. They immediately saw the sadness in their parents' faces, and Anna told them what had happened. They were young but already too familiar with death. They grieved with their parents.

After supper Iver rode to reva to visit with the minister while Anna did the chores that she had neglected. Iver informed him that Chris had passed and asked him if they could have the funeral on Monday. The minister said Monday would work fine for him, and that he would announce the funeral day and time during the upcoming Sunday church service. He added that it was cold enough for a body to keep, but that Iver was smart to have the funeral as soon as possible. He knew that most of Chris's friends would be in church Sunday, and that Iver would inform Odd and reidun in case they didn't make it to church. When neighbors suffered a loss, especially someone as beloved as Chris, the word spread rapidly through the ranching community.

It was a sad day at the ranch. Everyone loved Chris so dearly. Marjorie and the boys had hung on him, the only grandfather they had ever known, and he was like a father to Anna and Iver. There would be a hole in their hearts and an empty place at the table for a long time.

That night Anna told her children, "We might not have this ranch or even be here if it hadn't been for Grandfather Chris. He is the reason that your father came to South Dakota, so without him, life as we know it would've never existed. We owe him so much, and we will always love him dearly."

Iver then told his family about his first days in South Dakota and how Chris made him feel at home and helped him with buying land, homesteading, and getting his own Hereford herd started. Chris had practically given him the heifer calves that he had started with and had frequently counseled him on how to handle the challenges of the land and the climate. Deep into the evening, Anna's family exchanged stories of Chris, cherishing the time that they had been given with him.

After church on Sunday, Odd and a few of the men helped Iver dig a grave. They had started a little graveyard west of the church, and Anna picked a nice plot for Chris close to the church and in the shade of a tree. The ground had frozen on top, but after the first foot or so, the digging became easier. As they dug, Iver thought about Chris helping him try to chisel out a grave for his twin boys a few years earlier and how they gave up and stored them in the grain bin for the winter. Iver had never shared that story with anyone. As he reflected on their stillborn twin girls and digging their tiny graves, Iver started crying. The other gravediggers probably thought that he was crying for Chris. He was, of course, crying for him too.

Atypically for South Dakota, it was a still and sunny day in early December for Chris's funeral. Anna had him dressed in his best Sunday garments, and he looked peaceful. After a short service in the church, the neighbors carried him to his grave in the wooden box that Iver had made for him, a larger version of the ones he had built for the two sets of twins. Iver thought to himself that he was getting too good at making coffins, hoping to never have to make another. After the pastor was finished, Iver and Anna both said a few words at the grave site, as did a few of Chris's closest friends. It was a small and solemn but beautiful and reverent service. Afterward the men filled in the grave with rich, dark plains soil with Obert and art silently helping. The Dakota prairie had swallowed another of its children, and Father time had taken another soul. Anna silently prayed that Father God had Chris with him in heaven.

That night Iver and Anna wrote a letter to Iver's family in Norway and told them that their beloved Chris had died in his rocking chair, probably of a heart attack. They explained how much they would miss him and how much they loved him. It was a sad letter in ways, but it was also a letter of optimism and thankfulness. Mostly, they just wanted to let Chris's other relatives know that he had passed and that their prayers for him would be most appreciated.

In the spring of 1939, Anna had another stillborn baby, this time a little boy. If he had lived, Anna would have named him Iver Junior. Had all of her children lived, they would now have had eight children. Anna and Iver went on to have yet another premature and stillborn baby girl two years later. Their last two babies were buried alongside Chris at the reva cemetery. Anna's three living children were a great source of joy to her, but in thinking about them, she was reminded of their brothers and sisters and what should have been. She and Iver had buried six beautiful babies.

Anna's deep Christian faith, along with the hope that her children were in heaven with Jesus, was probably the only thing that got her through those deaths. *Anna was still wondering why, but she was past blaming God. She wasn't good at blaming others for her misfortunes. She silently and covertly shouldered those burdens all by herself, her shoulders sagging with the weight.* The lines of worry and pressure were etching themselves into her aging but still beautiful face. Time marched on, and Anna's eternal faith and optimism doggedly kept her marching with it.

Christmas and New Year's were difficult without Chris. It was like there was a big part of the ranch missing, but life on the prairie didn't afford a great deal of time for reflection, and the family was soon too immersed in work to have time to think about their loss. It snowed again this January of 1939 making the chores difficult to do. The bright spot was that Obert and art were now old enough for semi-heavy lifting, and they could almost do the milking and chores by themselves if necessary. They were taking a good share of the load, and now Anna could spend more time with Marjorie teaching her how to cook and clean and doing those things that mother and daughter enjoy doing together. Anna still had the chills and fevers, but only seldom were they severe enough to slow her down. She still dismissed them as "A slight cold" or a "bit of the flu." Her nightmares still occasionally came, but she had had them so often that she could almost dismiss them in her sleep, realizing that they weren't real.

Although the weather and the economic conditions had improved greatly, neighbors were still leaving. The hardships and the harsh years had taken their toll on the people of the prairie. Some families—their dreams shattered, and their hope extinguished—picked up stakes and left without even telling their friends and neighbors where they were going. They just vanished with the prairie wind, blending in with the trail of migrating farmers and laborers wandering the country in search of another dream, additional statistics of the Great Depression and the thirties. As a person of deep faith, Anna did the only thing that she could for the missing families—she prayed for them.

Anna, Iver, and their rancher neighbors along with the tens of thousands of people that had personally experienced the decade of the Dirty thirties and the Great Depression would never think, act, or be the same as they had been before encountering this era. What they had experienced was almost surreal. The feeling of being totally penniless with no hope for the future, watching their friends and neighbors leave their land in desperation with only what they could carry, and watching drifters aimlessly wander through the country was a life-altering experience. But it had been real, every dreadful day of it, and it had happened to them. They would always hold their money closely and guard their pocketbooks down to each precious penny. They would forever make sure that they had enough to pay for what they purchased, and they would never want to borrow from the bank. They would save every little possession that they had and live frugally, worrying about the future and their children and grandchildren. Knowing how uncertain life was, they would never take anything for granted. Those folks that lived off of the land, like farmers and ranchers, would anxiously look at every cloud forming on the horizon. Was it dirt? Was it locusts? Was it a dry lightning storm? Was it wind or hail? Could there possibly be some rain in it? For her family Anna's conservative nature would be reinforced.

It was why they went into the '30s and the Depression without any debt, enabling them to keep their land and livestock. They were simple people, not wanting to be a bother to anyone, but wanting to help everyone. The souls that came wandering through their lives were always met with dignity and grace and treated as equals. They ate what Anna was feeding her family that day, and, in return, most of them did whatever they could to help out. When Anna fed strangers, she was always the last to eat. If they had needs, she tended to them before helping herself. She was humble, and, as such, she was a natural leader. She was a living testament to her faith and her creator. She was a paradigm for how we should live our lives.

Glad Tidings

Anna was pleased to have most of the '30s behind her, and in 1939 she felt like the Dirty thirties, as they were being called, were finally coming to a close. She couldn't help but notice that the cold, severe winters were gradually getting milder, and the hot, dry summers were progressively becoming cooler and wetter. The dust storms were subsiding as farmers learned new methods of tilling the land, leaving more cover on their fields and planting millions of trees in shelterbelts to keep the wind from eroding the soil. The grasshoppers had run their cycle of destruction and were no longer devouring the precious plants that fed people, wildlife, cattle, horses, and sheep. Livestock markets were now open again, and prices had started rising. Anna knew that prices would increase sooner or later since there were now far fewer cattle and sheep to feed even more hungry american mouths.

Out of work citizens were finding jobs and going back to work, slowly at first, but more quickly as another war grew closer. It was looking like the "war to end all wars"—the Great War—wasn't going to live up to its reputation. Germany would soon invade Poland, Paris would fall, and auschwitz and the Nazi death camps would swallow their first prisoners alive. America, feeling safe and secure an ocean away, remained neutral. Even so, Anna was still troubled when she heard the war rumors. She had two sons who were rapidly becoming young men.

Since Anna and the other people of the prairie in western South Dakota didn't have electricity, they missed the Orson Welles radio dramatization of the H.G. Wells novel *War of the Worlds*. It was broadcast on the eve of Halloween, and the live performance most famously included news bulletins covering a Martian invasion that were so realistic that they sent scores of americans into hiding and caused widespread panic in large cities. Unaware of what was happening in the cities, Anna was just thankful that they had survived the '30s and the Depression, and she was doing her best to be optimistic about what the future held for them. Her faith and optimism had often made her visions brighter than the ensuing reality, but they were what had kept her going.

For some of the more fortunate folks, the dark days of the Depression were already in the rearview mirror, but for Anna's family it would take years to recover. Market prices increased rapidly, but they had virtually nothing to sell. Their cattle and horse herds had been whittled down to almost nothing with some of their cattle having simply starved to death. Their frozen bodies thawed in the spring and dried out under the summer sun while predators picked their carcasses clean. The prairie was littered with their bleaching bones along with those of the wild animals that were also victims of the devastating weather patterns. Many of Anna's neighbors had dispersed their herds for pennies on the dollar since they had nothing to feed them or had them sold by the bank when they foreclosed on their hapless owners.

Anna and Iver, like most of the ranchers who still had cattle, were down to a handful of animals, and it would take them years, maybe decades, to build their numbers back to where they were before the great devastation arrived. To Anna just staying alive—pure survival—had been the only thing that had mattered. Now she and Iver were virtually starting from scratch; they were rebuilding their lives, their herds, and their ranch. If the 1930s had been the time of the great tearing down, the 1940s would be the time of the great building up. Anna's faith and optimism were slowly regaining their rightful place in her life. Father time along with Mother Nature both seemed to be in a good mood and were smiling down on her family again.

One windy afternoon in the summer of 1939, Anna looked out her window and noticed some smoke in the yard. She went out to see what was causing it and saw that it was coming out of the woodshed. There were already flames, and she called to Iver and the boys to come quickly and help her. They all came running and formed a bucket brigade from the well to the shed. The shed was dry and burned easily, but they managed to save three of the walls and most of the wooden floor and roof. Iver was puzzled as to what might have started it. Obert left quickly after they had the fire out, but art, who was a couple of years younger, hung around looking sort of guilty.

Puzzled about how the fire had started, Iver finally asked art if he had anything to do with it. Art stammered around a while trying to think of something to say, but Iver saw right through his youngest son. "The truth is always the best, Son. If you have something to say, it had better be the truth."

"We were just lighting weeds, Pa; trying different kinds to see if any of them smoked good," art admitted. "The guys that come through always have cigarettes, and they seem to enjoy them so much. We was expermentin' to see if we could come up with a good one to give to them guys. They always seem to be out of cigarettes and are trying to borrow smokes from each other. They even pick the used ones off of the ground and try to get another puff of smoke out of them. I thought they'd be good, but they tasted terrible."

Since arthur had confessed and told the truth, he didn't get as long of a lecture as Obert did. Iver didn't even think about getting his belt out, knowing that the boys were getting too old for it. After all, they were teenagers now and did the work of a man. Even so, they still needed a little "guidance" occasionally.

From the time they were little tykes, it was easy to see that Obert would be the mechanic, and arthur would be the rancher. By the time that he was six, art had a herd of stick horses the size of Iver's herd of wild horses, and he fed and cared for and rode them daily. He had even culled the poor ones when times were tough and feed was scarce, just like his father had done with the real horses. He loved everything that had anything to do with livestock and the land. He could spend hours, losing all track of time, working with a new horse or checking the cattle. He loved difficult tasks, especially if they involved horses or cattle.

Obert, on the other hand, didn't take to livestock. He could spend hours on end in the shop tinkering with broken equipment in an effort to fix it or trying to invent or build something out of the old junk parts that were lying about. He had even made a race car when he was seven using an old log hollowed out for the body and round, wooden blocks for the wheels. All three kids could fit into it, and they pulled it up the hill and used gravity to race down. Obert's engineering on the steering mechanism wasn't the greatest, but it was usually sufficient to keep them on the road. When they had a crash landing, Obert had art and Marjorie blame the horses for any scratches or bruises, fretting that he might get the belt for endangering his little brother and sister with the car he made. If they got bruised or scratched up working with the horses, it was just a natural occurrence and didn't require a spanking Marjorie could hold her own, and she grew up tough having to fend off and keep up with two bigger and older brothers. One day she had been playing in the hayloft with her brothers, and the loft door was still wide open because Iver and Chris had been hoisting loose hay up to the mow to feed to the cattle during winter months. Obert and art looked from their sister to the open door and decided that they should give her a scare by pretending that they were going to throw her out the door, getting even with her for all the times she had gotten them into trouble. She was only six at the time, but she managed to escape from their grasp and ran off to the house screaming before they could catch her. She quickly found her dad and tattled, probably dramatizing the event a little. At any rate, off came the dreaded belt. Looking back at all of the belt incidents made the boys wonder why their dad hadn't simply bought another one so that he wouldn't have always needed to take his off. It would have been much more efficient, but probably not as effective, since watching their dad taking off his belt was almost as terrorizing as the spanking itself. Iver did it slowly and precisely, adding theater to the unfolding drama.

Marjorie was little Anna in many ways, both in her diligence and especially in her faith. She was always helpful in the kitchen, sometimes making the meals by herself when Anna was out working cattle, milking, helping Iver with a horse that he was breaking, pulling a calf, or any one of a thousand other ranch jobs. When Anna read the Bible to her children, Marjorie was the most attentive of them not wanting to miss a word. She even memorized a few Bible verses, reciting them to the Pastor on Sundays while her mom and dad listened in, their buttons popping with pride.

The last child is usually pretty spoiled, but there really wasn't any time or place for spoiled children on a cattle ranch. Obert, art, and Marjorie each had their tasks to do and suffered the consequences if they didn't get them finished correctly and on time. Anna's children had grown up quickly, mainly because they had so much responsibility. If anything that they were accountable for didn't get finished on time, the whole family suffered. They often had as much responsibility as adults, sometimes having to make life-or-death decisions instantly and on their own, as Obert and arthur had when Marjorie fell under their horse in the pond. If they hadn't reacted immediately, she surely would have drowned.

After work each evening, Anna's family often shared what they had accomplished for the day and went over the items that were scheduled for the following day. They had been discussing how well Iver recovered from the wagon accident one night, and it made them all think about the Christman family in Minnesota and how much they had done for Iver and their family. George had never sent a bill for any of the care he had given Iver. Anna remarked that it had been a long time since she had last heard any news from them, so she decided to write them a nice, long letter.

Dear George, Sarah, Gert, and family,

The year is winding down and so are we, it seems. I surely don't have the stamina that I used to, nor does Iver. It is a good thing that the boys and Marjorie are getting old enough to take some of the ranch duties upon themselves. Obert is so good at fixing our always-broken machinery, wagons, and anything mechanical. Art is a chip off the old Iver block and is our rancher in the making. Marjorie is my right-hand helper in the house and the kitchen. She often does the dishes for me, cleans the house, helps in the garden, or makes meals. She can already butcher a chicken and can the garden produce. She will make a wonderful wife for someone someday.

Well, that's enough bragging about my children. Their faithful watchdog, Daisy, is almost getting too old to keep up with them, but she still loves to go with Iver, either riding horseback with him or sitting beside him in the buggy or wagon. I swear that dog is almost human. We sometimes have to spell words out when we don't want her to know what we are saying, and even that doesn't always work. If I remembered my Norwegian better, I'd try that on her!

We are all in pretty good health. I still have chills and sweats and aches sometimes and seem to be prone to catching colds and the flu, but it doesn't happen nearly as often, or be as severe, as it used to be. You are the only people that I have ever told this to, but we have had two sets of stillborn twins along with a stillborn baby boy and girl since the birth of Marjorie. I have gone over their deaths in my mind a million times wondering what I did wrong that caused them to be stillborn and what I could have done differently to prevent it from happening. I sometimes think that if I had rested more or if I had taken better care of myself, they might be alive. I was ill quite a few times during my pregnancies, and, looking back, I probably should have tried to find a doctor or written to you to find out what to do. It sometimes nearly drives me out of my mind with heartache and sorrow. Maybe Father God just needed some beautiful babies for heaven and was sparing them all of the horrible things that can happen here on earth? Maybe it was something I did wrong, and He was punishing me? I'll probably never have an answer or know if I did something to anger Him, but not a day that goes by that I don't think of those beautiful babies and try to imagine what our family would have been like with them. It used to be unbearable, and I know that I took my sorrow and frustration out on Iver and our other children all too often. Now it is just a painful and dreadful enigma, a haunting memory that lives in my mind.

Our lives in themselves are a great conundrum it seems. When I think of all of the different paths my life might have taken, it's a wonder that I ended up here in South Dakota. I nearly stayed in Minneapolis with you. I loved all of you so dearly that it was extremely difficult to leave Minnesota behind to search for my Dakota dream. Speaking of wonders, Iver just walked in and is wondering when I'm going to come to bed. I guess it is way past that time, and the morning always comes much too early anyway, so I'll finish this letter in the morning or tomorrow night, if I can. Goodnight for now.

I'm back! The kids and Iver have been fed and are off doing chores. Art and Obert volunteered to milk my share of the cows for me so that I could have time to finish my letter this morning. We are milking our usual ten cows, and Art and Obert generally do three each while Marjorie and I each milk two of them. Milking makes for great family time as we can all chat while we are working. The boys still squirt each other occasionally, and Marjorie is no saint either. I've caught her squirting one of the boys when neither was looking. They automatically think it was the other boy, and the milk starts flying while she innocently giggles. We have one cat that loves to be squirted. Most of the cats run when targeted and stay out of range, but this one is smarter than the rest. It just turns around and starts gobbling the milk that is being shot at her! Our dog, Daisy, just endures it all, waiting patiently for her bowl to be filled.

When are you going to come and visit? Please, please, please. You keep promising, but we never see you. George, you must be about ready to retire or at least cut back on your work? The last I heard, that clinic of yours was rivaling Mayo. You need to put someone else in charge and come and see us. You still have a patient here, remember? You should come out and give him a check up and do some research on his recovery. You have met Iver, but he has never met you! He looks better shaved and with his clothes on, but you'll just have to come and see for yourself. He would love to thank you in person for all that you did for us and especially for him. We feel that we owe you his life, and to top it off, we never received a single bill for all the care you gave him. Oh, how we appreciated that. I don't know how we would have managed another bill!

The Mayo one was pretty staggering, and we know that you did a lot more than they did. As it turned out, we had to sell some of our cows to pay it, but thanks to the '30s, we ended up losing most of them anyway. Remind me to tell you about Iver's great hog enterprise sometime; it wasn't amusing at the time, but looking back, it makes me laugh. We will remain hopeful that you can come and see us.

I so wish we could come to visit you, but I don't know how we could ever get away from this place. It seems like every time we even think about leaving it to its own devices for a short time, something horrible goes wrong. Maybe someday one of the boys will take it over and let us have some time off. I remember that in Norway the farm—in our case, the ranch—always went to the oldest son, but in our situation, it will probably go to the youngest son, Art, as he seems to be the one most interested in it. I think Obert will be happy to move to the city and make his fortune there, but that will be his decision to make.

Please write back and let us know how all of you are doing, and please come out for a visit. It is the highlight of my year when I get word from you.

All our love, God bless you,

> *Anna, Iver, Obert, Arthur, and Marjorie*

A few weeks after mailing her letter, Anna received a reply from George and Sarah:

Dearest Anna, Iver, and family,

We have a lot of news, so I hope you have a cup of coffee and a comfortable chair to sit in while you read this. First of all, George has announced a partner at the clinic. He is a young doctor from Mayo Clinic. Usually, our good doctors go from here to Mayo, so this will be us getting even with them. He is a doctor that George consulted with on Iver, so Iver has already met him, although he probably can't remember it! His name is Dr. Sinclair, and George is going to let him take on most of the responsibility of running and overseeing the clinic. He was responsible for his own department at Mayo, so he should easily be able to take over here.

Luckily for us, he wanted to move to Minneapolis to be closer to his aging parents. So, with that being said, we should have time to come and visit next year! Can you make a slot for us around the first of July? Gert is taking her vacation then and will be coming along with us if it is ok and if you have room. We told her of the possibility, and she was so excited; it was all she could talk about in her return letter. I think she misses you more than she misses me, Anna. She still giggles when she tells us of how the two of you got from New York to Minneapolis, especially when you told her that you'd help her find the right train in Chicago when you had no idea how to do it yourself. This will be like a family reunion if you can make it work! I hate to bore you with children stories but here goes.

Both of our boys are going to be doctors, just like their dad. Who knows? Maybe one of them will be running our clinic someday. And to top it off, both of our daughters are now in nursing school. Our friends at church joke that we are trying to raise our own cheap labor force of doctors and nurses for our clinic. We are so proud of them, especially George. I guess it is the crowning achievement of a man's life to build something and have his family continue with it.

Speaking of medical problems, George has been researching what happened to you, Anna. How horrible, we had no idea. You shouldn't hold things like that in. Your soul will burst. He is looking into many possibilities and even has his new partner working on your case. He will probably write to you with questions after they have had time to do more research. So many good things are happening in the medical world right now with new techniques, new vaccines and medicines, and new medical equipment. George has difficulty keeping up with all of it and continually hires new doctors right out of college to help him stay abreast.

You are so right about my husband, though. George needs to be taking it a lot, lot easier. He is such a good doctor and father and works so long and hard at it and takes it all so seriously. If he loses a patient, he beats himself up over it for days and sometimes months wondering if he had done something differently or used a different approach, the person might still be alive. Being responsible for someone else's life can weigh heavily on a man. You know better than anyone how he feels; you've experienced WAY too much death in your life.

George is looking at new cars. He likes the Cadillacs and Buicks. The last I heard, you didn't have a car yet. Maybe the roads aren't very good there? Anyway, his main reason for getting a new car—or at least his newest excuse—is that if we come out, we would just drive all of the way. It would probably be a whole lot easier than taking the train to Hettinger and asking you to bring your wagon to fetch us from there. The kids are all out of the nest now and on their own so it would just be George, Gert, and me.

Along with everything else that is happening in our lives, we are buying a new house. The clinic outgrew our first facility, and we built a larger, more efficient building closer to the downtown area. It is a long drive for George from our farmhouse every day, so we need to find something closer. We are looking at a very nice ranch- style home that is only six blocks from the clinic. We also have someone looking for a home for Dr. Sinclair. He has a family of three just like you, two boys and a girl.

Now, I must tell on myself. I fell and broke my arm, but it is almost healed. George is taking the cast off next week. I was being silly and playing on some ice and slipped and fell on it. I guess my arm was in the wrong spot at the wrong time, and I broke my wrist and another bone. Oh well, if that is the worst to ever happen to me, I won't complain. Poor George, the kids used to keep him in business, and now it's me.

We drive by the farm where Obert used to live every chance we get. I still miss that old farmer so much, and I know how you felt about him. Such a gentleman, and he always had a gleam in his eye when he spoke of you. I think—well, I'm sure—that you were the highlight of his lonely existence after his wife died. I know that you wanted to have him come and live with you, and I know that you feel badly that you didn't get to show him his namesake, your first son, Obert, but you shouldn't. You made his life immeasurably better, and he loved you more than anything on earth. Being able to help you and give you his rifle and horse put a smile on his face that lasted until the day he died.

Now I'm the one that is getting too long winded. By the way, George wants to know what your favorite color is before he buys his new car. You'd think he'd ask me! I guess he knows that I don't care. I just don't want black. It seems like most of the cars are boringly black.

> *We can't wait to hear back from you,*
> *God's blessings and our love,*
> *Sarah and George*

Anna was beside herself with joy at the news that George, Sarah, and Gert were coming to visit them. She received the letter in reva, and Iver wasn't home when she got back, so she rode out to the pasture to find him and give him the great news. He was mending a stretch of fence when she arrived, waving and smiling and giving him a grand hug.

"What's this all about? Iver asked. "Did we win a million bucks or something?"

"Better than that, Iver! Much better! George, Sarah, and Gert are coming to visit us next summer over the Fourth of July. Here's their letter. I don't think that I've ever been happier!"

"I thought your happiest day was the day I asked you to marry me!" "Don't pout, Iver. You know what I mean."

"You might have to make it up to me tonight."

"We'll see," she smiled. "When will you be home for supper?" "What ya got cookin', good lookin?"

"Flattery will get you everywhere." "Everywhere is where I want to get!"

Anna had the letter from Sarah memorized by the time they went to bed that night. News like that was all it took to brighten up her life. She jotted a quick note back to them in the morning:

Dear Sarah, George, and Gert!

That is the most wonderful news I've had for years! No, not the part about your broken arm, Sarah, but the part that you all are coming to visit! I am overwhelmed with joy.

Don't you dare back out on us. We'll mark every day off of the calendar between now and the first of July next summer. You would break my heart if you didn't make it. I like red, George, but I also like blue, yellow, pink, purple, and green. I will love whatever color you get, just as long as the three of you come driving into our yard in it.

I'm getting this in the mail before you change your mind.

All our love,
May God continue to bless you,
Anna, Iver, and family

Anna was so happy that she wrote another short letter, this one to rasmus and astrid:

Dear Rasmus, Astrid, and family,

I have a little free time today and another letter to mail, so I thought that I would send you a short note too. I think it has been a couple of years since our last letter, but I know that Iver has been trying to keep you up to date on what is happening here in South Dakota.

We are so happy that the Depression is finally over, and that America is at last getting back on its feet. It seemed to last forever and was exacerbated here in South Dakota by the extreme summer drought and cold winters. We had so many storms and clouds of dirt that the news called us the Dust Bowl. We also had clouds of grasshoppers and clouds of lightning but hardly ever had any rain clouds. I don't think that we could have held out another year. Iver and I pray that your construction business didn't suffer, but it probably did. It seems like the Depression didn't leave anything or anywhere or anyone untouched.

Our sanctuary during the past decade has been our house and our three children. You made this house strong and tight, Rasmus. With the Dust Bowl and the clouds of dirt, other homes filled with soil quickly, but ours didn't. We honestly don't think that we would have survived the '30s in our other house. Like many other farm and ranch wives, I probably would have gone crazy listening to the wind howl through the cracks and watching the dirt sift in and accumulate around the windows and under the doors. We had drifts of dirt as high and deep as our winter snow drifts!

We used to promise folks that we would come back and visit, but we don't even do that anymore. We thought that we were so fortunate to own our ranch, but now realize that, in reality, it almost holds us prisoner. The cattle and other stock require attention 365 days a year and sometimes twenty-four hours a day. Since it is so difficult for us to travel, it is our hope and prayer that you will be able to come and visit us here sometime. It would be a dream come true for me to meet Astrid and to thank her personally for sharing you with us for the year that you came out and made our beautiful house. The guest bedroom is eagerly waiting for you, and, of course, so are we.

I'd best get this letter to Reva so it can make today's mail.

> *Our love and continual thanks,*
> *May God bless you both and all of your family,*
> *Iver, Anna, Obert, Arthur, and Marjorie*

15

Hope and Heartache

A nna, excited with the coming of her Minnesota friends and the new decade, found a renewed source of enthusiasm and optimism. The dreadful 1930s were over, and it was the spring of 1940, the start of a new decade for america. Anna's family, along with families all over the country, was confident about the future and that their country was becoming the land of milk and honey, the shining monument on the hill, once again. There were still rumors of war, but Anna did her best to dismiss them.

One of their neighbors, Harold Carlson, in his exuberance and optimism and in an effort to replace some of his old worn out farm equipment, took out a bank loan for enough money to buy a brand- new John Deere model D tractor and a mowing machine to pull behind it. As Harold said, "Out with the horses and in with the Deere's." Harold was so proud of his new equipment that he and his wife invited the entire reva neighborhood over for a demonstration of his new tractor and mower with a community picnic to follow after church on Sunday.

Anna's family hadn't been off their ranch for a few weeks, so they decided that it would be nice to go to church and then take in the picnic and farm equipment demonstration afterward. Obert and arthur were excited—maybe there would be some cute girls there?

Marjorie said that she would bake a pie for the big event. She already rivaled her mother in that department, but then she had learned from the best. Iver wanted to show off his new team of horses. He wasn't ready for the tractor era yet, but—he wouldn't admit it—he was thinking of possibly buying a little Ford tractor to pull the mower and rake. Obert was excited at the thought since he loved machinery, but art wasn't. Like his father, he still enjoyed doing the field work with horses.

As usual, Anna and Marjorie listened attentively to the Sunday church sermon, deeply thinking about each Bible verse and each heavenly statement. Iver and the boys had their minds on the upcoming tractor demonstration and festivities—Obert, because he loved tractors; Iver and art, because they were hoping it wouldn't start or something on it wouldn't work right, anything to make their horses look better. To them the sermon was always a little too long, but to the girls it was always a little too short. After the service almost the entire congregation went to the Carlson place to enjoy the long- anticipated community picnic dinner and festivities and then watch the tractor and mower demonstration.

As soon as they arrived, Obert ran over to see the new John Deere tractor and mower. Iver and art brushed their handsome team down. They were a matched pair of black horses—Beauty and Midnight— and Iver thought they were the best looking team he had ever raised and broken. Art agreed, although he hadn't been around to see all of the past teams. The ladies took their pies and fried chicken to the picnic table, joining in with the other gals in helping spread out the dinner items, organizing the meal into drinks, salads, main course items, and deserts. Most of the ladies there were ranchers' wives who were used to cooking for large families, and the overflowing picnic table displayed their talented culinary skills.

When Harold's wife announced that dinner was almost ready, there was a scramble to get as close to the front of the line as possible. Some of the wiser old-timers were already standing close by trying to outguess where the dinner line would form. The Pastor had been invited. He never missed an opportunity like this: a feast and a chance to visit with his flock and maybe expand it if the opportunity arose. All he had to do for admittance to the banquet was to say the mealtime prayer. He was as hungry as the rest of the men, so he said an unusually short and simple prayer of thanks for the food and the fellowship.

It was a segregated assembly with the men and boys gathering on one side of the yard and the women and girls on the other. Many of these neighbors hadn't had the opportunity to share what was happening in their little corner of the world for weeks, even months, so it was a very engaging event. The yard was alive with chattering and cheering as the delicious food rapidly disappeared, eagerly eaten by the hungry crowd.

Harold couldn't wait to show off his new equipment, but he wasn't having any luck in getting the men to leave the food table. The tractor would have to wait until the last piece of Marjorie's popular pie was devoured. It felt like an eternity to him, but finally the crowd was ready to wander over to his equipment and see his highly anticipated demonstration. Most of the women and their daughters stayed to clean up the dishes and the picnic tables rather than go to the exhibition because they weren't interested in machinery. After all, what could possibly be stimulating or exciting about watching a tractor?

As the men gathered around him, Harold gave a little speech about how great a deal the tractor and mower had been with the dealer practically throwing the mowing machine in with the tractor sale. To Iver's dismay, the tractor started right up, pop-pop-popping along in perfect rhythm. Then Harold showed the crowd the power take off shaft at the rear of the tractor which turned when he engaged the PtO (power take off) lever. He demonstrated how to hook the mower drive shaft to the PtO and then, after he had the mower connected to the PtO and had warned everyone to stand back, he turned on the PtO to demonstrate how the sickle in the mower slid back and forth along the sickle bar to cut the grass.

It was a grand show until the unthinkable happened. The men were crowding back around the tractor and mower, wanting to get close enough to see the sickle in action. Among the crowd was Harold's father-in-law, Henry Normanski. Henry was the closest to the sickle, in front of it, and his son-in-law, Harold, was standing by the tractor beaming with pride. Someone in the crowd accidentally pushed Harold, and instead of falling, he automatically reached for the nearest object to stabilize himself. His new John Deere tractor was equipped with a hand clutch rather than the old-style foot clutch, and when Harold reflexively grabbed the clutch lever for support, he accidentally engaged it, lurching the tractor forward.

The mower followed the tractor with nonchalant disregard for Henry's legs which were only inches away from the cutting edge. The sickle went through his ankles like a hot knife through butter, and Henry fell in a heap behind the mower along with the grass that also had been cut off. The other onlookers jumped the mower bar or dove away from it, and Harold chased the tractor down and managed to stop it. Art and Obert ran back to help Henry, holding his legs and trying to stop the blood that was rapidly spurting out of them in rhythm with his heartbeats. It was over nearly as quickly as it happened with Henry dying in art's arms, probably of shock as well as from loss of blood.

The horror of it all came crashing down on the formerly exuberant audience like a prairie wildfire roaring through them. It had all happened so quickly, yet in some ways it had seemed like a slow-motion scene from a horror movie. Cries of shock and alarm went through the crowd ending the day's festivities in sadness and despondency. After the accident, Harold was never the same again, going over and over the scenario in his mind until the day he died, trying desperately to somehow correct his blunder and undo what had happened. Anna, Iver, and their family stayed long after most of the others left, trying to console Harold, Harold's wife (Henry's daughter), and Henry's widow. Art and Obert washed the blood off of Henry, and then carried his lifeless body to a couch on the porch, covering it with a blanket from their wagon. Art went back to where the accident took place and found Henry's cut off feet and ankles and carried them to the porch, solemnly placing them with his body. With no more that they could do, they left for home.

As if nothing had happened, the milk cows were waiting in the yard to be milked. They had left Daisy home from church, and she had gathered the cows in anticipation of the work that needed to be done. The family milked in silence, Daisy probably wondering why they weren't visiting back and forth and squirting the cats that cautiously wandered by. The prairie had claimed another soul, leaving those still on its topside wondering why and how such a harrowing and heinous accident could have happened in their loving little community.

It had been a dark day for the ranching community, but Anna was determined that nothing would extinguish her happy anticipation of the upcoming visit of George, Sarah, and Gert. That night she prayed for Henry's soul and for peace for his family—especially Harold who had stared at Henry in sheer horror, begging his lifeless body to forgive him over and over. After that he hadn't said a word, overtaken with shock and distress. He needed healing along with the whole family, and Anna prayed earnestly for them. The rest of the family said prayers as well, Anna having trained them to never let a day go by without prayers of thanks to God for the day and all of the blessings that came with it, along with prayers for those who needed help, healing, and peace. Usually, the sound of goodnight, Ma, goodnight, Pa, goodnight, Marjorie, goodnight, Obert, goodnight, art echoed through their house at bedtime, but not that night. All thoughts were on what had happened that afternoon.

Along with the loveliness and beauty of spring came its drudgery, called "spring work" by the ranchers. Added to their usual chores and feeding routine were calving, fencing, and repairing everything that the winter winds and snow had blown over or broken. The winter snow usually piled up and froze on the fences with its weight tearing them down and breaking the wires. Wherever the fences crossed a draw or creek, the wires were almost always torn out and broken by the spring thaw and needed to be repaired. The usually dry draws and small creeks could turn into torrential rivers, and even cow paths, which were small trails across the prairie made by hundreds of sharp hooves as they followed the same route, turned into small creeks for a few days. Instead of tromping through winter snowdrifts, the workers now had to muck through the spring mud which clung to their boots and balled up under the horses' hooves. At least their feet didn't get as cold in the mud as they did in the snow.

Calving was the most difficult part of spring work and usually meant around-the-clock cattle watches with many sleepless nights. On one unseasonably cold night when the temperature dropped to below freezing, Iver came in the house with frozen blood and manure liberally splattered over his face and body. Anna felt sorry for him and let him thaw out and clean up in the porch rather than outside in the water tank. He had pulled three calves, one of them an especially arduous delivery. As he told Anna, the last heifer's calf might not have needed pulling, but he was so tired that he just pulled it out rather than waiting around for another hour or two to see if the heifer could manage it by herself. By pulling the calf rather than waiting, he was able to get an extra hour of coveted sleep.

Anna could hardly wait to hear her favorite spring songbird, the meadowlark. It always seemed to show up when she needed some cheering up, its song ushering in the end of winter and spring and the start of summer. She told Marjorie that its bright yellow chest and belly represented the sun—warm and cheery. Anna was a naturalist, loving everything outdoors with the exception of wolves which she respected but hated. She taught her children how to love and respect the prairie and its creatures. Wolves had begun to disappear from the prairie, and many years later when they were virtually gone from the landscape, Anna remarked that she *almost* missed them. Another critter that she could take or leave was the prairie rattlesnake. It was a relatively harmless creature when left to its own devices, but when it was surprised or cornered, it could also be deadly. Most folks were under the assumption that the only good rattlesnake was a dead rattlesnake, so they too were vanishing from the prairie.

Some of Anna's neighbors hunted and killed coyotes, the small cousins of the wolves, but Anna had never shot one of them. She loved to listen to them sing their mournful, eerie songs in the evening and hear their excited and often frenzied barking and yipping— which sometimes meant that they were having a family reunion or that they had killed some unfortunate rabbit or other small critter. Coyotes never bothered their cattle or horses except for pilfering the occasional afterbirth—the placenta and fetal membranes discharged after calving and usually eaten by the cow—or agitating the cows when they spotted one of them stealing their way through the herd. Chickens and lambs were another matter, and they were easy prey for coyotes, but rarely did a coyote venture into someone's yard. But any chicken that wandered off into the prairie was deemed fair game, and the sheep men had to guard their newly born lambs closely.

Obert and art were finally old enough to help with calving and the night checks, with art enjoying them and Obert hating them but diligently doing it anyway. If either of them found a birthing or any other problem on one of their checks, they usually got Iver out of bed to help. Anna gladly stayed in bed, going back to sleep with a huge smile on her face. It was such a blessing to be able to stay in bed rather than go out into the cold and dark night.

On one of those cold, dark nights, art came and woke his dad up. "The old gal is calving and has four feet sticking out, and I don't know what to do, Dad!" the calf was apparently bent over in the womb, and the cow had managed to shove four feet out with no way of pushing the entire calf out in that position. Iver called presentations like this fishing expeditions, always a puzzle. Which were the front legs? Which were the hind legs? It sometimes was one of each. Iver had to decide how to get the right two legs shoved back in and turn the calf to the proper position to be born. Sometimes the entire calf had to be pushed back in and turned around. If it was a backward calf, time was of the essence because those calves often started breathing and would drown in the placental fluid if they weren't extracted quickly enough. The only thing that you could be confident of with pulling calves was that when you were finished, you'd almost always be covered in blood and soaked with the other materials discharged from the back ends of cows. But if you were lucky, you'd have a live calf to show for it.

In June, calving season gradually gave way to foaling season which was infinitely easier for several reasons. First, it came later in the year so there was virtually no chance of a freezing rain mixed with snow or a late spring blizzard, either of which meant around-the-clock checks and the possibility of frozen calves. A wet, cold spring also seemed to promote scours which was a viral or bacterial infection resulting in severe diarrhea and often associated with pneumonia. When scours and pneumonia went through the calves, it was an around-the-clock battle to save them. Second, the horses were primarily on their own, foaling out in their pasture. On the very rare occasion that a mare had trouble foaling, it usually ended up as a case of survival of the fittest with the colt—and sometimes the mare—perishing if the birth was too difficult. A foal born out on the pasture virtually never had problems with disease.

The downside to foaling season was that it overlapped with the tail end of calving season and the beginning of the planting and farming seasons. Sometimes the mares had to go a day or two unchecked if it meant hurrying to get the crop planted while the ground was still dry enough and before the next rain came. Getting the crops timely planted was challenging, especially for ranchers that had cattle, sheep, or horses demanding their attention at the same time. Putting crops in too early often meant that the ground was still too cold, preventing the seed from germinating. When it germinated later, the ground was frequently crusted over preventing the new plants from emerging. Planting the crops too late normally meant that the newly emerged crop had missed most of the nice gentle spring rains that quickly grew them. If the plants weren't fairly mature by the time the hot, dry weather started, they dried up and withered before they had a chance to grow into a productive crop. Anna told her children that everything in the farming and ranching world relied on proper timing. This meant keeping perfectly in tune and in time with Mother Nature who often seemed to enjoy throwing a curve at them by being out of tune or time herself. She and Father time often seemed to have their own disputes.

While they were foaling and planting, the family worked on fencing or machinery repair in their spare time and on rainy days. This was where Obert shined, being by far the most talented mechanic on the ranch. He even had neighbors bring him their broken equipment for repair. Although Obert didn't want to be a farmer or a rancher, having him there to keep the equipment going was a real asset. He persuaded his dad to get a welder and an acetylene torch for their shop so he could patch up and weld almost anything that was broken. He jokingly complained that art purposely broke things just to keep him busy. Art would laugh and reply that he was helping him out by breaking so many things, keeping him out of trouble and in practice.

Anna and Marjorie were in charge of their area of farming expertise— tilling, planting, and hoeing the garden. They had it quite organized with the rooted plants like onions, carrots, beets, and potatoes in one section; those with vines like watermelon and muskmelon and squash and cucumbers in another area; and the peas and beans in nice neat rows ready for picking. They even had a variety of peppers which Anna loved to use in some of her recipes, and row upon row of sweet corn. It was a challenge to keep the raccoons, rabbits, and deer out of the garden. The scarecrow only seemed to serve as an opportune perch for the crows, but the ever-present Daisy faithfully kept most of the pesky critters out of their precious garden. As Anna had predicted, 1940 was turning out to be a better than average year on her prairie homestead with the crops and the livestock doing well and everyone in good health. Her bouts with the flu weren't as frequent, and Iver seemed to be complaining less about his arthritis and rheumatism. With the exception of the terrible tragedy at the Carlson ranch, the community hadn't had any serious misfortunes. Despite that disaster, Anna was happy, eagerly anticipating the arrival of her Minnesota family. As Iver put it, "When Momma is happy so is Papa."

Setting Out the Fancy China

Anna was getting more excited by the day waiting for the Christmans to arrive. She was making a list of all the things they could do with them like picnicking in the Buttes, horseback riding, showing off the new calves and colts, taking them to see the Sorum Dam that Iver had helped build, introducing them to Odd and reidun, fishing in the Grand river, looking for Indian arrowheads, showing them her house, visiting, and on and on went her list. On the bottom was written "Belle Fourche???"

Iver laughed when she showed the list to him. "How long do you think they'll be staying? I don't see a Christmas party on the list, but I see about everything else. If you get everything on that list done, they'll be here until New Year's!"

"Well," Anna replied. "I wouldn't mind if they did stay through Christmas and New Year's. I don't think I've ever looked forward to anything quite as much as their visit. I really do miss my old friends and wonder what they look like now and how they are faring. Friends like Donna who was as close as a sister and an anchor for me when I was all alone in New York after rasmus and I parted. Or the gang at the restaurant there, and the people I worked with at the café in Minneapolis. Our lives fly by so quickly, Iver. Although we may never see those friends again, they won't be forgotten. They will always be an important part of our lives that will forever be cherished and missed."

"Isn't that the truth, Anna? I miss the folks I met along the way too, but I especially miss my family in Norway. My mom was the most wonderful mom in the world."

"The second most wonderful," insisted Anna.

Iver smiled, "I won't argue that point with you, but I can truly say that I'm happy for you, Anna, knowing how much you are looking forward to this visit. I'll do my best to behave and be a good host. With both of the boys helping me and with Marjorie helping you, we should be able to find plenty of time to entertain them properly. Who knows, maybe we can get most of the things on your list crossed off? What did you mean by Belle Fourche with all of the question marks?" "I was just thinking that since they will be here over the Fourth of July, we might be able to take them to the celebration in Belle Fourche. I've heard that it is the best rodeo in the nation, and they even have a carnival and parade and other events celebrating our nation's birthday. Wouldn't that be exciting, Iver?"

"Come to think about it, Anna, we have never taken time to celebrate the Fourth and america's birthday. It's always the middle of haying season, and it would be at least a three-day affair with a day to get to Belle Fourche, a day there, and a day to ride back home. I usually put work over play, and you rightly remind me of that sometimes, but three days off in haying season is nearly impossible." "I know I do, Iver, but I almost think that we deserve to take a little time off to entertain our guests this year. They're what got me to thinking about it, Iver, because we will have a car this year. We could drive to Belle Fourche in an automobile! Wouldn't that be dandy?

And we could do it in one day instead of three."

"What are you talking about, Anna? I don't think we can afford to buy a car just now. We have too many other bills to take care of." "I didn't mean that you had to buy one, Iver. George is buying a new car for their trip to South Dakota. Maybe we could take his car to the celebration in Belle. I'm sure he wouldn't mind. This is his third car you know."

"No, I didn't know. Are you hinting that we should get one too? Do you know how much they cost?"

"Nope, and I'm not hinting, but I heard the Nelsons got one for under $500. It wasn't brand new, but almost," Anna replied.

"Well, I do, Anna. I heard that one of those new Cadillac 61s could set a guy back thirteen hundred bucks. We'd have to sell a lot of horses to buy one of them. I'd rather have some more land."

Iver had no sooner got the word *Cadillac* out of his mouth than they heard a horn honking in their yard. Anna and Iver went out to see what the commotion was. George, Sarah, and Gert were climbing out of their brand new 1940 Cadillac 61. It was red, of course.

Anna flew by Iver as if he was glued to the steps and threw herself at George, giving him the happiest, hardiest hug he had ever received. Then she went to Sarah and Gert, and the three of them had a long group hug, hopping around in circles. After what felt like half the afternoon to Iver, Anna called him over so she could introduce him. Of course, George had already met Iver, but Iver was unconscious at the time and until now had never seen the man to whom he probably owed his life.

"Iver, these are my dear friends—I should say family—from Minnesota. This is Dr. George, the man whose hands I put your life into and thank God every day that I did. This is his beautiful wife, Sarah, and her wonderful sister, Gert. This is the family that took me in like I was their own when I was nearly dying from loneliness and trying to reach South Dakota. Gert was my train and travel companion from New York, and she helped me find my way to Minneapolis."

Gert laughed at Anna's joke. She knew that it was the other way around.

Anna continued, "Welcome to our little piece of God's earth, our ranch. We are so happy to have you visit! You must be hungry and thirsty—and *tired*—from that long ride. I must say, George, that's the best-looking, fanciest automobile I've ever seen, and red is my favorite color. Will you take us for a ride in it sometime, please? It's beautiful."

George smiled, "Of course, my dear Anna! I'd be delighted to take you for a drive. How about you, Iver; do you like cars?"

"Guess I still fancy horses, George—they don't need gas—but I must admit that your Cadillac is one nice looking machine."

Just then Obert came running over from the shop. "Wow! a brand new 1940 Cadillac 61! How do you open the hood? I gotta take a look."

Anna interjected, "Mind your manners, Obert tenold. After you meet my friends and after you politely ask them if you can open the hood, you can do so—if they agree."

"Sorry, Mom. Guess I was just excited to see one of these. Sorry for being so rude, folks."

Anna introduced their first son, Obert, to the Christmans. Obert was hurriedly polite, and it was apparent that he was more interested in the car than the company. Art rode over from the round corral on the filly that he was breaking, looking like the genuine, handsome cowboy that he was. After fluffing up her pretty blonde hair, Marjorie came out of the house to meet them. Anna had a handsome family. Last, but not least, Daisy came over to inspect the car and size up the visitors. Even though she was a girl dog, she had to lift her hind leg and wash the dusty tires off. It was a dog's duty. She generally ignored other families but seemed to like these strangers. Maybe she sensed how much Anna loved them.

After all the introductions and hugs, Anna invited their company into the house. Sarah and Gert had already heard all about Anna's home—how and why it came to be—so they were anxious to inspect it in full detail. After the home tour, art and Obert went out and found the Christmans' luggage and carried the suitcases to the bedrooms where they would be staying. Afternoon coffee and lunch was a family custom on the ranch, so Anna asked everyone to the table for coffee and a generous piece of Marjorie's fresh sour cream raisin pie heaped with meringue. Iver called the meringue "calf slobber" because it looked just like the foam generated when calves were sucking their moms.

George said that the pie reminded him of the City Café in Minneapolis and of the days when Anna worked there. "That's still my favorite place to go eat, Anna. It was pretty much a dump that hardly anyone ate at before you took it over and transformed the place into the best eatery in town. You must have taught them well because they were able to keep the crowds coming after you left."

"I'm so happy to hear that, George," Anna said. "I wrote a letter to Herb once but don't know if it reached him. He was a nice guy, and all he needed was to learn how to greet and meet his customers … and some edible food didn't hurt anything."

"We didn't know you ran a restaurant, Mom," Marjorie said. "What else have you hidden from us?"

"Actually, two of them," Anna told her daughter. "But that was a lifetime ago. I started in a New York restaurant and did about the same thing in Minneapolis."

"She is being modest, Marjorie," Gert added. "Your mother's food was nothing less than famous in New York City. It drew customers from all over that area, and some of them had a lot more than food on their minds. Them New York boys knew a beautiful lady when they saw one."

As Anna blushed, Iver jumped in. "She sure was the most beautiful creature to ever come to South Dakota. Of course, you would've wowed us Dakota boys too, Gert!"

"I know flattery when I hear it, Iver," Gert teased.

Obert and art got up and excused themselves. "We'll do the chores up tonight, Ma. Why don't you and Pa show the company around the farmyard and just relax and enjoy the afternoon?"

"And I'll clean up the coffee dishes," Marjorie added.

George remembered how excited Obert had been about the Cadillac and added before the boys left, "Go ahead and look under the hood, Obert. I'll show you how to run it tomorrow and let you boys take a drive, ok?"

"Thanks so much, Mr. George!" Obert jubilantly ran out to inspect the Cadillac.

Anna asked their company if they would like to lie down for an afternoon nap, but they declined saying they were too excited to sleep, so Anna, Iver, and Daisy took them around the barnyard for an introductory tour. George asked about Iver's Uncle Chris, whom Anna had mentioned in one or two of her letters. They explained what had happened, and George apologized for asking.

"Don't apologize, George," replied Anna. "How could you have known? Besides, Chris is a wonderful memory, and we like to talk about him just like he was still here with us. We see him in everything we do."

The Christmans were all questions. What is this? What is that? How can two boys—we should say, young adults—milk ten cows all by themselves? Do chickens lay eggs every day? Do you have stallions? Do you have bulls? Is it always this nice here? How do you get hay in that barn? Do you have skunks and wild animals like wolves and mountain lions and badgers? Do Indians still live here? It was an endless stream of questions and answers until it was time for supper. Anna had prepared a big pot of beef stew that only needed warming up, and Marjorie spent the afternoon making fresh bread and some bread pudding filled with apples and raisins. Of course, there was a heaping bowl of whipped cream to smother it with.

"If we stay all week and eat like this every day, I'll have to add some extra air to the Cadillac tires so that it can support all the added weight," George said, patting his belly.

"And I'll have to diet the rest of the summer to get my girlish figure back," Gert giggled. Her giggle was contagious, and it spread to the whole family.

After the evening feast, they all went outside to enjoy the brilliant sunset which set the entire western horizon ablaze with dazzling displays of orange, crimson, two shades of blue, pink, violet, purple, and black. It was an evening that Anna would fondly think of for all of her days. After sunset, they went back in the house and drank more coffee. George got his pipe out and filled it with tobacco from his pouch. They sat around and exchanged stories until late in the evening, revisiting old events and sharing the newest pieces of their lives' puzzles. After they had all retired and gone to bed, the "good nights" echoed through their happy home for a long time. Good night, George and Sarah, good night, Anna and Iver, good night, Gert, good night, Obert and art, good night, Marjorie, good night, everybody.

Anna and Iver were up early as were Marjorie and her brothers. They were used to getting out of bed and having a huge ranch breakfast before going to work, but Anna didn't know what time the Christmans were accustomed to getting up. She didn't want to make two breakfasts, so she silently ushered the men out the door whispering to them that they could eat later with the Christmans when they got up. Art and Obert frowned— their stomachs were already growling—but off they went to start chores. Iver said he'd milk both Anna and Marjorie's cows, boasting to the boys he could milk four cows faster than they could milk three. The race was on.

An hour later, when they brought the full milk pails covered in foam back to the house, they discovered that their visitors had awakened. They could finally have breakfast. Art and Obert each usually had three or four eggs along with venison or sausage, half a loaf of bread smothered in butter and topped off with wild berry jelly, and maybe a stack of pancakes and syrup for dessert, all washed down with a glass—or two or three—of milk and a couple of cups of coffee. George, Sarah, and Gert watched with wonder as the two boys easily ate a quantity of food in one meal that would have taken them all week to finish.

"My, you two were hungry," Gert finally said in awe. Art looked up with his mouth full, "What? Huh?"

Anna giggled, "Guess you aren't used to big breakfasts like we are. Those boys will wear that off by mid-morning when they'll want coffee and caramel rolls or cake to tide them over until noon. I'll leave the morning lunch here for them, but they'll be on their own for the noon meal. I have a really special outing planned for you and Sarah and George today."

Anna had waited until morning to decide, wanting to search the western sky for any sign of a thunderstorm and to see if it was going to be windy. It had been negative on both counts, with cloudless blue skies and only a slight breeze blowing from the northwest. She had already decided that she and Iver would take their guests to the Slim Buttes today and show them the grandeur of western South Dakota as well as the canyon where Iver had first discovered the wild mustang herd. Iver already had the team hitched to the wagon, and they were in front of the house waiting, stamping their feet and switching their tails at flies. Daisy was sitting in the middle of the wagon making sure that she didn't get left behind.

Anna had already packed sandwiches and a fresh cake along with coffee and lemonade. To go with the sandwiches, she had even fried a few chickens. At the last minute she realized that she had made way too much food and left some chicken and sandwiches for Obert and art. Marjorie, who had been helping her, had already asked if she could ride along, so she ended up getting the day off too.

"This sounds so wonderful!" Sarah exclaimed.

"I've read in your letters about the beauty of the Slim Buttes area, especially those ship-shaped buttes out in the middle of the prairie, and can't wait to see them myself," Gert added.

"I've purchased a new camera just for this trip," George proudly proclaimed. He was always finding the newest, latest gadget and was already a camera buff. He had purchased one of the first Kodak roll film cameras right after George Eastman patented it and had recently bought a new Ihagee Kine Exakta 1, which was the first 35mm SLr—single lens reflex—camera made.

With everyone and everything loaded into the wagon, the group made their way out of the farmyard and onto the reva road and then turned the team of horses westward toward the Slim Buttes. Anna started their excursion with a history lesson. They were about a mile west of reva, halfway to the Buttes, and she pointed to the ravine and brush-lined draws south of the trail. "right here is where the Battle of the Slim Buttes was fought back in the fall of 1876. I think it was September. The US army, under General George Custer, had been defeated at the Battle of the Little Big Horn in the early summer, probably about this time of year in late June or early July. Custer and all of his men were killed in that battle, so the US army sent their best Indian fighter, Brigadier General George Crook, with orders to take control of the Dakota territory so that it would be safe for the onrush of settlers and fortune seekers."

George interrupted, "Guess you had to be a George to fight Indians, huh? If I had been born sooner, I might have been a famous Indian fighter, Sarah. General George Christman!"

Sarah laughed at the thought of her husband the doctor fighting Indians, and sighed, "Don't mind George, Anna. Please go on."

"Anyway," Anna continued, "The soldiers walked here in what history later called the 'Horsemeat March,' because it was one of the most grueling expeditions in military history and during it, they ran out of food and were forced to eat their own horses. When General Crook and his weary soldiers arrived, they decimated Chief american Horse and his village. It was a surprise attack on the Indian settlement, which was located right here at this very spot. The army then repelled a counterattack by chief Crazy Horse, the mastermind of the Battle of the Little Big Horn, and this along with a series of other smaller blows is what led to the end of the Sioux resistance to reservation captivity. The Indians were also forced to give up their most valuable treasure, the Black Hills."

Anna paused briefly and then continued, "Every time I ride by this vicinity where the Battle of the Slim Buttes was held, I close my eyes and attempt to envision the horror and terror of that life- or-death battle. It must have been a dreadful and chaotic scene with brave people trying to defend their homes and children. In the end, virtually all of the Indians and many of the soldiers lay dead, silently waiting for the buzzards and beasts to feast on their bloating bodies." the little troop was fairly quiet for the next mile, probably thinking about the gruesome battle, when they came upon the first of the battleship-shaped formations. The magnificent forms were actually huge sandstone and clay sculptures carved out of the landscape and scattered around a valley in the middle of the buttes.

The Slim Buttes themselves were pine- and aspen-covered hills with deep, hidden ravines and valleys and high plateaus with vistas of the surrounding prairies.

"Wow!" George exclaimed. "I had no idea they would be this grandiose. They are magnificent. Can we stop so I can get some camera shots? they actually do look exactly like ships sitting out here in the middle of the prairie, like they floated in on some long- lost ocean."

Anna added, "It's like they're still floating here, only on a sea of grass. There's a picnic spot right ahead where the road cuts through the buttes dividing them into a northern half and a southern half. We'll take time to explore a little here, and then I'm taking you up to the top to see all of God's creation and my very special valley."

"How suspenseful!" Sarah exclaimed. "What is so special about it?"

Anna answered that they would have to wait to hear about it until they reached the spot. Everyone was trying to guess what the secret was as they ate their chicken and sandwiches. George offered Daisy a piece of his chicken, but, un-dog-like, she turned it down.

"She doesn't like fowl meat," Iver laughed to George. "She's a beef eater. Smart dog."

It was now Marjorie's turn to shine, and she sliced the cake she made earlier and proudly gave everyone a large slice. George jokingly asked if he could take Marjorie home with him so she could teach Sarah how to cook. Marjorie shyly smiled at the thought. Wouldn't it be nice to visit the big city? the biggest town she had been to was Hettinger, North Dakota.

Anna interrupted her thoughts, knowing exactly what she was thinking. "Don't be getting any big ideas, Marjorie. We need you at home for another year or two."

After a little exploration with George finding what he said was probably a petrified dinosaur bone, they loaded into the wagon again, and Iver took them to a high plateau. From their viewpoint, the vista overlooked most of the western prairie states with the horizon stretching on indefinitely. Iver pointed out the Black Hills to the south, and George interjected that it sure would be nice to see that area too.

This was the opening Anna was hoping for, and she seized the opportunity. "Well, they have a huge extravaganza at Belle Fourche over our national birthday, the Fourth of July. I've heard it called the best rodeo in the nation with cowboys and Indians, bulls and broncs, trick riding, military displays, a carnival, a parade, fireworks, and everything else that I suppose comes along with festivities like that. We've never had the time to attend because it would be a three-day affair with the team and wagon, but if we had an automobile like your Cadillac, we could get there and back in a single day."

George took the bait. "Well, if that's all you're waiting for, I think we should head that red Cadillac toward Belle Fourche and take in their Fourth of July celebration. If you'll give the boys the day off, I think we could squeeze all eight of us in the car and even have room for Daisy if she wants to go along." Daisy wagged her tail enthusiastically at the mention of her name.

Anna looked at Iver, hoping for approval. He relented, telling everyone truthfully that they really should stay home and put up hay like they'd always done, but since this was such a special occasion, it wouldn't hurt to take a day off and see what the big city had to offer. "Are you sure you won't mind driving us all the way to Belle, George?"

"Not at all," George answered. "I promised everyone a ride in the Caddy anyway, so this will kill two birds with one stone. So, it is settled—I will drive everyone to the Black Hills on the Fourth of July. Now, I'm mighty anxious to see that special valley of yours, Anna."

The full, happy, and content group went about a mile south where Iver stopped the wagon. Anna had everyone get out and follow her to the top of the ridge which overlooked a deep and wide canyon covered with scattered pine, aspen, and cottonwood trees.

"This is where Iver captured my soul and forever won my heart!" Anna told them. "When he first lured me here with the promise of some grandiose secret, I thought that he was just full of you know what conning me into going to the buttes alone with him. Now, try this out. Close your eyes and imagine an entire herd of wild horses with mares, colts, and yearlings, magnificent mustangs of every color, with the stallion of the herd standing just above them overlooking his harem. When we first arrived, Iver and I silently worked our way up the hill on our stomachs and just lay there, peeking over the rim, watching them in wonder and awe. We left them there that day, not wanting to let them know that they had been discovered, with Iver wondering how he might possibly be able to capture them and keep them as his very own herd of mustangs. It was a lofty undertaking, but my husband managed to do it."

At that point, Iver interrupted her and told them that it was Anna that figured out how to accomplish the seemingly impossible feat. Then he went on to tell them the entire story of that long, cold, snowy winter and how they captured the wild mustang herd, saving them from almost certain starvation and the wolf pack that was picking them off one by one. He then added that he could show them that very same herd of mustangs tomorrow if they wanted to see them.

The visitors erupted in cheers making Daisy bark as she wondered what all the excitement was about. On their way back to the ranch, they stopped to view the first signs of another breathtaking western sunset, and then hurried the team for home. Anna had hungry boys and special visitors to feed, and, hopefully, Obert and art already had the milking and other chores finished.

It was another night of wondrous stories and tall tales ending with the usual family "good nights" echoing through the house when everyone went to bed. The Christmans almost beat Anna's family out of bed in the morning, eager to see the herd of wild horses. Marjorie and the boys stayed home from the wagon tour that day, promising to do the chores with Marjorie adding that she would have dinner ready whenever they got home. Art and Obert said they would finish stacking the hay in the west field if it had dried out adequately enough that it wouldn't rot or mold when piled into a stack.

George asked if Iver was sure that he could spare the time to go sightseeing, and Iver graciously told him that the cattle and horse herds needed checking anyway, so it was absolutely no bother. They saved the best for last, showing them the Herefords first. The happy and healthy already three-month-old calves showed off for the visitors, running around the wagon with their tails in the air and their concerned mothers looking on.

Sarah and Gert remarked how beautiful they were and wondered how anyone could possibly eat something that they had raised and loved and cared for.

Iver grinned and said, "Just the same way you do, one delicious fork full at a time." Anna pretended to scold him for the remark.

The horses were spread along Gap Creek enjoying the beautiful day and the sunshine. The Christmans watched them in awe telling Anna that they were probably having some of the same feelings now that she had when she first viewed them. The colts displayed their speed with their gangly legs flying through the grass, their long tails flowing behind. The mares showed off their colors and their colts, proudly standing guard over their offspring.

There was one mare left to foal, and Iver wanted to make sure that he found her before they left, so their tour was extended in search of her. They finally discovered her, away from the herd in a little ravine. She was in the process of foaling. Out slipped the slimy little creature looking like it was nearly all legs. Mom quickly jumped up and earnestly nudged her beautiful new creation, licking and nuzzling it into action. Before they left, the newborn baby had gotten its long and wobbly legs under itself, and the mare had guided the unsteady foal toward her milk supply. The foal was wagging its tail, eagerly having the first meal of its life on the prairie.

Gert wondered if Iver could possibly have planned the magnificent show for them, but Anna explained that there was no way on earth that even Iver could have accomplished that feat.

Iver didn't crack a smile as he countered, "Of course I could, and I arranged the entire show just for you, Gert. I have a way with horses, you know, and I asked that mare to hold off from foaling until we got to the pasture today. Horses always do exactly as I tell them."

Gert looked puzzled, but Iver couldn't hold off laughing any longer and gave himself away. "Okay, the joke is on me, but they look so intelligent that I probably would have fallen for your line, Iver. Please tell us more about them and how you break and train these wild horses. I'd love to hear a story or two about them."

"I guess I owe you at least that much after teasing you just a little," Iver laughed. "As you would probably guess, they are extremely resilient, athletic, and intelligent. They seem to have built-in instincts about almost everything including people and their motives. I've never tried to train an older mustang, but I find that the young ones that I take from the herd to break to ride and train are probably easier to work with than most regular horses. They are just so intelligent, and they seem to know what I want before I ask it of them. I've trained them for every aspect of ranch work and rodeo performance events, and they just adapt to whomever or whatever the task at hand is."

"Do you have any favorites?" Gert asked. "What else can you tell us about them?"

"There hasn't been one of them that I haven't fallen in love with, but there was one that seemed to be a bit more special than the others, maybe as much due to the extraordinary circumstances as the special abilities he seemed to possess."

"Tell us more!" George and Sarah joined in with Gert's inquiry. "Anna and I were checking the horses one frosty morning in February, and we found a newly born colt about a day or two old. It was freezing cold, but the little fella seemed fine and was playing hide and seek with us, using his mom as a shield and continually peeking around her to see what we were up to. We had no way to get the pair back to the barn and protection from what was left of the winter, so we just left him and his mom there to their own devices. He is the only colt we've ever had born out of the normal foaling season which starts in May and ends in July."

"Did he live? What happened to him?" Sarah, George, and Gert wondered together.

"Yes, he lived," Iver replied. "We named him Croppy because the ends of his frozen ears fell off. The temperature could have easily been below zero when he was born, and we can't figure out how he managed to survive with only ear damage. I brought him in from the pasture when he was a yearling and started training him for roping and general ranch work. He was a natural at everything, and I loved being with him and everything about him, so I decided to keep him for my personal riding horse rather than sell him. His short ears were distracting and would have made him difficult to sell anyway."

"Where is he? What became of him?" their guests were eager to know more.

"I truly was hoping that you wouldn't ask me those questions, because I feel dreadful about what happened to him. It is one of those things in life that I would give anything to do over again. Hardly a day goes by that I don't think about what happened to Croppy," Iver sadly stated.

"It might help you to talk about it, Iver," Anna said.

"Thanks, Hon," Iver looked at his wife. "You're probably right, painful as it is to even just think about what happened to Croppy; it might help to talk about it and get this off of my chest." Iver looked up and continued sadly, "Croppy quickly became my favorite horse, and we did everything there was to do on the ranch together. There wasn't any challenge that he wasn't up to, and I almost think he would have given his life for me. To make a very long story much shorter, he was five years old when a stranger came into the yard looking for a rodeo horse. I was riding Croppy, and the man immediately noticed how intelligent and well-built the horse was, asking me if I had ever roped off of him. Of course, I couldn't help bragging about Croppy, and the guy ended up asking what I wanted for him. I immediately told him that Croppy wasn't for sale at any price. This didn't deter the guy, and he offered me more than we had ever gotten for any horse before—more money than I would have dared ask even if I had wanted to sell Croppy. Anna and I desperately needed operating money, and we were behind at the store and bank, so I did something that I swore I would never do and something I will forever regret. I sold my best friend."

Anna looked thoughtfully at Iver and added, "Don't keep beating yourself up over it, dear. Selling horses is what we do to pay for the ranch. It's our business. You really didn't have a choice."

The visitors were anxious to hear more. "Is that the end of the story? Did you ever hear how Croppy fared?"

It was apparent that it was getting even more difficult for Iver to talk about, but he continued anyway, "I wish it were the end, but, unfortunately, there is more. The cowboy that bought Croppy was from south of the Black Hills, almost on the Nebraska border. It was late summer when he purchased Croppy, and we thought that we'd never see him or our horse again. Late that fall, we got word from a friend that the guy who bought Croppy—I think his name was Botcher or something like that—had lost Croppy and was looking for him. He had word out with law enforcement that someone had probably stolen his horse. We didn't think anything of it since there wasn't anything that we could have done anyway. One winter day a few months later, I had completely forgotten about the whole episode and was out checking the horse herd when, lo and behold, there was Croppy in with them."

"Wow! What did you do? How did he get there?"

"I couldn't believe my eyes and had to look several times," Iver said. "I was overjoyed to see him. I called out his name, and he ran over to greet me just as he always had in the past. I had tears of joy in my eyes as I greeted him and rubbed him down, itching all of his favorite spots and examining him for wire cuts and bruises. He had a few minor cuts, probably from jumping fences, but that seemed to be it. After visiting with him a while longer and giving him another rub-down, I gave him a final hug, and then happily rode home and told Anna the exciting news that my friend had returned to me."

"Croppy must have run away from his new home, wanting to be back here with me and his real family again. To do that, he would have had to cross the Cheyenne river and make his way north, either directly through the mountainous Black Hills region or by skirting around the mountains, probably on their eastern border. That would have been a much longer route but in all probability faster

And safer. Either way, he would have had to cross Spearfish Creek, redwater river, the Belle Fourche river, numerous smaller streams, and hundreds of fences and other obstacles. The journey would have been over three hundred miles, something that I never would have thought a horse could do by pure instinct, especially in country that he had never seen before. To cover that much territory in less than a year and be able to cross fences and rivers and navigate through mountains and valleys, avoiding covert dangers and enduring who knows what hardships and weather conditions—it wasn't a mild winter—and find his way home was nothing short of miraculous. But when I think about it, Croppy was a miracle himself, having survived birth in below zero winter temperatures."

"What did you do?" everyone wondered.

"This is where the story gets even harder to tell, and it still haunts me," Iver tried to hide the tears in his eyes as he continued. "I betrayed my friend a second time and got word out that Croppy had returned to our ranch. It tore my heart out, and I still feel like Judas must have felt when he betrayed Jesus. That horse trusted me with all of his heart and soul, and I betrayed his trust again."

"It was the only honest thing you could have done," Anna interrupted again. "And I remember that you were certain that you'd be able to buy him back."

Iver thanked his wife, and then slowly continued, "At any rate, the owner came back in the spring to pick up Croppy. Like Anna said, I tried to buy him back, but the guy wanted twice what I sold him for, which was more money than Anna and I would have possibly been able to come up with. We probably would've had to mortgage the ranch. I didn't recognize it in him the first time I met him, but the guy was a mean looking and strange acting fellow. He came close to accusing me of stealing the horse, saying that I must have had something to do with his disappearance. I detected the fear and hatred in Croppy when the man took him. I can still see the pleading and terrified look in that horse's eyes, and it tears my heart out to this day. If I had it to do over, I never would have let anyone know that Croppy had returned home. I would have hid him in my barn, for the rest of his life if necessary. I never saw or heard anything about Croppy again, but a few days later, we found that my roping saddle and some tack had been stolen from our barn. I think that same man was the culprit, but we'll never know."

"Oh, Iver, I'm so sorry. I'm crying for you," Gert said through teary eyes. Sarah and George were wiping tears away too.

"I've never told anyone else that story Gert, Iver admitted as he wiped away his own tears again. Maybe Anna was right (she always is) about me needing to get it off of my chest. But as difficult as it was to tell that story, it is a true testament to the heart, stamina, courage, and devotion of these wild mustang horses. I truly love all of them, and I'd give almost anything to be able to undo what happened to Croppy. It was one of those hard-learned life lessons that I will never forget and just one more thing on my long list that I have to find forgiveness for. But I do know one thing for certain—if Croppy ever came back, he would forgive me because those horses are just plain full of love."

17

Finding Forgiveness

It was a quiet ride home with sad thoughts of Croppy and Iver running through their guests' minds. Anna broke the silence by telling the Christman family about her trips to Belle to have Obert and art and other ranch stories about them. When they arrived back at the ranch, the two boys that she had been talking about were already waiting at the house, the chores having been finished. Since they hadn't had a proper afternoon lunch, they thought they were starving and were eagerly awaiting the delicious supper that Marjorie had prepared for everyone.

After supper Iver asked the boys what they thought about going to the Fourth of July celebration in Belle Fourche. "Do you two think you could get the milking done before daylight tomorrow so we could all be loaded up and ready to head out early enough to get to the celebration in time? George and Sarah have graciously offered to drive us to Belle Fourche in their Cadillac."

Obert and arthur yelled and whooped and grinned for several minutes, thanking George and Sarah over and over, along with their dad for letting them have the day off. For the ranching family, it would be a day of pure delight, one to forever remember. In the morning the boys had the milking finished along with all of the other chores well before daylight. They were so excited that they probably hadn't even gone to bed that night.

After cleaning up and having a light breakfast, they all crowded into the Cadillac, with Daisy hastily jumping through an open door onto arthur's lap making sure that the car didn't leave without her. The festive group in the red Cadillac left the yard, and George steered the car southwest. He flew over the bumps, pushing the Caddy pretty hard, not wanting to miss any of the activities in Belle. They arrived partway through the parade which extended for over a mile. There were floats, bands, clowns, candy-throwers, horses, autos, jugglers, oxen-pulled covered wagons, buffalo, and just about everything. There was even a cowboy with a pet coyote named tootsie who allowed the kids to pet her. The tame coyote was probably the most popular attraction in the entire parade.

When the parade was over, they went to the carnival where even Anna and Iver took a couple of the thrilling rides. Obert and art wanted to try all of them, but Iver said they were breaking him, and they still needed to buy rodeo tickets. George intervened and treated them and Marjorie to a few more attractions. Iver tried his hand at winning a teddy bear in the ball throw contest, which required knocking down all three bottles with three throws. After missing the first two throws, he gave art his last ball to toss. Art hit the bottles squarely and knocked all three down, winning the teddy. All the girls wanted it, but he ended up giving it to Gert. He liked her a lot despite the fact that she kidded him incessantly.

When it came time to get tickets to the rodeo, George paid the fare for everyone. "That sure isn't necessary, George," Anna said. "We should be paying for our guests, not the other way around."

"Nonsense, Anna. You are cooking and cleaning and entertaining us. This is the least we can do."

"Thanks, George!" all of the family said together. "That was really generous of you."

The rodeo was a wild and wooly affair, and everyone, especially art, enjoyed it immensely. Anna knew he secretly wanted to go on the rodeo circuit and ride the bulls and broncs, and he probably had as much talent as any of the professional riders, but he also knew that the ranch work would always have to come first. The broncs were rough, but many of the cowboys were just as tough, riding them for the full eight seconds required to get a score. The bulls were a whole different match, with all of the cowboys getting thrown off except for two. The clowns entertained the crowd throughout the event and protected the unfortunate contestants that were thrown off from the wrath of the bulls, but art and Obert were more interested in the pretty cowgirls than the rodeo clowns.

"Hey, art, the rodeo is in the arena in front of you," Gert said, teasing art as he tried to capture the attention of a cute cowgirl.

"Oh, uh, I guess something else caught my eye," art stammered. "We all know what that something else is, art," Marjorie joined in the teasing. "Those something else's have been catching your eye ever since we got here."

After the rodeo was over, they had hamburgers, fries, and cokes at one of the concession stands and then went to the gas station to fill up the Caddy for the trip home.

"Oh no you don't!" Iver told George when he went to pay for the gasoline. "You've been buying all day. I think it's about my turn."

On the way home George stopped and asked who wanted to drive. In ecstasy, Obert about jumped over the seat and managed to get the first leg. Art was next, and Iver even drove a few miles. Anna and Marjorie declined, so George took over again for the last fifty miles. It was a lonely drive for him, but the snoring from all around helped keep him awake. When they drove into the yard, it was hours past evening chore time, but Iver woke the boys and told them that, late or not, they had to be done, especially the milking. They yawned, stretched, and changed into their work clothes, not even grumbling. In the morning, the Christmans slept in, but there was no such luxury for the ranchers.

Over the next days, Iver and Anna took their company around to visit neighbors and friends. Odd and reidun took everyone to their favorite fishing hole in the Grand river. While they were fishing, Anna told the Christmans about her first encounter with the Grand river and how she had been so fearful of crossing it until she actually saw it. Iver shared his similar first experience and then told about the raging river it had become in the spring of '36.

Gert was the first to hook one, and she managed to land an eight-pound catfish. She was so excited when she pulled the fish close to the river's edge and saw how huge it was that she almost fell in. Iver went to help out by trying to grab the big fish by hand, and he did fall in, finally capturing the monster and helping Gert get the trophy to shore. In all, they caught five really nice fish and ended up leaving the entire smelly batch of fish for Odd to clean.

"Thanks so much, Iver," he jokingly grumbled. "You get all the fun catching them, and I get all the work cleaning them."

"It's what good neighbors do for their friends," Iver ribbed him back.

That night was somewhat somber and sad as everyone knew the Christmans would be leaving in the morning after breakfast. George had wanted to talk to Anna and Iver privately since his arrival but hadn't been able to, so he finally just asked if he could visit alone with them in another room.

"Anna, I know this will be extremely difficult for you to talk about," George began, "but I have been doing some extensive medical research and have found some information that you and Iver should know about. When Sarah showed me your last letter, the one in which you told us about having those stillborn babies, it set me to thinking about what might have caused it. You were, and even still are, a young and healthy woman and that just shouldn't have happened to you. Maybe one premature child with all of the stress and the workload that is heaped upon you, but having six stillborn babies after having had three strong and healthy children just doesn't make any medical sense. My new assistant (the doctor from Mayo Clinic) and I have done hours of studying on your case, and I think we may have finally discovered the cause of your miscarriages. You said that before your first stillborn twins, you had been down with the flu, is that right?"

Anna answered that it was and that she still occasionally suffered from similar symptoms, but they were no longer nearly as severe as they had been in the past years. "The first couple of times I came down with it, I felt like I was going to die. I had high fevers, aches, and pains in my back and groin so terrible that I couldn't eat or sleep, and I threw up continually. I lost so much weight that Iver said I looked like a skeleton."

"Now let me ask you this," George continued. "Did anyone else in the family have the flu? Where did you catch it? Was it going around the neighborhood?"

Anna thought about it for a long time. "It was so many years ago, and my memory isn't what it used to be. I'm pretty sure though that nobody else in the family caught it, because I was worried about that happening—and if it did happen, I think I would still remember. I do recall that my first and worst episode of the flu was late in the spring and that seemed unusual to me. Flu usually goes through in the fall and winter, doesn't it, George?"

"You're right, Anna; it isn't common to have flu outbreaks late in the spring—maybe a cold, but not the flu," George said. "One more question. Can you think back and remember what you were doing before you caught this flu?"

Anna thought about his question for a long while. "I'll try, but it seems like an eternity has passed. If I remember right, it was an extremely demanding season on the ranch. Iver and I were both particularly busy and behind on our work. I doubt that this matters but for some reason I do recall that the Fischer family wanted Iver to come over and check their sick sheep. I knew that he didn't have time, so I went over to their ranch for him. Their ewes had high fevers and severely swollen udders, and I didn't know what was causing it or how to remedy it. I helped them bring the fevers down, and I had them isolate the sheep that were sick from the rest of their herd just in case it was being caused by something in the corral or was contagious."

Anna paused and reflected for a while longer, deep in thought. "Oh yes, I recall something that was really unusual about that visit, something that saddened me deeply, and probably is the reason that I still remember the visit so vividly. The sheep were aborting their lambs, and there were tiny pink fetuses scattered about the corral. We didn't notice them at first, but once we discovered them and figured out what they were, we found several of them. It was an appalling sight, one that I doubt I will ever be able to fully erase from my memory. The sight of those dead fetuses has bothered me for years, so much that I even had reoccurring nightmares about them. My dead babies often frequented those nightmares."

Anna wiped away some tears and searched her memory for a while longer. "I'm sorry, but I really can't recollect anything else from that time frame. I have always felt that the reason I caught the flu then, and keep catching it, is that I let myself get run down and lower my resistance. I should have taken better care of myself. Iver suggested I see a doctor, and I should have heeded his advice."

"Your story pretty much proves my diagnosis beyond any doubt, Anna," George said. "I'm so glad that you could recall the incident with your neighbor's sheep because it is the clue I needed to prove my theory. First, let me tell you that you saved the rest of their lamb crop by having them isolate the ones with the disease. Yes, Anna, it was definitely a disease, and it is very contagious to other livestock and would have spread through the rest of the sheep with the same results. The disease's name is brucellosis, sometimes called *bangs* for short. It was named after a Doctor Bruce who first discovered the bacterial zoonotic disease. By zoonotic I mean that the disease can occasionally transfer from animals to humans. You caught brucellosis from those sheep, and the disease that you contracted caused your babies to be born prematurely and perish, just as it did in the sheep that you were helping. Bangs is usually chronic, meaning that you can have reoccurring bouts of it, sometimes for all of your life. You continued to have stints with it, and the same disease that caused your first twins to be stillborn caused the deaths of your subsequent babies as well."

George paused to let what he had told them sink in and then continued, "Knowing you, Anna, I'm guessing that you have felt depressed and guilty over what happened ever since, totally blaming yourself for the death of each of your babies." He didn't have to guess;

Anna was sobbing and in tears just from discussing it. George paused again to give Anna some more time and then added, "What I'm trying to tell you, Anna, and you, Iver, is that *it was not your fault.* Even with today's modern antibiotics and medicines, I doubt that I could have prevented the deaths of your babies."

Anna went to George like a broken creature, sobbing uncontrollably. She held him for several long minutes until she was finally able to speak. "George, you don't know what this means to me. I have nearly driven myself crazy trying to figure out why my babies died. I have carried that cross, borne that burden, since the deaths of our first twin boys, those beautiful baby boys, and the load has gotten harder and heavier with each subsequent birth and death. It has torn my heart out and sickened my soul. It has haunted my nights and occupied my days. I wake up at night crying, trying not to let Iver hear me. I sit in my rocking chair to sleep but only sob, wondering what I did wrong that caused their deaths. I have come close to losing my mind, and even though I try to hold it in, I know that it has affected my family. For a while I even cried out at the Lord, trying to put the blame on Him, asking Him why He allowed this to happen, all the while inwardly knowing that our Lord doesn't cause evil and is our only solace when it strikes. Never in my craziest dreams would I have thought that people could catch diseases from animals. I've never heard of such a thing. Are you sure?"

George gave Anna a fatherly kiss and told her again, lifting her chin so that she was looking at him. "It is rare, but it has been proven to happen, and you aren't the first victim. There have actually been several cases of this disease in humans. It has been with us for years, but until the disease was recently discovered and diagnosed, the women who contracted bangs and had stillborn children probably blamed themselves for what happened, just as you did. Again, it wasn't any of your doing, Anna. Without knowing about the disease or that it even existed, there was nothing that you could have done to prevent it. It wasn't anything that you did or didn't do, and it surely wasn't your fault—or anyone else's for that matter. Your neighbors had no way of knowing that what their sheep had could be transferred to humans. I'm sure that they, like you, didn't even realize that it was a disease. But now you and Iver know what caused your pain and suffering for all of these years, and now you can *stop blaming yourself*, Anna. You are good at forgiving others, *now it is time to forgive yourself.*"

George thoughtfully stepped out of the room to leave them alone, and Anna sat with Iver. They held each other and cried long after the rest of the household went to sleep. They cried for their dead twin sons, for their dead twin daughters, and for their other two stillborn children. They cried for what should have been, for the rest of the family they would have had, had it not been for a neighbor in need. There were tears of sadness but also tears of relief. It was a giant step toward the healing that Anna longed for and so desperately needed. With the revelation, the great gift that George brought to them, Anna finally began the process of forgiving herself and of healing her broken heart and soul.

Morning came quickly. After a huge breakfast, it was time to part—something none of them looked forward to. There were countless kisses and hugs and good-byes during which Anna pulled George to the side and whispered, "George, you are an angel that the Lord planted in my path, first to save Iver's life and then to save my soul and help me find forgiveness. You have lifted a mountain of weight from my shoulders."

George whispered back, "*It was not your fault, Anna*; now forgive yourself and let your heart heal."

The Cadillac and its three waving passengers slowly pulled out of the yard with George, as he put it, "heading his horses" back toward Minnesota. Anna's prairie family went back to work, the boys and Iver to the hayfield and Anna and Marjorie to the barnyard chores. One thing was certain. Time had been kind to them for the past few days, and there was now a renewed spirit of faith, optimism, and forgiveness in Anna's prairie world.

Anna said her prayers that night, as always. It was a special night, one that she would remember to her dying day. She sobbed as she thanked her Father God for letting her know what had happened to her precious babies. She prayed for their souls and for Iver and her living children. She prayed for their families in Norway and for the many friends that had drifted through their lives, especially George, Sarah, and Gert. She closed her eyes and slept peacefully through the night for the first time in years. Anna had begun the process of forgiving herself. Her broken heart was healing.

PART III

Time Marches On

18

Into the Forties

Anna didn't give much thought to wealth, but for most americans, prosperity—or at least the illusion of it created by the many government programs and handouts—continued to rebound in 1940. Unfortunately, this jubilance was being diluted by the threat of a war looming on the horizon. It would prove to be a challenging and harrowing time for a nation that was trying to recover from a depression and the Dirty thirties.

For the next two years americans debated about whether or not to enter the war. Charles Lindbergh, america's hero in flight, testified to congress that america should negotiate peace with Hitler, and later, he accused the Jews, Brits, and roosevelt of trying to push america into war. The already war-weary Winston Churchill tried, mostly in vain, to get help for his weakening nation from america, addressing the US Congress and forming the atlantic Charter. In the years following the war, the world would come to recognize that if it hadn't been for the brazen actions and sheer courage of Mr. Churchill, the whole world would probably have ended up speaking German and Japanese.

In South Dakota Anna went into the 1940s with renewed strength and vigor. With the burden of feeling responsible for the deaths of their babies mostly lifted from her shoulders, she was finally free to live without all of that guilt and anxiety hanging over her head. The drought seemed to be over, and the dust storms had subsided. The prairie and the life that it sustained were gradually being replenished, with the exception of the wolves. They had become so scarce that they, along with the other ghosts of the prairie, were almost being reduced to a recollection. To isolated ranch and farm families, Father time seemed to be ushering in a new and improved era. As she always had, Anna prayed to her Lord that better days and times were ahead. In her world there was no Lindbergh, Hitler, or Churchill. Protecting her family, doing the daily chores, and just surviving were her priorities.

As 1940 gradually became a memory, news of the European war became more frequent and finally reached western South Dakota, sending a wave of fear through Anna. She knew that her "boys" were actually young men and worried about america becoming involved in another war. She wanted to keep her sons at home with them. She and Iver needed their help to run the ranch, and they surely didn't want them being shot at in some war in some place that none of them had even heard of. Anna had lost far too many children, and the thought of losing another sent her into an additional round of anxiety and fear. As she had clung to her faith, she clung to her three children and her husband.

Haying had been slowed up a little due to the Christmans' visit, but they had been able to catch up and had gotten their calves weaned and sold with good market prices. For the second year in a row, Iver retained all of his heifer calves rather than sell most of them, as he had prior to the 1930s, in an effort to quickly rebuild his herd to the size it had formerly been. The income they would have received from their sale was sorely missed by the family, but they were accustomed to sacrificing for the future.

Under growing pressure from his family to purchase an automobile—especially from Obert and Anna—Iver finally relented, promising them that they would try to buy a used car and possibly even a tractor powerful enough to pull the farm machinery. Iver had already purchased a tiny Ford raking and mowing tractor, but it didn't have enough horsepower or traction to pull farming equipment. Other than their ongoing debate about cars and tractors, they were a contented family that Christmas of 1940, especially Anna and Iver. At the end of the year they made their New Year's resolutions, momentarily forgetting about the possible war and the problems of the world, having so much work and so many challenges of their own to deal with. Their ranch still had no electricity, running water, radio, or telephone. Western South Dakota was still in the dark ages compared to most of the nation.

The winter of 1940 slowly melted into the spring of 1941 and with spring came sunshine and warm weather. Anna looked out her kitchen window one morning and noticed that her garden was full of chickens scratching out her freshly planted seeds. She called for Daisy to come and get them out of the yard, but there was no response, so she got her broom and chased the hens out by herself. Daisy must be riding with Iver, Anna thought silently.

Later that afternoon, she saw Iver in the corral and asked him where Daisy was. He said that he hadn't seen her all day, but that she'd show up in an hour or so when it was time to bring the milk cows in for nighttime milking. But when milking time rolled around, there was still no sign of Daisy. It just wasn't like her; she had never before slacked on her duties. Iver got the cows in himself, calling for Daisy to come and help, but to no avail. Maybe she had gone somewhere with the boys?

Early that evening, art and Obert came in from their tasks and asked where Daisy was. She had always been on the porch waiting to greet them. They hadn't seen her all day. Anna flashed a worried look at Iver. They hadn't seen her either and neither had Marjorie. All of them went searching, thinking—hoping—that she had gotten locked in the shed or the barn. After looking inside the barn, Iver found the little border collie lying behind it as if getting ready to fetch the milk cows.

Daisy May, Daisy the Wonder Dog, had passed away. There would never be another like her. She had stolen the hearts of every member of the family. Once again, they made their long and sad march up the hill where they buried her beside the twins. They asked Daisy to watch over their babies as she had watched over the rest of the family and to guard them and play with them and keep them company. Anna prayed for little Daisy May, telling her Lord that *"If there is a place for dogs in heaven, Daisy should be the first one there. She is a member of our family."*

A few weeks after Daisy died, Iver was suddenly hit with severe and debilitating back, belly, and groin pain. After checking the cow herd, he had gone fencing with art where the pain crumpled him over in agony. Art was able to get him in his saddle, and both of them headed for the ranch, Iver almost falling off several times as he wretched in agony. Upon getting him home, they quickly decided to take him to reva and borrow someone's car to take him to the new hospital in Belle Fourche. Anna feared for his life, and finding a car to carry him to Belle seemed to be their only option. When they got to reva, however, they miraculously found a much better and faster option.

A man from North Dakota had landed his Piper Cub in the pasture behind the store, there to visit with a friend. Upon hearing about the emergency, he kindly offered to fly Iver to the hospital. Iver *never* would have gotten into that airplane under other circumstances, but right now he couldn't even speak and was in too much agony to object. Bill, the pilot, pulled the tie-down ropes from their stakes and got into the plane while art and Obert lifted Iver through the other door. Bill quickly fastened Iver's safety belt and his own and instructed Obert on how to prop the plane to get it started, telling him to be sure to *immediately* step back with each quick pull of the prop and, if the engine started, to keep stepping back and get the heck out of the way. An optimally functioning propeller could easily cut a person's head off!

The Cub started on the first prop revolution, and Obert and arthur jumped out of the way with Anna, Marjorie, and everyone from the store worriedly watching. Most of them had never seen a plane before, let alone watched one take off. There was a fairly stiff wind from the west, and Bill taxied the airplane into the wind for a few seconds, then went full throttle, raised the tail, and was in the air in less than five hundred feet. Iver was off for his first airplane ride, leaving Anna, Obert, art, and Marjorie wondering what they should do now. There wasn't anybody at reva who could drive them to Belle and going by wagon would take forever. Then and there, Anna told her family that they were getting an automobile, even if they had to sell a few cows or horses to do it.

Bill had promised to fly back to reva that day if he could, especially if he received any word on Iver's condition. Hoping that Bill would be back before dark, Anna decided that she would just stay in reva. He had told them that it would take about an hour and a half to fly to Belle, depending on whether there was a headwind, so he could possibly be back in four or five hours if the hospital could diagnose Iver right away. Obert stood there with his mouth open, astonished at the idea of getting to Belle in a little over an hour. Oh, how he wanted one of those airplanes for himself!

Anna sent the rest of the family home to check the horse herd which was foaling already, finish whatever other projects they had been working on, and do the rest of the barnyard chores. She asked each of them to pray for their father, which she already had been doing. She had never seen him in such pain and was fearful that he was having a heart attack. Iver was strong, but whatever this was had him begging for mercy. It brought memories of the wolf and wagon incident back to Anna. At least Iver was conscious when she sent him off this time.

Anna was waiting in front of the store, thinking about Iver and praying for him when, just before dark, an airplane flew over and waved its wings at her. Bill made an easy landing, as the wind had died down, and shut the engine off. Anna was already running to meet him, hoping to hear the positive news that she had been praying for.

Bill opened the door and smiled at her. "Iver should be fine. They are pretty sure that it is kidney stones and definitely not a heart attack. They told me the stones can plug a person's pipes. Sorry, I don't remember the medical lingo, but you get the idea, right? anyway, it causes severe pain, just like Iver had. I didn't hang around long enough to find out what they were going to do for sure, but they said if he didn't pass the stone or stones soon, they might have to surgically operate. Not to worry though, they told me that it is a fairly common and simple surgery, and they also said that, sooner or later, most folks do pass the stones without having to do surgery." Anna thanked Bill for his kindness and asked him what they owed him for his flying services.

Bill, in true South Dakota fashion, said he was just happy that he could help out and that he couldn't accept any compensation for doing a good deed. "Maybe next time I'll be the one needing help. I own a store in reeder, and if you ever get there, please stop in and say Hi. You can buy me a cup of coffee and that will make us even." "We certainly will, Bill. You saved my husband hours of agony today, and I'll forever be grateful to you. Can I do what Obert did to help get the airplane going?"

"I have no doubt that you could, Anna, but my friend in the store helps me with it all the time, and I'd be more comfortable having him do it."

After Bill had taken off, a greatly relieved and thankful Anna hurried home to tell the news to her children. "Iver didn't have a heart attack! It was kidney stones, which are extremely painful, but he is still alive and will get better. Don't forget to keep praying, though." after breakfast the following morning, they had a family conference and decided that Anna should go to reva and try to catch a ride with anyone she could find going to Belle Fourche so that she could be with Iver. Marjorie would do all of the milking and chores, art would care for the cattle and horses, and Obert would work on the haying equipment after taking his mom to reva. Later that morning Anna found a ride with some folks from Hettinger, and she was in Belle Fourche by noon.

Anna's new friends from Hettinger dropped her off at the hospital, and the front desk directed her to Iver's room. He was sitting up in bed and smiling as if nothing had happened. He had passed the stones during the night and was feeling like a new person.

Anna ran into the room and gave him a big hug while at the same time scolding him for giving them such a scare.

He apologized and gave her a kiss, saying that he had been as frightened and worried as she had been. "I really thought I was going to die, Anna. I was in so much pain that I didn't even thank the guy that brought me here, such a wonderful fella. That airplane of his really made fast work of the trip to Belle. How did you get here?"

"I went to reva and caught a ride with the Jorgenson family from Hettinger. They have a new Chevy car, and it got us here in a little over two hours. They just now dropped me off at the hospital on their way to Spearfish, so I'm stranded here just like you are. I don't know how we'll get home. I guess we'll have to spread the word and look for a ride going that direction. I was in such a hurry to find you and see how you were that I didn't think to ask the Jorgenson's when they were going back."

A doctor and two nurses came in to check on Iver, who introduced Anna to them. Anna asked how soon Iver could leave the hospital, and they told her that he would be dismissed later that day, but if they were in a hurry, there really wasn't any reason that he had to wait. Iver thanked them for their care and told them that he was needed back home and would leave right away. Anna had the presence of mind to ask if they knew of anyone going north toward Buffalo or reva. They didn't but said they would ask around.

Just then, Anna had another idea. "Iver, why don't we join the rest of the country and buy a car to drive home in?"

"What?"

"You know that we need one. What if another emergency comes up, and we have to get Marjorie or me or one of the boys to the hospital? We could cut the time it takes us to get to Belle by almost a day. We could drive it to church without having to harness the team to the wagon. I could drive to reva for supplies. We could use it to visit neighbors. It would save us so much time, Iver, something we never have enough of. It's going to happen sooner or later, so we might as well get one right now and drive it home. I'd rather do that than sit here waiting and begging for someone to give us a ride. Of course, that is, if you think you are capable of driving one." Anna added this, knowing that her husband would take the challenge.

"Of course, I can drive a car. You saw me drive that Caddy of George's. I could drive anything."

"Then it's settled, Iver—let's go car shopping."

"Well, errrrr, well, I guess we could look. It won't cost anything to look."

They spent the early part of the afternoon car shopping and after a few fairly animated conversations settled on a used 1935 Chevrolet Standard that had an "improved master blue flame six- cylinder engine and pressure cable brakes" for the bargain basement price of $310. It sold new for $465, and "The old man that bought it hardly drove it at all, so it is almost brand new." the dealer even threw in a "crash" course on how to drive "The thing," as Iver called it. The salesman took them to a little pasture on the outskirts of Belle and taught both Iver and Anna how to drive. It was a little tricky at first but became pretty simple once they got the hang of it. Anna even caught Iver smiling as they headed north on the road to reva, his arm hanging out of the rolled-down window and the wind flying in his face. She smiled too. It was difficult for them to part with that much money, but as the salesman told them, "This is an investment!"

They arrived home just before the sun sank below the western horizon. Obert was still in the shop repairing equipment, and art was in the round corral working with horses. Obert spotted the car right away, thinking that someone had given his parents a ride home, but nobody but them got out of the car. "Who loaned you the car?" "It's ours, Obert," Anna smiled. "We bought it in Belle so we wouldn't have to walk home."

"Miracles do happen; this is almighty proof!" Obert exclaimed as he looked for the latch to open the hood. "What's it got for an engine?"

"Darned if I know," replied Iver, "but it got us home. Pretty peppy if you ask me."

Art arrived about the same time as Marjorie, and they both jumped in with Obert. The three of them drove down the road for a test drive, calling out, "We'll be back for supper, Mom."

Now that they finally had a car, their family wanted a repeat of the year before and a trip to Belle Fourche for the Fourth of July celebration. Iver and Anna discussed it and finally relented. With all of the war talk and the uncertainty concerning the future, they decided that the ranch had still been there when they returned from Belle Fourche last year, so why not do it again while they could enjoy it as a family? the boys—really young men—said they would be up before dawn and have the chores finished so the family could leave at daylight. Anna and Marjorie made enough food for the entire day since the concession stands at the rodeo seemed so overpriced. Iver had purchased a fifty-gallon gasoline drum with a crank pump and kept it filled. After filling the car, they took an extra five-gallon can along, sufficient to get them home.

The happy family loaded their supplies, and the men donned their Stetson cowboy hats, looking forward to the parade, carnival, and rodeo. Anna remarked that it was one of the best decisions they ever made. Virtually everything that they did was accomplished together as a family, but it was usually associated with work or the ranch. This was family fun time, an extremely rare commodity. A year later would have been too late—by then, Obert was at the Fort Leonard Wood basic training facility awaiting his entry into the war. Fall was ushered in by the annual flight of the cranes and some nice gentle autumn rains. As the leaves changed their colors from green to gold, Anna and Iver found their colors shifting from golden to gray. Anna remarked that their lives were in autumn, just as the season was, and they were changing colors too. The fall rains kept the grass green longer that year, making the calves fatter and heavier. The price per pound was up from the year before, and Iver considered selling a few heifer calves but decided against it since they were still trying to build their herd numbers to where they had been before the devastating '30s. With the good price per pound and heavier than usual calves, their paycheck was respectable. It made both Anna and Iver smile. After so many years with no cattle check at all, it felt wonderful.

Obert told his dad that since they had a little cash, now was the time to buy a tractor large enough to pull the drills and the tillage equipment. "You could plow another eighty acres and plant more wheat, Dad, and get it done in a lot less time. This place needs more diversification and better equipment."

Iver had gotten used to driving the car and had already decided that modern equipment wasn't so terrible. He and Anna took Obert and art tractor shopping with them, leaving Marjorie home to watch over the ranch. They found a Case model L that they figured was big enough to pull almost anything. It was used, of course, but that was the only way Iver would have purchased it. "Why buy new when you get a barely used one for less money, and all the kinks have been worked out of it? It would be like buying an unbroken horse instead of a broke one."

"That's not the way it works, Dad," grinned Obert.

Though they didn't know it at the time, they had purchased their tractor just in time. As america moved into wartime production, tractors got higher and higher priced and harder and harder to find. America was between a rock and a hard place. It needed more grain and food to feed the military machine, but it also needed more war equipment to fight the Nazis and Japanese. Manufacturing companies that had previously made only farm equipment were now compelled to make military equipment for the war. Massey Harris would find itself making M24 and M5 tank parts and airplane wings along with their usual farming equipment. John Deere would be making tank and aircraft parts along with their already popular tractors. Allis Chalmers, another company that previously had only made farming equipment, would be producing ship propellers and steam turbines—even casings for the atomic bomb. The increased productivity and innovation of these companies would help usher in the upcoming revolution in farm productivity after the war, but for now, anyone in the farming business was fortunate to already have a good farm tractor.

Anna's family bought their tractor in Scranton, North Dakota, and Obert was happy to drive it all the way back to the ranch. It took him almost seven hours to make the drive. On their own way home, the rest of the family had to drive through reeder, so they thought they should stop at Bill Peck's business and thank him again for flying Iver to the hospital. It would be nice to buy something from his store or take him out for that cup of coffee that they owed him, and Iver wanted to shake his hand and thank him personally.

When they arrived, they went in and browsed a little before asking the lady at the counter if Bill was in the store. She was silent for a moment before asking them how they knew Bill. Iver explained that Bill had flown him to the hospital and had saved him hours of pain and agony and that he was indebted to Bill for his kindness. They said that they knew how busy he probably was, but all they really wanted was to say Hi and maybe buy a few items from the store as a way of saying thanks and take him out for dinner or coffee if he had time. The lady said that she was so sorry to have to tell them that Bill had recently passed away. She explained that Bill had his "home" in an apartment above the store, and his assistant found him shot to death on the stairway one morning about a month ago. The authorities assumed that Bill had interrupted a robbery, and the thief or thieves, whom hadn't been caught yet and were still at large, had killed him rather than be apprehended. Anna, Iver, and art sadly left after offering their condolences to the lady and thanking her for letting them know.

"What a terrible tragedy, Iver; he was such a nice man and was so kind to us. He more than likely treated everyone the way he did us. It just doesn't seem fair. How could something so evil happen to such a good person?"

Iver was angry. "It isn't right, Anna. An honest and decent person is dead, and the wicked ones that did it are still running free. I wish I could get my hands on them; they'd pay for doing this to Bill."

"Vengeance should be left to the Lord, Iver."

"You're right, Anna, but I'd sure like to help him out this time."

Into the War

November and thanksgiving came to the ranch with Anna and her family still having much to be thankful for. There were turkeys in abundance in the buttes again, offering ranching families a change of pace from beef and venison on thanksgiving Day. Anna didn't know it while they were celebrating and giving thanks, but their peaceful world would soon be taking a drastic turn.

A few days later, on December 7, 1941, america's argument about whether or not to enter the war ended with Japan's cowardly surprise attack on Pearl Harbor followed by an american declaration of war on Japan. Four days later, on December 11, america declared war on Germany and Italy, and they, in turn, declared war on america. The United States immediately became the world's paramount hope in fighting the tyranny and hatred that came along with National Socialism and the Nazi party that represented it.

Everything in america was drastically different after the war suddenly and somewhat unexpectedly enveloped it, even in Anna's world. The United States, though unprepared, found itself totally immersed in the conflict instantaneously. To Anna's dismay, the draft age changed from twenty-one to eighteen, making Obert eligible by a few months. But rather than being drafted, Obert and millions of other american men entered the military by volunteering—in his case against Anna's wishes. By the end of the war ten million american men would be inducted into military service. All the men between eighteen and sixty-four were required to register for service, even Iver, although only those from eighteen to forty-five were subject to military service. Anna thanked God that art was too young. She would keep one of her sons home. Art would later qualify for an agricultural deferment, class II-C, if he wanted to stay out of the war. America soon found itself needing farmers almost as much as it needed fighters.

Christmas and New Year's were solemn occasions that winter for Anna's family because everyone dreaded the coming months. Obert would be leaving for basic training at Ft. Leonard Wood, Missouri, right after the New Year holiday, and after that he would be heading to war and God only knew where.

When it was time for Obert to leave for basic training, the whole family took the Chevy to Hettinger where he would board the same train that had carried Iver to Minnesota. Anna did her best not to cry, but her best wasn't good enough. Obert was her first child to leave the nest, and although she had known that he would be leaving, she hadn't sufficiently prepared herself. How had he grown up and become a young man so quickly? It seemed like only yesterday that she brought him home from Belle Fourche as a baby and named him after her friend in Minnesota. The time when he could barely walk yet escaped from the house, and she found him and Daisy out in the west pasture, somehow crept into her mind. His whole life went blurring by. What had happened? How could her baby boy be marching off to war?

As hard as she tried to stop them, Anna's tears fell anyway. The brave and fearsome Anna, the same Anna that ran away from home as a child and came to america by herself, the same Anna that fiercely attacked the wolves that were threatening her livestock—was the first to cry. Marjorie broke down too, and Obert tried to console both of them, telling them that he would be fine and promising that he'd write letters home whenever he could. He hugged and kissed them, even wiping the tears from his mother's face as she tried to smile, then bravely shook hands with and hugged his father and brother before boarding the train. The remaining family of four watched the train as it slowly got up to speed and moved east, taking their son and their brother off to war. As he left, Anna was already praying for his safe return.

After Obert departed, there was more work for the others. Each of them had to do a little of what he had done with art taking the lion's share.

Obert had been the caretaker of the equipment, and now they had a car and a tractor added to the list. Art had been the livestock man—along with his dad—but now he would have to be the shop foreman and mechanic too. The women of the house took over the milking by themselves to allow the men more time for their tasks, and Marjorie did most of the cooking and cleaning since Anna was more capable with chores and ranch work. There were four now to do the work of five. Odd and reidun felt the war too, as James had entered a week before Obert. Both of their first-born sons were at war. They should have been courting girls, not guns.

The war dominated the news in 1942, even in Anna's rural america. William Hitler, adolph Hitler's nephew, moved to america and joined the navy to fight against his uncle, and the first american forces landed in Europe. At home, Japanese-american citizens were interned, and their property seized while their former countrymen in the Japanese Imperial army were invading the aleutian Islands of alaska and firing on Fort Stevens in Oregon. The alaskan highway was finished, and Edward O'Hare became america's first WWII flying ace.

Back in South Dakota, art discovered that he wasn't such a bad mechanic after all. He dearly missed his brother Obert, but he would have to manage without him.

A terrible late-spring blizzard blasted its way through western South Dakota that year killing hundreds of thousands of spring calves and lambs. Anna and Iver had been moving their calving date to later in the spring as they got older, realizing that their bodies couldn't suffer the demands of early spring calving forever. It was just so much easier not to have to fight Mother Nature. Thanks to that decision, they only had about a dozen calves on the ground when the storm hit them. It struck without warning, catching them and all of their neighbors off guard. Fortunately, it started mid-afternoon, giving them adequate daylight to find the calves that had already been born and move them and their mothers to the barn before the calves froze to death.

They usually checked heifers every three hours around the clock while they were calving, but with a storm like this they checked all of the cattle every hour on the hour. They wanted to catch the cows *before* they calved so that the cow could carry the calf to the barn and birth it there, out of the freezing blizzard. If they missed a cow that was calving and she calved in the storm, they needed to carry the slimy, bloody, and half-frozen calf to the barn while trying to get the cow to follow them. This was extremely difficult with the cow often running back to where she had the calf and their having to go back to look for her. Finding the right cow was almost impossible when you were looking into a blinding blizzard with snow and ice freezing your eyes shut and all the cows looking the same—like white, snow- covered mounds. When they did find the right cow, they had to fight her each step of the way to the barn since every instinct in her body was telling her that she couldn't leave her calving spot, the place where her calf was supposed to be. When they did get the cow to the barn, it was sometimes difficult to get her to claim her calf. *This one can't be mine! Mine's out in the snow drift.*

The storm lasted three days then switched directions and came back at them for another two days. When it finally broke, the whole family was totally fatigued from sleep deprivation and exhaustion. They lost six calves, but neighbors that calved earlier in the year—and those that didn't watch their calving herd around the clock—reported losing up to half of their calves. Sheep losses were even heavier.

Anna knew firsthand that the worst killer storms in South Dakota were like that, always striking without warning and when they weren't expected, then lasting longer than they should. She recalled the year when a mid-fall storm hit the Dakotas with heavy snowfall and high winds causing the usual blizzard conditions for several days. Cattle weren't in their winter pastures or around the farmsteads yet, and since they were still out on the prairie pastures with no protection, they drifted with the storm. It was sufficiently cold to freeze the dams, but the ice wasn't thick enough to support a cow's weight yet.

One unfortunate neighbor of theirs lost his entire herd when the blinding snow pushed it onto a large body of water and the ice broke under them drowning every animal he owned. After the storm some ranchers found their cattle up to forty miles from where they should have been. The cold and hungry cattle drifted with the wind, pushing through fences or piling up in fence corners until the snow had been trampled sufficiently for them to go over the fence and then drift on … and on. If they found a highway or road, they just followed it aimlessly, walking with the wind until the storm abated. When the storm had finally blown itself out and moved on, it took men on horseback days, sometimes weeks, to find the remnants of their scattered herd and bring what was left of it back home.

Obert had been keeping his promises to write home. He wrote his first letter upon arrival to Fort Leonard Wood and his second just after basic training. Anna received each letter with great joy, reading them over and over to Iver until she had them memorized. She missed her first son desperately and worried about his welfare deeply. She wrote to him every day that she could, with art, Marjorie, and Iver adding notes.

After he graduated from basic training, Obert entered the Military Police. He served with the 720th Division, Company B. He wasn't deployed until a couple of years later, and it was to Japan. He still attempted to write letters, but wartime correspondence wasn't easy. He tried to hide it in his letters, but it was plain that the war was like "hell" and that if he and his companions made it home in one piece and alive, it would be nothing short of a miracle. Anna fervently prayed for that miracle every morning, night, and day, and often in between, for over three years.

In one of his letters, Obert put it this way: *"America entered WWII unprepared, and we suffered the consequences. However, as the war waged on, our American will to prevail took over, and our military might and sheer determination gradually began to overcome the Japanese and German war machines."*

One astute Japanese leader, admiral Yamamoto, said this: "I fear all we have done is to awaken a sleeping giant and fill him with terrible resolve."

In South Dakota the Great Depression was officially ending, and Anna's family was able to sell their calves at the Belle Fourche stock market again. Iver smiled to himself thinking about his banker's stock market in New York that didn't even have cattle. It was an average year income-wise and weather-wise for South Dakota ranchers, and art, now a part-time farmer as well as rancher, plowed up another eighty acres of virgin prairie soil to plant wheat to help the war effort. American farmers and ranchers took their role in the war seriously, saving every scrap of food that they could to send to the soldiers and pushing their production capacity to the limit.

Obert continued to write letters home relating to his family some of the war news. In his latest letter, in 1944, he wrote: *"Our troops captured the Marshall Islands, and we sent another 155,000 men to Normandy for*

Operation Overlord to liberate France and weaken the Nazi position in Europe. I am doing fine, but the food is terrible. Of course, I had the best cook in America at home, so I went into the war pretty pampered. I'd give anything for one of your apple pies, Mom."

By now, many american families had received those horrific letters from the war department saying that their sons were either dead, captured, or missing. Anna continued to pray fervently for the war to end and for Obert, along with all the american fighters, to come home.

Iver and art struggled to keep up with the work, and many tasks fell on Anna while Marjorie went to college for a semester. Marjorie met a girlfriend there from east river—South Dakotans divide their state into east river, which is east of the Missouri river, and west river, which is west of the Missouri river—whom she liked a lot and let her see several photos of her brother arthur, the cowboy. The weather that winter was wicked again, almost a repeat of the winter of 1935-36. It was cold, snowy, and seemed to last forever. In the west river, South Dakota roads were blocked from January to mid-March with no supplies reaching any of the remote outposts, including reva. Anna and her family just endured and outlasted it like all of the other hardy west river ranching families.

The year 1944 was the turning point of the war, and Obert's letters reflected the prairie optimism he had inherited from Anna. On May 8, Obert posted another letter: *"We won!! The Germans surrendered today! Now we can focus on those Japs that got us into this mess. But when I think about it, God may have planned for us to enter the war since the world would surely have been overtaken if we hadn't."*

In 1945, President roosevelt was in his fourth term as President but suddenly died, and his Vice-President, Harry truman, took over. Soon afterward, the trinity test detonated the world's first a-bomb, and a month later, President truman approved an order to use one of those bombs on Japan. It was a tormenting decision for american leaders, knowing that it would kill thousands of innocent Japanese people, but also perceiving that if it ended the war, it would save thousands upon thousands of american— and Japanese— soldiers. On august 6, 1945, the a-bomb named Little Boy was dropped on Hiroshima, Japan, wreaking utter destruction there. The obstinate Japanese still wouldn't accept defeat, so on august 9 another a-bomb, named Fat Man, was unleashed on Nagasaki. Five days later, Emperor Hirohito finally surrendered on what became known as VJ Day.

Since Obert was in Japan, he saw much of this firsthand, and while there he bought a new camera and took dozens of superb wartime photos. In another letter he wrote: *"Here are some photos that I took of the devastation after Little Boy and Fat Man destroyed Hiroshima and Nagasaki. Everywhere I go there is total destruction. I don't know how anyone could possibly have survived. Most of the people that died here were innocent victims of their leaders whom these poor indoctrinated people actually thought were gods. Satan must have been here in person to bring this foretaste of hell to earth."*

Anna and Iver were overwhelmed with joy when they found out that the long and horrible war was over. The good Lord had finally brought peace to the world again. Good triumphed over evil, and after devastating much of the world, the long and merciless killing spree had finally ended. Those horrific WWII years had dealt a permanent blow to america, killing over 400,000 of our strongest, bravest, and best men.

When Obert came home, Anna was overcome with relief. Only a mother can know what had probably been going through her mind during those war years, but her fears and doubts were reinforced by years of sorrow. Every time she thought of Obert in the war, it brought back memories of her six dead babies. She was too accustomed to death. It seemed to shadow her life like a black cloud hanging over her, and she prayed daily that Obert wouldn't follow that pattern. Anna didn't think that she could possibly survive losing another child. When Obert finally came home and she saw him in the flesh, she got down on her knees and thanked her Lord even before giving Obert the biggest hug of his life. Anna smiled through tears of happiness while she told him how handsome he was in his uniform, how deeply she loved him, and how proud she was of her war hero.

The reva community held a celebration for him and for James Larson who had also returned safely. Two of the community's first sons had returned to South Dakota, unharmed and underweight but healthy. Anna and Iver wouldn't have to deal with another dead child.

Heaven already had an ample supply of their children.

After a few days at home, Obert knew for sure that his heart wasn't in ranching. It never had been. He knew that his brother wanted to be a rancher and always had. Like his father before him, it was all art ever wanted. Obert had dreamt of being a businessman and owning his own store, so he moved to Belle Fourche to find his fortune and, hopefully, a wife. Anna was sorry to see her first son leave the ranch, but at the same time she was very happy for him. She knew that he was pursing his own course in life, being his own man. She also knew that their little prairie ranch wasn't big enough to support both brothers, so it was almost a relief to her when one of them didn't want it. Anna was content with the outcome.

20

Their Lives in Letters

Iver enjoyed going to reva for the mail, and he came home wildly excited one day. "Anna, you have a letter, Anna! Let's open it!"

"Hold your horses, Iver, I'll be right there. Who's it from? Where's it from?"

"I think one of your sisters, Anna! the return address says Harriet, and it's from Norway!"

Anna's heart skipped a beat and then nearly leapt out of her chest. She had left two sisters and a brother when she ran away from her father and stepmother, fleeing Norway at the tender age of sixteen. Her siblings were younger than she was, and she thought of them nearly every day, wondering how they were doing. She made a few attempts to write to them, once from Minneapolis and twice from South Dakota, but she never knew whether they had received any of the letters. This was the first letter she had ever gotten from home, and Anna's heart was now pounding like a trip hammer, so hard that she thought it might explode. She hurriedly, yet very carefully and lovingly, opened the letter making sure she didn't damage the contents. It was written in Norwegian which Anna found difficult to translate after speaking and writing English for so many years.

Dearest sister Anna,

I have been trying to track you down since the war ended. I probably never would have found you, but we just now received a letter that you wrote to us several years ago.

We moved from the address you mailed it to, and it was forwarded to a wrong address and then sent back to our old post office. A schoolmate of ours works there and held it until now, knowing it was important and hoping to find me. I was the happiest girl in Norway when I received it! From what you said, we know that you have written other letters that we have never received. I feel so badly that we haven't written, but we wouldn't have had a clue of where to send a letter to until receiving yours. There is so much to say that I don't even know where to start, so I'll start with the worst news and work my way up to the best.

The war was horrible. We were occupied by the German Wehrmacht for 5 years until the war ended. Our fascist party, headed by Vidkun Quisling, set up a pro-German puppet government during the war, but fortunately, King Haakon VII and most of our pre-war government and Parliament were able to flee to Britain, escorted by some of our war ships. The Germans came in and took control of our city following only a marching band. It was disgusting and humiliating. Our poor King, before he escaped, was in the village of Nybergsund when the villagers heard German bombers coming to kill him. The King and many others fled into the woods where they stood knee deep in snow and watched their town being destroyed.

After the Germans took over our country, it was unsafe for women to go anywhere for fear of being raped and killed. The Germans had several hundred thousand soldiers here in Norway. It seemed like there were more Germans than Norwegians, but the Germans weren't the only enemy as many of our own people collaborated with them. Several of our police even worked for them, and you never knew who to trust. Some of our men went so far as to volunteer to be Nazi soldiers. I know for a fact that the Nazis sent those misguided boys straight to the Eastern front where the poor traitors were the first in line to be shot by the Allies.

We had many heroes too. Patriotic Norwegians set up a resistance that became known as the Milorg. These brave patriots gathered intelligence and raided German posts and facilities. Our courageous sister Ingrid was one of their leaders! Not only did she help the resistance, but she hid Jews that were trying to escape to the UK and Sweden. She was in the middle of it all, helping fight the Germans and assisting those poor Jewish families that the Nazis were trying to exterminate. When it looked like the war was finally turning in the Allies' favor, she became even more brazen and shot a few German soldiers. After the war, King Haakon and Queen Maud honored our sister as a war hero and gave her a huge medal of honor to wear! We were so proud of her! Now she is helping our government get reorganized and works directly with the King and Parliament. She has never married, and I doubt the brave girl ever will since she is too busy helping Norway recover to look for a husband.

Iver interrupted the letter reading at this point. "If she's as good with a rifle as you are, Anna, I bet she could have taken on the whole German army. Isn't that something about your sister being honored by the King and Queen? Don't you wish you could have been there for that ceremony?"

"Oh, my brave little sister Ingrid! It's hard for me to imagine her grown up and fighting in the war." Anna's heart had slowed down, and she was savoring every life-giving word in her sister's letter.

Anna's world was expanding with each sentence. Her family was alive, and she was in contact with them again! It felt like heaven. Anna continued to read through her teary and happy eyes:

After the war, we went over to Sweden for a while to help some of those folks. Did you know we had relatives there? The Germans had what they called the Scorched Earth Policy, and they burned everything to the ground when they retreated rather than leave it usable for the people left behind. Those devastated families were left with nothing, and we tried to help them rebuild shelters for the winter.

Dad and our stepmother have passed on, and I don't have any idea what happened to our stepbrothers and stepsisters. Our brother has married and has a family of his own. They live in Bergen and have a small market store there by the ocean. My family of five lives in Oslo. I'd brag about each of my children, but having never known them, you would be bored. Now my husband and I are eagerly waiting for some grandchildren. My husband is a doctor, and we live in a nice house in Oslo where most of his relatives are from. I was going to nursing school when we met. We keep really busy since Norway has a severe shortage of medical personnel.

Compared to other countries, we didn't have a lot of physical war damage, but we have had our share of psychological wounds. Our King is trying to restore our faith in mankind and in our fellow Norwegians which the war greedily stole from us. We still don't like associating with the people that collaborated with the Germans, especially the socialists. I feel particularly exasperated when I think of all of those unfortunate war babies. They are like children in search of a family and a country. The Germans set up a Lebensborn program and basically treated Norwegian women as cows, using them to make German babies. There are several thousand of those children, Anna. They are generally despised, along with their mothers, but it really wasn't any of their doing, and we should be helping them rather than holding it against them.

The war was atrocious, and I have already said too much about it. I still go to our church, but I often wonder why God lets people like Hitler be born. I think that he was Satan himself in disguise.

I am so anxious to hear from you again. How I would love to visit you in America and see the wonderful country that helped liberate our people! We miss you so much and dream of the day that we might see you again with our own eyes and hold you again with our own arms. My hero, my big sister, the adventurous Anna, the one that made it to America all by herself. You have always been my idol, and even though you weren't here in person, you helped me make it through times that I wouldn't have survived without your memory pushing me along. Getting your letter has given Ingrid and I renewed hope. She says to send her love and that she will write too. She is too modest to have told you about her awards and achievements, but I'm not!

Now, if you get this letter, you will have our correct address, and you can be fairly certain that your correspondence will reach us.

> *My husband, Reidar, sends his love too. Please write*
> *soon and often; I miss you more than the world,*
> *Lovingly, your sister,*
> *Harriet*

Anna didn't wait to write back. "Iver, could you ask Marjorie to make dinner for everyone today? I'm going to stay right here and answer my sister's letter and take it to reva so it gets in tomorrow's mail."

My Dearest sister Harriet,

When my husband, Iver, brought your beautiful letter home to me, I was so happy that I cried. I opened it with trepidation—you never know whether letters will have good or bad news. It was mostly wonderful news!

Until now, I have never known what happened to our family. It is almost impossible to think of you and Ingrid as grown women, and all I can see are the two little girls that I left behind. Time has stood still for me where you are concerned. I still see you and Mom in our little home in the North Sea. I always thought that you would grow up to be the beauty of the family, and it sounds like you surely have. Marrying a doctor and becoming a nurse yourself, how amazing. And to think of our sister, the war hero! She was the tiniest one in the family when I left, and she grew up to fight the German invasion!

It must have been so horrible for you to endure being occupied by people that killed and raped our women. The thought of our own people helping them makes me sick, but I suppose that in times of war people do things they normally wouldn't do. I pray you never have to put up with that wicked Fascist Party again.

Here on American soil we saw virtually nothing of the war, but our boys, the ones that came back, came home with horror stories. My son Art was too young for war, but my son Obert went into the military right after the Japs wickedly and cowardly attacked Pearl Harbor. Obert was in the Military Police and served some of his time here in America before being deployed to Japan. He returned from the war unharmed, in answer to my many prayers.

My husband, Iver, and I are also waiting for grandchildren. We have our own ranch here in South Dakota with horses and cattle. Along with our two boys, we have a beautiful daughter, Marjorie, and many ranching friends. We have several Norwegian neighbors along with some Swedes, Germans, and Dutch. This can be an unforgiving land one day, and it can be bountiful the next, just as I had imagined it when I first dreamt of coming to America and living here. I couldn't have met a nicer, more honest man than my Iver, and I couldn't have found a better place to raise my family.

Sometime soon I am going to write you a very, very long letter. I will tell you of my adventures in coming to America and traveling through it and the friends I met on my journey. I will write about South Dakota and ranching stories of horses, cattle, wolves, rattlesnakes, Indian families, the Grand River, the Slim Buttes, and the Black Hills. I could go on and on, dearest sister, and I will when I get time. Right now, I just wanted to get a letter posted back to you so that you know I received yours and felt the love that it contained.

Please give all my family in Norway and your husband and children my love and hugs and kisses. It would be my greatest dream come true to see all of you again, to hold you and to feel your love and have you feel mine. For now, I will settle for the sheer joy and peace that your letter brought, knowing that you are well and happy. Tell my little sister Ingrid that we stopped reading and cheered when we read about her exploits and heroism. I left Norway in good hands with her.

All my love to you, and more.
May God bless and keep you for me,
Your loving sister, Anna

Anna and her sisters wrote several letters back and forth. They weren't just letters, they were love. They were treasures greater than gold, lifelines to their families containing the greatest gift of all, knowledge that the people they loved were alive. The mail service eventually improved, and they diligently kept each other informed about the events in their lives.

Harriet did try to visit Anna somewhere around 1947, but, tragically, she died on the ship that was bringing her to america. It was never certain what happened, but it was reported that she contracted flu and pneumonia on board the ship and didn't recover. It was just one more trial for Anna, one more promise of happiness that turned to tragedy, one more test of her faith. Her sister Ingrid remained in Norway for the rest of her life and never did marry. Anna wanted desperately to go to Norway to see her and the rest of her family, but she was never able to. Their family reunion would have to wait for heaven.

All through the 1930s, Anna had been teaching Iver how to write in English. He made friends with rasmus when he was there building their house and wanted to keep in touch with him. Anna helped him write his first letter to rasmus, hiding the fact that she still thought about him too. How can a heart completely dismiss its first love?

Dear Rasmus,

It has been a busy winter, and I've wanted to write to you sooner but just haven't found enough time. Besides that, I didn't know how to write until Anna started teaching me.

Today was fairly nice, and the chores went quickly so I'm in the house early. The coal furnace that we have really cranks out the heat and keeps us nice and warm. You built the house really solid! It has taken winds that would have blown over homes that weren't this sturdy, and it did its best to keep out all of the dirt that blew in with the dust storms that continually pounded it. The hordes of locusts that came through ate most of the paint off the walls, but it is easy to re-paint.

Anna loves the kitchen and dining room, but maybe the porch, where her rocking chair is located, is her favorite room. We let Chris stay in the guest bedroom during the winter months so that he didn't have to walk over for meals, and we didn't have to heat another house. It is a great bedroom but sits empty now that Chris has passed away. It needs some visitors to stay in it.

How is your family doing? How many houses did you build this year? Is the construction business doing ok, or has the awful economy affected you like the rest of America? Since the Depression, we haven't had much rain, and the market for our livestock has dried up right along with the prairie and everything else. Many of our neighbors have moved away looking for greener pastures, I guess. Anna and I have a steady trail of drifters to feed during the spring, summer, and fall. They stop in and stay for a while, then move on in search of something, anything that will give them some hope and maybe even a job. Times are tough, but Anna somehow always finds something for them to eat. She takes care of each of them as if they were kin, but we usually have them stay in the barn. It sounds harsh, but the barn is much better than the road ditch.

We are hoping that you can come and visit someday. Anna has good friends in Minneapolis that write to us and invite us to visit them, and we sure would like that. Anna would also like to see New York again and visit you and her other friends there, but I don't know how we could leave this ranch for as little as a day. A trip like that would take a month, and we have to milk the cows every day. It seems there isn't a single day of the year that we can take off without something dreadful happening. I used to think that I ran the ranch, but I have come to realize that it probably runs me.

I'd better go stoke the coal in the furnace for the night and get the kids tucked in.

Sincerely,
Your friend,
Iver Tenold

Iver and rasmus wrote a few letters back and forth, but they never did get to see each other again. Anna still saw rasmus in the occasional dream, but he was just a good friend now. She no longer felt guilty about dreams that included him and willingly let them enter her sleep. Sitting in her rocking chair, her mind drifting back to Norway and her adventures, rasmus occasionally returned. He always would.

Like Anna, Iver exasperatingly tried to correspond with his family, but it wasn't until the 1940s that the mail service became sufficiently dependable to rely on. Iver received this letter from his brother John after WWII:

Dearest brother Iver,

My wife and I were so happy to hear that your son Obert survived the terrible war. Our children are all fine. How happy we are to have our country and our farm back. Now we need to heal as a nation. Some Norwegians helped the Germans during the war, and there is a lot of hatred for those people. There are hundreds of German babies, poor children. They are despised since they're half German, but it was no fault of theirs. I am so glad that we were able to hide our own daughters, along with a few Jewish families that the Germans wanted to ship to their death camps. We took them to caves in the mountains and made living quarters for them there.

My sons joined the resistance and were able to keep ahead of the Germans. Fortunately, they know these mountains and the valley of Tenold so well that they had dozens of hiding places and could easily stay away from the enemy. The Germans stole our livestock and crops, and we barely had enough food to stay alive ourselves, so now that they are gone, we are trying to rebuild our herd. At least they didn't burn our buildings like they did to the people in Sweden and other places.

That is enough about the horrible war. Mom is really old but doing well and enjoying her grandchildren. I wish Dad was still here to do the same. Maybe someday our families could have a reunion. Wouldn't that be wonderful? I try to imagine what you look like now; you were so young and handsome when you left for America. I'll never forget seeing you bravely leave on that ship. Mom went down to the docks and cried every day for months after you left. The folks at Vik still say the water there is the saltiest in the ocean because of all of her tears.

If she is even close to as beautiful and wise as you say your wife, Anna, is, she must be amazing. I am happy that the two of you have a son to take over the huge ranch that you have there. I would love to see America and you and your family someday and to show you my family. We feel very blessed to have 6 grandchildren and to have survived the German occupation and have our family farm back.

Please write back to us when you get time,
Our love,
Most sincerely,
Your brother John and family

Although they had good intentions and desperately wanted to, neither Anna nor Iver ever saw any of their family in Norway again.

Their last glimpse of them was when they left as teenagers. Faith and optimism kept their hopes up, but the time and distance between them was just too extensive to overcome. Their lives were in their letters.

21

Arthur and Adeline

It was postwar and dating days for Anna's children. Unlike most moms, Anna had no intention of trying to choose their mates or interfering with their choices. She simply prayed that they would find someone to love and to be happy with. Obert found a beautiful young lady from North Dakota, and their relationship was serious, but when it came to marriage, art beat him to the punch. Marjorie had brought a good friend of hers home from college one weekend, and she and art hit it off immediately. Art had that romantic cowboy image and appeal, and she was a beautiful and alluring college girl. They dated for a few months and then decided to become engaged. Her name was adeline—addie—Olinger, from the east river portion of South Dakota.

Anna and Iver were thrilled, both at the thought of having a daughter-in-law and at the thought of having art at work full-time again. Anna knew that she was entering another season of her life. Her children weren't children any longer. They were dating and would soon be married and have families and lives of their own. Like all changes in life, it was a little sad, but Anna was more happy than sad. Her family could grow again. She would have two more daughters and another son! and Grandchildren if the Lord was willing!

Art's mind certainly hadn't been on ranching since he and addie had started dating, and it wasn't easy to get any work out of him in that state. With Marjorie off to school most of the time and art not being able to concentrate on the ranch work, Anna and Iver were almost back to running the ranch alone again. One day after art had been out courting addie, Anna and Iver sat him down in the dining room for a long, serious discussion. Anna had made cinnamon rolls, and they were still hot. She poured coffee for the three of them and chose her words carefully.

"Art, if you're sure that she's the one that you want to live the rest of your life with, you should get married—sooner rather than later. Your dad and I are getting too old to run this place by ourselves, and our bodies just can't keep up this pace. We've had two cattlemen from texas here trying to the buy the ranch. Of course, we turned them down, but it started us to thinking about our future and yours. Obert has decided that he doesn't want to be a rancher, and he wants you to have the outfit. If you do want it, and if you get married, we could stay here and help as long as we are able. But it is a big decision, and we don't want you to rush into something that you might regret later."

Art was surprised, "What do you mean, if I want the ranch? I've never in my life wanted anything else. ranching is all I know and all I've ever wanted. I love this ranch and the horses and cattle, and I've even grown fond of farming. If I marry addie, she will move here with me and help with the ranch work."

Art was on his third cinnamon roll. Anna continued, very seriously, "Have you asked her if she wants to live on a ranch? She's a city girl, art, and she'd have a lot to learn. City folks aren't used to working daylight to dark, freezing in the winter and drying out like the prairie grass in the summer. They like town jobs and short workdays, along with regular paychecks and weekends off. They want certainty in their lives. We never know from day to day what might strike us next, and our paycheck only comes once or twice a year. We don't know in advance what it will be or if it will cover the expenses. We seldom get a day off, and weekends are no different than weekdays except we try to take time for church. Not many college girls would settle for that kind of a life, Son."

Listening to his mother, art finally got it and pushed his plate aside. "You're right, Mom. I need to put all the cards on the table for addie to see. Not many town girls would understand what they would have to give up to live out here. We've discussed matrimony but haven't really talked about living on the ranch. I just took it for granted, but she probably hasn't even given it a thought. Marjorie did say that addie told her that she really liked the ranch, but I admit that ranch life appears a lot nicer and more romantic from the outside looking in. When all you see is the pretty land, the horses, and cattle, you don't realize what kind of grit it takes to live here or try to make a living here. I'll be seeing her again this coming weekend, and I'll discuss everything with her and see how she feels. Please don't sell the place to any texans! I don't think I could possibly live anywhere else on this earth than here. I do know how much I owe you two. You're the reason that this ranch is here for me to take over."

Later that day, Iver was up on the barn repairing some shingles when he slipped. Sliding all the way down the steepest part of the barn, he fell onto its lower slope and from there all the way to the hard earth below. Anna saw it happen from her garden and ran over to see if he was alright, nearly certain that he had broken a bone or two with a fall like that. He had already gotten up, embarrassed that she had seen him fall. He was trying to act like it was nothing, but when he put pressure on his leg, he almost fell over. After checking it closely and finding that it was probably just a bad sprain rather than a broken ankle, Anna scolded him for being so careless.

Iver leaned on her shoulder, and together they hobbled to the house where Anna made them some coffee. They visited about art and his fiancée and how complicated it might be to have another family on the ranch to support. They realized that they weren't getting nearly as much work done in a day as they had in the past and that it was getting difficult to keep up. Anna was worried. What if art and addie got married, but addie wouldn't live on the ranch and they moved to town? How would they ever get the work done by themselves if that happened? Marjorie was sweet on a college guy that wanted to be a minister, and if they were married, there certainly wouldn't be any prospects of ranch help from them. Without help, she knew that at their age they couldn't work the ranch. Anna's heart and soul were in that ranch, but at the same time she knew that everything under heaven actually belonged to God. If need be, they would return it to Him.

For Anna, growing old wasn't easy, especially when she had so much work to do and so little time and energy to do it. Anna and Iver had kept the names of the texans, but they had never even thought of having to call one of them someday. After Iver's fall off the barn and with his past history of accidents and health issues, Anna paused to reflect on his mortality, and hers. Anna knew that they weren't the strong young ranchers they had once been and that they had to face the fact that they wouldn't live forever. Father time was knocking on their door.

As if Providence was trying to prove a point, Anna had a similar scare that week. There had been a leak in the porch ceiling during the last rain, and she was determined to patch it before it rained again. Art and Iver had ignored her pleas for them to check on it, so Anna decided to do it herself. She gathered a few shingles, some shingle nails and a hammer, and a couple of other things she thought she might need. Then she found the old wooden ladder and leaned it against the porch wall. She loaded all the supplies in a bucket and took them to the top of the ladder and put them on the roof, along with the shingles that she had already carried up.

It took about an hour, but she replaced a few worn out shingles where she thought the leak had originated, then went to her bucket to get the tar and finish the job. She found that she had forgotten the tar, so she scurried down the ladder to get it. Her foot slipped on a smoothly worn ladder rung and down she fell, crashing through the ladder and hitting the rock-solid ground with a thud. She just lay there for some time, wondering what she might have broken or injured. Finally, slowly, she got to her feet, relieved that she could stand and thinking that she had gotten off easy.

However, when she turned to fetch the tar, she found out otherwise. There was a sharp pain in her side and chest, and it was laborious to breathe in and out. She felt her ribs, and the pain shot through her chest. She immediately knew that she had broken one or more of them. It was painful, but she hid it well, never admitting what had happened. Life on the ranch had made her an expert at concealing pain. Art came by later, and she nonchalantly asked him to finish her roof job. "All that's left is tarring the new shingles that I have already nailed on. I was interrupted and couldn't finish the job."

"Yes, Mom; it'll just take me a few minutes," art replied. "Are you still going on a date tomorrow, Son?"

"Yup, and I promise I'll tell addie everything you told me to, Mom."

"You'd better. You wouldn't want her coming here to live and then be disillusioned and unhappy with ranch life. If anything, make it sound worse than it really is—if that is possible—so she positively knows what she's getting her pretty little self into."

Art came home from the date beaming and told his parents the great news. He and addie were going to be married that fall in her church in Salem, South Dakota. He was the happiest man on earth, finding the girl he loved and getting to be a rancher to boot. He had told addie everything about ranching and living on the prairie—well *maybe nearly* everything— and she had agreed that she would *just love* to make her home on that *simply adorable* ranch and live *happily ever after* there with her cowboy.

Anna was a little skeptical of art's summary, but at the same time ecstatic about the upcoming first marriage in their family. She immediately began a list of people to invite knowing that it was too far for most of them to travel but wanting to let them know the good news anyway. At her first opportunity, she took addie aside and welcomed her into the family, while at the same time revealing a few of the details of living on a ranch that her son might have forgotten. Anna's life was starting to feel complete, and seeing her son this happy filled her heart and soul with gratitude and contentment. Her prayer that night reflected it.

Art and addie were married that fall according to plan, and after a short but memorable honeymoon in the Black Hills of South Dakota, the blissful newlyweds moved to the ranch. Their first home was in Chris's house, which Anna and Iver had cleaned up and prepared for them. Anna did her best to make addie feel at home and took her under her wing like a daughter. Most girls have to learn how to cook and clean on their own, but addie had Anna to help, at least when she asked for it. Anna was careful not to interfere with addie's life unless she was asked. It was the perfect time for the couple to be newly married since it was the easiest time of the year for ranchers. Anna knew that art would have his head in the clouds for a few weeks, or maybe months, so she and Iver planned to do most of the work until he came back down to earth. It brought wonderful memories back to Anna, memories of her marriage to Iver and their first home and the birth of their first child. Anna had finally forgiven herself for the deaths of her babies and now welcomed memories of her past years on the homestead.

Anna was seriously surprised one morning when addie showed up at milking time and said, "I've been here for almost a week now, and it's about time that I learn how to help with the chores, especially the milking. I know that you probably think that I'm just a lazy city girl, but I grew up with six brothers and no sisters, so I'm not as helpless as I might appear.

Those brothers treated me like a boy, so I'm no sissy." addie found a stool and bucket and asked Anna to help her get started.

"I will certainly appreciate the help, addie. Let's see, first we use the washcloth soaked in warm soapy water to bathe the cow's bag and teats. Well, not really first; first we put the cows in the stanchions where they put their heads through those slats to get the grain in the pans waiting for them. The slats close behind their heads and hold them still. Next, we tie their tails to a post with twine. That is for pretty obvious reasons, but if you forget and get a mouthful of wet cow tail soaked with you know what swatted across your face and into your mouth, you won't forget the next time! When the cow is washed up and clean, you are ready to start milking. Just put your stool as close to the cow as you can comfortably sit and tuck your head down into her flank and start milking, dear."

"I'm pulling, Anna, but there isn't any milk coming. How do you get the milk to come out?"

Anna demonstrated the process of how to squeeze as she pulled a few times, and addie soon had the process down. For the first three or four weeks, addie milked one cow while Anna milked four or five, but she gradually grew better, and her hands became stronger. Within a couple of months she was able to double her quota. Anna admired her determination and grit. It took no time at all for addie to learn the chicken chores, and she surprised Anna one day by butchering one of the roosters all by herself.

Addie asked her mother-in-law to teach her how to ride, and Anna asked her why she didn't ask art. "I want to surprise him. He still thinks I'm a tenderfoot and too 'dainty and fragile' to do things like rope and ride. I want to prove that I can handle myself."

So, in their spare time, Anna taught addie how to catch a horse—and, just as importantly, which horses *not* to catch—and put the halter on. After tying the horse up, Anna showed addie how to brush it and put the saddle blanket and saddle on slow and easy and gently tighten up the cinch. Next, Anna showed addie how to open the horse's mouth with your thumb and carefully place the bridle bit on top of its tongue before pulling the bridle gingerly over its tender ears. The last step was to slowly put your left foot into the stirrup, hold the saddle horn with your left hand, and pull yourself up and onto the saddle. Addie was a good student, and within a few weeks she was riding by herself and had found a favorite gelding. All of this was accomplished while Iver and art were out getting the hay moved to the stack yards, fixing fences and corrals, hauling manure, and checking the cattle and horse herds.

It brought a smile to Anna's face, and addie asked her what she was thinking about. "A few years ago, Odd had me trying to break a horse that he thought I'd never be able to ride. Iver and I tricked him into feeling bad enough about it that he gave me the horse, thinking it truly was unbreakable. We had the horse saddled and bridled, hidden around the corner from his view, and I rode it past him just as he was begging for forgiveness. We laughed all day!"

At the end of her lessons with Anna, addie surprised art by asking him if she could ride along while he checked the cows. He said he was running late today, but that as soon as he had time, he'd give her some lessons, and they could go riding together. To his utmost surprise, she saddled up her horse and asked what was taking him so long—she had chores to do and couldn't be sitting around all day waiting for him to get his horse ready. The cowboy had a cowgirl.

Even Iver was surprised at how quickly addie had taken to ranch life. He admitted one day that he hadn't thought that she would last six months, but now that she was holding her own and even doing things that they hadn't thought of, it looked like she was truly a "keeper."

That winter addie was in the hayloft helping art fork hay down to the cows below. He thought back and laughed as he told her how Marjorie had always gotten him and Obert in trouble by tattling on them, and they decided to get even with her by pretending to throw her out the barn door. Addie whacked him with the blunt end of her pitchfork and told him that his story wasn't a bit funny. Her six brothers had done the same to her, only they weren't pretending. They threw her out the door, and she fell twelve feet to the hard ground below. She hadn't broken any bones, but she'd limped for a long time. As her dad was belting her brothers, they kept saying, "We just wanted to see if she could fly, Pa. We didn't think it would hurt her none."

It was 1947, and the honeymoon was over. Anna was pleased that her son was taking more responsibility in running the ranch. Art was noticing that some of their neighbors were getting Black angus cattle along with the typical Herefords. One day he asked Anna and Iver if they could try some angus too.

Iver seemed pretty irritated at art for even asking, saying, "Why would anyone take a perfectly good and pure herd of Herefords and mix angus with them? We have one of the best herds of Herefords in the country, Son. Chris and I worked diligently to keep these cows pure and to keep improving the herd by getting better bulls and strictly culling the poorest animals. I've heard that those angus are just fence crawlers and are as wild as coyotes."

"I've heard that too, Dad, but I've also heard that in many ways they are more trouble-free than Herefords. Do you remember that late spring snowstorm last year? When the sun came out after the storm, the reflection off of the snow burned our cows' udders and teats. What a mess that was! I had to rope and tie down several of those cows every day and *make* them let their calves nurse until I finally got their sunburned udders healed up. Since the angus cows have black udders and teats, they don't have that problem."

Iver had a quick comeback, "Well, that just proves what I've always said; we just have to calve late enough to avoid all of the snowstorms."

"Another thing, Dad, I have to sew up several prolapsed cows every calving season. We've culled every cow that has prolapsed, but it never seems to solve the problem. The neighbors say that the angus cows hardly ever have that problem. Wouldn't that be great? I hate the bloody mess of trying to push everything back in while the cow tries her best to push it back out again. I had to sew up one cow three times this spring."

Iver wasn't swayed. "You just have to catch them right away. It's easier if they haven't had it hanging out for a long time, and it isn't swollen up and crusted over."

"Maybe, but I don't care if I never see another prolapsed cow, Dad," art tried to persuade his father. "And if I never have to cut another cancer eye out, that will be fine too. That last cow took months to heal up after we took her eye out. What a disgusting mess. The neighbors say those Black angus don't get cancer eyes either. Another good thing about them is that they don't have horns. Wouldn't that be great not to have the extra work of dehorning the calves? all in all, they sound pretty trouble free to me, Dad."

"*Maybe* angus aren't as much work, Son, but they sure aren't as pretty to look at. I just don't get why you'd want to mix them with our Herefords. They've produced a line of Herefords without horns called Polled Herefords. Maybe we should look into them?"

Anna laughed at them, arguing back and forth about whether or not to get some angus. She could see both sides of the argument and wisely didn't interfere. Since it wasn't a matter of life or death, Anna didn't concern herself with the outcome.

The year 1947 started out nicely without any bad spring storms, just the usual snow, rain, and cold weather. Art was complaining about taking all of the night heifer checks, so one unusually mild and warm spring night, addie said she'd go out and help him. He beat her to the corral, but she showed up a little later, still in her nightgown. The wind was blowing, and her white nightgown was flapping. The heifers must have thought that she was the ghost from hell, because they spooked and stampeded through the corral fence, shattering it to escape the great white demon. Art took the somewhat embarrassed addie back to the house and got Iver out of bed to help him gather the heifers. It was nearly impossible in the dark, so they just went back to bed and waited until morning. Fortunately, there hadn't been any calvers that night, so no harm had been done—except to the corral. Later that year, when Art brought the incident up to addie, wanting to tease her about it, she turned the tables on him by saying, "Well, how do you know that I didn't do that on purpose? You didn't ask me to help you with another heifer check all year!"

Anna overheard the conversation and laughed and added, "I think that girl you married might just be smarter than you are, Son!" addie beamed with pride. She knew she had an ally with Anna, whom she had come to admire and love. She even found herself thinking of Anna as her mom.

Art was always neighborly, friendly, and just plain loved to talk. When neighbors stopped in, he dropped his work like it was a hot iron and started up a conversation. Iver sometimes got irritated with him and told him to quit gabbing because "we got work to do, and daylight is wasting."

Art even visited with salesmen and usually invited them in for lunch saying, "You got to eat somewhere, so come on in; we always have plenty."

After several salesmen made it a point to be there for dinner, addie got fed up with feeding the moochers. "The next salesman you bring in for lunch, I'm going to throw both of you out the door, *ARTHUR.* I'm tired of the extra mouths to feed, and we can't afford it, *ARTHUR.* I like having dinner with just our family, and I'm getting sick and tired of you always bringing some salesman home with you, *ARTHUR.*"

Two days later, the feed salesman came into the yard trying to sell art some newfangled cow pellets, stalling around and waiting for art to invite him in for dinner. Twelve o'clock came and went with no offers from art, who was trying to think of some excuse. Finally, he told the guy that he didn't need any feed and that addie wasn't home to cook dinner, so he'd just have to eat at the café in Buffalo today. The usual trail of "come at dinnertime, salesmen" started to dwindle as word of addie's ultimatum got out. Like her mentor, Anna, she could handle herself.

22

Grampa's Girl

A nna remarked that 1948 came in like a breath of fresh spring air with an ample supply of sunshine softly descending on the prairie people. Father time and Mother Nature were both being benevolent, and it would prove to be a year of healing and prosperity for all the western South Dakota ranchers and farmers—especially Anna's family. They still didn't have electricity or telephones, but how could you miss what you had never known?

Anna and addie were doing the milking when addie mentioned that she might be pregnant. Anna almost tipped her milk bucket over, quickly leaving her cow to give addie a big hug. "Are you sure? Have you told art? You can't imagine how happy this makes me. Having a new baby on the ranch will enrich my life, addie—all of our lives. This will be my first grandchild. I'm so happy for you and my son! Can I tell Iver? He'll be ecstatic too."

Anna didn't admit it, but along with the joy she also felt a sharp twinge of apprehension. The news of a new baby brought many memories back to her, and not all of them were good. The last several children born on the ranch were in the graveyard, and she couldn't keep from thinking about what had happened to them. There was hardly a day since their deaths that she didn't wonder what her family would look like now if they had lived. A new baby would be wonderful, but what if something bad happened again?

Anna interrupted the unwanted thought with a prayer for a healthy baby. As she finished milking, she decided that she wouldn't let anything keep her from being happy at the news. After all, a baby was a gift from God, and it was in His hands. What could better than that?

Addie asked Anna not to tell Iver until after she told art. When she did, art was beside himself with joy. The proud father was so elated that he couldn't wait to make the announcement at church, interrupting the minister with news that art thought was just as important as the pastor's message of salvation. Anna had already told Iver who was giving his son a run for his money in the boasting department. Not wanting to be outdone by the blissful news, Mother Nature cooperated and produced a mild January and placid February, the kind of weather that leaves smiles on ranchers' faces and makes the livestock and wildlife content. Anna viewed the nice weather as a gift from God and a sign that their lives had indeed made a permanent turn for the better, and that the new baby would be happy and healthy—and *alive.*

Calving came and went like a summer breeze with hardly any losses or problems. The mild temperatures combined with no blizzards or heavy snowfalls were Anna's dream-come-true. With a touch of skepticism she mentioned that usually a period of weather this nice meant that you would soon "pay for it," but not in 1948. April brought warm april showers, and the prairie soaked them up like a cold Black angus cow soaks up sunshine. The grass and wildflowers shot out of the ground like rockets reaching for the stars. Foaling and farming days were wet and mild, and the mares munched on abundant green grass while they roamed Gap Creek looking for their favorite hiding places to foal.

Art had become an excellent farmer and meticulously prepared the ground for seeding. Then he tested the newly prepared soil for just the right temperature, saying that if you could pull your pants off and sit your bare bottom on it, the ground was warm enough for planting. They planted over 300 acres of wheat along with some oats, barley, and corn that spring. Anna and addie were impressed with what their husbands had accomplished and planted an extra-large garden to try to keep up with them.

Anna watched the spring rains graduate to summer rains while the prairie continued to blossom and bloom, as did addie. The calves and colts grew fast and fat, and the hay and wheat stretched to record heights as their crops reached for the sun. Art laughed that a short person could almost get lost in his tall fields of wheat and oats, and the whole family made trips to the farm ground to admire the thick, lush crops. Anna and addie good naturedly complained that with all the extra green grass, the cows were giving more milk than they normally did, making the milking take longer. Their abundant and extra-large garden looked like the Garden of Eden in the heavenly year of 1948. The deer and antelope, the coyotes and prairie chickens, the skunks and badgers, and all of the creatures under the beautiful blue prairie skies were enjoying the unusually mild, rainy, and productive year. Anna again remarked that 1948 was becoming the best year of her life.

Art and Iver started haying in June, but it was so wet that every time they mowed a field, it rained again. They finally got one field raked into windrows only to have it rain on the rows of hay for a solid week. When they at last were able to start piling the hay up, the new crop was already growing through the top of their windrows. They gave up and said they'd try again later in July if it wasn't still raining. As if to make the summer even better and more productive, if that was possible, Mother Nature stopped the rains just long enough for them to harvest more hay than they had ever had on the ranch. It was better than money in the bank, as Iver often told his sons.

The grain crops were exploding with growth, and the heads of grain at the end of their golden stalks were so heavy that they drooped over like old men with worn-out backs. The granaries and bins overflowed, not able to hold all of the grain they harvested that fall. Iver had to go to Scranton, North Dakota, to hire extra trucks to haul the excess grain to town. To crown the bumper crop, grain prices were high. The rancher's rule of thumb was that if prices were high, you didn't have any to sell, and if prices were low, you had a lot to sell—but not in 1948, heaven's year of healing. It was the once-in- a-lifetime year when both nature and time smiled on them, making faith and optimism soar. Without a doubt, 1948 was a golden year for prairie people.

For Anna and all of her family, the pinnacle of the year was the birth of her first grandchild. She was a healthy and happy little girl that addie and art named Marlene. Anna said that the happy little girl reminded her of Marjorie at the same age. She held the newborn child with all the love and pride she had showered on her own children, loving her with all of her huge heart. Having a new baby on the ranch had indeed been an answer to her prayers, and she thanked God that the curse had been broken and that this baby had been born alive.

Marlene had the Norwegian hallmarks—those chubby cheeks and golden Scandinavian locks that turned to light brown as she got older. She was the apple of everyone's eye, but especially her grandparents'. They just couldn't seem to get enough of their first grandchild. The years had been so cruel and difficult for them when their own children had been growing up that they had missed much of their childhood, but now they vowed to make up for lost time with their first granddaughter.

The last four months of 1948 were equally pleasant. Anna was living the dream, life was *oh, so good*. Thanksgiving Day came, overflowing with blessings to be thankful for. Anna always had a thankful heart, but this year was exceptional. Abundance like this was a rare occurrence on the prairie whose current benevolence was helping heal the hearts of all those souls that had survived the Dirty thirties, the Great Depression, the Dust Bowl, locusts, extreme drought, killing winters, the days of despair, the year of the wolves, and the terrible war. America was indeed the land of milk and honey again, and South Dakota was diligently working to get electricity and telephones to rural farmers and ranchers in the western portion of their state. It would finally arrive in the 1950s.

Anna joyously and thankfully wrote in her journal that 1948 had been one of the easiest, happiest, and best years of her life. It went out like a lamb, perfectly ending the ideal year. But as often happens in South Dakota, 1949 ended the honeymoon and came in like a wild beast that was very eager to devour the lamb that preceded it. The snow and cold struck on January 2, and the winter wind came with it. It wasn't just wind but a gale with hurricane-force winds that ranged from fifty-two to ninety miles per hour, flash freezing everything in its path. Snowfall and the accompanying snowdrifts paralyzed South Dakota, and pilots were hired to fly in hay for starving livestock that couldn't be reached by any other means. The snowfall ranged from two feet to several feet, with eight times the normal snowfall in western South Dakota. The rapid City, South Dakota, weather station said that the January storm was the most severe blizzard in the history of the Black Hills. Anna took it all in stride. Nothing could diminish the new joy she had in her heart.

Iver and art did their best to feed their livestock. They had the cattle close by the barn and hay, but it was still virtually impossible to get them fed. When the winds were blowing up to ninety miles per hour, and snow and sleet were coming at you horizontally with hurricane force, it was nearly impossible to open your eyes to see where you were going. Even with them just barely cracked open, art couldn't see more than a few inches. The cold blasted through his hide and he almost felt naked, like he didn't even have clothes on, and his limbs almost instantly went numb. About all he and Iver could do was stay inside and hope for the best, which was having the cattle stay in a protected area without drifting off.

Anna warned art, "If cattle drift away from protection in a storm like this, there will be no way for them to get back to it. Even if you find them, there will be no turning them back into the fierce storm. They'll just drift with the blizzard until the wind quits blowing, or they freeze to death, whichever happens first."

Iver had checked the horses the day before the storm, and they were in the breaks by Gap Creek where they had good wind protection and grass. Anna and her family hoped and prayed that they stayed there. At times when the wind subsided to the fifty-mile-per-hour range, art went out and pitched hay to the cows until he couldn't take the cold any longer, hoping he had pitched sufficient hay to keep the cattle content enough to stay where they were. Coming back to the house, he walked with the wind to his back, which was a blessing since he was physically too exhausted to walk against it.

The storm lasted for three and a half days, a long time for a storm of that magnitude. When the wind at last died down sufficiently to get to the cattle, art found most of them blind with ice and snow covering their eyes. He knew they could startle easily in that condition, so he went and got his mom to help him, knowing that the cattle would recognize her soft voice. Together they walked through them, talking to them quietly and moving as slowly and carefully as possible. One by one, they rubbed some of the ice off their eyes so they could see again.

As often happens in South Dakota, a severe winter with an abundance of snow will be followed by a hot, dry summer. As Anna once observed, "We usually only get a certain amount of moisture per year, and if we have an abundance of snow, there probably won't be very much rain." Following those guidelines, the summer of 1949 was hot and dry, but it produced a couple of timely rains, and the family's crops looked like they might make nearly normal yields.

It was getting close to harvest time with less than two or three days until the wheat and barley would be ripe and ready to combine. Anna knew that they desperately needed the crop. The crop of 1948 had been abundant, but its riches were long gone, used to pay off old operating loans and repair equipment and purchase ranch supplies. Iver estimated that the crop yields wouldn't be good, but they hoped to at least pay off their credit at the store and buy some gasoline and coal for the winter with the proceeds. Iver planned to save enough grain for seed for next spring and sell the rest right after harvest. Anna prayed that they might even have enough money left after paying their bills to get addie and Marlene some new clothes and buy the washing machine that addie had been eyeing.

"That new washing machine would be wonderful," art said. "I know it sounds extravagant, but I'd like to get a new saddle. I've been patching mine for years, and it needs to be relined again. I see Dad's is in even worse shape though, and he should come first."

Iver added, "We'll just have to see how much we get for the grain. Prices are decent, and I have the harvest crew lined up to be here Monday."

That was on Friday afternoon. Saturday was nice, but very hot, as was Sunday morning. Hot days tend to generate storms, and on Sunday afternoon a large and ominous bank of clouds started building in the west. It started as a squall line, which rapidly closed ranks and formed a solid mass of thunderstorms. Forceful fifty- to seventy-mile per hour winds came with the storm, and when it arrived, it didn't rain, it hailed. With almost hurricane force winds, the hail didn't come straight down. Each large hailstone came horizontally at the speed of the wind, like tiny Japanese kamikaze pilots, each hailstone wiping out several plants instead of just one. After the storm had released all of its energy and wrath on their crops, it moved out to the east and created a beautiful rainbow, as if to make amends. There would be no harvest for Iver and art, and Anna and addie's garden had been completely destroyed. The women mourned the loss of the garden almost as much as the loss of the crops.

That evening, Anna told her family, "At least we had one bountiful year, 1948, to remember. We will get through this; we always do. This certainly isn't even close to the worst thing to ever happen to our family." the year 1949 had been a wreck with most of their work that year for nothing, but the ever optimistic and faith- filled Anna prayerfully thanked her Creator for what they still had. With His help they would survive, just as they always had.

The next few years found western South Dakota farm and ranch families entering the era of electricity and with it came radios, telephones, and televisions. Anna excitedly watched the rural Electric association—rEa—building electric lines across western South Dakota. She liked her old kerosene lanterns and candles but had heard about lighting a house with light bulbs and listening to a radio, and she was eager to see how those things worked. As usual, Iver was reluctant to try new technology, but thought it would be worthwhile if it helped make Anna's life easier. Indeed, life for the following generations would seem almost effortless when compared to the hardships that Anna and Iver endured.

Marlene was growing quickly, and Anna and Iver weren't going to miss one minute of it. Art jokingly stated that he should rent her out to them like a cash crop. He kidded that Iver spent so much time with his granddaughter that he just wasn't getting any work out of him anymore. In reality, he truly enjoyed seeing his parents so happy. Art's philosophy, sometimes to Anna's dismay, was that "The work will always be there waiting for us, so let's go fishing." He was a simple man, working when necessary, but his family was more important than getting the chores done on time. When Iver and Anna were first married, Iver had said, "The most important thing in life is to take care of your loved ones and spend as much time with your family as possible." Years later, art helped his father realize the truth of that statement. He and Iver worked well together as did Anna and addie, and doting over Marlene kept all of them occupied. Iver and art knew how much the little girl loved animals, and they were always on the lookout for an exotic pet to bring her. According to Anna, they were acting like two teenage boys competing for the admiration of a pretty girl. She sometimes scolded Iver, saying that addie had enough work to do without having to take care of a menagerie of pets.

One afternoon Iver was in the shed and thought he heard some rustling in the attic. Peeking through a cracked board, he discovered a small litter of raccoons. They were recently born and still had their eyes shut. That was the perfect age to make them a pet, so he carefully snuck one of them out through the broken board hoping their mom wouldn't miss it. He proudly carried the baby coon to the house and showed it to Marlene and addie. Addie didn't want it in the house, but her daughter put up such a fuss that she relented. Marlene had a toy baby bottle, and with Grandma Anna's help, she mixed some cereal with milk and honey which the little coon loved.

Before long "Willy" was following Marlene around the house like a kitten, getting more mischievous with each day.

Willy loved to steal addie's mop. As Willy got older, he began to think the pretty yellow mop was his girlfriend, and addie would catch Willy taking her—the mop—up the stairs to his favorite room. *Thump, thump, thump* the mop handle would go as Willy pulled his girlfriend up the stairs. If addie caught him, the mop went back to the broom closet, and Willy would have to go find Marlene to play with him. He loved hide-and-seek, and he always looked for her in the last place that he had found her. If Marlene wasn't there, he would search until he discovered her, and then they would roll around and wrestle. When it was Willy's turn to hide, he would often leave his butt end and tail exposed. As long as his head was covered up, he figured the rest of him was hidden too!

Anna loved watching them, and often came over to their house to watch Marlene's game of hide and seek with Willy. "Wiwwy? Wiwwy?" Marlene would tease when she saw the big lump under the covers with the coon tail hanging out. The covers would heave up and down faster and faster as Willy tried to stay hidden but got excited anticipating the moment of discovery. Finally, Marlene would pounce on him, and the hysteria and the wrestling match would resume with Anna giggling as much as the two wrestlers.

Willy also liked to play with art. He would climb on just about anything and jump down to art, who would catch him and ruffle up his hair and tickle him, which Willy loved. One afternoon art was on the porch talking to Anna, and Willy climbed on the roof to play his game of jump and catch. Art was so busy visiting that he hadn't noticed Willy climb on the roof. All of a sudden, a brown flying object came hurtling out of the sky at art and his mother. They both ducked, and Willy crashed on the porch with a big thud. Willy looked up and gave art a surprised and betrayed look as if to say: "You were supposed to catch me. That wasn't very nice of you." art asked for forgiveness and gave Willy a nice rubbing down. Willy climbed to the roof again, and the next time he jumped art caught him. Anna laughed but had to ask art if he didn't have anything better to do than play games with Willy.

Willy stayed all summer and fall but eventually started wandering off with the other raccoons as they traveled through. Anna had shown Marlene how to imitate raccoon trilling, and Marlene could even get wild coons to come to her. She could even convince baby coons to leave their mothers and come to her. If it was nighttime and they saw coon eyes shining in the field, Marlene would trill and call out, and if Willy was with them, he would happily leave the pack to greet her. He was easy to spot since he was the fattest coon in the field. Addie made him pancakes with butter, syrup, and eggs, so he looked like he needed to be put on a diet.

One night they came home late, and Marlene spotted a raccoon on the porch. "Da da, Wiwwy is sick. Wiwwy is so skinny," she cried out. Art and addie came to look, and sure enough, Willy looked like he had lost twenty pounds. He was a shadow of his former self. Then the real Willy came waddling around the corner. They watched him try to impress the scrawny girlfriend that he had brought home to dinner. He did tricks, rolling over and hanging with one paw from the railing, but nothing impressed her until Marlene and addie brought Willy's pancakes out with syrup and butter. Willy must have been starving from being out courting all night, and he started to eat the delicious meal. But as soon as Marlene left, Willy's girlfriend came over and pushed him away from the bowl so that she could have it. Poor Willy, his new love didn't want him; she was only interested in his dinner.

Not to be outdone by Iver's raccoon, art brought a little fox pup home. He was so cute that even addie and Anna took to him. He followed Marlene everywhere she went, and the two were inseparable. The problem with fox puppies, Anna warned them, is that they grow up to be foxes. Sure enough, the pup grew quickly and soon developed a taste for chickens. Addie told art that he had better do something about it right away or he wouldn't be having any more fried chicken for Sunday dinner. Art didn't like chicken—he called it fowl food—anyway, but figured he'd better help out since he was the culprit that brought the fox home.

He retrieved an old cream can, which he partially buried in the yard, and put the little chicken thief inside. The fox liked the idea of having its own den but wasn't crazy about the collar and leash. He could only go about fifteen feet before he ran out of leash, but Freddy the Fox wasn't about to miss any chicken dinners. He quickly learned exactly how far his tether could reach and crouched in his cream can waiting for one of those juicy fat hens to wander close enough to nab. Once his target was within reach, Freddy would pounce out and, presto, another chicken dinner.

Addie noticed that her hen population was still dwindling but didn't suspect the innocent Freddy because he was, after all, tied up and couldn't leave his den. Marlene was playing with him one day when she saw chicken feathers in his cream can. "Look, Mommy, Freddy has made himself a fedder bed." She didn't know that she was betraying her fox friend. When Marlene went to play with Freddy the next day, he was gone. Art guiltily told her, "Freddy must have slipped his collar and went out to visit his mom and dad; he'll probably come back pretty soon." He didn't.

During haying season, Iver and art always searched the field closely so that they didn't accidentally mow some innocent little creature with the wicked sickle bar. One day Iver noticed an antelope kid hiding in the field and caught it for Marlene. It wasn't any bigger than a jackrabbit, but it bleated loudly when Iver caught it. He anxiously looked around to see if mom was coming, but she was nowhere in sight. He knew that antelope and deer moms usually hid their kids and fawns until lunch time, and then they came out of hiding to feed their babies.

Iver took the gangly little antelope home, and Marlene had another pet. Grandma Anna was consulted on what to feed it and out came the baby bottle again. Before long, Anna's granddaughter had a playful little antelope that they called "Lopey" following her everywhere. Lopey was a great pet, and Marlene loved to play around the yard with him. Lopey made mad dashes around her, running in circles as fast as his skinny little legs could carry him, cutting corners so sharply and quickly that it was hard for your eyes to follow.

Lopey's spirited frolicking was cute, but Lopey also liked to play head bunting. Marlene, and everyone that ventured into the yard, quickly learned that Lopey had a harder head than they did and not to play that game with him. When nobody would play head bunting with him anymore, Lopey changed tactics and started attacking the other end of the human anatomy. Nobody was safe from getting rear-ended by Lopey. Just bend over, and Lopey would come out of nowhere at full speed with his hard and pointy little head aimed dead center—and he never missed. That got to be more than annoying and downright painful as he got bigger, as Anna found out one day when she was bent over picking weeds out of the garden. Anna warned the little goat to behave, but he didn't listen.

The final straw for Lopey was when he noticed addie's clothes hanging on the clothesline to dry. They made great, almost human- like targets, and Lopey attacked them with a vengeance. He learned that he could even run down the line and mow several of them over with one charge. Alas, it was definitely time for Lopey to join the herd. He was eating grass by then, and art figured he was old enough to be weaned, so he and Iver loaded Lopey in the wagon—when Marlene wasn't looking—and headed to the field that always had antelope in it. Lopey probably looked for the clothesline and Marlene for weeks. Marlene was told that Lopey probably missed his mama and poppa and went to visit them but that he would more than likely return. He didn't.

Other pets followed like chicken hawks, rabbits, a deer fawn, and even a baby badger, which actually made a great pet. Anna called the place Marlene's zoo. When the estranged range creatures ran out, Marlene made use of her time by taming wild barnyard cats. She soon had a herd of them that followed her to the house. Anna and addie finally got so tired of so many cats on their doorstep that they started dousing them with water, sending them back to the barn. The cats were quick learners, and soon Marlene couldn't get them to follow her home anymore.

Over the year Anna noticed how much Iver seemed to be slowing down, so she asked him if he was feeling okay. Iver assured her that he was fine, but she thought that it seemed as if he was trying to hide something. Actions spoke louder than words, and Anna didn't think her husband was acting like he felt as good as he claimed. She told him to take it a little easier and not work so hard.

Iver just laughed at her and said, "I'll start slowing down just as soon as I see you doing the same, Anna dear."

"You know how much work we have to do, Iver tenold," she replied.

"That's exactly what I'm talking about, Hon. There's no way I'm sitting around and watching my wife do the work."

It was a draw.

Art was aware that his dad had experienced some off-and-on chest pains but knew that his father was too stubborn to tell anyone about them. The more art tried to talk him into taking a few days off or slowing down, the more determined he seemed to be to prove that he could still do anything that he could ever do. Anna was just as obstinate as her husband when it came to relaxing or doing anything other than work. When addie told her that she and Iver should take a vacation, Anna brushed it aside saying that there was too much work to be done to take a *silly* vacation.

The debate continued in that fashion until in desperation art and addie hatched up a scheme to get Anna and Iver to take some time off. Obert was living in Belle Fourche, and they included him in their little plot. Art had sold several furs that winter and saved the money for something special. What could be better than giving his parents a vacation, even if they had to trick them into taking it? Obert would have to do most of the legwork, but he agreed. First of all, he needed to send his parents an official looking letter postmarked from Belle Fourche informing them that they had won an all-expenses-included vacation to the Black Hills of South Dakota from the Black Hills tourist association—there was no such organization, but art and addie thought it sounded good—to promote tourism in that area. The *free* vacation would include *free* lodging and meals, *free* tickets to Joseph Meier's famous Black Hills Passion Play in Spearfish, plus a movie of their choice in rapid City. There had been an official drawing, and their names were selected. All they had to do was to take the *free* vacation sometime that fall and keep track of their expenses which would be reimbursed by the tourist association.

Addie was at the reva post office when the official-looking letter arrived. When she got home, she gave it to Anna. "This letter sure looks important, Anna. What do you think the tourist association could be wanting from you?"

"Probably a donation, like all of the other organizations," Anna huffed. "They must think that money grows on the trees out here." Anna set the letter aside, and addie was wondering how to get her to open it when Anna finally picked it up again. She opened it and read the contents. "What's

Honoring Anna

it got to say, Anna?" addie asked. "It says that we won an expense paid vacation to the Black Hills.

I've never heard of such a thing, have you?"

"Oh … yeah, I've talked to others that have won that contest," addie fibbed. "It is the real deal, and they say all you have to do is keep track of your expenses, and sure enough, the association of tourism sends you back cash money to pay for all of your vacation expenses. All they want in return is for you to tell everyone what a great time you had in the Black Hills."

"I'll show it to Iver tonight. If it really is *free*, we might just do it. They didn't say anything about gas money; I suppose that's the catch."

Marlene giggled, she could only barely talk, but it seemed to be a show of support for the free vacation. "Oh, that is a minor part of your expenses; maybe they just overlooked it. They say it is entirely *free*." the following day art and addie anxiously waited to hear something from Anna and Iver. They finally told art about winning the trip. "We've never won anything in our lives, Son. This sounds too good to be true, don't you think?"

"Naw, addie said they do events like this all the time to promote tourism. She says that you should do it as soon as you can, though.

There might be second place winners that would like to steal your spot."

"Well, do you think that you and addie could handle the ranch for a week? We don't want to run out on you and make you take more than your share of the work."

"We can handle it for a short while. It would be extremely difficult without you two here, but we'll somehow make it work," art enticingly added.

Anna looked at Iver and said, "Maybe it would be good for you to take a few days off."

"I was thinking the same thing, only it's you that needs the time off, not me," he replied. "You work too hard for a lady your age."

"I'm younger than you are, old man."

"You're both absolutely right," art broke up their dispute. "I know that neither of you want to miss any work, but it would be very loving and respectful of you to make this *sacrifice* for each other."

"Okay. We'll think about it, Son," they replied. "But you have to promise that the place will still be here when we get back. You know it won't be easy for us to be away from Marlene for a whole week either."

Anna and Iver left the following week for their *free* vacation. They kept track of all of the expenses and mailed them to the tourist association—whose address happened to belong to one of Obert's friends. Sure enough, they received every penny of their expenses back from the Black Hills tourist association. In return, they fulfilled their promise and told all of their friends and neighbors about the great time they had vacationing in the Black Hills. Most of their friends whispered to themselves, "I wonder what got into them, taking a vacation after all these years?"

A year later art talked his parents into taking him and addie and Marlene to the annual Belle Fourche roundup and rodeo over the Fourth of July. Art told Iver that they had enough leftover hay for a year or two and a little time off would be good, for the women of course, and that they could visit Obert while they were there. Anna and Iver caved, and they all went to the roundup and had a great time.

Anna, always thinking of others, thought that they should personally thank the Black Hills tourist association for the vacation that they gave them. "We should go and thank those nice folks, Iver."

"We don't have that much time, Ma," art objected.

"It wouldn't take that much time, Son. Their kindness deserves a personal thank you."

"I already thought of that, Anna, but they're closed through the 4th of July," addie fibbed, but saved the day.

Iver and Anna finally learned how to relax a bit, and the family made a yearly habit of attending the Belle Fourche Fourth of July celebration. Other than that, they didn't get much farther away from the ranch than Hettinger, North Dakota, but it was a nice one-day vacation once a year. Anna remembered and cherished every minute of those family trips on the Fourth of July. Anna admitted that without being pushed, she and Iver might not have taken the time to go and that they were wrong. "I guess I just wanted to prove that I could still keep up with the work and to impress on you young folks how important it is to glue your noses to the grindstone. I was wrong, and you two should take as much time as you can with your family. If I've learned anything at all over the years, it's that you'll never get all of the work done anyway."

Anna kept noticing that Iver wasn't quite feeling right, and he finally admitted that he had been having some chest pains. Like his wife, he was too stubborn to go to Belle and visit the doctor. Over the next two years, his chest pains kept coming, but he ignored them. Iver and art had an ongoing, never-ending argument over who would do what on the ranch. Iver wanted art to do everything that had anything to do with tractors and machinery while he did the manual work. Art kept telling him that driving the tractor was easier than manhandling a shovel or pitchfork and that Iver should let him do the hardest tasks. In some cases, like cleaning the barns and chopping the ice in the winter, Iver obliged and let art do the work. He even let art and addie do the night checks on the heifers and most of the herd riding. Art had his dad's talent with horses, and although the horse business had severely fallen off from the heights it had reached prior to cars and motorcycles, they still sold a few broke geldings annually. Like his father, art was always in the mood to do a little horse trading.

Stacking the hay was one thing that Iver wouldn't give up. He still didn't like tractors and didn't want anything to do with them, but without a tractor haying was now virtually impossible. First, the hay was mowed and raked into windrows, all with tractor-pulled implements. Then a tractor with a hay basket on the front of a loader scooped and pushed the windrows into small bunches of hay called bucker piles. When the piles were cured out, they were pushed and piled into huge ten-ton stacks. To make these stacks truly nice and weather tight, someone had to work in the stack while someone else pushed the bucker piles to it and lifted them onto the stack with the loader on the tractor. The person on the stack arranged the loose hay neatly around the edges with a pitchfork and stomped it with their feet to keep it tightly packed. That person meticulously and gradually sloped the hay inward as the stack got higher and higher until they had a huge round dome of tightly woven, weather-tight stacked hay.

Being the person in the stack was difficult, dirty, and strenuous work. Art strongly objected to letting his dad do it, but Iver was stubborn and insisted that it was his job. Art kept trying to keep him off of the haystacks but always gave in to his father's wishes. His dad was the boss even if it wasn't in his own best interest.

One afternoon art was lifting a bucker pile onto a stack, but his dad hadn't finished the last pile, so he stopped and asked if he could help. "Dad, want to rest for a spell? How about sitting in the shade with a cool drink while I pack and sort out these last few bucker piles?"

There was no response. Puzzled, art climbed up the loader and jumped onto the stack. Iver was lying there unconscious for the second time in his life. Art pushed enough hay aside so that he could hold his dad and slide down the side of the stack with him. He then ran to get the farm truck, lifted his dad in, and frantically drove him back to the house.

At first Anna thought they had come home for an early supper, but then art yelled to her to come at once and help him. She ran over to the truck, and her heart sank when she saw Iver lying on the seat. Together she and art carried him to the bedroom, the same bed that he had been carried to—unconscious—after the wagon accident years earlier. Anna told her heartbroken son that there was nothing more that he could do, so he might as well go home and tell his family. She promised to watch over Iver all night and come and get him if she needed help. After he reluctantly left, Anna got some towels and washcloths and warm water, and began to wipe the sweat and dirt off of her beloved husband. He was still breathing lightly, but Anna somehow sensed that in all likelihood she would never see him walk or hear his voice again. She cried as she whispered to him. She lovingly washed him again and combed what was left of his thinning hair, rubbing oil on his sunbaked, leathery skin. She sang his favorite hymns and said his favorite prayers. She hugged and kissed him and told him how much she loved him, over and over. She begged him to get up and tell her how much he loved her. She got on her knees and pleaded to her Lord to let her have him for a few more years.

Anna stayed at his side, talking to him, loving him, and praying for him, until early the next morning when she realized that he was no longer breathing. When her tears briefly stopped, she said the Lord's Prayer over him once more and lay down beside him, not wanting to ever leave. She was still there, lying at his side, when art and addie came to see how he was doing early in the morning.

At first art thought his dad was just sleeping, but when he realized that he had passed, he walked to the bed and helped Anna get up. She started sobbing again, still trying to fend off the realization of what had happened.

Art gave his mom a hug and a kiss, and addie did the same. None of them said anything; their tears and actions said it all, but they knew that for them life would never be the same again.

Art never did forgive himself for letting his father stack hay that day. It tore his heart out to even think about what had happened, bothering him for the rest of his life. He went over and over the day in his mind always trying to make it come out differently, but there was really nothing that he could have done to prevent it. When it came to work and looking out for himself, Iver had been his own worst enemy. Later in the morning, Marlene searched the house for Grampa Iver. She wanted a horsy ride and knee bounces. There were neighbors in their house, and they brushed her aside and told her to go outside and play. The little girl knew something strange must have happened, and Anna finally, tearfully, explained to her that Gramps had left for heaven and that he wouldn't be coming back.

Marlene gave her grandmother a hug and said, "Of course he'll be back, Grams! Gramps never misses dinner."

23

Honoring Anna

Anna was lost. Iver's death had been unexpected, and she hadn't had time to prepare. She wished that she had been able to hold him one last time, to tell him how much she loved him and how proud she was of everything that he had accomplished once more. As she thought about him, memories of the wolf attack and his wagon catastrophe flooded her mind. He had been unconscious for nearly a year after the accident but had, in time, fully recovered. That, and the fact that their two small sons hadn't been killed in the incident, had been a miracle. As she prayed for Iver's soul, Anna thanked the Lord for bringing him into her life and for blessing her with those extra, precious years that she had been given to be with him after he recovered from the wolf attack.

Anna willed herself to get out of her rocking chair and wipe away her tears, and then she went to work to prepare for Iver's funeral. Obert and Marjorie had already gotten word, so they were on their way home; meanwhile, art and addie told Anna they would help make the funeral arrangements and notify all of Anna and Iver's friends. Anna reminded them to send funeral announcements and letters to their families in Norway, along with Nils and tove, Donna, rasmus and astrid, and the Christman family.

Anna knew it would be a large funeral, so she started baking enough bread to serve beef and ham sandwiches to at least 150 people. Anna was heartbroken, but the work made her feel better. When Marjorie arrived, she helped with cakes, cookies, and pies, taking time to hug and hold her mother between jobs. Friends and neighbors were already stopping by, trying their best to comfort and support Anna and her family by bringing condolences, food, and other gifts.

As Anna worked in her kitchen baking for Iver's funeral, even under these circumstances, she couldn't help but smile. Iver had worked diligently the year before to bring running water to the house, saying that he didn't want his Anna to carry one more bucket of water. They had gotten electricity in 1950, and the conveniences that came with it were like gifts from heaven. For all of her prior life, Anna hauled water from the well. Now all she had to do was turn on the faucet in her kitchen! She thought back to all the times that having running water in the house would have been so nice, like when she and Iver came home from pulling cows out of the icy pond. Iver was suffering from hypothermia and desperately needed hot water to warm up with, but, first, Anna had to haul water from the well, bucket by bucket, and then heat it up. Now there was plentiful water at her fingertips right in the kitchen. Oh, how wonderful!

She smiled again as she thought about another of Iver's labors of love, getting electricity and light to her house. He and art had placed a pole by their house with an electric wire that ran down it and into the house and installed lights in the entryway and the kitchen. All Anna needed to do for light was to pull the string attached to the light fixture. Soon they wouldn't need their kerosene lanterns! He was in the process of installing a sewer and indoor plumbing when he died. They both had dreamed of the day that they wouldn't have to go out into the cold, dark night to the dreaded outhouse. To sit in the warmth of your house and go to the bathroom! How good and how easy could life possibly get? If only Iver were still here to finish the job and enjoy it with me. Anna smiled at the thought.

Obert had arrived, and the entire family worked together on the ranching duties while preparing for Iver's funeral. Under normal conditions, it would have been pleasant family time, reminiscent of when the kids were younger. Anna couldn't help wishing that Iver was still there to enjoy it. Odd, reidun, and their family stayed with them for an entire afternoon, a long time to be away from their ranch. Odd, the hardened rancher, cried nearly as many tears as Anna. He and Iver had been closer than brothers, and almost all of their ranching careers had been spent helping and consulting with each other. On the day of the funeral they stopped in with more food and offered to keep Marlene for the day. By now, Marlene probably realized that Gramps wasn't coming back, but she kept searching the house for him just in case. His favorite place was the porch, so she looked there often.

As Anna expected, it was a large funeral, showing how much the community loved and respected Iver. Art and Obert dug their father's grave, and together the brothers made the coffin. It was simple in the fashion of the caskets that Iver had crafted for their brothers and sisters. It was just what Iver would have wanted—a coffin lovingly made by his children. They slowly lowered Iver's body into the grave as Anna and Marjorie held each other and cried. The rich prairie soil solemnly accepted another of its children, reminding everyone attending of their mortality. God was taking Iver home, and time wouldn't be making an exception for any of them.

Anna was still sad, but her unyielding faith reminded her that the Lord had prepared a place for both her and Iver in heaven, and they would be together again soon. Eternal faith and optimism were woven into her, an integral component of her body, mind, and soul. It was a never-ending fountain that had kept her going through the death of her mother in Norway, through the deaths of her children, through the Dirty '30s and the Depression and the war, through the loss of Daisy and Blue and rain and countless friends, through Iver's encounter with the wolves and his absence from the ranch for over a year, through blizzards and droughts and hailstorms and all of the calamities that the prairie winds hurled down on her. Her prairie roots went deep and held her securely, as did her faith and belief in God.

Months passed, and Anna's oft-broken heart was yet again on the mend. It was late afternoon, and she was enjoying sitting in her rocker, relaxing and reflecting. It was a time of refreshment for her, a time to think about what she had accomplished that day and what she might achieve tomorrow. She sat and rocked, her mind going back in time. She found herself in her home with her parents in Norway, the country she fled to become an american, sadly contemplating how much she still missed her mother. She reflected on the ship and the ocean voyage and the glory of first seeing Ellis Island, the Statue of Liberty, and america. She saw rasmus, Donna, and Nils and tove. She re-visited her train ride across america, going through Chicago and Minneapolis, and meeting Gert.

Her adventures in Minnesota and living with George and Sarah came to mind, along with the old man that she came to love and call Gramps— the old gentleman that she named her first son after, the selfless old man that gave her his horse and his rifle. That horse, Blue, accompanied her to South Dakota, where she met so many wonderful people like Odd and reidun. She thought about meeting Iver for the first time and falling in love with him. He had shared that golden surprise with her, the wild and beautiful mustang herd that he had discovered hidden in a valley in the Slim Buttes, starving and being hunted by a wolf pack. There was so much to be thankful for starting with her wonderful marriage to Iver and their children and grandchildren. They were living in the beautiful house on the prairie that rasmus had trekked across america to build for her, honoring an old promise that most men would have easily swept under the carpet. Her thoughts formed visions which drifted in and out of her dreams. Anna was smiling when her tranquil interpose was interrupted by her granddaughter, Marlene.

"Gramma, you have company!"

"Who is it, Sweetheart?"

"I don't know them, Grams."

"It isn't some pesky salesmen looking for a free lunch is it?"

"Oh no, Grams. He's an older gentleman, about your age, and he has an elderly lady with him. Their license plates are from New York." "Oh, my goodness! Stall them for a minute while I take off my apron and make sure the kitchen is clean. I think that I know who they are!"

THE END

Epilogue

Do you ever wish that you could go back in time and do things differently? We wouldn't be human if we didn't. We live our lives thinking that they will never end, but history has proven that they always do. Like everything under the heavens, we get old, and with age we usually have regrets. Why didn't we allow more time for our children? Why didn't we take more vacations? Why didn't we sit and listen to our grandparents and our parents and ask them questions about their lives? time is an elusive entity; it keeps indiscriminately marching on. Few mortals use it wisely, spending it foolishly, wishing they could somehow buy it back when it is nearly depleted. Some try to save it, but in doing so, end up losing it. Father time must be amused by our antics.

My wife, Marlene (Molly), lived with Anna for a year while she attended high school and certainly wishes that she had asked her more about her incredible life. What tales Anna had to tell! tales that were gleaned mostly from Anna's three children; stories that should have come from Anna herself. Wouldn't it have been awesome to have sat with her and gotten all of these stories firsthand, and to have had actual quotes from her for the book? I guess we assume that life will never end and that making our own history is more important than listening to the history that has already been made by our fathers and forefathers. I now know how much richer my life would have been if I had integrated it with the wisdom and history of my parents and grandparents. Time relentlessly passes us by, and those opportunities usually come only once. Molly, the little seven-year-old girl at the end of this book, is now 71 and has several grandchildren of her own. Her grandmother Anna, the truly great american immigrant who is honored in this book, passed away March 18th, 1976, after 86 extraordinary years of love, honor, and faith. Molly's beloved grandfather Iver has been gone for over sixty years.

I was fortunate to have known Anna before she passed. When I first met her, she was a really nice and pretty elderly lady. If only I had known then what I know now! the life of adventure and the stories that lay hidden behind those bright blue eyes of hers! Anna was quiet and reserved and probably would have construed telling someone about her life as boasting, so her story was an enigma of sorts. Her life was truly remarkable, a voyage of honor and faith combined with volumes of wisdom, a gift waiting to be discovered and passed on. My only prayer in writing this book based on her life is that it will adequately honor Anna and her family and do justice to that entire generation of immigrants that did so much to make america what it is today.

Soon after Iver's death, Anna moved to a very modest house that she and Iver had purchased in Belle Fourche. She didn't want to "be in the way" at the ranch and gave her home there to art and addie. When Marlene was ready to go to high school, the nearest one was thirty miles from the ranch, and since there weren't school busses in those days, art and addie asked Anna if Marlene could stay with her in town while she attended her first year of high school. Anna was delighted at the prospect of being able to spend more time with Marlene again and happily accepted. Marlene said that during that time, Anna continued to enjoy her late afternoon moments in the rocking chair, asking Marlene to turn her noisy music down and pull the shades so that she could rock and relax, think about life, and say her prayers.

Molly relayed the following amusing story about Anna that happened while she was going to high school and living with her in Belle Fourche: Being a cute country girl, my future wife started receiving a few looks from the high school boys. One of them decided to do more than look and asked her to go to a movie with him. When Marlene arrived at Anna's house after school that day, she informed her grandmother that she had a date and that he would be there to pick her up for the movie later. Anna asked Marlene if art and addie knew the boy or his parents, and Marlene said, "No, don't be silly Grandmother; how could my parents know these people from Belle Fourche?" Nothing further was said, but later that day when the boy came to take Marlene to the movie, Anna was on the front steps with her broom. She pretty much swept him off of the steps and told him not to come back! the bewildered kid probably never asked another girl on a date for years.

Art, my father-in-law, later told me that Anna said she really liked me. I'm not sure what I did to win her over, but I'm sure glad that I did.

Sweeping must have been imbedded in those Norwegian genetics though, as her granddaughter sure swept me off of my feet! art was one of those rare people that probably didn't have many regrets in life. He always took an abundance of time for his family and hardly ever let work get in the way of an afternoon of family fishing. When I was dating his daughter, he met me with a broad smile and usually had something that he wanted to show me or to do with me. It may have been a ploy to keep his daughter in the yard rather than out on a date, but I construed it as just plain friendliness. It often involved making homemade ice cream. He poured ice into the bucket while I turned the crank and listened to him. I had about four or five "dates" with Marlene before we finally went on a real date and to a movie. To accomplish this, she made her dad stay hidden so that we could actually get out of the yard. Nevertheless, he couldn't help himself and came out to " just say Hi" but quickly went back into hiding when Marlene gave him the look—the same one I still get occasionally. We miss his smile and friendliness and always will. Art died of alzheimer's in 2003.

Addie was quiet and reserved, and Anna's conservative nature rubbed off on her. Using the precedent set by Anna, she moved off of the ranch so that her son Gene and his wife Janice could take it over. Addie moved to Spearfish when art was first diagnosed with alzheimer's and lived there until her death in 2012. We once gave her a $100 bill for some occasion, probably her birthday, telling her to buy herself something nice with the money. She neatly folded it and put it into her purse. Years later, Marlene found it, still neatly folded up, still in her purse.

After forty years of ranching and farming, Molly and I moved to Spearfish to retire and to care for addie and my father Henry in their later years of life. My mom, ava, passed away during heart surgery at the Mayo Clinic in 2004. Henry died in 2009 from a stroke. All we have left of that generation is memories. Father time moves on. Life is indeed just a fleeting moment, an enigma, a blink in the eye of history.

> Yet you do not know what your life will be like tomorrow.
> You are just a vapor that appears for a little while and then
> vanishes away. (James 4:14 NaSB)

> So teach us to number our days, that we may present to
> You a heart of wisdom. (Psalm 90:12 NaSB))

Acknowledgments

I would like to thank my wife Molly, Anna's granddaughter, and my daughter andrea, Anna's great granddaughter, for their assistance in reading my rough draft and making suggestions about possible improvements. Also, a very special thanks to Anna's great-great granddaughter Bri*anna* Hoff for volunteering to help Gramps— me—edit this book. She is 16 and attending the South Dakota School of Mines and technology, having already graduated from Liberty University, receiving her high school diploma and associate's degree simultaneously.

We are incredibly proud of both of our children, Brian and andrea, and their families. Brian's wife is Sherri, and their beautiful daughters are BriAnna (mentioned above) and anari. Anari is our youngest grandchild and is a high honor student in high school. Andrea's husband is aaron, and they have a beautiful daughter, aubrey, who is a sophomore in college taking speech pathology, and a handsome son, aJ, who is ranked no. 1 in his high school class of over 200 students.

Although they have now passed, I would still like to thank Anna and Iver's children, Marjorie, Obert, and arthur, for their help and time in sitting with me for hours and telling me the stories about Iver and Anna's lives. Without their time and those stories none of this would have been possible. Also, I have a confession to make about the ending of this book. I don't really know if that happened. I think it did, I hope it did, but I'm not sure. I asked Marjorie and Obert if rasmus and his wife came back to South Dakota to visit Anna after Iver died, and they weren't sure. Marjorie thought that they did. She seemed fairly sure. Art already had alzheimer's so he couldn't help, and addie couldn't recall either. That is why I pretty much left the ending up to you, the reader. And finally, I would like to sincerely thank each of you so much for reading this book. I truly hope that you enjoyed it and will pass it on to your children and grandchildren to read! Every generation needs to learn our history and know how indebted we are to the incredible immigrants that came from around the world to make america their—and eventually our—home.

In keeping with my last book, *Honoring Anna*, here are a few poems that I wrote and will dedicate to those people in our lives that we think back about and wish that we had spent more time with. Those people whose visceral memory has been forever imprinted on our hearts and souls and minds and whom we will dearly miss and remember for all of our days:

MA AND PA HARDEN

In nineteen and two, the spring was past due,
The winter had been a hard one.
Then a Chinook wind came, and that's what they blame,
For the deaths of Ma and Pa Harden.

Was the first day of May, and the old man did say,
I'm tired of living on hard tack.
So he hitched up the bay, to the wagon that day,
And told Ma he'd hurry right back.

The sun had gone down when the old man reached town,
And he had to wait for the morning.
He bought him a room, not knowing what doom
Would catch him with hardly a warning.

With his breakfast o'er he went to the store
And bought his bacon and flour.
An old friend said there was a storm to beware,
So he left town within the hour.

The blue skies turned gray, so he hurried the bay,
But quickly the clouds were snowing.
And the wind has to blow, on the prairie you know,
And soon a blizzard was blowing.

The prairie they say, has its very own way,
Of weeding the weak and the aging.
The strong stay alive, but the weak don't survive,
And around Pa the blizzard was raging.

The cold and the snow, had dealt their best blow,
And he could not last any longer.
The wicked old wind, didn't know it had sinned,

It just blew a little bit stronger.

Meanwhile back home, in her house made of loam,
Ma was knitting a sweater.
In a dream she saw the storm bury Pa,
But she prayed he was doing better.

The old milk cow, was past due right now,
And a calf would die without shelter.
It was getting late, but Ma couldn't wait,
She'd have to go out and find her.

With her strongest yarn, she left for the barn,
Using the yarn as a life line.
The yarn was strong, but it didn't last long,
And she drifted out past the coal mine.

Ma knew she was lost, and she knew what cost,
She'd pay if the storm didn't stop soon.
But the storm had its way, for another full day,
And the snow didn't melt 'till past June.

Douglas Hoff

WHY CAN'T IT RAIN

Why can't it rain on this here high plain?
One of these days gonna' go insane!
Looking to the west, looking for a cloud,
But all I see is dust, for cryin' out loud!

Why can't it rain on this crop of mine?
I keep looking to heaven for some sign.
The clouds always split and go north or south,
It looks like we're in for another drought.

But one of these days, when it's too late for the crops,
The rain'll come down, in great big glorious drops,
And wash away some of these tears we cry,
While we thank the Lord, instead of wondering why,

Can't it rain on this here high plain?
The water would sizzle on my sun-soaked brain.
I keep on looking up, but all I see is sky,
The sun keeps beatin' down, and I keep wondrin' why,

Can't it rain on this field of grain?
The Lord must think that I always complain.
The grass is dyin' and the crops are dead,
The dams are dryin' and the streams have fled,

The cows must think that they've gone to hell.
Their feed is gone, so we'll have to sell.
But the worst is watching the prairie die
For lack of rain, and always wondering why,

Can't it rain on this here high plain?
I keep on praying but it seems in vain!
Well, I had a dream just the other night,

It was pouring rain—such a beautiful sight.

When I woke up, the sun laughed at me,
'Cause it hadn't rained on the dry prairie.
But one of these days the heavens above,
Will quench the thirst of this land we love.

The prairie ponds will come to life again,
Like a long-lost soul just cleansed of sin.
The grass'll turn green and the prairie will play.
Our prayers'll say thanks and we won't have to say,

"Why can't it rain on this here high plain?

Douglas Hoff

THE OLD MAN

I looked into the mirror, and I was shocked to see,
That there was an old man, staring back at me.
His face was worn and weathered, his hair was turning gray,
And I couldn't help but wonder how he came to be that way.

'Cause once upon a time, in another life it seems,
He was a young man, and his heart was filled with dreams.
He dreamt his dreams on visions, like those that angels send,
He lived his life on wonders that he thought would never end.

But now he's trapped inside a body bent with age,
And indignantly cries out from within his mortal cage!
How could this be the fate of a free and gentle spirit?
That keeps crying out for help, doesn't anybody hear it?

The young man looks up, as the old man cries in vain,
For a moment their eyes meet, and they feel each other's pain.
A tear rolls down my cheek, as I turn my eyes and say,
Goodbye to the young man, and his dreams of yesterday.

Douglas Hoff

FAIRY TALES

Not so very long ago,
I told her that I loved her so.
In my eyes she did no wrong,
She knew it well and played along.
Grams and Gramps spoiled her too,
It seemed the proper thing to do.
She was ours to hug and hold,
Our fairy girl, our pot of gold.
Fairy tales come true it seems,
She lived with us, not in our dreams.

She roamed our fields in ballet dress,
With cats and cows to impress.
Behind her bro and BB gun,
Dreaming of deeds they'd get done
Known for their bravery everywhere,
Getting home for lunch, their only care.
I was the tickle monster way back then,
I made fairies giggle again and again.
Fairy tales come true you see.
How else could one have lived with me?

When fairies get older, they lose their wings,
And start to dream of different things.
Ballerina dresses get packed away,
Along with games they used to play.
The tickle monster can't touch them now,
Only certain young men might be allowed.
But I see right through this new disguise,
'Cause fairies live forever in their daddy's eyes.
And fairy tales come true I know,
'Cause one lived with me not long ago.

Douglas Hoff

TIME

Once upon a rhyme,
There was no such thing as time.
Tomorrow was today,
And today was yesterday.
No one could grow old,
That's the way that it was told,
And no one could be sad,
For there was no such thing as bad.
Happy was forever,
And sadness was for never,
For there was no such thing as time,
Once upon a rhyme.

Douglas Hoff

GONE

In the blink of an eye,
Your life will go by.
Gone like the rent,
Each day of it spent.

Was it wasted and vain,
For only your gain?
Or did you help others,
Take care of your brothers?

When you face God,
Will He see a fraud?
Or will He say, Son,
Your life was well done.

Douglas Hoff

About the Author

D ouglas Henry Hoff was born in 1948 and graduated as valedictorian of his high school class in 1966. He attended and was an honor student at Black Hills State University and the South Dakota School of Mines and technology. He and Marlene (Molly) were married in 1968 while attending SDSMT. When his parents considered the sale of the family ranch, Doug and Molly decided to give ranching a try and later bought it, eventually tripling its size. While on the ranch, they had two children, Brian and andrea, and started a herd of angus cattle that became world renowned. To help with their cattle research and assist their bull customers in marketing their genetics, they also created a cattle genetics and research company named angus america, which they later sold to Cargill Corporation.

While ranching, Doug received the National ralston Purina Youth of the Year award, the South Dakota Young Farmer of the year award, the North american Beef Improvement Federation Seedstock Producer of the Year award, the 2000 US Livestock Man of the Year award, and graduated from the South Dakota agriculture and rural Leadership Program. He and Molly enjoyed and lived a robust ranching career, selling semen, embryos, and cattle around the globe, with cattle from their cow herd dispersal going to five continents. Doug brought his expertise and his in-depth agricultural experience to this book, helping to produce a unique perspective of the demands of agriculture and living on the prairie.

This is the house that rasmus came to sd and built
for Anna with iver's help, in truly remarkable acts of
honor and love to Anna from both of them.

Some of the built in cabinetry and crown
molding rasmus put into the house.

Some of the Mares

**The Author and his wife, Anna's grand
daughter marlene (molly) in Anna's house**

Art haying the Herefords with Marlene & Eugene

Art & Addie hunting

CPSIA information can be obtained
at www.ICGtesting.com
Printed in the USA
LVHW090801020621
689128LV00007B/135/J

9 781954 168572